To John,
Thanks for reading.
Best of everything.

Jim Tompson

Tuyết

A Novel By
James M. Thompson
Lt Col, USAF (Retired)

Copyright ©2018 by: James M. Thompson
All rights reserved
ISBN 9781729762929

This is a work of fiction. The characters names, events, views and subject matter of this book are either the author's imagination or are used fictitiously. Any similarity or resemblance to any real people, real situations or actual events is purely coincidental and not intended to portray any person, place or event in a false, disparaging or negative light.

Dedication

This book is dedicated to the women of Viet Nam who courageously strove to care for their families during the terrible times of war—particularly those women who were forced into prostitution to survive. My sincere wish is that they have found the same happiness Tuyết finds in my story.

I also wish to acknowledge the contributions of my critique group, the many friends who encouraged me to keep writing and most importantly my lovely wife. Without her help this book would not have been possible.

Introduction

One of my most interesting assignments during 23 years in the United States Air Force was as an advisor to the Vietnamese Air Force at Bien Hoa Air Base from August 1971 to September 1972. During this tour of duty, I gained a true appreciation for the Vietnamese people. They suffered a great deal to preserve their freedom but lost everything when the United States abandoned them to their Communist oppressors.

War has always produced camp followers and prostitutes who live by the needs of men far away from home. Our tiny officers club for advisors called the ***Auger Inn*** was frequented by several of these ladies during my year in country. All of them were attractive, and many of them absolutely beautiful. Vietnamese women are like delicate porcelain dolls, and very desirable. I could easily understand any man's attraction to them.

Several officers I knew, and some enlisted men had Vietnamese mistresses. One in particular was very beautiful. I met her on a few occasions and wondered what drove her and the other women I'd seen into a life of prostitution. This book is my concept of those circumstances and what might result from them should the woman escape the Communists and make it to America. Would she find love? Would her life be happy? Would old lovers be her salvation or her disappointment? Read on and see what might have happened to Tuyết.

Chapter 1

I need to rest. I put down my basket and lean against an old French post. I curse the war. I curse the politicians who keep my husband away from me to fight their stupid war. Don't they know the rack of loneliness is relentless. Click by click it stretches my nerves nearer the breaking point. I need my husband here with me. The children need his strong hand, and I need his soft touch. Then, I hear hope.

You can't mistake the sound of a helicopter for anything else. The rotor blades flog the air into submission, and the crack of their whip can be heard for miles. My mind dares to grasp the thin thread of hope for my lover's return. My heart floats in a warm sea of anticipation. I pull off my straw hat and wave it at the noisy metal flock.

I look up, straining to see the pilots' faces—in vain. He told me to look for his helicopter, but all helicopters look the same to me. One pilot waves. Is that Chinh? I can't tell. It has to be him. Who else would wave back to me.

Dare I hope for an end to this torture? Does he realize what loneliness I suffer? Only he knows my soul. Only he can taste the tiniest hint of the bitter flavor our parting leaves in my heart. He must share some of the same feelings, but he has his work and the war forces him to concentrate on his own welfare. He has little time to think about the burdens his absence places on the wife he left behind to care for her parents and his children.

How many times have I prayed for his safety? I've seen too many women wailing for a lost husband, and too many children crying in vain for their father. The longer the war goes on, the more likely the chance I will join them in grief.

The helicopters vanish behind some buildings, and I know I will have to wait for a seeming eternity until he comes through the door, but I jump up and run toward the small part of sprawling Bien Hoa Air Base allotted to the families of its pilots. Our house is one of dozens, all the same. Cinder block construction with one large window facing the broad square for the market. We're lucky. We have electricity, a range and a refrigerator. These are luxuries in Bien Hoa City.

I burst into our quarters and find mother working over a pile of sewing. She's still a viable woman at nearly 50 though her beauty is only evident by its ruins. She's had a hard life, but she never complains. The money she earns is small, but every bit helps. Father is working a construction job on the other side of the base and won't be home until later.

"Mother, I just saw Chinh. He waved to me from his helicopter. He's home." I lift her up from the sofa and dance her across our tiny living room.

"Daughter, let me go. I'm glad Chinh is back, but I have work to do."

"I'm sorry, it's just that it's been so long."

"The important question is, did you have any luck finding some greens?" she asks.

"Not much they've been heavily picked over. There won't be many more until after the next rain. Who cares about greens? I'm just glad Chinh's home."

"Do you really think it was Chinh? You've been disappointed so many times."

"I know it was him this time. Wait and see. He'll be coming through that door any time now."

I'm lucky to still have my parents. They help relieve the loneliness, but only temporarily. Their love has limits even though they would not say so. The nearness of their own death and the loss of passion haunts their thoughts, and their daughter's troubles are small matters by comparison. I'm sure they are also tired of hearing about my problems.

I take my basket to the cooking area where my peace is shattered by my daughter, Anh.

"Mother, mother, Bao hurt me."

I pick her up and kiss her. She's four and growing fast she's almost too heavy for me anymore.

"What did he do?" I ask.

"I didn't do anything to her," Bao protests as he enters the room carrying his soccer ball.

"Yes he did. He hit me with his ball."

"Is that true?"

"I was kicking my soccer ball, and she got in the way," Bao protests.

"Bao, you must be more careful. You could have hurt your sister. Now you two go play nicely while I fix dinner." *Chinh, Chinh I need you to help manage Bao. He's seven now, and he thinks he can get away with anything. He needs your strong hand to guide him.*

My children are poor company. They live in their own little worlds, each according to their age. Love for me will only blossom in the direst of circumstances or when they finally come to realize the contributions to their lives I'm responsible for.

The voice of Mai, my neighbor, calls from the open door. "Tuyết, are you home?"

"Come in, Mai. I'm cooking dinner."

She enters holding a bowl. She's my age with two small children of her own. Her husband is also a helicopter pilot in Chinh's squadron. Mai is far from pretty with a long body and short legs. What she lacks in looks, she more than makes up for in compassion. She's been the one I turn to for solace while Chinh's away.

"Do you have any extra nuóc mắm sauce? I didn't realize I was so low, and I don't have enough for tonight's dinner."

"Yes, I have plenty." I go to my pantry as I think about the value of friends. They only dip their toes in the vast lake of my loneliness. They can say kind words and offer temporary respite, but in the end, they have their own troubles to combat.

"I heard some helicopters a while ago. Do you suppose your husband is back?" she asks.

"I know it was him. He waved to me."

"Thoung tells me all the pilots wave to women. Don't get your hopes up yet."

"This wave was special. It's him."

"I know this is hard on you. Thoung comes home to me almost every evening, and I'm lucky to have him with me. I don't know what I'd do if he were gone as long as Chinh."

"You'd do what I do, hope and pray until he does come home."

I make sure there are several cold beers in the refrigerator, and I put on one of my best ao-dais after supper, but Chinh doesn't come.

Thoung and Mai come over as soon as he's home.

"I'm sorry, Tuyết. That was me who waved to you today," Thoung says. "Chinh is still at Nha Trang. He asked me to give you his love and tell you he's been extended there another month."

I can't help it. I sit down and cry. Mai sits down beside me. "Don't cry, Tuyết. It's just the war. You know he loves you more than his own life," she says.

"I know. I just don't know how much longer I can go on without him."

I don't fall asleep quickly that night. I pray to whatever gods there are that Chinh will come home soon. I miss the touch of his hands on my face. I miss the pungent-sweet smell of his body after a day's flying. I miss the feel of his skin; tough and leathery where it's exposed to the sun, then velvety soft over the hard muscles of his chest and stomach. I even miss the reassuring sound of his snoring when I awaken at night.

I recall our good times together and savor the emotions and thrills of each moment alone. Before the children came, we'd often go to a movie then walk home hand in hand to relive the love scenes. We would shut out the war for a few moments while we buried ourselves in love for each other. Once Bao arrived, he made as many demands on our time together as the war, but the war seemed to grow jealous and began to draw Chinh away more and more often. Then Anh came, and the war became a demanding mistress. Now, Chinh has been away for nearly four months. I curse the war until I grow tired and fall asleep in spite of my anger.

*

I don't know how long I lay there before going to sleep, but I'm awakened too soon by the crump of rockets. I count, expecting the usual six the VC send over each morning; but this time they don't stop at six. I hear Bao and Anh crying and rush to comfort my children.

"Mother, Father, wake up." I call to rouse them, but they come from their room dressed and carrying bags of necessities. The noise grows more intense and the explosions are now mixed with the wail of sirens. I open the door on a swarm of people racing for the bunkers, Mai and her children among them, and close it at once.

"Never mind, Father. I think it would be safer to stay here than fight the crowd. One of us could get lost too easily in that mob."

It's as much the idea of spending several hours huddled inside the dark, musty bunkers as the thought of being trampled by the crowd. They are horrible caves of wood and concrete covered with the dank red earth. Centipedes and lizards are everywhere and there is no place for anyone to relieve themselves without venturing outside.

He looks out the door to see for himself before agreeing. "I think you're right, daughter. The fighting doesn't seem to be close to us, and these walls make good protection." He pats the cinder blocks as if to test their capacity to stop bullets.

"I think we would be safer in the back of the house away from the windows," I say.

He nods his approval, and we huddle together in a corner of the sleeping area. I pile mattresses around us as Chinh instructed me to do.

The sirens finally stop, but they're replaced by the sound of more airplanes and helicopters than I've ever heard before. Louder explosions add more worries to my already terrorized mind, but I have to be strong for my children. I hold them tightly and purr assurances softly in an effort to staunch the flow of their tears.

"It's all right. Listen, do you hear those helicopters? That's our soldiers going to protect us. They won't let the VC harm us."

At that moment, a shell explodes just outside the house, shattering the window. Shrapnel bounces off the walls and rips into the mattresses with a soft "plop" sound. I can't hold back my tears any longer. Bloody images fill my mind. I can almost feel the pieces of iron tearing through my body and hear the shrieks of my children as they're ripped apart by the lethal fragments. How random it is. The VC aren't shooting at us, they're just shooting, and anything that happens to be in the way suffers the consequences. I should have taken them to the bunkers. Will the next shell hit closer? I was foolish to stay, but I can't let my children suspect my uncertainty.

"You are a brave boy, Bao, and you're brave too Ahn." I hold them closer and begin to coo an old lullaby.

The fighting lasts all morning. The sun is high before we venture out of our makeshift shelter to assess the damage. Broken glass covers everything, but nothing else is damaged. Outside, I can see the small crater created by the shell. I look back at the house and see hundreds of tiny pockmarks from the shrapnel and count my blessings–none of us have been hit.

People with dazed looks begin to filter back from the bunkers, but their expressions brighten when they see their homes still intact, though needing some repairs. Smoke rises from several places in the direction of the airplanes and their hangars. Ambulances hurry back and forth on the road with lights flashing and sirens blaring away.

For the first time the war brushes against us. No one was hurt this time, but when would it be our turn to suffer as so many others had and are doing even now? Mai's husband appears in the entrance to the housing area.

"Tuyết, Tuyết!" he shouts as he runs toward me. "Have you seen Mai and my children? Are they okay?"

Thoung is not a handsome man, and his pained expression only exacerbates the high cheek bones and narrow chin. Hair matted by his helmet clings to his forehead. His flight suit is black with sweat from the waist up and blood stained from the knees down.

"You have blood on your legs, Thoung. Are you hurt?"

"No, no; I just got back from a medical evacuation mission. It's from the casualties. Have you seen Mai?"

"I saw them go to the bunkers, but I haven't seen them come back. I'm sure they're fine," I say, trying to reassure him. "Do you know anything about Chinh? Is he alright?"

"I haven't heard a thing. There was no time for anything but fighting the VC. I'm sorry. I can check with operations after I find Mai."

"I'm sorry. I was being selfish. Go find her."

"I have to find her. Maybe one of the shells hit the bunkers." Thoung runs back the way he came, and I pray his fears are unfounded. The thought of losing Mai is more than I can stand on top of Chinh's absence.

I go back into the house to make tea and help Mother straighten out the mess from the broken window and the pile of mattresses. Thoughts of Chinh dead or wounded fill my mind. I barely notice Bao playing with the pieces of shrapnel littering the floor.

"Bao, put that stuff down. You'll hurt yourself," I scold.

"It's okay, Mother. It's not sharp," he protests.

"I said put it down."

"Oh, all right." He throws the pieces of metal to the floor and stomps away.

Just then, Thoung appears with Mai and the children. "I found them, Tuyết. They're okay. After I get them settled I'll go check on Chinh.'"

Mai has a weary look from her ordeal of trying to keep two children from crying while deathly afraid herself. I run to my best friend. "Are you really okay?"

"We're fine. The children were so frightened, but they behaved well. The military police wouldn't let us pass for a while. When they finally allowed us to use the road, it was horrible. There was blood everywhere, and the bodies of the VC were lying in the fields and on the barbed wire. There were hundreds of them just lying there." She breaks into tears and her husband holds her close.

"Tuyết," she says, regaining her composure. "I'm so happy you're okay. I didn't see you at the bunkers, and I thought you might be injured."

"We decided to stay here rather than risk getting trampled by the crowd. We're fine, but both of our houses are damaged. A shell landed just outside in the open area where they set up the market, but all it did was knock out a lot of windows."

"Will they come back?" Mai asks her husband.

"I don't think so. They suffered heavy losses today, and I don't think they will be able to recover for quite a while. They say there is still some fighting in Saigon and up North in Hue, but it's over nearly everywhere else."

I breathe a sigh of relief. We've managed to survive this one, but what if they attack again? Chinh, Chinh, come home to me please. I couldn't bear to think I had to endure more of this hell without you. I need the words you always have that renew my strength.

I put up a good front today, but I know I can't keep it up if the attacks continue. This was the best place to be today, but will it always be so? What if Chinh is hurt? What will I do without him?

Mai sees my concern and embraces me. "Be strong, Tuyết," she whispers to me. "Chinh will be home soon, and if you need anything, don't hesitate to call on me."

Her kind words are little reassurance, but our only choice is to go about trying to put our lives back in order as best we can. "Thank you, Mai. I will do my best until Chinh comes home, but it's good to know you're there for me."

We part tearfully, and I continue the task of cleaning up. Thoung leaves to check on Chinh.

He's gone what seems to be an eternity, but soon returns to tell me Chinh is okay. I feel a dark cloud part above me and feel the warm sun of assurance bathe me in comfort once again.

I had to pay for a new window and the repairs to the outside of our home. I thought the VNAF would be responsible for the repairs to on-base housing, but the men working on the other houses tell me I'd have to wait a long time for that, and I can get the work done now if I pay them directly.

I think I've been taken advantage of, but I'm not sure. Chinh would know. He'd handle it well. I need him so much.

We're counting đồng (pennies) carefully now. Prices rise almost daily, and I wonder how long we can last.

Chapter 2

I don't hear from Chinh until several days after the fighting. I'd heard there was a lot of action near Nha Trang, and I worry until his letter arrives.

I tear it open with anxious fingers.

My dearest Tuyết,

I have some good news. I'll be home next Thursday for a few days. I'm to receive a medal for some action I was in during the recent fighting. I'll tell you all about it when I get home. My medal will be presented to me by Vice President Ky himself at a big party on Friday night. You don't know how much I'm looking forward to seeing you and the children again. I'll only be home a few days, but we'll make the most of the time we have.

It's been so lonely here at Nha Trang without you. The other officers here take advantage of the women hanging around the bar, and I won't say I haven't been tempted, but none of them compare in beauty to you. They all seem so artificial with their make-up and silk ao-dais. Don't worry about any of them stealing my heart, even for one hour.

I have to leave for a mission now, but by the time you get this letter it won't be long until I hold you again.

With all of my love,

Chinh

*

"What does he say, daughter?" Mother's question brings me back to the present.

"It's wonderful. He'll be home next week, and he's to get a medal for his bravery." I can't contain my elation. I smother her in a bear hug and dance her around the room.

"Tuyết, let me go!" she shouts half-seriously.

I let her go and wave the letter at her. "Isn't this wonderful?"

She straightens her clothes and smiles at me. "It is wonderful. I always knew you married well, my daughter. He's a fine man."

"Yes, a fine man, indeed," I agree.

That evening in my bed, I think about our wedding day. It was a lovely Buddhist ceremony with many of the rituals and costumes of the traditional way. I wore an Áo Mệnh phụ for the ceremony at the Buddhist temple, but changed into a regular ao dai for the reception at the hotel. Chinh wore a rented tuxedo for the whole affair. We didn't do the traditional visits to the family houses since Chinh's family lived in An Loc and my family was in Saigon. After the reception we were escorted to the bridal suite for our wedding night.

Chinh was so gentle with me. He made the night wonderful and has never stopped being a tender lover. I know how much he loves sex, and he's been gone a long time now. I wonder if he misses our sex. If so, does he have women at Nha Trang. Our Buddhist ethics require us to be faithful to each other, we both know infidelity is bad karma.

For my part, waiting for him is a normal way of life. Yes, I miss his touch and his kind words, but I do not burn for physical love. Is it the same with men? Certainly, movies and books tell of men going mad for want of a woman. Some of them, at least, must feel that kind of irresistible urge to find satisfaction some way.

I think of the possible ways. Seduction would probably be their first choice. That might be the safest way. Patronizing whores would be the easiest, but the risk of venereal disease is always there. I don't think Chinh is the type that would turn to rape no matter how much he burned.

Do I really want to know if he has a woman at Nha Trang? I decide I do not. I know he will be only mine once he comes home, and after all, he is the one who will have to live with the bad karma of his peccadillos. I'm content to wait for him.

*

When Chinh arrives, I run to his arms and kiss him with all the pent-up passion I've saved only for him. His thick black hair is in disarray, and his flight suit smells of perspiration, but his chiseled face and deep black eyes still make my heart pound faster. Not even a day's growth of beard can mar his charm.

I'm glad he's tall, almost 180 centimeters, because I'm tall for a woman. He folds me in his muscular arms and presses me against his broad chest. "I've missed you so much, Darling," he whispers. "You don't know how I've longed for this day."

I hold him as close as I can. "How long will you be home?" I ask.

"I'm afraid I only have three days here before I have to return. They need me very much at Nha Trang. As I told you in my letter, I came home because there's going to be a big party for Vice President Ky, and my commander said he would award my medal there."

I sit down with Chinh, but I keep one arm around him. "Tell me all the details. How did you get your medal?"

His face melts from joy into a somber expression. "It was during the fighting at Tet. My flight was carrying supplies to one of our Army units when I heard an American Captain call for help. His unit was ambushed and taking heavy casualties. His commander said there were no American helicopters to help him, but I broke in on their frequency and offered my birds. We'd just dropped off some supplies and were headed home, carrying some of our wounded. Three of our choppers were empty, so I got his coordinates and went to help. We took a lot of hits on the way in, but we managed to get them out without losing one of our own birds even though it took two trips. The American Captain wanted my name and my unit. He said I should get a citation for what we did. His outfit was in bad shape. They had a lot of dead and wounded to carry out. It was pretty bloody."

He takes a deep breath and seems to return to his usual, cheerful self. "Anyway, a few days later my commander called me into his office and told me I was to get the Gallantry Cross with Gold Palm from Ky himself. I was glad to hear it because it meant I could come home for at least a short time."

I throw my arms around his neck and kiss him. "I'm so proud of you. Can I be there to see it?"

"Of course. The party's tomorrow night."

"Oh, but Vice President Ky will be there, and I don't have anything fancy to wear," I protest.

"Wear that blue ao-dai you save for special occasions," he says.

"That thing is so old. It's almost an antique," I protest.

"Nonsense, it's a lovely ao dai. Besides, you're beautiful in anything." He kisses me, and my troubles seem to melt away now that the man I love is with me again.

My parents arrive and greet Chinh. Mother takes his bag while Father brings him a cold beer.

Mother calls the children in from play, and they run to join us.

"Daddy, Daddy, you're home," Bao shouts.

"What'd you bring me?" Anh pleads.

"Children let your father relax a bit before you start in on him," I scold half-heartedly.

Chinh laughs and reaches into his pocket. "This is for you, Bao." He holds out a small plastic bag. Bao takes it at once but stares questioningly at the black mass of material inside.

"What is it?" he asks.

"It's licorice, American candy. I thought you might like it. Try a piece."

Bao opens the bag and recoils in disgust. "It smells terrible," he says.

"It tastes much better than it smells," his father assures him.

The boy pinches a small piece from one of the tangled strands of black rope and puts it in his mouth. He savors it like a connoisseur would a fine wine before a smile spreads across his face.

"It's delicious," he proclaims as he pulls off an even larger piece and stuffs it in after the first one.

"And here's something for my little girl," Chinh opens his briefcase and produces a small box wrapped in shiny blue paper.

"What is it? What is it?" Anh shrills as she tears off the wrapping.

She opens a small box to reveal one of the ugliest things I've ever seen. It's a small doll with grotesque features and a shock of purple hair standing out from its head in all directions.

"It's a Troll Doll," Chinh laughs at her puzzled expression. "My American advisor tells me every little girl in the United States has one. I think they must be for good luck or something because they're too ugly to be real dolls."

Anh quickly overcomes her initial revulsion and is soon quite taken with the thing.

I call the children back to me. "Your father is to receive a medal for bravery from the Vice President himself. You should be very proud of your father."

"That's good, isn't it?" Anh says. Even at her young age, she knows about military things. I curse the war inwardly.

"Did you kill a lot of VC?" Bao asks around a mouthful of licorice.

"No, I just rescued some Americans," Chinh says.

"But it was very brave of your Father to do that," I say to the children. I turn to Chinh. "You're being too modest," I scold.

"Anyone would have done the same thing I did. I just happened to be leading some empty Hueys a few minutes from their position."

"Still, children, your father is a brave man who deserves his medal," I say.

"We know he's brave without the medal," Bao says as he returns to his licorice, and Anh goes back to her new doll.

Chinh laughs as much at me as the children and takes a long swig from his beer bottle before continuing.

"I'm sorry I have to go back. We lost quite a few pilots in the fighting, and they're afraid the VC will regroup for another attack soon. Everyone says I'm the best instructor pilot in the outfit, so I have to do it."

"Can't we join you there? Nha Trang is not that far away," I ask.

"There's no good housing there, or I'd take you all back with me. I spoke with Colonel Dai the other day, and he said you could continue to live here while I'm at Nha Trang. Besides, you'll be safer here at Bien Hoa if there's any new offensive."

"Can you send any more money? It's very hard making ends meet now, and If Father should lose his job we wouldn't be able to make it."

"Don't worry about that. There'll be plenty of work for him, cleaning up after this attack. I'll send you as much as I can, but I have to live too, you know."

"Does living include buying drinks for the bar flies in the officers' club?" I ask as I punch him in the chest half playfully.

He stiffens a bit at my remark but recovers quickly. "A man must have some fun from time to time," he says cheerfully as I pummel his arm with my fists.

He pulls me to him and kisses me tenderly. "You know you're the only woman in my life," he says between kisses.

That night we make love with a fervor I hadn't known since our wedding night.

*

The next evening Chinh puts on his dress uniform for the medal ceremony. I fall in love with him all over again when I see him. He's so handsome, and though he doesn't need a uniform to look like a military officer, he seems to stand a bit taller when he's wearing it. I'm almost afraid to embrace him for fear of spoiling the image, but he solves my problem by embracing me.

"You look beautiful tonight," he says as I've heard him say so many times before.

I blush and turn away. "How can I be beautiful?"

He takes my shoulders and turns me to face the mirror. "Look at you. See, you're as tall as I am. You have a great body and wonderful legs. Your skin is the color of aged gold, and your hair shines like polished ebony. I'd almost take you for an American by the shape of your face and the delicacy of your features. Beautiful? You're more than beautiful. Every man in that room tonight will want to take you home." He pulls me into his arms and kisses me gently.

I see truth in his eyes, and I feel confidence in his touch. What a wonderful man I have. I survey him from head to foot. "And you look like the hero you really are," I reply.

Chapter 3

The next morning, I ask Chinh to take me to a nearby restaurant for pho. Over the meal I bring up the forbidden subject.

"Do you really have to go back to Nha Trang? Can't you just stay here?"

"Darling, you know I have to go back." He continues to eat his pho as if it were a closed matter, but I persist.

"Can't you talk to someone, some high-ranking officer here? I miss you so much, and the children need you. Besides, it's very hard for us, financially, when you're gone."

"I'm a military man. I must do as I'm told. I've talked to everyone who could make a difference, and not one of them will help." His tone turns angry. "I've told you all of this before. Why do you keep asking?"

"Why can't you find us something at Nha Trang? I hate this being apart."

"I'm on temporary duty now. I can't get housing there unless I'm assigned permanently. Even if I were, there's nothing there as good as you have here. I'll be back as soon as I can, and that's all there is to it." He slams his chopsticks on the table and turns away from me.

"Then, resign your commission and find a civilian job." I've never said this to him before, and my tone convinces him I'm serious about this.

"You don't know what you're asking. Ignorant woman. Do you know how many people are out of work in our country? Do you have any idea what kind of bribes it would take to land even the most menial job? No, you don't. Eat your pho and keep quiet."

I know enough to stop arguing at this point. We finish in silence and walk home without another word. That night, he makes love to me, but it's as if he's a soldier doing his duty. He rolls off me and goes to sleep immediately.

In the morning, Chinh is apologetic. "I'm sorry, darling. I'll make another try at getting back to Bien Hoa."

"Thank you. I'm sorry if I made you angry, but I love you so much, and I want to be near you all the time."

He kisses me tenderly as the truck arrives to take him away.

"Goodbye, my darling. Know I love you with all of my heart," I say before he lets me go and boards the truck that will take him away from me again.

I start to cry, but a red rage of anger washes over my body stifling the tears. Damn this war. Damn the Air Force. Damn him. A sudden thought forces everything else out of my mind. *I've seen the officers here on temporary duty. I've seen them pawing every woman they can get close to. I've seen them drinking and gambling while their families are just as hard pressed as we are.* A picture of Chinh leaning against a bar telling some loose woman how brave he is feeds the fire growing in my belly. He's not suffering the way we are. He's not worried about where the next meal is coming from.

My love overcomes the anger. He can't help his situation. He must obey orders. I know he loves me. Why should I doubt him? He's relying on me to carry on, and I can't let him down. I go back into our house sad but determined to find a way to meet this challenge.

*

Nha Trang Air Base
February 25, 1968

My Dear Tuyết,
Things are back to normal here at Nha Trang, but I'm busier than ever training new helicopter pilots. I was hoping my promotion to Major would qualify me for a staff job back at Bien Hoa, but that didn't happen.

It was so wonderful to be home if only for a few days. I miss you so much, but it's hard for me to take leave to see you and the children. I'm glad your father has work. I know I don't send you enough money, but it's all I can spare. You won't believe it, but I've stopped buying drinks at the officer's club to save money. My roommate has a small refrigerator, and he lets me keep some beer in it. That's the extent of my drinking these days.

I can't tell you much about what we're doing here for security reasons, so there really isn't much to say except how much I wish I were back with you and the children. Colonel Xiem wants to transfer me here. If he does, I'll try to find a place for us to live. I should know about that in a few more weeks, and I'll let you know as soon as anything's final.

Give the children my love. I know Bao's birthday is coming up, and I'll try to get one of the American advisors to buy me some new toy for him. If that doesn't work, there's a Sergeant here who makes toy helicopters out of junk he finds around the shops. He doesn't ask a high price for them, and I know Bao would like one.

Write when you can. I love your letters.
With all of my love,

Chinh

*

Several weeks pass without any problems, then one day, Father comes home earlier than usual. The look on his face tells me all I need to know.

"What's the matter, Father?"

"I've lost my job, and there's no more construction work. The Americans are bringing in Korean companies for their jobs now. This is my last pay." He hands me the envelope. "I will try to find something else, but most people will not want a man my age."

"Father! You're not yet 60, and you're in good physical condition. With all the young men off in the army, you're bound to find something."

"I'll keep trying, daughter, but I fear the bribes I need to pay for any job may be more than we can afford."

I sit down, stunned by the news. Without his income, there's no way we can keep going as we are. I may have to find a job myself, but I don't want to leave the children as a burden on Mother. Perhaps something will turn up.

Mother comes in and rushes to her husband. "I'm glad you're home early today." She embraces him but draws back on realizing his dejected state. "You're out of work again, aren't you?"

"Yes, wife. I fear the Americans are really serious about leaving our country."

She turns to me almost in tears. "I've dreaded this day even though I knew it would come before too long. I'll get a job cleaning for the Americans."

"No, Mother, it would kill you. Besides, I am the best one in the family to look for work. You can stay home and watch the children for me. If Father finds work, you'll be the only one available to watch them. I'll start looking for a job in the morning. We'll just have to tighten our belts until then."

Dinner that evening is more silent than usual. Even the children seem to sense our fears.

*

Bien Hoa Air Base
April 29, 1968

Darling Chinh,
I had some bad news today. Father lost his job with the American construction crew and can't find work elsewhere. Without his income, there's no way we can buy enough food to keep us going. Our small garden and the few chickens we have help some, but we still must buy rice and pork. Father fishes, and that helps also, but we will need more money soon.

I go to our temple when I can and pray to Green Tara to protect you and White Tara for help with our money. I know you can't send any more money, but I can pray for your quick return. More than the extra money, I need you and your warm touch. I need your firm voice with Bao and your sweet understanding with Anh. Above all, I need you beside me each night. Come home soon. Is there any word on your possible transfer?

I just remembered Xuan. You know, the widow who lives two units down from ours. She works in the big American store they call a BX. She must make good money there because she never wants for anything. I'll talk to her. Maybe there's a job there for me. I know you don't want me to work, but I fear we will be hard-pressed without another income.

I'll let you know what I finally do. Come back as quickly as you can, and always know I love you with all of my being.

My love forever,

Tuyết

*

The next evening, I watch for Xuan. I know she works at the big store the Americans call "BX" on the other side of the base. She also works as a bartender in the tiny officers club the American advisors maintain on the Vietnamese side. I'm hoping this is one evening she doesn't go to work in the American club. Luckily, I spot her coming home from her job at the BX. I call to her as she rides her moped past our house.

"Xuan! Please come for some tea. I need to talk to you."

She stops and looks at me with a suspicious expression. "This is the first time you've ever invited me into your home. I suspect you want some kind of favor."

"I can't deny it. I need a job, and I was hoping you could put in a good word for me where you work."

"I'd be glad to. In fact, one of the girls didn't show up today, and I don't think she'll be back."

"Why is that?"

"Someone's been altering checks at the cashier's cage, and I'm sure she's the one. An American Major showed up yesterday making inquiries, and she's gone today. Come in tomorrow, and I'll see you get the job."

"That's very kind of you, but how do you know they'll hire me?"

Xuan laughs shrilly. "I'll threaten to quit giving the manager blow jobs if he doesn't hire you. Of course, he'll have to be bribed also."

I have to hold back my revulsion at the image of Xuan and the manager. Do we have to stoop to this to exist? Have we become little better than whores? "I understand. How much will he want?"

"I suppose you could go to bed with him instead of giving him money, but I don't think you'd like that option."

I shudder at the very thought of sex with a strange man. "No, not at all. How much money does he want?"

"Oh, 5,000 Piasters should swing it. Can you afford that? I'll loan it to you if you can't."

"I can afford that. I'll go in with you in the morning."

*

Nha Trang Air Base
May 6, 1968

Dear Tuyết,
You know how I feel about you working. The children need their mother. I know your mother is capable, but she also has work to do tending the garden and the chickens and earning money by sewing. Please, don't go to work unless it's absolutely necessary.

I miss you so much here, and I wish I could come home, but Colonel Xiem says I'm critical to the success of the war here, training helicopter pilots. As long as this war continues to go on, he'll keep me here, and I don't see any end to this cursed war anytime soon.

Things are quiet now all over the country. I think we bloodied the VC very badly at Tet. If the war stays this calm for a while longer, I may be able to talk Colonel Xiem into some leave time. He's still working on my transfer, but nothing's firm yet. I've been looking for a place for us to live, but I haven't found anything suitable. The Americans have been building up their forces here, and they are taking everything nice.

I must go now. I have three students to take up on check flights this afternoon. Always know I love you forever.
Your loving husband,

Chinh

*

I get the job. Mother watches the children while I work, and I ride to work on the back of Xuan's moped. All goes well, but my first payday at the BX is quite a shock. I catch Xuan at our break.

"Xuan, is this right?" I show her the money.

"Yes, that's what I get," she replies.

"But, it's so little. How do you manage to have so many nice things on just this?"

She laughs as she lights a cigarette. "I guess you're the only one on Bien Hoa who doesn't know what I do for my extra money."

"You have another job?"

This comment elicits even more laughter. "I guess you could say I have five other 'jobs'."

"I don't understand."

She turns serious and takes my hands in hers. "Tuyết, I have five American boyfriends."

I'm not that naive. I quickly understand what a "boyfriend" is. "No, you mean you're a whore?"

"I like to use the term 'mistress'."

I really don't want to offend her. I hold back my revulsion at the idea of having sex with five different men, but my sense of morbid curiosity compels me to go further. "How do you do that?"

"It's easy. Each one is a different night. They don't care what I do on the other nights as long as I take good care of them on their night."

"I meant, how can you stand to do it with five men?"

She blows a smoke ring and grunts. "It was hard, at first, but the money and the presents made me a good life. I soon decided it was better than limping along on a widow's pension, and I learned to swallow my disgust. After the first two, I found one man was much like another. They're simple creatures. All they want is a good meal and a quick orgasm."

"But, five? I would think one would be jealous and beat you if he found out about the others."

"I had one who got mad, and I quit going to him. I found a replacement for him inside of a week."

I lean back against a stack of boxes to digest what I just heard. She's so casual about it. You would think she's talking about learning a new recipe. I shake my head in disbelief. "I could never do that, Xuan."

"You don't know what you'll do when times get really bad. I'm even beginning to like the thrill of a new man when one of my boyfriends goes home."

"Well, I don't condemn you, but I still don't know how you do it."

Our conversation ends with the end of our lunch break. I don't bring the subject up again.

*

One week, Xuan is sick, and I'm forced to wave down rides to work. Most people don't even slow down, and I'm late for work twice before a VNAF (Viet Nam Air Force) jeep stops. I'm surprised to see an American officer driving it and hesitate to get in.

"Do you speak English?" he asks.

"I speak little English."

"Where are you going?"

"I go BX."

"Get in, I'll take you there." He pats the passenger seat of the dusty jeep, creating a small brown cloud, and I'm glad I wore my light brown ao dai. I climb in, and the jeep starts off toward the American side of the base.

"My name's George. What's your name?" he asks.

"My name Tuyết."

"That's a pretty name. What does it mean?"

He's an advisor. I can tell by the Vietnamese Major's rank he wears and the patches on his fatigue top. That's probably why he asked what my name meant.

"It mean snow."

"Snow, how unusual for this part of the world. Have you ever seen snow?"

The mopeds and motorcycles zoom around us. He seems to be going rather slowly, and I wonder if I'm the cause of his dawdling.

"I no see snow."

He smiles at me. He has a very kind face, not hard like the other advisors I'd met, but he's Air Force, and they were Army. Maybe that's the difference. The Army officers seem to have a disdain for us. Most of them have been here once or twice before, and Chinh tells me they've seen a lot of combat, and that makes them hard.

"It's beautiful. It comes down in tiny white flakes like ashes from a fire and covers everything. It clings to the trees and paints a coat of white on the whole world. You're as beautiful as new-fallen snow."

I blush. I'm not quite sure, but I think he's just paid me a compliment.

"Thank you, Thieu Ta."

His eyes light up at the sound of me pronouncing his Vietnamese rank.

"Yes, I'm a Thieu Ta. We Americans say, Major."

"I know, my husband Thieu Ta, Air Force."

We continue our conversation all the way to the BX. The Major leans over the seat as I start to leave. His hand touches mine as if to hold me back. My instincts tell me to pull away, but his touch is so soft and warm I let it stay.

"I'll pick you up tonight, if you like. What time do you get off?"

"I go home six thirty, but you clean seat." I point to the dusty cushion as I brush the dirt from the back of my clothes.

The Major laughs. "I'll take care of it today." He waves as he drives off.

I look after him for a while. Is he trying to become familiar with me? I shake off the feeling. He's just being cordial. I shouldn't read too much into a ride to work and a brief touch.

Xuan comes back to work two days later, and I'm glad to have a ride with her again. George was very nice, but I was never comfortable in his jeep. I always had a feeling of impending danger around him. When I told Xuan about him, she only smiled, "See how easy it is to snare a good-looking American? It sounds like he'd be a good boyfriend if you wanted that."

*

Bien Hoa Air Base
May 15, 1968

Dearest Chinh,
I got the job at the BX. The pay is wonderful and takes care of all our needs with a bit to save for bad times. I ride to work with Xuan on her moped. While she was sick, an American Thieu Ta picked me up. He is an advisor, and a very nice man, but I went back to riding with Xuan as soon as she was well.
Everyone seems to be doing fine now. Inflation continues to eat into our money, but so far, we don't have any problems. Oh, if you could only come home. I could quit my job, and we would be a family again. The children miss you and ask about you often.
I miss you terribly, and I love you always.
Your wife forever,

Tuyết

*

The weeks pass, and Chinh does not come home. Bao asks, "Mother, when will Father come home?"

"I don't know, but I do know he would come home if he could. He's a soldier, and he must obey his superior officers."

"Why?" he asks.

"Why do you obey me?" I ask.

"Because you will punish me if don't," he says.

"It's the same with him. His superiors will punish him if he does not obey their orders."

"How can they? They aren't his mother."

It's hard for me to keep from laughing at his simple view of the world, but I know he would only take it as ridicule of his budding intellect.

"No, but it's the same kind of thing. As children obey their parents, soldiers obey their superior officers."

"I think his *super* officers are mean people," he protests.

I can only agree with him, but I must put a better face on the matter.

"Do you think I'm a mean mother when I must punish you sometimes?"

This question requires some thinking on his part, but he finally looks up at me and smiles, "No."

"Do you know I love you?"

This question brings a wide smile. "Yes."

"Do you know why I must make you do something or forbid you to do something else even though I love you?"

"No."

It's an honest answer, and an opportunity for me to help him understand.

"It's because I know more about the world than you do. I know what is wrong and what is right. I must teach you and Anh the right ways and punish you to teach you not to do the wrong things. Do you understand?"

"Yes, Mother. I understand. Father's super officers are older and wiser than he is."

"Yes, they are, and that's why he obeys them. Now go and play."

I usher him out the door.

*

Nha Trang Air Base
June 6, 1968

Dear Tuyết,
My life here grows lonelier and lonelier each day. I ache for your touch, but there is no leave allowed for any of us. My transfer came through last week, and I'm now stationed here permanently. I've looked into moving you and the family here, but I haven't found any decent housing.

Be careful of the Americans. I think they are all oversexed from what I see here. I hear many stories of Vietnamese women who are seduced by them and become addicted to the money and gifts they're able to give them. Don't fall into their trap. I know this warning isn't necessary in your case, but please be careful.

Tell the children I love them. I'll be home as soon as I can.

Love,

Chinh

I was dreading this news. I sit with his letter in my hand fighting back the tears. I know he will do all he can to move us to Nha Trang, but he never has good news about housing. All I can do is hope, but hope seems to fade faster with each discouraging letter.

*

As time passes, inflation becomes worse. Soon, even the BX job isn't enough. The children must make do with badly worn shoes and school uniforms they are outgrowing. I barely manage to keep food on the table. I have no idea how to earn more money, and Father's attempts at finding work produce no results. I quit taking a lunch to work. The children need the food more than I do.

Xuan notices I'm not carrying my usual lunch pail and asks, "Where's your lunch?"

"I'm not bringing any lunch these days," I decide to lie, "I have to lose some weight."

She stops the moped and turns to face me. "You're as skinny as sugar cane. You don't need to diet. What's wrong?"

"I drop my face into my hands and begin to cry. "My children need the food more than I do."

Her face takes on a stern expression. "Listen, if you go hungry it will affect your work, and you'll get fired."

She opens her bag and hands me money. "Take this and buy some lunch today."

I push her hand away. "I can't take your money. I can't repay you."

"It's a gift for now, but what will you do in the future?"

I dry my tears on some tissues from my bag and compose myself. "I don't know. I'll try to find a second job, I guess."

"Jobs are scarce these days. Don't you think I tried to find something?"

"I can't do what you do."

She stiffens a bit but recovers. "When your children get hungry enough, you will do whatever it takes to feed them. Don't belittle what I do. It may be bad karma, but my boyfriends treat me nicely, and I've come to enjoy their company. They provide me with a life worth living. I'm not begging." She turns back to the road and continues on to the BX. I sit silent until we arrive.

As I dismount I grasp Xuan's shoulder. "I'm sorry. You've been a good friend to me, and I didn't mean to hurt you."

She places her hand on mine and smiles. "I understand," is all she says.

*

Bien Hoa Air Base
August 22, 1968

Dear Chinh,

Inflation grows daily, it seems. It's harder and harder for us to eat well. We're getting by, but just barely. If you can't send any more money, I don't know what we'll do. There's still no work for Father, and Mother is charging as much as she dares for her sewing. Xuan steals cigarettes from the BX and sells them on the black market, but I can't bring myself to steal anything.

I hate to bother you with our troubles, but I must tell someone, and you're the only one who cares. Everyone has the same problem, and I'm sure you do too.

Enough of bad news. The children grow every day, it seems. Bao is going to be a strong boy. He plays soccer with his friends and is always scoring more than anyone else. Anh is a good girl, and I think she is going to grow up to be very pretty. Mother and Father are both well and send their love.

Please come home soon. My soul aches for you.
Love,

Tuyết

Chapter 4

The tenuous nature of our existence becomes apparent one morning when my Father awakens me early.

"Get up, daughter, your Mother is very ill."

I rise on one elbow. "What is it?"

"She has a fever and is delirious. I fear it may be something serious."

I dress rapidly and go to her side, placing one hand on her forehead. "She's burning up. I'll get a basin and some cloths."

The children are roused by our activity. "What's wrong, Mother?" Bao asks.

"Your grandmother is ill this morning. Help Anh get dressed and Grandfather will find both of you something to eat. I need for you to take care of your sister until I can help you. Can you do that?"

"Yes, I can do that."

"Good. I'll be with you as soon as I can." He leads his little sister back to their sleeping area, and I carry a basin of cool water and the cloths back to Mother. Father is in a state, and I know the best thing is to keep him busy.

"Father, go fix the children some breakfast, then send Bao off to school"

He obeys as if he were one of my children himself.

I kneel by Mother's bed and place a wet cloth on her head to stem the raging fever wracking the poor woman. Father comes in again and begins comforting his wife.

"My poor Ngon. Please don't leave me alone."

"I don't think she can hear you, Father." I look behind him. "Where's Anh?"

"She's busy with her dolls. What can I do to help you?"

I sit back and sigh. "I don't know. I don't know. I usually just give the children aspirin and keep them hydrated, but this looks much more serious."

I hear Mai's voice from the doorway. "What's wrong, Tuyết? Bao said his grandmother's sick."

"Yes, it's Mother, she has a terrible fever, but why did he tell you?"

"I was seeing my children off to school, and I guess he felt he had to tell me. You know how children his age are." Mai comes to the bedside and inspects the patient.

"I think you'll have to get a doctor, Tuyết. I've seen this before, and you won't be able to break the fever without medicine," Mai offers.

I sigh and sit back on my heels. "I think you're right, but I don't know any doctors."

"I know of a good man in the city who might come. He came once when my children were sick. Perhaps he'll come to your mother. I have our moped today. If your father could watch her for a while, we could go into the city and talk to him."

I turn to father. "Can you watch Anh and tend to Mother also?" I ask.

Mai breaks in. "It's best to keep the children away from her. I'll take her to my house. My aunt is watching my youngest, and Anh will be no more trouble."

I instruct Father in the proper care of Mother while I'm gone. "Keep the wet cloths on her head, Father; and try to get her to drink something. She needs to stay hydrated. Also see if she'll take some chicken broth I have in the kitchen. She needs to keep up her strength."

"I will care for her properly, daughter. You go get the doctor."

Mai takes Anh to her house, and we mount her moped for the trip into Bien Hoa City.

The doctor's tiny waiting room is full of people. As we wait, Mai tries small talk to help pass the time, but all I can think of is how much money will be involved. Will I save my mother's life only to have her starve? I alternate between wanting her to live and a secret wish pops into my head that she should die and save us the expense. We wait over an hour and a half until our number is called.

Doctor Nguyen is a small, skinny man whose chiseled face and graying hair gives him a look of distinction. I'm a bit intimidated by such an impressive fellow, but Mai speaks first.

"This is my neighbor, Tuyết, Doctor Nguyen. Her mother is very ill and cannot come here because we don't have a car, and..."

"Slow down and tell me exactly what her problem is," he says.

"I'm sorry. I'll let Tuyết tell you." They both turn to me.

"She has a bad fever with chills and trembling, and Mai thinks it's very serious. She says she's seen it before."

Mai breaks in. "Yes, Doctor, I remember three years ago when many people had the same symptoms. They said it was typho, or something like that."

The doctor thinks for a moment before answering. "I remember that also. It was typhus. This could be serious. I must see your mother to be sure. One of you must ride with me in my car. You will need to vouch for me to get past the guard at the base," He says.

"I will," I volunteer.

"I will be finished here in about an hour. Just take a seat outside, and I'll call you when I'm ready."

We go back to the nearly empty waiting room. Mai wants to wait with me, but I insist she go back to her children.

It's over an hour before the doctor emerges from his office and leads me through a series of rooms and hallways to a black Toyota. He opens the heavy wooden gates and drives out before locking them again behind the car.

I'd been in open-sided jeeps, but never before in a closed car. How luxurious it seems with the fine leather-like seats and the carpet on the floor. I think how wonderful it must be to be rich.

He threads his way through the city to the base gate where he shows his identification to the guard. I vouch for him after showing my ID also, then direct the car to my house.

The presence of a non-military vehicle creates quite a stir as we park. The children cluster around and place their hands on it as if to verify that it's not some sort of mirage. Mai Is watching for us and comes out of her house to shoo the curious urchins away, but they only back out of her reach and continue to stare at the unusual sight. Father reluctantly takes over the chore of guarding the car while we go inside with the doctor.

At mother's bedside, Doctor Nguyen listens with his stethoscope and pokes and prods various places. He feels her pulse and takes her blood pressure and temperature. He asks several questions, and I provide the answers since she's either asleep or delirious all the time the doctor examines her.

"I believe your mother has Typhus," the doctor pronounces. "Do you have a problem with rats?"

"No, I haven't noticed any."

"Typhus comes from lice, and the lice usually come from rats. If there are infected rats in the area an epidemic could start. Has she been anywhere where there might be rats?"

"She went to the dump the other day to see if there was anything there we could use. She washed as soon as she came back, but she did complain of itching on her hands."

"That must be it," the doctor said. "I will notify the Base Commander to have the dump sprayed immediately. I just hope we can catch this before an epidemic begins. Typhus can be very deadly. Of course, I couldn't be absolutely sure without more tests, but you would have to take her to a hospital for those."

"We can't afford the hospital, doctor."

"I didn't think so. To cure her you will need antibiotics; and they're only available on the black market. Do you have any money?"

"Our savings are almost gone, but I have a little. How much do these things cost?"

"More than a month of your husband's wages, I'm afraid," the doctor's voice shows his frustration at trying to practice medicine in a country still working under the old Mandarin system of bribes, kick-backs and black markets.

"Will she die if she does not have them?" I ask.

"There is a good chance of that. Some people recover fully from this disease, but at her age and state of malnutrition, the odds are not good."

"Then we will buy the medicine."

He takes out a note pad and scribbles a message. Tearing off the page, he hands it to me saying, "Take this to the apothecary next to the market place. Do you know it?"

"I do." Mai volunteers.

"Good. Take 15,000 Piaster with you and pay no more than that. If he wants more, come to my office, and I will find you another source."

"How much do I owe you, doctor?" I say as I hand the prescription to Mai.

"Do you have a spare chicken?"

"Yes, I will kill one for you."

"Never mind that right now. Bring it to me cooked if your mother recovers. If she doesn't, eat it yourself. I must go now and alert the authorities."

"Thank you, doctor. You are very generous."

"It's the least I can do for our soldiers. Goodnight."

He leaves, and Father enters as worried as ever. "What did he say, daughter?"

"He thinks she has typhus and needs medicine."

"Medicine is very expensive, but if the doctor says she needs it to live, we must get it. I will go into the city. Tell me where to go."

"Wait a moment," I tell him and turn to Mai.

"You have a moped, and you know where to go. Will you get the medicine for me?"

"Yes, give me the money. I'll go now," Mai says.

I go into the back area of the house and open the hiding place for our money. I remove the small pile of paper notes, leaving the coins. I count it out, 17,000 Piasters. What I thought was so much just yesterday will be mostly consumed in one transaction, but Mother must have the medicine. A tear forces its way out of one eye in spite of my resolve to hold it back. I take the money to Mai.

"This is all we have, Mai. There's 17,000 Piaster there in case he wants more."

"I'll do my best bargaining, Tuyết." Mai takes the money and leaves the house. The buzzing of her moped is a reassuring sound.

An hour later, Mai appears carrying a small brown bag.

"This is all you get for 15,000 Piasters," Mai says holding the bag out to me with one hand and offering the change in the other.

"If it saves my mother's life it is worth it." I shove the money in my bra and open the bag to find a small plastic bottle full of pills.

I stare at the medicine. It represents nearly all of our savings, and there is very little food in the house. I'll probably lose several day's work tending to Mother, reducing my pay considerably, and Chinh's payday is still two weeks away. After sending a chicken to the doctor, we won't have much to eat until then. I pray to our ancestor's spirits to help us in this hour of need.

*

The first day I can leave Mother and go back to work Xuan is sick again. George picks me up.

"I've missed you. Have you been sick?"

"No, Mother sick. I take care her."

"I'm sorry. Is she better now?"

"She better now, but medicine cost much money." I mentally kick myself for saying that. It makes me look as if I'm asking him for the money.

"How much money?"

"15,000 Piaster, but I pay okay."

"I know that's a lot for you to pay." He pulls the jeep over and produces his billfold. "Take this."

He hands me a large stack of bills. "This too much," I protest.

"Take it all. I was going to give it to one of my counterparts, but you need it more. It's not that much in American money. I can afford it, and you need it."

He smiles at me, and I almost see Chinh's face in his. He is a handsome man, even for an American, and he doesn't smell like most of them. The others have a new baby, sour milk smell about them, but George has a fresh, manly smell in the mornings and an almost sensual aroma of masculine exertion in the evenings. I take the money.

Bien Hoa Air Base
September 9, 1968

My Darling,
Mother contracted typhus, and it took almost all our savings to buy her medicine. We now live hand to mouth. Please come home. I beg you to come back not because I'm lonely or the children need you, but because any increase in inflation or any other setback will mean we will begin to starve. I'll ask for more money from the BX, but I think that's hopeless. Father is still looking for work but has no luck. Mother is still weak from the Typhus. She says she can go to work as a maid when she's well, but I need her to watch the children. Father is there for them now, but they need a woman's touch.

Your superiors must be made to understand. We need you here. We need you now more for the money than anything else. It's horrible to say that. I love you so much, and I ache for you, but those feelings are now secondary to our need to survive.

Please come home now.
Love,

Tuyết

Mother is recovering nicely from the typhus. She's sewing again and feels strong enough to do the shopping at the local market once a week. One week, she comes home with her shopping bag only half full. I see her light burden and open it to inspect the contents. "Is this all you could get?"

"Prices have nearly doubled on everything. There's barely enough rice here for three people, let alone five. I killed the last chicken yesterday, and meat is impossible on our budget now. I hear the Americans are passing out some dried milk. I will go there tomorrow and get some for the children," mother says.

"I'll just have to find another job. Otherwise, we'll have to start begging."

"I wish you more luck than your Father's had."

The children burst into the house followed by Father. "Mommy, Mommy, look what Grandfather found," Bao yells as he holds up two dead rats.

"Bao! What are you doing with those?" I recoil from the sight of the horrible beasts. "Get them out of here. Rats made your grandmother sick."

Father steps forward with two more rats. "It's all right, Daughter. I caught them near the American quarters, and Hau says the rats there don't have bad lice. Besides, there was no Typhus outbreak after your mother was ill. I think they're safe to eat."

"Eat? You expect us to eat rats?"

"Daughter, I told you we can't afford meat, and the chickens are gone," Mother says.

"I will skin and clean them. They don't look so bad without heads or tails, and they're not bad to eat once you get over what they are," father says. He takes the rats from Bao and leaves the house by the back door.

I shake off my revulsion and grab the children. "Come, we must wash your hands very well after handling those creatures." I drag them to the kitchen and scrub them thoroughly.

The rats really didn't taste that bad at dinner.

*

The next day over the lunch hour, I sit in the back room of the BX with my head in my hands, praying to Tara for an answer to the problem.

"Why so glum, Tuyết?" Xuan asks.

"It's money. I don't make enough here to make ends meet these days, and Chinh can't send me more than he is already. I don't know what I'll do. The children need more than I can feed them, and my parents are almost skeletons. I need another job, but there aren't any available."

"Like I told you before, the Americans have money," Xuan offers.

"You know I can't do what you do."

"With your looks, you could have them standing in line to pay you four times what they pay me."

"Why would they do that?" I know there is no way I can do what Xuan does, but again, my curiosity overcomes my revulsion.

"You're tall, I'd say about 170 centimeters,"

"168," I correct her.

"Okay, 168. You have long legs and good boobs, but more importantly, you have a western face. They really go for women with western faces. They'll give you lots of money, and all you have to do is cook them a good meal and fuck their brains out."

"What are you saying? You don't have a husband—I do." As soon as I say it I want to take it back. It's a very cruel remark. Xuan's face falls a bit from her usual cocky smile. "I'm sorry. I shouldn't have said that. Forgive me."

"Nothing to forgive. I know exactly how you feel. If Duc were still alive, I probably couldn't do it either. At least, not as long as he was with me, but if he were gone as long as Chinh's been gone, I might think seriously about it."

"I can't even think about it, Xuan."

She shrugs her shoulders. "Suit yourself. All I know is, if you're willing to put aside your prudish feelings, you can have more money than you could use just for an hour or two on your back once a week, and you wouldn't have to worry about your family starving."

"You're Catholic. Doesn't it cause you problems with the church?"

She inhales and blows a smoke ring. "I don't go to confession any more, and I haven't been to mass since Duc was killed. You're Buddhist, you should have no problem with it.

"I couldn't do that. It's very bad karma. Besides, Chinh would kill me."

"He's not here; is he? What he doesn't know won't hurt him."

"What about my children and my parents? They'd surely suspect something if I was sleeping with an American."

"You can be clever about it. Say you're just cooking for them, or doing some cleaning, or something like that. They can't prove you're fucking them."

"They'd know. I'd look so guilty. It's silly anyway, the very thought of it's revolting, and I could never betray Chinh."

She smiles at me as she produces a tissue and wipes my eyes. "How sick do your children need to be before you change your mind?"

I know she's right. They are already beginning to suffer from their diet of rice and greens with no meat except fish or rats on rare occasions. They don't understand why there is so little to eat. If Chinh would only come home, all of our problems would be solved. The money he needs to live at Nha Trang would be available for the whole family. Tears roll down my cheeks again, and I taste their salt as they run into my mouth. Maybe she's right.

"I wouldn't even know how to go about getting an American boyfriend, Xuan." I begin to cry again at the thought of cheating on Chinh.

Xuan smiles and puts a comforting arm around my shoulders.

"What about that handsome Thieu Ta you rode with while I was sick?"

"He's a very nice man, but I don't think he's interested in me in *that* way. Besides, he's happily married himself."

Xuan laughs. "If he isn't interested in screwing you, he's not human, and, by the way, all of my boyfriends are happily married. They all need sex after a few months, and you're exactly the kind of woman they dream about. The officers are nice to you. The ones you have to watch are the Sergeants. They don't think you're human, and most of them will knock you around a bit. I don't fuck with them anymore."

Xuan seems so confident about the matter. Maybe I could have any American I want, but I can't bring myself to even think about having sex with them.

"I'm sorry, Xuan. I appreciate your good wishes, but I just can't do that."

At that moment the manager calls us both back to work.

Nha Trang Air Base
December 22, 1968

Dearest Tuyết,
I've spoken to my commander about your plight, and he has sympathy, but he can't release me yet. He offered to pay me for playing my dan ghi-ta phim lom[1] for the cai luong theater[2] he owns, and I've agreed. It gives me more money to send to you and keeps me out of the officers' club at night.
I still miss you terribly and I yearn to see my children again. This war seems to have no end, but we must win. I can't imagine life under the Communists, that is, if they let us live.
Be brave and believe that I'm doing all I can to help you and to return home as soon as possible.
All my love,

Chinh

1. A guitar with the neck scooped out between the frets.
2. A form of Vietnamese folk opera.

Chapter 5

One evening I walk into our house and smell a strange cooking odor. I follow it to the kitchen area and find Mother busy at the range.

"What are you cooking, Mother?" I ask.

She continues to batter and fry something that looks like fish as she replies, "Your Father killed a snake today. He says it's good to eat. I haven't tried it, but I remember my mother saying snake was good for you."

I have to fight back my revulsion. I know many people eat snake. Why should I be repelled by the idea? At least it's protein for the children. They won't know it's not fish. I reach for one of the fillets cooling on the counter. It's cool enough to try, and I take a small bite.

"What do you think?" Mother asks.

I savor it for a moment. It does have a taste hinting of fish, but more like the frog's legs I had at a restaurant once.

"Not bad. Some nuóc mắm sauce should help it a lot."

At dinner, the children eat it with no complaints. I'm glad to see it. They were beginning to look a bit too thin, and I was beginning to find stray hairs in my own brush more often. Most of them are black, but some are showing gray. The meager diet is affecting all of us.

Even our clothes are beginning to show our plight. The children are outgrowing their school uniforms, and I can't afford to buy new ones. Mother tailors them as best she can, but it's easy to see they've been let out.

*

I'm surprised when Xuan quits her job at the BX. She says she doesn't need to work that hard for what they pay us. I know that's not the real reason. She steals enough to make up for our low pay. She says she can make more by taking on another boyfriend. Whatever the real reason, I'm left without a ride to work and forced to wave down rides. I'm not surprised when George stops for me.

"Where have you been? I've looked for you every day," he says.

"I ride moped with friend, but she quit." I settle into the jeep, and he pulls away.

"I'll be glad to take you both ways, if you like."

I have to think about this. I can certainly use the ride, but what will he expect in return? What can he do? His only answer to my refusal to have sex with him is to stop picking me up. I feel safe in my ability to avoid being backed into a corner.

"Okay, you pick me up same last time, okay?"

"Sure, it will be nice to see your beautiful face again each morning."

*

It seems there is no end to our suffering. The children miss more school due to illness, and they grow thinner before my eyes. Our money buys less and less, and Father is hard pressed to provide any supplement to our diet as everyone is searching out wild sources of meat. Sometimes a neighbor will bring in one of the small deer from the forest to share among us. They find them while on missions into the bush.

I see Xuan from time to time, and she reminds me of my opportunity with the Americans. I still can't bring myself to do what she does, but I wonder how much longer I can hold out.

That evening on the way home from the BX, George senses my uneasiness. "What's on your mind, Snow?"

"Is nothing." I can't possibly talk to him about my discussions with Xuan.

"Is it money again?" he asks.

I don't answer. I don't want to take his money again. I feel like a beggar.

"Okay, I understand how you feel, but what if there was a way for you to earn the money?" he says.

I look at him, knowing how he expects me to earn the money. "Jhorjhe, I no go bed with you."

He pulls the jeep to the side of the road. The Hondas and mopeds swirl past us as he continues to stare out the windscreen.

"I would not ask you to do anything you don't want to do, Snow. I will buy you something you can sell on the Black Market. It will be something that doesn't cost me much money, but it will be something I know will bring a good deal of money

43

for you. It will be better than me giving you money directly. Do you know about the Black Market?"

I remember Xuan has some connections there. "I have friend who know."

"Good, I'll order you some baby bottles. I know my counterparts sell them to raise money. It'll take me a week, or so, to get them. Will you be okay until then?"

"Yes, I be okay."

*

We don't talk about money the next week. George asks me about Chinh and when I expect him home. He wants to know about Bao and Ahn and how they do in school. He tells me about his home in America. I feel my guard beginning to slip a bit, and I have to keep warning myself not to become too familiar with this man.

In spite of my misgivings, I begin to relax with George. He never uses harsh words, even for the swarm of mopeds around him. He has such a kind face, and he's always smiling. He doesn't talk down to me, and I feel like an equal with him.

The next week, he announces the arrival of the baby bottles.

"The bottles came in today, they're back at my trailer."

"Thank you, Jhorjhe," is all I can muster.

As we drive to his trailer, a dark voice in the back of my head keeps telling me not to go while another lighter voice assures me it's all right. What will I do if George really does ask me to have sex with him? I can't betray Chinh, that's all there is to it. I'm grateful to George for the money he's given me, and he doesn't seem to expect anything in return. The dark voice insists it's a trap, but I'm confident I can refuse sex with George without creating problems. I have faith in him as a gentleman. Still, I see no point in putting myself in an awkward position.

"You bring bottles out, then we go my house."

"Don't you trust me, Snow?"

He says this sincerely, but he never takes his eyes off the road. How do I answer that? If I say I don't, won't that cloud our friendship? There's only one answer.

"I trust you. No need for me go inside. I no want cause you trouble."

"Look, I want you to come in because I think we should toast the start of our new venture."

"Okay, but I no can stay long. Children wait for supper."

"This won't take long."

We drive on in silence. I can't help but think about what I'll do if he wants sex. Will he overpower me and rape me? No, that's not the man I've come to know. He'll understand if I say "no". He has to.

Chapter 6

George drives me to a complex of trailers in the American compound under the big water tower on the Vietnamese side of the base. It's a maze of bunkers and trailers seeming to stretch on forever, but George opens one of the doors to reveal a tiny room so cold I shiver as we go inside.

I know about air conditioning from the BX, but it's never this cold. I wonder how he can stand it, and I think it must be this cold all the time in America if he sleeps in such a frigid environment here.

He notices me holding my arms around my body and says, "Oh, I'll turn down the air conditioning. The maids turn it up during the day while they're working."

He moves to the unit on the opposite wall and turns it off, then produces a large box from the doorless closet.

"Here they are, Snow," George smiles as he places the box on the bed.

"Thank you, Jhorjhe," I always have trouble pronouncing his name correctly, but he seems to think it's cute. I sit down on the bed and open it carefully.

The box contains a dozen baby bottles and all the accessories needed for feeding babies. I've heard of the American's plastic bottles, but I used glass ones for the children. These are truly marvelous because they won't break if a baby drops them.

George produces a bottle from his refrigerator and two wine glasses from a cabinet. The bottle is champagne, and he opens it with a loud "pop". He pours two glasses and hands one to me.

"Here's to a new venture just between us." He raises his glass, and I follow suit.

The champagne is cold and effervescent. The bubbles squish in my mouth, and the wine goes down smoothly.

He smiles. "One of my counterparts told me they fetch a nice price in Bien Hoa City."

"Okay." I really don't have any idea how to go about selling them, but I'm sure Xuan will know.

George sits down on the bed next to me and moves the box to the floor. I feel his warmth in the chilly room, and I fear what surely comes next.

"I've grown to love you over the last two months, Snow. You're such a beautiful woman, and so delicate. I'm afraid to hold you too tightly. I fear you're really fine porcelain and I'll shatter you with a rough touch."

He takes my hand in his, and I inhale sharply as the need in his grip surges through my body. I know what comes next, and I can't do it. What will he do if I say no? He pulls my face to his and kisses me gently.

My mind reels. He's a nice man, and very attractive, for an American. I wouldn't mind having sex with him if I were free, but my conscience screams out in opposition. Xuan's words echo in my brain, "What he doesn't know won't hurt him." His kiss is gentle and warm. So far, it isn't as bad as I'd imagined, but the worst is surely to come. I must refuse him now before we go any further and hope he understands. I break off the kiss and push him away.

"No, Jhorjhe. I no do this. You nice man, but I no want boyfriend. I married. Please, I go home now."

"I know you love your husband. I love my wife, but I've got seven more months to do on my tour, and I'm about to go crazy. I can't bring myself to patronize the bar girls or visit the base massage parlor. When I met you, I thought I'd found a woman who might understand my problem because she was alone too. Please stay."

Why do men think we need sex as much as they do? Yes, I miss Chinh, but sex is secondary. I miss more things about him than our sex.

"I no same like you, Jhorjhe. I wait. Chinh come home soon."

"You told me he didn't know when he could come home. Please?"

Once more he takes me in his arms. I look into his eyes and see a burning need gnawing at his insides. If George quits giving me money, and Chinh doesn't come home, we'll eventually starve. I don't know what the bottles will bring on the black market, but I believe him when he tells me they'll bring good money. He kisses me again, and I don't resist this time. He's so gentle.

I want to say no, but a vision of my family thin and sickly blocks the words. It overcomes my natural revulsion and causes me to wrap my arms around him. He seems to understand and kisses me with a loving passion I haven't known since Chinh left. *No, no,* my brain screams; but the sound can't escape my head. His tongue parts my lips and searches my mouth. I fight back the urge to gag then slip deeper and deeper under the spell of the moment. A wall of passion seems to block out all opposition.

I can't believe what I'm doing yet I can't bring myself to ask him to stop. The sin is already committed, and I have nothing more to lose. I don't resist as he pulls off my top and removes my bra.

He kisses each breast and suckles my nipples. I feel a surge of desire rising from deep in my body. It rides rough-shod over my inhibitions. He lays me down and removes my pants and underwear. Somehow, the room doesn't feel so cold anymore. He kneels by the bed and kisses my body. Each kiss is like the touch of a hot iron.

He stands up and undresses. I close my eyes not wishing to react with revulsion at the sight of his naked body. He lays down beside me, and I can't move. He kisses me more aggressively as he enters me.

I surrender to the moment and pull him closer to me. The erotic sensation I haven't felt in months sweeps away my reasoning, but I recover enough to remember a condom. I push him away.

"You use rubber. I have baby, I die."

George overcomes the initial shock and begins to laugh. "I don't need them, Snow. I've had a vasectomy."

I have no idea what he's talking about. Is this some kind of American ruse to fool the gullible Vietnamese?

"I no know, vasecomy," I mispronounce it.

He points to his testicles and explains the procedure, but my look of utter disbelief remains.

"My wife and I don't use them anymore; and my youngest kid's sixteen. The Air Force does the operation free. Besides, I don't have any rubbers."

I have no way to prove or disprove what he says. He seems to be sincere, but I know men can lie like dogs when it comes to sex. There's no alternative but to let him proceed. Xuan will surely know of some possible remedies if he proves to be a liar.

"Okay, you go ahead; but if I have baby, I die."

He resumes his attentions, and I feel sensations I've never experienced with Chinh. I marvel at the things he does to me. The same overwhelming force causes me to abandon all inhibitions and savor the pure joy of the moment. My mind rebels at this. How can I enjoy being unfaithful to my husband? I want to push George off me, but demonic laughter from some distant realm revels in the announcement that there's no going back now. A wave of shame washes over me, and I want to cry, but I hold it in, thinking I can't let George see me react this way.

He finally spends himself and rolls off to lie beside me.

"That was wonderful," he says before falling asleep.

I lay in that strange bed thinking more clearly now. The dark clouds part, and the devilish voice falls silent. I've done something terribly wrong, but I push those feelings away, and my practical side takes over. I think of how much money the bottles will bring and the food that money will buy. *Oh, Chinh; I'm so sorry to do this to you; but I have no choice. I know you will never forgive me, but even if I should lose you for this, my children will survive.*

My mind shifts gears. *Chinh doesn't ever have to know. Who will tell him? Only George and I know about this.*

Wait, this isn't a one-time thing. Now he'll expect me to continue doing this for him until he leaves. Can I manage to pull this off over several months without Chinh ever knowing about it? I'm as clever as Xuan, and he's in Nha Trang. If he comes home, I can break it off with George quickly.

There's no love here, only sexual service for a lonely man. I'll need to think up some kind of story to convince my parents I'm not having sex with George. I'll work that out with George when he wakes up.

His snores tell me he will sleep for a while, and I manage to climb over him without awakening the pale giant. I go into the tiny bathroom and look in the mirror. A different woman looks back at me. I've taken that first fatal step over the edge of a cliff, dropping into an abyss I can't fathom. I step into his shower and let the water run over me for a long time, hoping it will wash away my shame.

Chapter 7

I dress and awaken George.

"I go home now. You take me, please."

He's groggy but responds with a smile. "Sure, let me get dressed."

He drags on his pants. As he reaches for his top, he asks, "When can we do this again?"

I knew this was coming. Once begun, a man expects it to go on forever. The only way out is to stop now. Xuan says I will get over this feeling of revulsion, but will I?

"Did you hear me, Snow?" he asks.

"I hear you. I think."

I have no choice. I need this arrangement, but I need to set the boundaries on this activity. "I come once week. What day?"

"How about each Thursday?"

"I come Thursday. I bring food. I tell parents I cook for you, you give me money. Okay?"

"I wasn't expecting a meal, but I'll gladly accept one. I like Vietnamese food You can cook whatever you like. If your cooking's as good as your sex, it'll be great. I'll be glad to pay you for cooking."

I can't believe what he's saying. I was little more than a stiff mannequin, but if he's satisfied, so am I.

He drops me off at my house, and my Father is waiting in the living room.

"You're late coming home. Your Mother had to feed the children and me, but there's some left for you. Why are you so late, and why are you coming home with an American?"

"The American Thieu Ta who takes me to work and back gave me a special gift." I set the big box down and show him the bottles.

"Why bottles?" he asks.

"They're to sell on the black market."

He looks at me with an accusing expression. "You aren't screwing him, are you?"

"Don't be silly. He's just a nice man who wants to help us. He's asked me to cook for him once a week, though. He says he gets tired of mess hall food."

I knew this was coming, and I'd rehearsed my answer many times on the way home, but I can tell by his expression he doesn't believe me. I'm sure he wants to, but he's a worldly-wise man.

"Daughter, no man does what he's done for you without expecting something in return."

"The Americans are all rich, Father. I see them in the BX every day. They buy expensive things, one after another. They have money to give away if they want to. My Thieu Ta is just very generous, that's all."

He eyes me with suspicion, and I fight hard to suppress my guilt while looking him squarely in the eye.

"Just make sure you don't wind up in his bed, daughter."

He leaves it at that, and I'm very glad he accepts my explanation.

*

I lay in bed that night thinking of Chinh. If he ever found out about this, he'd leave me in an instant. His pride would overcome his love for me. I still love him as much as ever, but I know he'd never understand. It would make no difference to him that his children were starving. He would only see a whore. Is that what I've become? The word hits me like a bullet. It ricochets through my brain, wounding every moral fiber in my body. I pray for another way to make money, but no answer comes. I will not see my children starve, and if this is the only way, so be it.

Bien Hoa Air Base
January 16, 1969

Dear Chinh,
We're doing the best we can without you. Father and Mother are well, and the children are healthy, but there is no money to spare beyond what it takes to feed us.

The kind American Thieu Ta I told you about has asked me to cook for him once a week. He says he'll pay me well for a good meal, and he loves Vietnamese food. I think this is the answer to my prayers. The Americans have so much money, and George (he taught me how to spell it, but I can't pronounce it), the Thieu Ta, is very generous. He says it's his contribution to American foreign aid.

Speaking of that, I've found the Americans also distribute many things through their aid office here on Bien Hoa. I can get powdered milk and some cheese plus some canned goods. The canned goods are American food, but I can use it as part of some recipes.

Our bellies are full, but our hearts are still empty waiting for you to fill them with your love. Please come home.
All my love,
Tuyết

*

Friday, I trap Xuan after her work at the advisor club. "I have a set of baby bottles George gave me. How do I sell them?"

She smiles at me knowingly. "Does he fuck good?"

How can I possibly avoid discussing this with her? "He's very gentle," I whisper.

She laughs. "That's okay, but I like a good, rough fuck every now and then."

"Let's not talk about that part. How do I sell the bottles?"

"Very well, I understand. I have a man in Bien Hoa City who buys my things. I can take them to him if you like."

"How much will he give for them?"

"The last bunch I sold, he gave me 20,000P."

"Is that all? They're worth twice that from what George tells me."

"Hey, you have to realize that he must make a profit too."

"Don't you bargain with him?"

"Not on baby bottles. I can get a little better price out of him on things like radios, TVs and cameras, but not on bottles."

"I guess I'll just have to settle for that. When can we go see him?"

"We can go tonight if you like."

"Is that safe? They tell me the 'cowboys' are out at night," I say.

"Mr. Huyn will protect us. The 'cowboys' know me, and they know not to mess with me. You'll have to get the bottles and things out of that big box and put them in bags. You can't carry that big box on my moped."

"I can do that. What time? I can't go before 7:30, I have to make dinner and clean up."

"Make it 8:00, then. I'll come by for you at 8:00."

I hear Xuan's moped promptly at 8:00. The bottles are ready in the bags I use for shopping at the market.

"Are you sure you want to go into Bien Hoa City at night, daughter?" Father asks.

"Xuan says it will be safe. She goes in several times a week."

I kiss the children and join Xuan outside.

"Ready for a wild ride?" she asks.

"Let's go," I say.

We ride out of the base gate and into the city. The first part of the ride is normal. The moped's light cuts a tiny swatch of daylight into the dark enveloping us, and there is little traffic on the road until we enter the lights of the city.

The first two motorcyclists zooming past us only shout bawdy suggestions, but a lump of bile rises in my throat. We are defenseless against any attack. The next motorcycle carries two ominous-looking fellows who crowd close to us. The pillion rider reaches out for me, but Xuan swerves to avoid him and slows the moped so they zoom past us.

These are the dreaded "cowboys" who haunt the streets at night. Theft is the least of our worries. I've heard stories of gang rapes and torture. The motorcycle comes back to cut us off, but a jeep comes up from behind us and threatens to run down the cowboys. They speed up and soon vanish into the city. The jeep pulls alongside, and the driver waves.

"Chao Co Xuan," he shouts.

Xuan waves to him and allows him to pull ahead of us. Only then do I notice a man in the passenger seat cradling a submachine gun on his lap.

Xuan turns back to me and shouts, "That's Mr. Huyn. I told you he'd protect us."

We follow Huyn to a shop near the marketplace where the jeep pulls into an alley. Xuan stops the moped at the shop door, and we wait for Huyn. He soon appears accompanied by his bodyguard.

"Who is this lovely lady with you?" he asks Xuan.

"This is Ba Tuyết. She has something for you," Xuan replies.

"I hope it's more than the baby bottles you mentioned in your phone call," he says as he strips me bare with his eyes.

Xuan slaps him playfully. "Are you tired of my services? If you dump me for another woman, I'll never bring you anything again."

"You know I love only you," Huyn says as he pats her softly on the bottom.

He opens the door, and three of us go inside while the bodyguard remains outside guarding the jeep and Xuan's moped.

Huyn turns on a dim light and takes a seat at an old desk. "Show me what you've brought."

I lay the baby bottles on his desk along with all that came with them. Huyn inspects them.

"Ah, they've not been used. My usual price for these is 15,000P." He opens a cabinet containing a safe and begins to dial the combination.

"You crook," Xuan says. "You always give me 20,000P."

"I have a cot in the back if this lady wants 50,000P," he says.

"I don't do that kind of thing," I say.

Huyn turns serious. "Yes, you do. I know how you got these bottles. You're the same as all the others. Take 15,000P or fuck me for 50,000P. That's my final offer."

"I'll take the 15,000P," I say.

He counts out the money from his safe and hands it to me.

Xuan breaks in and forces his hand away. "No you won't." She turns to Huyn. "Give her 20,000P or you'll never get another blow job from me."

He smiles and counts out another 5,000P. "It's good you have a friend so loyal, Ba Tuyết."

The jeep follows us to the Bien Hoa Air Base gate, and Huyn waves as he turns back to the city.

*

The next Thursday I bring a meal that's one of Chinh's favorites. It's called Ga Kho Gung and consists of chicken thighs and legs glazed in a special sauce. The recipe calls for nuóc mắm sauce, and I add very little I don't know if he likes it. It's served over sticky rice. It's the least expensive thing I can cook. We now have several chickens, thanks to George's money and gifts, and my family prefers the breast meat. Legs and thighs are not missed.

*

Ga Kho Gung

Nuóc mắm Sauce
2 tbsp sugar
¼ cup water

Add water to sugar in a deep skillet and cook over medium heat until caramelized.

Cut two thighs and two legs into smaller pieces and add to nouc mau sauce, coating the chicken pieces.

Add 1 tbsp nuóc mắm sauce, 3 tsp sugar, ½ tsp salt, 1 tsp ground black pepper and I cup water.

Add 2 diced shallots, 4 cloves of garlic, minced, 2-inch ginger knob, sliced.

Cook 40 minutes or until thick carmel sauce forms. Add water if needed.

Serve over sticky rice.

*

I walk the short distance from our home to the American compound, and the man at the gate insists on escorting me to George's trailer. He only leaves after George confirms he's invited me.

"Good evening, Snow."

"I bring food." I hold up the containers.

"Go ahead and use whatever you like in the kitchen." He waves a hand toward the tiny kitchen area of his trailer.

I go to work on the dinner, exploring his drawers and cupboards for the pots, pans and other utensils as I need them. I say nothing, and the silence is like a thick fog in the chilly room. As I cook I look around. The bathroom is off to my right as I face the small range. The main room is behind me with the bed near the far wall. I remember that part of the room well.

George finally breaks through the fog. "Are you sorry we had sex?"

I have to think about my answer. Yes, I am sorry—sorry I'd betrayed Chinh, but there's no way I can say this to George. "No, I no sorry. You nice man. You not hurt me."

"Why would anyone want to hurt you? Was any part of our sex painful?"

"No, sex good, but friend tell me some American hurt women."

"I can't believe it, but I have to admit it's possible."

He sits staring at the wall for a moment, and I continue to prepare the meal. I have no idea of what to talk about with this man. He finally breaks the silence.

"How is your husband? Is he coming home any time soon? I'd hate it if you had to stop visiting me."

"Husband say he no come home soon. He…"

I break at this point and begin to cry. George moves to me and takes me in his arms.

"It's all right, Snow. You don't need to say any more. I know this is hard for you."

"I cook." I turn back to the stove, and he sits down again. Another long silence follows.

"Is there anything you'd like to know about America?" he asks.

I hadn't thought about this subject. It would be a safe topic, and I am curious about some things. "Why Americans have much money? You buy much at BX. Spend lots money."

He breaks into a merry laugh, but I know it's not because he thinks I'm stupid for asking.

"No, we're not all rich. We buy things in the BX because they cost less here than they do in America. We're taking advantage of the lower cost and shipping the items back home. I'm going broke saving money."

I don't understand all of it, but I get the gist.

"Is there anything else you'd like to know?"

I'm dying to ask him if he feels badly about cheating on his wife, but I hold my tongue. I suddenly remember a question Chinh would ask. "You have car in America?'

"Yes, I have a Ford station wagon."

Chinh will know what he's talking about, but it's just words to me. I make sure to memorize them for my next letter to Chinh. "It big car?"

"Yes, it's big. You've seen some of the cars the Air Force uses, they're station wagons."

"I see many jeep—some truck. No see big cars."

"Well I'll point one out to you if I see one on the way to or from the BX."

The room falls silent again. I lift the lid on the rice pot and see it's done. I find plates and bowls and set the small table in the end of the room opposite the bed. "You sit. I serve."

George takes one chair, and I place a bowl full of rice in front of him. The chicken and vegetables go into the only big bowl he has, and I find a large spoon for that. Cups of tea round out the meal, and I sit down opposite him.

"You don't mind if I say grace, do you?" he says.

"What grace?"

"I mean pray."

"Why you pray?"

"It's an American custom. Do you mind?"

"I no mind."

He bows his head and sits silent for a moment. Then he speaks, "Father we thank you for this food. Bless the hands that prepared it and bless it to the nourishment of our bodies. Amen."

He looks up at me and smiles then picks up his fork. I couldn't find any chopsticks among his utensils. He takes a bite of the chicken, savors it for a moment, then nods his head to one side.

"This is delicious." He smiles then takes another bite.

He seems to be pleased with the food, so I begin to eat my portion with a clumsy fork, making a mental note to bring chopsticks next time.

I clean up after the meal, leaving the dirty dishes and bowls in the sink. He can wash them after I leave. I know what comes next, but I don't know how we move from now to naked. George solves my problem.

"I have a nice item for you this time." He beckons me to the bed and pats the mattress, indicating I should sit down. I do as he indicates. He pulls a box from under the bed and I recognize it from the BX. It's a combination radio and tape player.

"This should bring a good price on the black market," he says.

I know it will, but I still dread the next move.

"Thank you, Jhorjhe." He turns my head and kisses me. This is the beginning, but I can't stop him even though my brain is screaming at me to push him away. Once more the black cloud of lust pushes all thoughts of fidelity from my mind.

"Your lips are so soft," he says.

He removes my ao dai and top, then unfastens my bra and lays me back on the bed. He begins the ritual I know from the last time, and my tongue won't form the words to protest. I soften under his touch, and I even begin to enjoy his attentions. He does everything so expertly, so smoothly. I marvel at the sensations. I fall under the spell of passion and catch myself responding with moans and Vietnamese words he doesn't understand but can guess their meaning.

He moves with a simple rhythm, slow at first, then building slightly. He seems to be waiting on me, but I urge him on. I can't help myself. He's sending rivers of fire through me and I orgasm.

*

Nha Trang Air Base
January 26, 1969

Dearest Tuyết,
I hope your Thieu Ta appreciates your cooking as much as I do. It's the second thing I miss. You know well the first thing. You must charge him a lot. You are an excellent cook.
Just one word of warning. He may try to seduce you. Be on your guard and quit cooking for him if he tries to bed you. I'm sure there are other Americans who would appreciate your food.
I'm glad your life is back to normal, but there is still no way I can come home, even for a day or two. I'll keep trying—even if I can only get home for a few hours, I'll do it.
Always be sure of my love.
Your loving husband,

Chinh

*

George surprises me one Thursday by producing a funny looking razor and shaving off my pubic hair. He explains this is the kind of razor used for shaving women before they have babies. I'd never heard of such a thing as both of my children were born at home with a midwife in attendance. I deduce he wants me to do this to make his kissing my private parts less repulsive, but what he does feels so good, I'm glad to make it easier for him. As a reward for my compliance, he gives me a television set. Its sale funds a month of groceries.

The weeks pass quickly. Chinh still writes that he can't come home. I begin to suspect he has a mistress at Nha Trang. He's a virile man, and if George needs sex, Chinh must also. It helps me justify my evenings of infidelity.

*

Slowly, I lose my inhibitions with George. If I'm going to be a mistress, I might as well enjoy the role. I also learn a lot about making a man happy from him. He teaches me many moves and positions Chinh and I never tried. I love Chinh, but his technique can't compare to George's.

*

My mother is waiting when I come in the door that evening.

"Why are you still up, Mother?" I ask.

"Your children were asking for you tonight, and they asked why you stay away so late each Thursday."

"What did you tell them?"

"I told them you were making money to buy food so their bellies would be full."

"Did they accept that?"

"They did, but I don't."

"What do you mean?"

"I mean I think you're doing more for this American than just cooking for him."

I can't tell her she's right, but what can I say? There's only one possible reason for me to stay with George so long. "He's an advisor, and he wants to learn Vietnamese. He helps me with my English, and I'm teaching him Vietnamese. My English is getting much better, he says." Mother doesn't speak any English, so it would be hard for her to tell if I'd improved or not. She gives me a doubtful look.

"As long as you aren't going to bed with him."

"Believe me, Mother. I'd not cheat on Chinh."

"Very well, I'll accept that explanation for now. Goodnight daughter."

"Goodnight, Mother."

*

It's getting closer to the end of George's tour. I'm dreading that day for only one reason—the end of the money. I'm secretly relieved that I've managed to keep this up without my parents, or Chinh, becoming too suspicious, and I can only hope that my husband will be transferred back to Bien Hoa before the money I've managed to save runs out.

The Thursday before he leaves, George seems sad. He's quiet through dinner and makes love to me more tenderly than he ever had before. When we finish, he leans on one elbow and speaks softly.

"I go home tomorrow, Snow. I'll miss you, and I want to thank you for being a surrogate wife."

I don't understand 'surrogate', but I can deduce the meaning, and understand he won't be there next week.

"I no like you go, Jorjhe." His gifts and money are all that stand between my family and starvation. I'll have to find another American lover. I won't go back to living from hand to mouth again.

"I have to, Snow. Here, here's some money to help you out until you can find another lover." He hands me a stack of Piasters larger than any I'd ever seen. There has to be at least 50,000P there. "It's all they'd let me exchange right now."

I bury my head in the pillow and begin to sob. George probably thinks the tears are for him, and some of them are, but I cry more for the loss of food for my family.

"Don't cry, Snow. My replacement is here already. I'll tell him to look for you in the morning when he drives to breakfast."

I dry my tears. My problem may be solved. I can only hope his replacement is as kind as he is.

*

Bien Hoa Air Base
March 21, 1969

Dear Chinh,
Things are going well for me now, as well as they can without you. The children are growing by the day. Bao is doing well in school, and Anh will start next year. Father and Mother are both healthy, and Father can sometimes find temporary work without paying too high a bribe.

Every time I hear helicopters overhead I pray you're in one. Come home to us soon.

With all of my love,

Tuyết

*

With George gone, I'm forced to wave down rides again. I'm happy to see the same familiar jeep stop for me once more.

"You must be Snow." the driver says.

The man is a Major, like George. I can tell because he also wears Vietnamese Major rank insignia besides the black American patterns I've never been able to decipher.

"Yes, I Snow."

"Hop in, and I'll give you a ride to the BX."

As we drive, I study this new American. He's the direct opposite of George. George was nearly two meters tall, and this man is much shorter. George was stocky and athletic, while this Major is slim. His hands are almost as delicate as a woman's where George's were stubby. George was a white American, and this man is one of the black Americans. A large, gold ring gleams on his right hand, and he wears no wedding band.

"I'm Tom Wilkins," he extends his right hand.

I take his hand softly.

"I pleased meet you, Major Wirkins."

He laughs lightly. "Just call me Tom; I know the 'l' is hard for you to say."

He's not a handsome man by any means, but he smells so good I think he must have a bouquet of flowers in his pocket. His jet-black hair is the same color as mine but kinky curly. I've never met a black American before, and I wonder if he looks the same as George without clothes.

"Okay, Tom, how you know I Snow?"

"Major Morris told me about you," he says. "He told me you'd be looking for a ride, and I should pick you up."

"What else he tell you?"

"Only that you're a good cook. I could really stand some home cooked meals if you wouldn't mind. I'd pay you well for them."

I'm sure George also told him I'm an easy woman, but I have to pretend he didn't say anything about our sex, even though I've crossed that threshold and must live with the consequences.

"What food you like?"

"Anything as long as it doesn't come from the mess hall or the officer's club. What do you say?"

I survey the man beside me and think about having sex with him. I know exactly what's in store for me in his trailer. The spirits must truly be looking out for me to provide a replacement for George so quickly and so easily, but I still dread the new experience and the continuing subterfuge it will require.

"Okay, I cook for you. What night?"

"How about Wednesday night?"

"You show me your trailer; I come." I smile at him and am pleased to see his face light up with joy.

"I'll pick you up at the exchange tonight and show you where I live. What time do you get off?"

*

Thus, I begin my second affair, which proves to be no easier on my conscience but every bit as profitable as the first one. Tom is surprised to find I have no pubic hair, and I explain that George did it and gave me the razor to keep it off. I tell him I thought it was just one of those things peculiar to Americans. Tom explains it was only peculiar to George, but he finds it very pleasant and asks me to continue.

*

Nha Trang Air Base
April 5, 1969

Dear Tuyết,

It's now been over a year since I last saw you. I burn for your embrace, but I smother the flames before they can consume me. I've told my commander that I must get home soon. He understands, and he says he'll try to give me some leave. I'll let you know as soon as I have a firm date.

You told me your Thieu Ta left. I hope you've found another American to cook for. I know you need the extra money because the Piaster is worth less and less every day. Hopefully, I will be able to end our separation soon.

Kiss the children for me and tell them their father loves them.

With all my love,

Chinh

*

Xuan is pleased to discover I have another American lover.

"How many boyfriends do you have?" she asks.

"Only one. Why should I have more than one?"

"More money. These Americans are stupid when it comes to sex. You can have a different one every night if you want, I do. You just make each of them think he's the only one you're screwing even though you may have five or six more. Like I told you before, they don't care as long as you do a good job when it's their turn."

"I already feel like a whore with one lover. That's enough to get what I need to feed my family."

"Don't you want to live better than you do now? Why not enjoy some of the finer things in life? One lover, six lovers, what's the difference?" Xuan reasons. She lights one of her cigarettes and blows the smoke out in a ring, as she always does to emphasize her point. She's back to work at the BX and back to her old habit of stealing things.

"I understand what you're saying, but I think I'll stick with one at a time. If Chinh comes back, it'll be easier to stop with just one."

"Suit yourself. How are you fixed for rubbers?" Xuan asks.

"Tom has plenty, and he's very good about using them. He's a black American, and I'd die if I had his baby, not only from the shame, but for what that child would have to live with the rest of its life."

"Most of them are scared to death they're going to get some kind of horrible disease from you, but every now and then you get a brave one. I'll steal you a couple dozen this week."

"George didn't use rubbers. He'd had a vasecomy, or something like that." I never did learn the correct pronunciation.

"You mean a vasectomy," Xuan laughs. "You have to watch out for those guys because they might give you a disease. Be sure you douche good after you fuck 'em."

*

Tom replaces George as my ride to and from work, but I encounter a new prospect in the BX one day.

"Hello, Miss. Could you tell me if you're going to get in any more of those pot and pan sets like you had last month?"

The questioner is a tall, thin man who must be in his early fifties. He too is an advisor. His rank is Dai Ta, or as Americans say, Colonel.

"I go check," I say and go to find the manager. He tells me they've just received more sets but they're not out of the container yet. I talk him into getting one out and pricing it. The box is too heavy for me, so he offers to take it out to the Colonel for me.

"We just get in. Manager open big box for you." He hands the large box of pans to the Colonel.

"I wish I knew what to do with these. My wife does all the cooking back home, and I'm sure getting tired of the mess hall food. Are you a good cook?"

"Everybody say I cook very good." Perhaps this is not an invitation to sex. He's much older than the other Americans. Maybe all he wants is a cook?

"Would you be willing to cook for me once or twice a week? I'll pay you very well."

"Sure; I do for you. What night?"

"Well, how does tomorrow night suit you, for starters?"

"That fine, you pick me up here six o'clock. Okay?"

"It's a deal. Do I need to get you any particular kind of food?"

"No, I bring everything."

I tell Tom I won't need him to pick me up tomorrow night because a friend is taking me home on his moped. He seems to take it in stride.

The Colonel, whom I learn is named Watts, proves to be different than the other officers. He never asks me to have sex with him. He never even makes an unwanted advance. I start out cooking once a week, but he expands it to twice a week. He wants me to teach him how to cook and will pay me double for an extra day. The only problem is, that would mean three nights away from my children. I don't have to think too long. I can't pass up the extra money, and I agree to teach him on Monday nights.

Bao is the first to complain. As I prepare to leave for my Thursday with Tom, the children come for my goodnight kiss.

"Why are you gone so much, Mother? I miss you," he says.

I take him in my arms, and Anh runs to join in the embrace. "I'm sorry, my darlings. I don't want to leave you, but I have to. Remember when we had to eat the rats?" Both of them nod their acknowledgement. "Did you like them?"

"They tasted funny," Bao says.

"I didn't like them," Anh says.

"I leave you to cook for the Americans. They pay me very well. I use the money to buy our food, so we don't have to eat them again. Do you understand that?"

Nods, again, are their response. I pull them closer to me and begin to cry. I cry because I despise what I have to do to feed them. Anh kisses me on the cheek.

"Don't cry, Mother. We still love you," she says.

Her words seem to release the tears pent up behind the dam of practicality I've erected to hide my shame. I quickly mend the breach. I can't appear in Tom's trailer with red, swollen eyes.

"I love you both very much. Give me a goodnight kiss."

They both respond with more love than I ever thought possible.

"Now, off to bed with you." I shoo them toward their grandmother, waiting just outside the sleeping area.

I wipe my eyes and head for the door, but Father is waiting just outside.

"Tell me, daughter, why is it you are gone for three hours on this night and only two on the others?"

"Major Wilkins eats slowly, and he wants me to watch an American television show before I can leave. He says it will improve my English. Don't read anything sinister into what I do."

"Just be careful. Men talk about their sexual conquests, and the word will soon make its way back here. I don't condemn you for what you do. I understand why you must do it, but eventually, you will have to pay the price for your actions. Take care, my daughter." He places a hand on my shoulder then turns to enter the house.

As I walk toward the American trailer complex, I think about my situation. Yes, I hate to betray Chinh, but, why should I feel guilty? Chinh doesn't seem to be too concerned about getting a trip home, and I begin to be angry with him for putting me in this position. I have to blame somebody for my sins, and it isn't hard for me to make him the cause of my mental torture.

I fight back more tears. I can't cry now. I can cry later, in my bed, alone, without my husband to console me. Console me, hah! If he knew, he'd throw me out into the street. There'd be no compassion in his mind, no mercy, no forgiveness. His male pride and superior attitude would leave no room for such "un-manly" emotions. Men, bah!

Maybe it's only Vietnamese men. Both of my American lovers have been kind to me and generous with their gifts. Even my colonel buys me gifts from the BX, and I haven't had sex with him. Generosity seems to be an American trait, and I wonder if they would forgive their wives for being unfaithful while they are here, half a world away. Maybe men are the same all over the world.

I've quickened my pace out of anger, and I slow down. I must allow time for my face to return to normal. I must not show anger or remorse to Tom. I'm like an actress. I must put on my stage face. I'm glad I don't wear any make-up except for some lipstick. It's easier to change from the inside out than from the outside in.

Why doesn't Chinh come home and save me from this false life? Deep inside me I fear the reason for his absence is that he knows about my affairs. Father may be right. George or Tom might have mentioned me to their VNAF counterparts. If they have, the word would surely get through to Chinh at Nha

Trang. Yes, that's it. He hates me now. He's staying away because he doesn't want anything to do with me.

Another thought hits me like a monsoon rain. What will I do when the Americans go home? Where will I be then—no Americans and no husband to welcome home and share my bed for the rest of my life? I'd be a woman alone with no hope and no way to support my family.

I brush the thought from my mind. I've told him I'm cooking for them, and he seems to believe that. I know other officers in his unit go to Nha Trang, but most of them don't even know about my cooking ruse, and the ones who do seem to believe it. Even if he does know, he'd give me a chance to explain. He must still love me, and he'd surely try to forgive me.

I can only think of one other reason he's staying away—he has a mistress at Nha Trang, and he doesn't want to leave her. What else could it be? The war doesn't seem to make the same demands on other pilots I know, and that's the only other force strong enough to compel his absence. Yes, that's it. He's screwing another woman and prefers her to me. I wonder if he's giving her money and presents like the Americans give me. Yes, that's why he can't send more money home—he's spending it on his mistress. Well two can play that game. I compose myself with that resolve as I enter the gate at the American compound.

*

The next day I go to the market in Bien Hoa City to sell the wrist watch Tom gave me the night before. I wrap it in brown paper and place it in my market bag out of sight of casual observers or the young thugs that sometimes patrol the streets of the city in search of victims. I catch Trung's small mini-bus and pay him the 100 Piaster fare. I transact my business and hide the American scrip under the produce I buy as a cover activity.

Back home, Father sees me unload my vegetables and take the scrip to my cache. One of the cinder blocks in the sleeping area wall is loose, and I take advantage of it to store the money I'm saving. The scrip is used for buying items on the black market or as bribes. Those are the only things it's good for. Xuan uses scrip to repay Americans for buying her extra things from the BX above those her clients give her. I haven't started that yet. I'm surprised when Father asks, "How much do you have now?"

I quickly push the block back into place. "Not enough."

"How much is enough? When will you be able to end your whoring?"

The word strikes a nerve. I turn to him and raise my hand, ready to slap his face, but I hold back. He recoils in anticipation of my blow. I drop my hand and fall at his feet.

"Forgive me Father. I would never strike you, but I'm not a whore. The Americans pay me for cooking. That's all."

"Only a fool would believe that, but I will play the fool for you because I understand why you do it. I just don't want you to think I really am a fool."

My tears run freely as I lay there. "Does Mother also think I'm a whore?"

"I don't know. I haven't asked her. She tells me she's happy that you've found a way to make more money, and I will continue to share her happiness, but know that I am not fooled, and I don't think she is either. She plays her part, just like I do."

I hear his footsteps as he walks to the door and goes outside. I compose myself and continue with my usual housework.

*

That afternoon while we're busy washing clothes in the community laundry, Mai asks, "Tuyết, are you screwing the Americans?"

"I'm only cooking for them. Don't read any more into this than there is."

"You're living very well these days, and I've seen you selling things to the black marketeers. Cooking seems to pay very, very well. Don't try to con me, Snow. We've known each other too long."

She's right. I know what it looks like to her, but I have to maintain my cover.

"You don't know the Americans. They have money to burn. We think it's a lot for a meal, but they think they're getting a bargain. They tell me the food in their mess hall is bland, and the meals in their officers' club are too expensive. Why shouldn't I take advantage of their generosity?"

"Tuyết, do you think I believe it takes you three hours to cook a meal, wait while he eats and clean up afterward? I've seen you feed your family and be done in half that time."

It's useless. She's my best friend, and I can trust her with my secret.

"Do you swear you will never tell anyone?"

"I swear on my parents' spirits. May they make my life miserable if I ever tell anyone," Mai replies.

"Not even your husband—especially him?"

"I swear," Mai says.

"Yes, I have two American boyfriends—a Major and a Colonel. That's how I can make the money it takes to live these days. I hate doing it, but I must if we are not to starve. Things cost more and more all the time, and our money is no good; but the American scrip is better than gold, Mai. I can buy a hundred times as much with it."

"You're fucking an American Colonel?"

"No, I really only cook for him. The Major is my only boyfriend. They're nice men and they don't mistreat me at all."

Mai sits for a while in shocked silence contemplating my admission.

"I knew you'd changed, and I suspected you were having sex with them. I just kept hoping I was wrong, that you hadn't become…"

"Say it—a whore."

"I didn't mean it that way, Tuyết."

I know she can't condone what I'm doing, even though she may understand what drove me to it. Her husband is home most of the time, and they have enough money to live on if not enough for any luxuries. She saw my children grow weak with hunger until I began to bring home the gifts from the Americans. Who is to say she wouldn't do the same thing under the same circumstances?

It's a silly idea. She would never have that option because she's not pretty. The Americans don't like her kind of woman–the kind with long bodies and short legs–the kind with flat faces and half-closed eyes. No, they go for the tall, long-legged kind with thin lips and almost round eyes—women like me. The randomness of human genetics dooms her to one fate and blesses me with the tools I need to survive.

*

Bien Hoa Air Base
April 12, 1969

Dear Chinh,
I miss you so much. I understand your duty comes first, but please try to find a way for us to be together again. The children are beginning to forget about their father. I show them your picture and promise them you'll be home soon, but they've heard it so often the words just don't sink in anymore.

Thankfully, I found two new Americans to cook for. They love my cooking and pay me well for it. One of them even pays me for teaching him how to cook Vietnamese food. Americans have so much money they don't care how much I charge. They even pay me with things I can sell on the black market. We're doing well again. The children are healthy and growing daily. My parents are looking ten years younger, too.

You must convince your commander to let you come home, even if it's only for a day or two. I remember your handsome face and your special smile. Most of all I miss your touch. Please come home soon.
All my love,

Tuyết

Chapter 7

Why won't he come home? I can't believe the demands of the war are so severe that he can't be spared for a few days every now and then. Other men manage to get home quite often—some almost every day, like Thoung.

Chinh, Chinh, I can't believe you have a mistress. Maybe these Americans' wives believe the same thing, yet their husbands are taking me to their beds. I don't understand men. Can their lust be so strong that they betray their sacred vows? My American lovers all seem to be decent men, but…

"Snow, we've got customers waiting." The BX manager wakes me from my reverie.

"Yes, sir," I respond and return to my job.

*

Wednesday evening, I come home from the BX to find Chinh having a beer with my father. He stands and holds his arms open to me.

"Chinh!" I shout and run into his embrace. We kiss with the passion of newly-weds alone for the first time and he holds me so close I think I might suffocate, but even death in his arms would be heaven to me.

"It's good to be home again," he whispers.

"I've missed you so much."

I let him go, and we sit down to talk.

"Is there any way we can join you at Nha Trang?" I ask.

"I'm afraid not. There's no housing there I would ask you to live in, and if the VC do launch a major attack, Nha Trang will be a primary target. They aren't strong enough yet to attack Bien Hoa, so you're much safer here."

"I miss you so much, Chinh. I wish this war would be over so we could get our lives back to normal."

"I'm trying to get assigned back here, but I can't promise anything. It could be a long time."

Father interrupts. "Don't you have to cook for the Americans tonight, Tuyết?"

"Then you'd better go. You won't want to disappoint them, and I know you need the money." Chinh's voice has a hard edge, and I know he's suspicious about the cooking story, but I pray it's only suspicion.

"My husband is home. My first duty is to him. The Americans will just have to do for themselves tonight," I say.

"They may miss your *company* more than your cooking," Chinh says.

Fear grips my insides. He knows, and he's only waiting for us to be alone to confront me.

"I only cook, Chinh. The American advisors like home cooking. I've learned to make some of the American things, and they even like some Vietnamese food. They pay well for it."

"I know I don't send you enough to live on, and the BX job can't make up the difference with our current rate of inflation. What if the Americans fire you?"

"They won't do that. They like my cooking too much. I've not shown up before, and they kept me on. When the children were sick I didn't cook for nearly two weeks, and they welcomed me back as if nothing happened. It'll be all right."

The rest of the evening is strained, but the children do not seem to notice. They're only glad to see their father and scream with delight over the presents he's brought from Na Trang.

Finally, we're alone together, and Chinh doesn't accuse me of infidelity. My prayers have been answered. He doesn't know for sure. As we undress for bed, Chinh notices my pubic hair is gone.

"What happened there?" He points to the spot where a thatch of black curly hair should be.

My mind goes blank, but the words come automatically. "Do you like it?"

What did I just say? It's the same thing I say to my new lovers when they first react to my bald pubic area.

"I don't know. Why did you do it?"

"Xuan said she did it once to please her husband. I thought you might like it."

"But, you didn't know I was coming home."

"No, I borrowed her razor two days ago to try it just to make sure it wasn't uncomfortable or itchy. If it was okay, I was going to do it for you when you did come home. I hope you like it?"

Chinh strokes his chin and cocks his head to one side. "I think I'll tell you later, darling."

In bed that night we make love with an ardor I never experienced with my American lovers. Afterwards, Chinh seems aloof.

"What's wrong, darling?"

"It's nothing," he replies with an obvious lie. "I was just thinking of how I have to go back to Nha Trang so soon."

"That's not it. Something's bothering you besides that. What is it?"

"It's silly; I'll be okay in the morning," he says.

"Something's bothering you, and I need to know what it is."

"It's just that you're…different." Chinh turns his face away from me.

"In what way? I'm the same woman you left over a year ago."

"In many ways, you are, but you seem harder. You're not the same wife."

I hold back on telling him he seems different too. There's no point in starting an argument over the subject. It would only reinforce his doubts about me.

"I've had to make a living for our family, Chinh. I never worked while you were home, and I never had to deal with the black market before. I've learned a lot these last few months, and that's probably made me harder in some ways; but I'm still your wife, and I still love you."

"You've changed other ways too," his voice breaks a bit as he says this.

I'm not sure what he means, but the possibility that sex with the Americans has changed me in some physical way crosses my mind. Could he tell some subtle, physical differences in me?

"What ways?"

"You make love differently," he says between clenched teeth.

"How? We always had good sex. What is different now?"

"You move differently. I can't explain it; it's just different somehow."

"I'm only glad you're home. It *has* been a long time, you know. It's probably because I've shaved." I hope he accepts that explanation. It's possible I am different. The Americans like some things Chinh and I never did together, and I'm not sure if I'd managed to screen them out during sex with him.

"Maybe that's it," he sighs. "It's okay, don't worry about it." He rolls over and kisses me good night. I think I see a tear about to fall from his eye, but he rolls back away from me before I can be sure.

I lay awake thinking about his remarks as he snores beside me. If I am different in some ways now that I'm having sex with the Americans, maybe he recognizes his mistress in my actions. She's probably screwing more than one man, too. That's it, I'd wager a large sum on it. Anger boils up inside me, but I must hold it in check until his departure.

*

Chinh kisses me goodbye in the morning. I say I'm sorry to see him leave again, but he seems to be less sad to go.

Chapter 8

Inflation continues to eat into the money I make from the Americans. Tom tells me he's going home in a week, and I dread the thought of taking on a new lover. My colonel has two months left, but with Tom gone, I won't have enough coming in to feed us well. I find another client, as I call them now, from the Americans at the small officer's club the advisors have on the Vietnamese side of the base. He has no jeep or truck, and his quarters are too far to walk. I also need a ride to work, and my Colonel says there's a new rule forbidding Vietnamese civilians in military vehicles. I can ride to work with Xuan but getting to my new clients is still a problem. My prayers are answered when one evening I notice Dai Ui (Captain) Hien has a "for sale" sign on his moped. I knock on their door, and he answers.

"Ba Tuyết, what a pleasant surprise."

I feel his eyes trying to penetrate my clothing. He knows Chinh is gone, and I see unbridled lust behind his eyes.

"I've come to ask about your moped."

His face falls a little, but I can still see the gears of sex turning behind his gaze. "I've been transferred to Da Nang, and I must sell it. I'm only asking P90,000 for it."

"How does it run?"

"Get on and take it for a ride." He hands me a key.

I've never ridden a moped before, but people have told me they're just like a bicycle only you don't have to pedal as hard. I've seen several of the women at the BX starting theirs, so I turn on the key and go through the same procedure. The little engine purrs to life, and I find riding it is easier than I thought. There are no gears to shift like a motorcycle. I ride out of the housing complex and down the main road for a while before turning back. It all seems in order, and I pull up to find Hien waiting for me.

"It seems to be okay," I say. "I'll give you $150.00 in American scrip."

His eyes light up with greed instead of lust at my offer of scrip.

"Where would you get American scrip?"

"The Americans pay me well for my cooking."
"In scrip?"
"I demand payment in scrip. It buys hundreds of times more than Piasters at the market."

He rubs his chin and smiles luridly. "You must *feed* them well."

"That's my business. Is it a deal?"
"Make it $200 and it's yours."
"I can only go $175."
"Okay, but you buy the new license."

"Done." I now own a moped, making my commute to and from the BX and my clients' trailers much more comfortable and it also gives me more time at home since I don't have to walk to my clients or pay for a ride to the market.

*

I have to keep reminding myself that this life of prostitution is only temporary until Chinh comes home, but deep in my inner being I began to think more and more that he's deliberately avoiding me. His letters are more infrequent now, and he never speaks of coming back to Bien Hoa even for a short visit. I know deep in my soul I've lost him. He may not have any proof of my lovers, but he has enough circumstantial evidence to convict me of my crimes. He's only taking a neutral path until he can be sure. I mourn his loss for I still love him dearly, but I also have to be practical.

The Americans love to talk about the things they like, and I learn a great deal about America from them. My English also improves considerably through those conversations. I find myself becoming a more polished woman to please the Americans. Xuan teaches me how to do makeup, but I don't like the artificial look I see in the mirror.

*

Bien Hoa Air Base
August 7, 1969

Dear Chinh,
You haven't written very often since you were home for that one night. Did I do something to offend you? I can't

understand why you don't write. Please tell me what's wrong. I'll do anything to make it right again, but I can't deal with the problem if I don't know what it is.

I love you, and I don't ever want to lose your love. Please, please write to me.

Your loving wife,

Tuyết

*

Chinh doesn't answer my letters. I begin to worry that he's wounded, and no one has informed me. Mai's husband tells me he's seen Chinh at Nha Trang and he's well. I know I have the right address for him, but I ask Thoung to hand carry a letter to him when he goes to Nha Trang again.

Thoung does take one of my letters to Nha Trang, and he tells me Chinh received it from him personally. Two days later I finally hear from Chinh.

Nha Trang Air Base
September 4, 1969

Dear Tuyết,
I'm sorry I haven't written sooner, but I just couldn't find the words to tell you the sad news. The commander here says I'm critical to his mission, and I can't be re-assigned back to Bien Hoa.

I'll try to find someplace for us to live here, but there's very little housing I would ask you and your family to live in. A few of the old French family quarters are still here, but the more senior officers have them. If one of them becomes available, I am the first name on the list.

I'm sorry about this turn of events. I will try to get back to you as often as possible, but I'll continue to send you as much as I can each month.

I'm glad you have some help from the Americans. I know they are enjoying your cooking and your pleasant company. Be sure to charge them what you are really worth. I know how wonderful your cooking is.

Sincerely,

Chinh

Now, I know I've lost him. It's not hard to read between the lines of his letter. He knows what I'm doing, and he's letting me down as easily as possible. It's just like him to be gentle with me. That night I cry myself to sleep.

*

The next morning, I awake with a resolve to make the best of my life without him. I know my parents are aware of what I do, but they choose to pretend belief in my facade. Only the children still love me as their mother. Their unquestioning trust and love is the only anchor in my sea of troubles. I'm like a building with a bright façade that's been gutted by an explosion. My soul lies in ruins, but I must go on.

I feel falsely accused like Guan Yin, and I pray to her for help. I know what I do is wrong, but I am forced to choose between bad karma and the misery of my parents and children.

I ride my moped to the market and leave it with Cuong the black market contact I use now. I know he'll keep it safe. As I shop the stalls, I notice several women huddling near the fish vendor. They speak in whispers, and now and then, one of them looks my way. I recognize them from the base housing area. A woman named Diep seems to be the central figure. I deliberately approach the group.

"Chao Ba Diep. Is there any good fish today?"

Two of the women nod to me and go about their marketing, but Diep and one who I know is a close friend of hers, remain.

"Ba Tuyết, it's good to see you. Yes, they have an excellent selection today. The prices are high, but someone like you can afford the best."

"Am I different?" I pretend to be ignorant of her meaning.

"I don't know where you get all your money. Does working for the Americans pay that much?"

"I work two jobs to earn enough money to live. Your husbands are with you, mine is at Nha Trang."

"We know about your job at the American BX, but what else do you do for them to merit all the expensive items you sell to Cuong?"

"I cook for them, that's all."

They both smile and bid me good morning. As they walk away together, I see them whisper to each other and cover their mouths while they giggle.

*

There's enough money now, thanks to my clients, and what Chinh still sends me each month. Perhaps he feels he must still provide for the children even if he no longer cares what happens to me.

I continue to write to him anyway. I tell him of the children and my parents and the people he knows here at Bien Hoa. He never responds, and as the months pass with no word, I find my feelings for him turning from love to anger. If he knows I'm having sex with the Americans, why doesn't he accuse me? I could deal with that, but this silent treatment is unfair. I don't even get a chance to beg his forgiveness.

A thought hits me. What if he's waiting for me to admit I'm having affairs? He can only suspect me now because he has no solid proof to confront me with. It would be much easier for him if I incriminate myself. A black cloud shadows his image in my mind. Red rage begins to rise from deep in my gut. That bastard. Now I only feel he's getting what he deserves.

Just in time a deeper emotion takes control. It's not his fault. He's not the one engaging in sinful activity. Even though this is the only way I see to solve my problems, I still love him, and I must believe he still loves me.

I must go on. This is my new life. I've made it, and I must live it, but I'll do my best to be the most successful whore in Viet Nam. I have a new calling.

*

One afternoon Bao comes home with a black eye and several bruises.

"What happened to you?" I ask.

"I got in a fight with Sanh."

"What were you fighting about?"

"Are you a whore?"

The word is like a bullet to my brain, but I don't believe Bao knows what it means.

"Do you know what a whore is?"

"Sanh says it's a dirty woman who does evil things with men."

I sit down and pull him to me, pretending to inspect his eye. "A whore is a woman who sleeps with men for money. What she does is not evil, and she's not dirty. Sanh doesn't know what he's talking about."

"He says you fuck them. What is fuck?"

"That's a dirty word for an act of love between a man and a woman. I don't want you to use that word ever again. Do you understand?"

"Yes, Mother."

"I'll punish you severely if I ever hear you saying that."

"Yes, Mother." He hesitates a moment before his next question. "Does Father give you money when you sleep with him?"

"It's not the same thing. We're married."

"So, being married makes, that dirty word, not dirty?"

I sigh. I was hoping to put off this discussion until he was much older. "Sit down, I need to tell you some things about life."

We have a detailed discussion about the "birds and the bees".

*

My lovers come and go. I continue to restrict myself to two at a time so I can be with my family in the evenings as much as possible. There's enough money with only two, though Xuan keeps urging me to take on more.

"How many lovers do you have now?" Xuan asks during our lunch break.

"Only two. I don't want any more. That's enough time away from my family."

She looks at me with a disgusted expression and shakes her head. "You could be making a fortune with your looks and shape, and you wouldn't even have to cook for them."

"I have to cook. It's my cover story."

"Hah," she laughs. "Everyone knows what you're doing. I hear it all the time from the other women at the laundry and in the market. They don't talk to me much because we're the same kind in their eyes, but I overhear them. They want me to hear what they say. They talk too loudly to want their views to be secret. Like I told you before, one or six, what's the difference?"

Her words ring true in my mind. I know she's right, but I have to do this my way to keep any sense of dignity.

"It makes a difference to me, Xuan. I can't explain it, but it does."

"Suit yourself. I think we need to pile up as much as we can to be ready to get out of Viet Nam before the Communists take over."

I can't deny I've had the same thoughts. Surely, Chinh will have some plan for saving us all if that time comes to pass? I've saved all I can from and the sale of my lover's gifts on the black market, but will it be enough? Chinh claims he's unable to save any money, so I can't count on him. I smile inwardly. Here's another justification for my actions. I'm earning the money we'll need to escape the wrath of the Communists.

"I know what you mean, but it will be hard for me to leave my homeland if it comes to that."

"Hard? Do you know what the Communists will do to you and your family? They'll line Chinh up against a wall and shoot him, if he's lucky. They may decide to torture him first just so they can hear him scream. As for you, they'll chain you to a bed and rape you to death. They just cut your children's throats and bayonet your parents for practice. I saw what they did in the village I grew up in. I know them. That's why my father moved us out as soon as he could. That's why I married an Air Force man, so I could live on the base. No, leaving here won't be hard for me if it comes to that."

"I know you're right, but you've talked to the Americans just like I have. Their country is so strange and rich. I don't know how I'd live there."

"I'll live there just like I do here—on my back."

"I wouldn't want to do that in America. Besides, I'd have Chinh with me then."

"Dream on, Tuyết, dream on."

We must return to our work, and the conversation ends there.

*

Nha Trang Air Base
January 17, 1971

Dearest Tuyết,

I'm sorry I haven't written very often. My duties keep me flying long hours, and I fall into bed at every opportunity. I barely find time to eat these days, and I hear there may be a big Communist offensive soon. I wish I could be there to protect our children, but I think they will be safe on Bien Hoa.

You asked about my plans should the Communists win. I don't have any because they won't win as long as the Americans are with us. We don't need their help in many ways these days. All of us are very good at what we do, thanks to their training. We only need supplies, parts for our planes, ammunition and some food. As long as they continue to support us, we can beat the Communists.

Don't worry about getting out of Viet Nam. The Americans are now bombing Hanoi, and we expect the Communists to give up in a year or two. Things will be wonderful then. We can live together again, and you won't have to work so hard to live.

Love,
Chinh

His letter gives me some hope, but I still save as much as I can. If his dream comes true, what I have will buy us some of the nicer things in life.

*

My American major leaves in February, and he says there will be no one sent to replace him. The men at the small club all seem to have girlfriends, and I don't want to wave down rides again. I begin to think I may have to take on Vietnamese clients, but I dread that day.

One morning my moped breaks down on the way to the BX. An American pick-up truck stops for me with the most handsome officer I'd ever seen at the wheel. He's tall—I can tell that by the fact that his hat brushes the top of the cab. The loose-fitting fatigues hide any hint of his build, but sturdy, muscular arms show beyond the short sleeves of his uniform top, hinting the rest of his body follows suit. Salt and Pepper hair, cut military style, peeks from under his cap, but it's his face that generates a feeling deep in my body I hadn't known since my first meeting with Chinh.

If I had to carve a bust of the ideal American officer, this man would be my model. Every detail of his appearance is chiseled perfection, and his sea blue eyes are almost hypnotic. His mouth curves into a perpetual smile revealing even white teeth.

"Good morning. Do you need some help?" he says. His voice is deep and masculine yet soft and inviting.

"My moped stop running, I be late for work."

He gets out of the truck and moves to the moped. He checks it over and tries to start it with no better luck than I had. "Looks like you're going to need a mechanic." He thinks for a moment. "I've got a sergeant who's pretty good with these things. I'll bet he can get this running for you in no time. If you like, I'll let him have a look at it."

I certainly don't want to spend any money on the bike, and maybe this man will do what he says and not charge me. "Okay, how you take to him?"

"Easy."

He drops the truck's tailgate and lifts the front wheel onto it.

"Here, steady it while I get it into the bed." He nods toward the seat.

I steady the seat as he climbs into the bed and pulls the bike aboard. He lays it on its side and jumps down. "There, where are you going?"

"I go BX."

"I'm going to the mess hall. Get in."

"Thank you." I get into the truck, and he drives on.

"Do you work at the BX?"

"Yes, I work there."

"Your English is good."

"Thank you. I have lot of practice." What did I say? Oh well, I think I want him as a client anyway.

He turns his eyes from the road briefly and smiles at me. "A woman as lovely as you should be riding in a limousine."

"What is limousine?"

"A big, fancy car with a chauffeur."

I laugh, and he cocks his head to one side. "Why do you laugh?"

"I no know chauffeur either."

He laughs in response. "It's a driver, like me. I'm your chauffeur today."

We drive on in silence for a moment.

"My name's Mel Jenkins." He extends his hand to me, and I take it. His grip is soft, and his hand is almost delicate for being so large.

"My name Tuyết."

He seems to be reluctant to release me, but he must put his hand back on the steering wheel.

"That's a lovely name."

He thinks for a moment then says, "If I get your moped fixed today, how can I get it back to you?"

"You maybe bring BX tonight?"

"What time?"

"I go home 6:30."

"I'll see you there one way or the other. If your moped's fixed, I'll take you to it. If not, I'll give you a ride home."

He drops me at the BX, and I hope he can't get the moped fixed. I'm looking forward to seeing him again. I don't know why. Maybe it's the way his eyes brighten when he says my name or the soft smile when he looks at me. I shake it off. If he's going to be a client, I can't afford to have any feelings for him.

*

That night he's waiting for me outside the BX. I don't see my moped in his truck, so I open the door and get into the cab.

"Moped no fix?" I ask.

"Yes, it's fixed, but he had to put fresh fuel in the tank, and I can't lay it on its side. It's back at my trailer. I'll take you there."

Here I go again. This has to be a trap, but I'm prepared for this one.

"You ask me come into trailer, yes?" I ask as we drive.

He smiles at me, and for the first time I see the glint of lechery behind his smile. "Only if you want to."

"Maybe I do. You like that?"

He laughs. "And, here I thought I was going to have to seduce you. Thanks for saving me the trouble. You must have had American boyfriends before."

His statement strikes a nerve, and I rebel at his implication. "That none of your business."

He takes my hand and squeezes it gently. "I'm sorry. I can't believe I'm lucky enough to find a girlfriend just because her moped broke down. I've been here for two months now, and the girls at the advisor's club were beginning to look good. You're the most beautiful woman I've seen since I got here, and I found you by sheer good fortune."

His face takes on a lecherous glow, and I wonder if I've made a mistake in offering my services. "If I go bed with you, you pay me good money, give me things sell Bien Hoa City, okay?"

His expression sobers a bit, but he's still smiling that same wicked smile. "I see, you're a call girl."

"What is 'call girl'?"

"It's a beautiful woman who has sex with men for money."

"I cook for Americans, too. Maybe I cook for you?"

His eyes sparkle with lust as he turns to face me. "You could cook for me every night of the week."

"I only cook one night each week. What night you like?"

"How about Wednesday?"

"Wednesday good. I come Wednesday."

"I can't wait to see you *privately*."

His emphasis conveys the extent of his lust, but what should I expect? This is my life now.

"You like Chinese food?"

"Oh yes, I also like Indian food, but I don't like Korean or Japanese."

"I fix you Chinese now, Vietnamese later."

"Sounds good to me. I'm really looking forward to our time together."

At his trailer, he shows me the moped on its stand near the big barracks at one end of the compound.

"Sergeant Ramey was keeping an eye on it for me. He said you just got some bad fuel and fouled your spark plug. He cleaned it and put in some good gas and oil mixture. It's ready to go."

"How much I owe you?"

"No charge. I took care of everything. See you Wednesday. Come around whenever you get back from the BX. My trailer's the first one down on the first row."

I mount the moped and start it. "I see you Wednesday. Good night, Trung Ta (Lieutenant Colonel)."

*

Wednesday night I bring Mel a dinner of spicy chicken prepared the way I know Americans like it. He opens the door before I can knock.

"I heard your moped pull up. Come on in." He holds the door for me while I carry in my food containers.

His trailer is the same one another of my clients used, so I know where everything is. I go directly to the kitchen area and place the containers on the small counter. "I bring good chicken dinner."

"Wonderful, I can't wait to try it." He follows me into the kitchen area and slips his hands around my waist.

"Mmm, you smell wonderful. What perfume is that?"

I pry his hands off my stomach. "You no go so fast. Make drinks, I heat food. I like Scotch, water. You have?"

He takes a step backward. "Sure, sure, I drink Scotch too." He busies himself with the drinks while I put the food that needs warming in the oven and turn it on low. I find plates, silverware and napkins and set them on the coffee table in the living room area of the trailer. He's on the couch, so I sit down opposite him and he raises his glass in a toast.

"To a pleasant evening, and a long relationship," he says. I lift my glass from the coffee table and raise it to his. I take a tentative sip and find it's not too heavy on the Scotch. My clients usually think they have to get me drunk before I consent to sex and mix me strong drinks until they find out it isn't necessary.

"I make tea for dinner. That okay?" I say.

"Tea's fine," he responds.

"How you day today?" I ask as I take another sip of my drink.

"Oh, the usual things. A lot of paperwork. The VNAF doesn't really need my help these days."

"I hear Americans soon leave Bien Hoa."

"I'll probably be the last maintenance advisor here. The US side of the base is already on skeleton staff. We're turning everything over to the Vietnamese as fast as we can."

The kettle whistles, and I'm very relieved when I rise to finish dinner. I take the plates with me and dish out servings. I place the dishes on the table and return for the tea. Mel digs into the meal with gusto, complimenting me on every other bite. I'm flattered, but I know it's his way of softening me up. We finish, and I take the plates and cups to the sink. When everything's clean and back in its place, Mel takes me in his arms and presses his face to mine. I'm surprised that his lips are so soft given the strength of his embrace. I relax and return his kiss.

"The bed's back this way." He leads me to the rear of the trailer.

*

He's a good lover, and we lay together afterward for a moment before he speaks.

"You're wonderful. I've never had anyone make love to me like that before."

"You do good too," I say as I stroke the graying hair on his chest.

"I'd love to tell everybody I know about you, but a gentleman never tells about his lovers."

"Especially wife," I joke. To my surprise, he turns suddenly sullen.

"My wife, hah. She doesn't care who I have sex with as long as it isn't her."

"You no have sex with wife?"

"Twice on our honeymoon, and that was it."

"Then you no have children?"

"No, she never wanted any children. She said she wouldn't subject children to a military life. She wanted me to leave the Air Force, but I wouldn't do that. It's been a sore point with us for the two years we've been married. I want children, but she won't cooperate. She thinks the best method of birth control is total abstinence."

"I no unnastan wife no have sex." It doesn't make sense. How could a woman live with a man as handsome as Mel and not want to make love to him?

"It's true. I'd been married before to a real bombshell in the bedroom, but she left me for some oil tycoon when we were stationed in Texas. I married Meg two years ago in Tacoma, Washington. I thought she loved me, but she only wanted a meal ticket and a way out of town. I was really fooled."

"You no divorce her?"

"I've threatened to, but she tells me she'll take me for everything I have if I do, and I believe she could."

"Wife no have sex good reason for divorce." I still can't believe his wife could be so cruel.

"Not in California. I came here from March Air Force Base in Riverside, California, and I'll be going back when I leave here. What about you? Do you have children?"

"Boy 10, girl 7."

"Do you have a husband?"

This question has come up many times before, and early-on I decided to lie. "My husband helicopter pilot. He killed in war two year ago."

"I'm sorry. It must be hard on you, a woman alone with two kids." He seems to be sincerely sorry, and I hate lying to him, but I'm not sure how he might react to me cheating on my husband. I'd also found the lie produces even more expensive presents.

"Mother, father live with me. They help with children."

"That's good. I'm sure they're a big help."

"That enough talk about me. Wife no have sex, I your wife while you here," I joke as I slap him playfully on the chest.

He rolls over on top of me and smiles. "No, not a wife. Wives nag, and I won't keep you around if you nag, no matter how beautiful you are. No, you're my call girl, but if I had to pay you on the same basis as a call girl in the States, someone as lovely and talented as you would be way above my pay grade." He kisses me gently.

I remember he told me a "call girl" is a woman who has sex with men for money. I'm not really sure, but I think it's a compliment.

"Okay, I be your call girl, but pay with things, and money. I take all money you give me, but things from BX bring much money on black market. More than cost in BX. You come BX, I show you what buy for me." I pull him back into my embrace and we make love again. I'm very relieved that he hasn't mistreated me. My fears about him begin to fade.

*

The next day, Mel comes into the BX, and I show him some things I can sell. He buys a small TV set and says he'd have it for me the following Wednesday. My other clients continue to treat me well also, but Mel's image keeps popping into my head when I'm with them. I find myself actually looking forward to his nights.

Chapter 9

At our next meeting Mel gives me the TV and 20,000 Piasters before I leave for home. His gifts keep getting more expensive as the weeks pass, and one evening near the American Christmas holiday he presents me with something special.

He has a small artificial tree on his dresser hung with multi-colored balls, and Christmas songs are playing softly on his tape machine. There's only one package under the tree, and he passes it to me.

"I got this in Bien Hoa City today. One of my counterparts told me these things are prized by Vietnamese women."

I quickly tear off the brightly colored paper and open the box to find a solid jade bracelet.

"Oh Mel, it is beautiful."

"I'm glad to see you've learned to use some of the little words in English," he says.

Mel has really helped improve my English. He keeps correcting me about what he calls the "little words", like it, the, and, to, of, am and many others.

"You teach me good," I say.

"Well, Snow, well. Say it again."

"You teach me well."

"Very good. Can you fit the bracelet around your hand?"

I have some trouble slipping it past my hand, and Mel produces a bottle of baby oil to help get the job done. These bracelets are usually given to young girls. By the time they are grown, it's almost impossible to remove them. After the woman dies she's buried wearing the bracelet, and it's removed when she's dis-interred after her body has decomposed enough to allow removal.

"What do you use baby oil for?" I ask him.

"It was here in the trailer when I moved in, but I can guess what the previous resident used it for."

I knew the previous resident very well, and I couldn't imagine what he would use it for. Mel must have noticed my curious expression. He reaches to his crotch and pumps his fist back and forth. We both erupt in laughter as it dawns on me what he means.

*

The next morning my mother notices the bracelet.

"Where did you get that bracelet?" she asks as she points to it.

"My Americans pitched in together and bought it for me as a Christmas present. I think that was very nice of them, don't you?"

"Very nice. I'm surprised the men you *cook* for know about each other."

Her meaning is unmistakable. I bristle at the implication. "Why shouldn't they? I'm only cooking."

"I know, I know, you're a very good cook." She walks away without saying any more

*

By the start of 1972, I'm fighting back my feelings for Mel. I think I'm falling in love with him, but I can't do that. Each time I'm with him I can't help but feel him filling the empty space in my heart left vacant by Chinh. He treats me as an equal even when he's correcting my English. He never talks down to me on any subject, and he often asks my opinion on the war and the political news. He seems truly interested in how we Vietnamese feel about each new development.

He's a good lover, and always tender with me. He gives me as much as he expects me to give him, without complaining or demanding. I teach him some things to improve his technique, and he seems grateful.

His gifts of money continue, along with items from the BX. My stash of scrip is growing because I demanded payment in scrip for the items I sell. I can only hope the Americans don't replace it with a new issue before I can use it to purchase the things I need that only the black market has. I can't remember the last time that happened, and Xuan says it was years ago. Mel says they won't change it now because the Americans will be leaving Viet Nam soon, and it would be too costly to make the swap for the short time remaining. I have to use it all before they leave because it will be worthless after that.

I laugh at myself for worrying. The Piaster will also be worthless once the Americans leave. Only the American green money will have any value, and I have none of that. I've seen the green money, but I have no idea how to get hold of any. Mel tells me the Americans aren't allowed to have any while they're here. I'll just have to deal with that when the time comes.

I shudder at that thought. If the Communists win I know what my fate will be. I can only hope that Chinh will be back before then. Maybe he'll have a plan to get us out of the country, even if he doesn't want me anymore. He'll surely want to rescue his children, and he'll probably take me along just to care for them, if for no other reason.

One evening, Mel surprises me completely. "How would you like to go home with me when I leave Viet Nam?"

"What do you mean?" The question doesn't contain enough information for me to formulate an answer.

"I mean you and I go to the States together and continue there just like we are here."

I look at him not believing what I'm hearing. He wants me to be his lover there just like I am here. I do what I do to feed my family. If he took me to America, I'd want to stop this life and begin anew.

"I will not be your lover in America. I have a family and must care for them. I will not leave them behind. The only way I would go with you is as your wife."

"I'm already married, and a divorce is out of the question." His face grows flushed, and he stares at me with almost pure hatred in his eyes. "Besides, why would I want to **marry** you?"

His insinuation strikes a nerve. I rise and slap him hard. "I know what I am, you do not have to remind me." I turn to leave.

He rises and grabs my arm. "I had that coming. I'm sorry. Please don't go."

"Mel, I thought you were a very nice man, but now I know your true feelings. I do not want to talk about this anymore. Goodbye."

He tightens his grip on my arm. "Mel, you are hurting me."

"Oh God, I'm sorry, Snow. Please don't go. I'll make it up to you, I promise. I really didn't mean what I said."

Yes, he did, but now I must choose between my pride and his gifts. My childrens' health wins.

"Okay, I will stay, but promise you will never talk to me like that again."

"I promise, believe me, I promise. Why should I screw up a good thing like this?" He takes me in his arms, and we kiss tenderly.

We make love very passionately that night. I had almost come to love him, but tonight he destroyed those feelings. I realize I love only Chinh, the father of my children and the man I must go back to if he will still have me. Mel is only a client again, and I must go on with him until he leaves

*

In April 1972 the VC launch a major offensive. Mel is busy all the time, and he can't let me come on Wednesdays. American airplanes and men flood into Bien Hoa to stop the Communists, and the units deploy from the States so rapidly, there's no time for the men to change their green money for scrip. I make a fortune working the advisor's club exchanging my scrip for their green. They need scrip to spend at the officers' club and the BX. I only keep enough scrip to use for what I need on the black market and stash the green in a new hiding place in my house. I'm inundated with propositions for "one-night stands" with the new Americans but refuse them until one Major offers $500 in green money. I take him but say no to all the others. I'm now confident I can bribe my way out of the country if the end comes and Chinh is not there to help.

Chapter 10

I keep on writing to Chinh even though my letters become increasingly impersonal.

*

Bien Hoa Air Base
August 30, 1972

Dear Chinh,
Why don't you write? Thoung says he sees you from time to time, and he says you're well.
My parents and the children are fine. Bao liked the birthday present you sent him.
It was very busy here during the spring offensive, but I'm sure you know all about that.
That's about it for now.
Sincerely,

Tuyết

*

I continue to see Mel for the rest of his tour, and he never brings up the subject of getting me out of the country again. My feelings for him remain strictly business, but I'm still dreading the loss of his gifts and money.

When it comes time for him to go, all of his friends are there at the air terminal to see him off, and he has to spend some time with them. He finally excuses himself and takes me to another part of the big room to tell me goodbye.

"I'm sorry I have to leave you, Snow."

"I am sorry too. You a big help to my family."

"I'm sorry you couldn't accept my offer to go home with me, but I understand why you refused. If the Communists win, what will you do?"

I shake my head. "I not know. I no have husband to help. Maybe someone else help me. I not know." It's what I must tell him, but I still hope Chinh will have a plan.

"I want you to know that if you do manage to get to the States, I'll be there for you. You know where I'm going. I'll be there for at least three years, and if I don't get promoted, I'll retire. I like southern California, and I'll probably stay in that area. In any case, the Air Force can always find me. No matter what happens, you only have to call, and I'll come to you."

At that moment they call his flight, and we're distracted by a commotion in the main part of the terminal. I turn to see another Vietnamese woman lying on the floor. She's crying piteously and clinging to the legs of an Army Sergeant, trying to hold him back. The Sergeant is cursing her and doing his best to free himself. Each time he succeeds, she renews her grip with the tenacity of an octopus. He drags her a few feet until the security police at the gate make her release him. She lays on the floor sobbing until he boards the jet liner. It's a pathetic sight, but if he was as generous with her as Mel has been with me, it's understandable behavior. If Mel never showed me his true side, I might be doing the same thing.

Mel takes me in his arms one last time.

"Goodbye, Snow." He kisses me gently, and I once more feel a hint of love in the touch of his lips, but he pushes me away and shakes hands with his friends before walking to the gate. I watch him until he waves at me before vanishing from sight, then I fall into a chair and let the tears flow freely. I tell myself I'm not crying for him, only for the loss of his gifts, but a small part of my soul is telling me I'm lying.

Another officer I know on his staff sits down beside me. He puts his arm around me and holds me for a moment.

"Are you ready to go home?" he asks.

I nod, and he helps me to my feet. We go to his truck and he helps me inside. As he starts the engine, I say, "I will miss him."

He sees me digging in my purse for a tissue and passes me his handkerchief. "Here, I think you need this," he says.

"You have to get over him, Snow. He's out of your life forever now."

"He very good to me. Do you know he want take me to the States?"

He pats my shoulder and says, "I'm sure he did."

He drops me off where I'd left my moped, and I start to hand him his handkerchief, but it's very wet with my tears. I ask, "You want this back? It very wet." I hold it up to indicate what I'm talking about.

He starts to reach for it then pulls back. "No, you keep it. Goodnight, Snow."

I think this is the darkest day in my life, but darker days are ahead.

Nha Trang Air Base
September 16, 1972

Dear Tuyết,
Things look bleaker every day. Many of our helicopters are down for parts, and it's taking longer to get them from the States. We barely have enough flyable choppers to move the army, and we can only do that by cannibalizing parts from one helicopter to repair another one.

The army units we carry say they only have enough ammunition to give each man two clips and one grenade. I don't know what the Americans are thinking. We can't win if we have nothing to fight with. The Communists seem to have all the arms and ammunition they want while we must ration our bullets. I begin to despair of our chances for winning.

Many of my friends are beginning to plan for leaving the country if it gets worse. I can't leave without the children and you, and I don't know how I can get back to Bien Hoa to get you. I'll work out something, I promise.

Stay safe until I can be with you again.
Love,
Chinh

At last, I have some hope that Chinh will come to get us if the worst comes. Even if he knows about me, he will come for the children. I can't wait to open each new letter. Maybe one of them will show the way to freedom.

*

After Mel's departure, I begin receiving offers from Vietnamese officers. They knew they had no chance with me as long as the Americans were here, but now they flock to me.

Colonel Huong is the first to ask. I know of Huong from Xuan, who had briefly been his mistress. She said he has a mean streak that only comes out when he's drunk, and he's drunk most of the time. I wisely turn him down.

Other offers follow, but I decline them all. I have no interest in any Vietnamese lover, and I've managed to accumulate enough money and black market items to keep us alive until the Communists take over. Everyone knows what life will be like after that, and anyone related to the armed forces is sure to receive "special" attention from that bunch. Each family begins planning some way to get out of the country once that happens.

My neighbor, Mai, says her husband has an escape plan, but he won't tell her what it is. She tries to assure me that Chinh will also have a plan, but I can't see how he can help us if he's still at Nha Trang when the end comes.

The inflation is so bad now the black market people are only taking American green money in payment. When my Father becomes sick, I have to use nearly a fourth of my green money to buy medicine.

*

I lose my job at the BX when it closes, but I find another job helping Xuan tend bar in the small officer's club for the advisors. Only a few of them are left, and they're mostly army officers now. It keeps me away from my children more, but I need the money. I have no American clients now. The officers remaining all have girlfriends, and no new Americans are scheduled to arrive.

Xuan teaches me about the various liquors and how to mix the drinks the Americans order. I find that I've been drinking a poor quality of Scotch. The difference in taste is remarkable, and I quickly move to a quality brand when I sneak in a drink for myself from time to time.

One of the advisors tells me what I learn here will be very useful if I do manage to get to the States. He says there are always taverns looking for good bartenders, and beautiful bartenders are in particular demand. I wonder if I will ever see this remarkable place they call "The States".

*

The Vietnamese propositions keep coming in, but I still refuse them. I know they would not be kind to me like the Americans, and they would expect me to do much more for less money. It is not until General Quang approaches me that I finally relent.

The occasion is a formal party I attend with another VNAF Dai Ta I'm considering as a possible client. Quang is immediately drawn to me, and wastes no time making my acquaintance. He begins in Vietnamese.

"Ba Tuyết, I believe?"

"Yes, General; I am Tuyết."

"My name is Quang," he extends his hand.

"I know who you are, sir," I take it in a gentle grip; and he immediately raises it to his lips.

"I have heard many good things about you from the Americans. Why did you restrict your services to them?"

"They were good to me and gave me a lot of money. My family needed food, and they helped me provide it."

"Inflation is worse now, and you must soon need money again. What will you do then?"

"I will make out as best I can. I fear the end of our country is near, but my husband will have a plan to take us to safety when that time comes."

"I understand your husband is at Nha Trang. If he can't help you, you will need an ally here at Bien Hoa."

"Do you know my husband?"

"No, but I do know who he is and where he is. Even if he comes back, he will not want to keep you when he knows what you are."

"And what is that, sir?"

"A prostitute, basically. You have sex for money. I think that defines the term."

I've learned to live with this label. Men have no idea what it's like to see a child hungry. They go off and fight their wars without ever thinking of their families at home. They have full stomachs and women like me to service them. What is the term for these men? Whatever it is, it's worse than whore. I did what I did to feed my family; they are only satisfying their lust.

"You are right, General. I am a whore, and I would do it again and again rather than see my children starve."

At this point, he switches to English since his wife comes within earshot.

"I don't condemn you, Tuyết. I only point out the facts. If you would take care of me, I could use my influence to help your family get out of the country, if that becomes necessary."

"Influence not feed my family."

"Oh, there would be plenty in it for you too. I can't pay you in green money, but there would be food and enough Piasters to buy some nice things from time to time. All of this for, let us say, two nights a week."

I think of the alternatives. There really are none except slow starvation and persecution when the Communists take over. I have no outside income now. The small officer's club has closed, and he is my only hope of help. This General might be able to get my family out of the country if Chinh doesn't come back. Why not cultivate him?

"I see if your deeds as good as your words, General. We do Tuesday, seven o'clock?"

"I will clear whatever is on my calendar. Come to my command trailer. Do you know where it is?"

He tells me how to reach the trysting place. He can hardly bring me into his house, and a hotel room in Bien Hoa City would be expensive, and far too dangerous for someone like him. The VC would soon know his routine and take advantage of it to eliminate him. The command trailer is only used for emergencies or large offensive actions, but it has sleeping facilities.

*

Bien Hoa Air Base
  December 30, 1974

Dear Chinh,

All the Americans have been gone for some time, but I finally found a job taking care of General Quang's children. His wife is very ill, and she can't cope with them. Once more we do not have to do without.

Have you had any luck with a plan of escape? The war news is bleak, and we can even hear cannon fire here on the base from time to time. I know you are doing all you can, but any hint of what you plan to do would help buoy-up our spirits. I don't know what we'll do if you can't help us.

Write soon.

Tuyết

*

General Quang is as good as his word, and he keeps me provided with the things I need. The only problem I face is a cover story now that the Americans are gone, and the cooking ruse is not viable. I change my role to that of caretaker for the General's children. Never mind that I haven't been in his house; my parents accept this lie as readily as the last one. By now they are ignoring what I do to keep them fed and healthy.

I haven't heard from Chinh for a while. I can only hope he has some plan for us. I'm sure he knows about me, but he must take me with him for the children's sake. If he can't help us, Quang is a good back-up plan.

The war goes from bad to worse. Every day we hear of more and more defeats for our army. Mai's husband tells her Nha Trang has been attacked several times, but the army managed to drive off the VC and their Northern allies each time. He can't explain why Chinh hasn't written lately, but Thoung vouches for his safety and good health.

As the end draws closer and closer, I begin to fear for my family. The VC will be ruthless in their reprisals, and officers and their families will be the first to feel their wrath.

We've heard stories of the VC raping women brutally before killing them in bizarre ways. It's well known that they like to use children for bayonet practice while their parents watch.

Mai and I talk about what we might do, but neither of us has a workable plan without our husband's help. We don't even have a good way to kill ourselves without some kind of firearm. She thinks her husband will try to get them out of the country and to America, but she isn't sure. I turn to Quang for an answer.

"My dear General," I coo in his ear one evening. "It may soon be time for you to use the influence you once promised me. It appears the VC will win, and what will become of me when the Communists take over?"

"What makes you think they will win?" he counters.

"We both know it is only a matter of time now. One of the officers in our compound says they are just outside Bien Hoa air base even now, and they are only waiting for enough ammunition to launch an attack."

"He is a fool to think we would let them take Bien Hoa so easily," Quang responds.

"Only a fool would believe it to be so difficult for them, and I do not think my General is a fool. I know you must have some sort of plan in the event our world collapses around us. I have some American money I would be willing to use in a plan to see myself and my family safely out of the enemy's reach."

"I would not dream of leaving you behind, my darling. I will let you know what to do if the time comes. In the meantime, I must take care of some officials who can make our escape possible. The Americans only issue papers to those people they think are important to them, but they rely on we Vietnamese to tell them who those people are. When the time comes to leave, you must have one of their special letters to enter the embassy grounds in Saigon or you will be left behind. The bribes are costly. How much do you have?"

"I have over $1,500.00 American green money, and I could get more from the black market people if I sell them my moped and some other things the Americans gave me." It seems like a fortune to me, but if it will buy safety for my family, it's worth every penny.

"I will list you as my personal secretary on the American forms. They've assured me that all members of my household staff will be welcome at the Embassy in Saigon when the evacuations begin. They've given me a code word to be broadcast over Armed Forces Radio. It will mean we should get to the embassy as quickly as possible. I've already made sure there will be a helicopter available to take us there, and..."

I interrupt him at this point, "General, I must take my children and my parents with me. What about them?"

"I'm sorry, Tuyêt. The money you have is not enough to cover everyone. It's barely adequate to cover one person, considering the people I must bribe to get you included with my family."

"I can't leave them behind." I begin to cry, and he holds me close.

"Now, now. The Communists will not harm your children, and your parents are too old for them to bother with. You and I will have a good life in America. It's a wonderful place. I've been there, and I know. Leave the past behind and start a new life with me. I know some powerful people in America. We will live well."

My tears won't stop flowing. All of my hopes rest on this man and the influence he claims he can bring to bear on the problem. Now my hopes are dashed on the rocks of his lechery. He only wants me to join him and continue as his mistress. I have to admit that the life he describes does sound exciting, but how could I ever live with deserting my parents and my children? There is no way I can do what he asks. If I wouldn't do it for Mel, I certainly won't do it for him.

"I'm sorry, sir. I will not go without my family. I'm also sorry this means the end of our relationship. I can't continue on with you if there's no hope for the ones I hold dear." I rise to leave, but he stops me.

"Wait, Tuyêt. There may be another way to take care of your whole family for the money you have."

"What is that?" My heart races. Perhaps he is as good as his word after all.

He sits pensively for a moment. "Yes, you would be eligible as the family of critical military personnel. Providing, that your husband manages to reach Bien Hoa so that he is part of your group."

"Would Chinh fall into that category? He's only a helicopter pilot."

He waves a hand at some phantom barrier. "If I say he is critical, the Americans will believe me. I'm pretty sure I can get all of you passes for $1,500 under those conditions."

"Oh, thank you, my general. I know Chinh will do everything he can to be here with me. I'll bring you the money when you tell me."

I go home that night confident I've done the right thing in sleeping with Quang. Somehow, I know Chinh will get back in time. I pray he will be with me before the end comes, but I have no way of knowing since he has not written to me in several months.

Only a few days later, Quang tells me to prepare. I sell everything at the ridiculously low prices offered by the black marketers and count out 1,500 American dollars for Quang. I only hold back $1,000 for our personal use. I have no idea what life in America is like or how much it costs to live there. I only know I'll need some money, and this will have to be enough.

The next night the General takes my money and tells me to come back in two days for the papers. The hours seem to drag by, and the war news is worse and worse. People are streaming into Bien Hoa hoping the big base will provide a way to break the Communist onslaught. The parking ramps fill with airplanes and helicopters, but Chinh does not appear; and there is no word from him.

Two days later Quang hands me official looking documents in English. He says they are passes for me and each member of my family.

"What do I do with these?" I ask him.

"Come to the headquarters building tomorrow at noon. Bring only what you will need to live. Leave everything else at home. We will have trucks with armed men here. They will take us to helicopters that will fly us to Saigon. Don't be late. We will not wait for you."

I thank Quang for his help and vow not to be late. I fly home to tell my family about their good fortune. I gather them all together in the big room.

"General Quang's obtained special passes to get us into the American embassy in Saigon. There's even one here for Chinh," I show the official looking documents to my parents. Father doesn't read English, but he scrutinizes them carefully before pronouncing his agreement concerning their authenticity.

"We must be at the headquarters at noon tomorrow, but we can take no more than a few things with us. Everyone must select those items they prize most and things that will be of the most use to us in America. I don't know what our life will be like there, but I know exactly what it will be like if we stay here. I'm sure it would mean separation for the children and death for us if we do not leave."

The children begin to sob softly as I speak. I call them to me.

"It's all right, children. We have American passes, and they will see us safely out of danger." I hold them close to me and dry their tears.

That evening we pack carefully. Each time I think I have only the barest necessities it seems there is still too much to carry. In the end, I only take my jewelry, a picture of Chinh, the last of my American money and a few clothes. The children's bags are mostly clothes with only one toy allowed for each one. My parents cry as they leave behind things dear to their hearts.

I find it hard to sleep that night. All I can think of is what it will be like to live in a strange land. My English is considerably improved through contact with the Americans, so I'm not worried about that aspect of the new life; but I remember my lovers telling me of strange and wonderful things in America. How Americans live in houses bigger than two of their trailers and drive cars everywhere.

One of my Americans was from the city where cars are made, and I loved to hear him talk of how they were put together a piece at a time as they came down a big line. He told me a new car rolled off the end of that line every minute. How can any country use so many cars? The city he told me about is much bigger than Saigon, and he told me there were many cities in the United States even bigger than this "Detroit" where the cars are made. What could I do in America to make a living for my family? Maybe there are exchanges there too. I know there are bars where I might find work. I will find something, I'm confident of that.

I think of Chinh, and how long it's been since I heard from him—Chinh of the wonderful hands and the soft voice. I close my eyes and try to remember the gentle way he looks at me after we make love. Chinh, why did you have to leave me alone? Come to me now, and I will send the children to America with their grandparents. I will stay here with you and face whatever our fate may be. As long as we are together again, nothing else matters. I have done such horrible things, but I managed to save our children. Even if you hate me, I will be content just to die by your side. Chinh, Chinh, I love you so. I weep softly into my pillow, so the children will not be frightened. Sleep finally comes as I exhaust my supply of tears.

*

The next morning, I prepare a good meal. so we'll have full stomachs the whole day. There's no way of knowing when we might be able to eat again. I pack some dry food in my own bag for the children's lunch. A last-minute check of the bags proves all is ready. I make a final call on Mai, next door.

"Dear Mai, I will pray for your safety. I wish there was some way I could have gotten passes for your family too."

"It's all right, Tuyết. Thoung says he will come for us when the end is near. He says he has a plan for reaching safety, but he will not tell me what it is. He told me to be ready to go at any time, and we've packed our things. I'm happy you'll be safe with the Americans."

"You've been a good neighbor, Mai." I run to my friend and embrace her as tears run down both of our cheeks.

"We'll never see each other again, Tuyết," Mai sobs.

"We'll find each other in America, I know. I won't forget you."

"And I'll never forget you, my good friend. Good bye."

I run out the door and back to our house where the family stands ready.

"We must leave now to be sure to get to the headquarters building by noon," Father says.

"I know, Father. Come children."

Chapter 11

As we approach the Headquarters building, I'm surprised by the size of the crowd around the entrance. People are everywhere waving papers just like the ones I have, and a young Major is holding back the crowd with the aid of several armed men.

"What is happening?" I ask another woman.

"That Major says our papers are no good. He will not let us get on the helicopters."

I couldn't believe what I heard. I'd received my papers from General Quang's own hand. Surely, they're good. This woman must have been swindled by some lower ranking official. I push through the throng and up to the Major.

"Please, sir. My papers are from General Quang himself. I'm sure they are good." I wave the sheaf of forms at him.

"Let me see them," he says.

I hand him the papers, and the Major looks each one over carefully before handing them back to me.

"Yours are just like all the others. They're forgeries. The Americans will not honor them."

"How can that be? He gave them to me himself. Where is General Quang? I wish to speak to him personally. He will know me. Tell him it's Tuyết."

"General Quang is gone, lady. He left for Saigon an hour ago."

I fall back in a daze. I've been swindled too. Quang has taken all of these people's money. What a fool I was to trust him. It was silly to think that just because he was screwing me, I rated some kind of special treatment. What can I tell my family? I've sold everything but what we're carrying with us. I even gave away what food we had left. At least we can go back to the house. There's still a roof over our heads. I stagger back to my parents and the children.

"What is wrong, Daughter?" Father asks. The look on his face tells me he already knows.

"Our papers are forgeries, Quang made a fool of me. We have no way out now."

"The VC will kill us," Bao mutters and bursts into tears. Anh copies her brother's emotion and begins to sob quietly.

"No they won't," I shake him back to his senses. "We still have your father to protect us. He will be home soon once he hears we need him. We will go back to our house and wait for him. Come children."

I lead the sad little band back to our house to find it ransacked. The good furniture is gone, and every possible hiding place in the house has been pried open. Cinder blocks are torn from the walls. Tiles in the kitchen area are ripped up. The only thing left is a small porcelain figurine standing on the window sill. I pick it up and throw it at the wall.

"Damn you, Quang," I yell as it shatters into tiny pieces.

Mai runs over when she hears the noise.

"What happened? Aren't you going to Saigon?"

"It was a trick. That bastard Quang tricked me. The papers are forgeries." I throw the worthless forms to the floor. "What happened to our house?"

"Everyone thought you were gone for good. The moment you left they broke in and took whatever they wanted. They tore the place apart because they believed you had a hidden stash of gold."

I try to hold back the tears, but the realization we are destitute forces them out. "Oh Mai, what will we do?" I fall to my knees and sob bitterly.

Mai takes me in her arms. "You must be strong for the children. You can't let them see you falling apart. We have some extra things you can use, and maybe some of those people will bring your things back when they see you're still here. You must have courage, Tuyết."

"If only Chinh would come home. He'd know what to do. I have no plan at all now. We will be at the mercy of the VC."

"I'll talk to Thoung. He is due back any time now. Maybe he'll be able to get word to Chinh."

"I hope so; it's our only chance." I dry my eyes and begin to attempt making a home out of the shambles around me.

*

The next morning, Thoung appears–armed to the teeth–his flight suit soaking wet with perspiration.

"Have you seen Chinh?" I assail him as soon as he comes in the door.

"He was on a mission when Nha Trang fell, Tuyết. I was barely able to escape with my crew. I have just come from the flight line, and no one has seen him there or at our operations office. I don't think he got out, and I fear anyone who's not here now is either dead or a captive of the Communists."

I bury my face in my hands and cry without shame.

"I'm sorry. There was no other way to tell you."

"What will I do now? How can we escape? You must take us with you," I say.

"I can't, Tuyết. My helicopter can't carry any more than my own family plus my crew and their families. I have no room. I'm sorry," Thoung says.

My father comes up to us. "My daughter, you need not worry about us. We are old and ready to die if we must, but I don't think the VC will harm us. We are too old and useless to be any threat to them.'"

I look to Thoung with pleading eyes. "You don't know what I did for the Americans. The Communists will not treat me or my family well when they take over. You must help me."

Thoung turns away and looks down at his boots. "I do know, Tuyết."

I knew it was inevitable that Mai would tell him about me, but I was still disappointed that she betrayed my confidence. Maybe Thoung will refuse to help me on the grounds that I've betrayed a friend of his.

"Then you know you must help me leave."

He shakes his head and turns to face me. "I don't care what you had to do to live. It's not about that. I told you, my helicopter is overloaded now. I can't take on any more passengers."

Mai comes in behind her husband and rushes to my side. "We must help them get out with us, husband. The children do not weigh much," Mai begs. "And Tuyết will not bring any more than the few things you see here. We can't leave her behind. She helped the Americans, and the Communists wont deal easily with her. You know the fate awaiting someone like her."

Thoung thinks for a moment. "Well, if I leave the door guns and ammunition I could take you, but that would make us vulnerable to the frenzied crowds assaulting anything offering a hope of escape. The only thing holding back the mob now is an occasional burst over their heads from the door guns." He thinks for another moment, "All right, but come quickly. We will not be able to hold off the mob much longer."

I embrace my mother and father and kiss them goodbye with my tears flowing freely. They hug the children who join me in crying. My heart breaks as Thoung helps us into the back of his commandeered truck. The children squeeze into the cab while we women sit in the bed along with one of his crew carrying a nasty looking machine gun. As we leave the housing compound, I wave to my parents as long as I can see them. The grief at leaving them behind fights with the terror of the unknown future for possession of my soul. I manage to push back the terror, at least for the present, but the pain of parting with the love that created me and nurtured me throughout my life can't be pushed into a back corner of my being. I make a vow to myself to bring them to America if I manage to get there myself. Now, I must concentrate on the safety of my children. I must push all other thoughts from my mind and keep up a good front for their sakes.

We speed across the parade field and plow our way through crowds pressing against the guards on the gate. Periodic gunfire is the only thing holding back the flood of humanity, yet a trickle of people penetrate through the hangars and some holes they manage to cut in the fence.

Once on the parking ramp we easily dodge the people running about trying to find some way out. The airman in the back of the truck uses the butt of his machine gun to knock away those who try to climb aboard. I wince each time I see the hard metal smash into another face. Those poor souls are only trying to save their own lives.

It's a scene from hell. Thoung's helicopter hovers just off the ground ahead of us, but a circle of people stalk it like a pack of hungry wolves. The door gunners menace the mob, and fire if they get too close. Thoung lays on the horn, and one of the door gunners picks up his machine gun and jumps to the concrete. He fires into the crowd to clear a path for the truck killing several people before the rest melt away in panic.

Thoung speeds into the tornado of the rotor blades and stops the truck next to his helicopter. We clamber aboard with our few bags while the gunners keep their vigils. When all are aboard, Thoung takes his place in the right seat and the chopper lifts off. People clamber to grab the skids, and a few manage to leap into the air and catch hold as the bird lifts away from the base. I'm horrified when the gunners pound at their hands until they let go and fall to their deaths.

The helicopter is full of people. The seats have been removed so they can be packed in as closely as possible. I loose count at twenty. At Thoung's command the gunners throw away their machine guns and several boxes of ammunition. At the next order all of their side arms and rifles are discarded along with any other loose equipment they can find. The noise is too loud for me to hear anything being said, and the screams of the frightened children drown out what little does come through. I hold Bao and Anh close to me for fear the gunners will throw them out to save weight. The steady flop-flop of the rotor blades seems to have a calming effect, however, once we're clear of the base and over the green countryside.

As the children calm down to only sobbing, muffled by their parent's embraces, Mai leans closer to me and shouts into my ear. "Thoung's plan is to fly out to sea and find an American ship. He thinks he knows where they are. Maybe he can find one of the large ships where we can land on the deck, but if he can't we'll have to set down in the ocean next to one. Can you swim?"

I hadn't bargained on this. I never swam in my life, and the children don't even know what the ocean is. I've heard stories of large fish capable of swallowing ships in one bite and fierce sharks that tear their victims to shreds. Drowning is horrible, but it's the least of my fears. "No, none of us can. What will we do?"

"It's all right. Thoung told me what to bring, and I have some for you too." She pulls several large, plastic bags from her suitcase and hands three to me. "Before you go into the water blow these up like a balloon. They will help you stay afloat. Do one for each of the children and tie it with these." She hands me three pieces of plastic like those I'd used in the BX. I know to push one end into the holder and pull it tight, and I also know it will not loosen once it's set. Knowing we have something to help keep us afloat is a bit more comfortable, but fear of being in the water for any length of time makes me tremble.

We reach the seashore, and I keep the children distracted by pointing out the beach and the little fishing villages we pass. Soon there is only the monotonous ocean below us, and I begin to wonder if we will ever find a ship in this vast desert of water. I'm busy trying to figure out how I might be able to spare my children the misery of a slow death when Mai shakes me and points out the front window.

There ahead of us is the biggest thing I've ever seen. A ship as large as a city with a broad, flat deck filled with gleaming white airplanes. Thoung turns around in his seat and points to it, smiling broadly. He brings the helicopter down smoothly on the deck, where it is immediately surrounded by armed Americans. The engine whines to a stop as the rotor blades continue to flop through the air slower and slower.

We pile out of the bird to be met by a group of sailors, while more sailors search and question the men. As they herd the women and children into a group, I see a huge machine pushing the helicopter over the side of the big ship. How symbolic it seems. The last tie to my mother country is severed, and I am now a stranger among what I hope are people as kind and generous as the men I knew so well. What lies ahead for me? I resolve that whatever it is, I can face it and conquer it. I've survived a war, and I know the future has to be brighter than the past.

Chapter 12

"Do any of you speak English?" A tall sailor asks.

"I do," I reply, as I leap to my feet and wave my arms. Sleeping with Americans was wrong, but I'm thankful it improved my English.

The sailor sighs in relief. "Thank God. Will you tell your people they will not be harmed, and that we'll take them to a safe place. We'll give them food and water and a doctor will help them with any medical problems. Do you understand?"

"Yes, sir. I'll tell them." I assure the shaking women and crying children that all is well. Most of them have had no past contact with Americans, and they're sure they'll be thrown into the sea after the helicopter. With this news, the mothers are able to calm their children a bit.

"Good," the sailor says. "Now follow me, and I'll take you below decks."

I relay his instructions to the group, and we walk to an area near the side of the ship. Mai stays close to me. As we walk, she asks, "Where are they taking us, Tuyết?"

"I don't know, but I trust the Americans. They won't mistreat us."

"I hope you're right. I've heard stories about American soldiers doing horrible things to people in the villages."

"I've heard those stories too, and I asked my American clients about them. They told me the people who did those things are criminals, and they've been punished severely." I only knew my clients, and I'm sure they are typical of all Americans.

"Did he say when I'd get to see Thoung again?"

"No. We must be patient for a while longer. You know what I was, and you know I know something about Americans, and they would never harm children or keep families apart any longer than necessary."

"I trust your experience with the Air Force people, but are you sure about their Navy?"

"I don't think they'd be any different, Mai. Be patient."

As I speak the deck begins to give way beneath our feet. The women scream, and the children break into new fits of crying. The sailor turns to me.

"Tell them it's just an elevator. They're safe. It's okay."

I have to shout to make myself heard over the noise of the machinery and the wailing of the mothers, but they calm down a bit as they see the thing is not intent on dumping them into the water.

The elevator stops at a lower deck, and the sailor leads us into what appears to be an airplane hangar. All around us men are working on the same kind of airplane we'd seen on the upper deck. Most of them act as if we aren't there at all. Only a few stop their work to look us over. We reach a roped-off area where armed men in different colored uniforms stand guard. The sailor tells me to instruct the people to sit down in this area, and they are not to leave it until they've been inspected by the doctor. I relay the information to the others, and we wait.

Another group of sailors bring trays of food and bottles of water, and the frightened mothers and children take the water but shy away from the food. I recognize the American thing they call a sandwich and explain it to them. I take a bite myself and give them to my children before they consider them safe to eat.

Once they know they won't be harmed, it's hard to contain the children. The older boys are fascinated by the airplanes and the burly men with curious haircuts guarding us. The younger ones don't understand why they can't have the run of the place and give the guards a difficult time keeping them confined to our designated space.

It's not long until the medical team arrives to set up an inspection station. A Vietnamese man is with them, and I recognize him as Doctor Nguyen, the one who treated my mother when she was ill. I run to him.

"Doctor Nguyen," I call to him, and he smiles as he recognizes me.

"I don't remember your name, but I could never forget so beautiful a face," he says.

"I'm Tuyết, you treated my mother for typhus. I'm glad you were able to get out," I say as I embrace him.

The American doctor looks impatient. "Doctor Nguyen, we need to process these people. You can speak with her later."

"He's right. I'll find you later. Right now, I have to interpret for Dr. Reiman, here."

"I understand. I'll see you later."

I return to my children and Mai. "That's Dr. Nguyen, isn't it?" she says.

"Yes. He said he'd talk to us later."

"It's comforting to see him here," she says.

They began to process us, and as they finish with a family, they're led away through a steel door. Mai turns to me with a worried look.

"What's behind that evil-looking door, Tuyết?"

"I don't know, but don't be worried. See, all the other doors are the same as this one." I point to two we can see from where we sit.

"I'm so frightened. I wish Thoung were here to explain all of this."

"It's alright. I know the Americans. They will not harm us, and you know Dr. Nguyen would not allow it."

As we speak, another group of women and children arrive. I don't know anyone in that group, but they are just as frightened as our people.

"I must speak to them, Mai. Watch the children for me." I move to them and speak.

"You will be alright. The Americans will not harm you. Be calm."

One older woman speaks up. "Who are you, and what do you know of Americans? I remember the French who used to feed us before they tortured us."

"My name is Vien Nouc Tuyết. I'm from Bien Hoa, and I worked with the Americans there. I know them well. They only want to check us over for any diseases before they let us inside their ship. Be patient."

They calm down a bit, but the old woman speaks again. "Mark my words. We will all wind up sleeping with our helicopter before this day is over." She sits down and continues to brood.

"Whatever they do, it can be no worse than what the Communists would do to us. Think of that," I say.

The doctor inspects me and my children before it's Mai's turn. While he does that, another group of sailors go through our meagre baggage. They take any food we'd brought along but leave the clothes and keepsakes. As they lead us away, I shout, "It's alright, Mai. I'll wait for you."

We go through the door, and I ask the sailor with us if we can wait on Mai's family. He agrees.

It's not long until Mai and her children join us, and the sailor leads us to a large room with cots and tables holding more food and drink. What I think are Filippino men in white uniforms stand behind the tables serving the people who were there before we arrived. A Vietnamese Thieu Ta in a flight suit speaks to us.

"Find a vacant cot and leave your things there. The bathrooms are there." He points to another door. "If you need new clothes, the Navy people will try to find you something to wear. The food is excellent, and you may have all you want, but I'd advise you to take it slowly. The American food is quite different from what you're used to. If you need to speak to an American, I will translate for you. Do you have any questions?"

"I speak good English, sir," I say. "Can I help you translate?"

"Thank you, but you have children to care for. That is your first job, but if I need you, I'll find you."

"Please, one more thing," I stop him as he turns to leave.

"What is it?" he says.

"Were you at Nha Trang? Did you know my husband Thieu Ta Chinh?"

His smile changes to a grim expression. "Yes, I was at Nha Trang, but I didn't know your husband. I'm sorry."

We find cots for everyone in both our families while Mai finds the bathroom. The only place to keep our things is under the cots, and I fear any valuables will be gone if we leave them alone for any length of time. I study our surroundings and notice several basketball goals suspended from the ceiling and some markings on the metal floor.

"This must be their gym, Mai," I say when she returns.

"Yes, I saw lockers in the bathroom. The toilets are American style, too. I'll have to teach the children how to use them."

Once the rest of the refugees are processed, a Vietnamese Dai Ta (Colonel) enters the room and moves to a microphone. He taps on the mike before speaking, and the room falls silent.

"I'm Dai Ta Tran. I've spoken with the Captain of this ship, and he tells me he will take us to the Philippines where we will board airplanes for Guam. The Americans have set up a permanent base there to process all of us for entry into the United States."

This announcement is met with cheers from many of the people in the room, but quite a few remain silent. He waves for silence before resuming.

"We will be aboard this ship for a little over 24 hours before reaching the Navy base in the Philippines. He expects that we will not be there more than another 24 hours before leaving for Guam. Those of you waiting on your husbands and fathers will have to wait a little longer to see them. The Americans are de-briefing them now, but they will be with you soon. Make yourselves comfortable, and if there's anything you need, or you have any questions, just ask one of the English-speaking officers. Is there anyone else here who speaks English?"

Several of us raise our hands.

"Please stand up so the others can see who you are," he says.

We all stand.

"You may also use these people as translators. I'll see you at Guam."

He leaves the microphone and joins his family in another part of the gym.

A half hour later Thoung arrives, much to Mai's relief.

"Did they torture you?" Mai asks as he embraces her.

Thoung laughs. "No, they only asked a lot of questions, most of which I couldn't answer."

"Do you think there will be any more helicopters?" I ask.

"No, I think we're too far out to sea now. I was almost out of fuel when we landed, but two more came in after me. I doubt any others make it." His face takes on a sober look, and he looks away for a moment before turning to me.

"I know what you hope for, and I have to tell you that you need not look for Chinh. One of the pilots in the other helicopter was a man I knew at Nha Trang. He said he saw Chinh's helicopter go down after it was hit by an RPG. I fear he's either dead or captured by the Communists. If he's a captive, he probably won't be alive for long. I've heard stories that they are executing any officers they capture. I'm sorry, Tuyết."

"Thank you for telling me." I turn away and let the tears flow freely. My children nestle close to me, and I hold them tightly while we all weep. Bao is now 14 and Anh 11. They are capable of understanding everything, and I'm glad of that. I know it's hard for them to realize they'll never see their father again. I can't believe he is dead. Something deep in my soul pours hope into my heart.

Chinh, my beloved, are you really gone? Not being certain is worse than seeing your bloody corpse stretched out on the ground before me. I know what he says is true, yet I will continue to hope. I must be brave for my children's sake.

"Do you think father's dead?" Bao asks.

"I think he must be dead. I know how much he loves us, and he would be with us if he were alive." We gather together and weep for a long time.

That night I lay on my cot thinking about our situation. We've escaped the Communists, but what lies in store for us? When will we get to America? What will happen when we get there? I'm confident in my English, and I know what my clients have told me about America, but I begin to imagine various fates that may await us there. I'm an ignorant woman with no husband. What could I do in such an advanced culture? Will people such as I be little more than slaves? Who will help us there? I have no relatives in America to take us in. Where will we go? I eventually fall asleep to the lullaby drummed out by the ships engines.

Chapter 13

Our next stop is the Philippine Islands where we spend the night in tents until being herded into the largest airplane I've ever seen. It's all overwhelming. Everything is so large. First, the aircraft carrier, then the huge naval base, and now an airplane so big I can't believe it will fly. They tell us our destination is an island named Guam. I have no idea where it is or how long it will take us to get there.

An American Captain accompanying us asks me to translate for him and tells me the flight will take about four hours and that there is a two-hour time difference, Guam being two hours ahead of the Philippines. I pass the information on to the other people, and we settle into uncomfortable canvas seats arranged in four rows. Two rows are fastened to the sides of the airplane with back-to-back seats of the same type down the middle. What little baggage we have is stacked in an open space toward the front of the plane. The cabin is longer than the walk from my house to the local market, and it ends at the long ramp we used to enter. As I think of it, the ramp raises to close off the outside. Panic begins to spread among the women and children, but the military husbands do their best to calm things down.

The engines start, and the noise makes it hard to talk to my children. They're so frightened, just like all the others. The helicopter flight was different. The sides were open, and we could see what was happening. Here, we are like meat in a can. I know this is a common thing for the men, and they feel safe, but I can't help but worry.

The plane lifts off, and we finally settle down for a long, uncomfortable ride. The crew passes out box lunches at noon, but several people are too airsick to eat them. The men and those passengers who are not sick gladly consume the unwanted meals.

It's mid-afternoon when we land on Guam. An Air Force officer tells us we will be taken by bus to some temporary housing until we can be processed for entering the United States. Again, I act as translator for those with no English. He asks if anyone is not interested in going to the United States, but all of us are hoping that will be our final destination. I'm still with

Mai and her family, and I ask if we can be housed together. It turns out that we are placed in tents on opposite sides of the base. We manage to meet again and vow to stay as close as possible.

Here we're given a few clothes, consisting of American Army issue items that fit the men and some of the women, but not the little ones. Some donated items arrive for the children, and I manage to find some pajamas for Anh, but none of it is big enough for Bao. We still eat American food which isn't too bad except for the eggs. We used eggs in recipes in Viet Nam, but we never ate them by themselves. The children seem to adapt more easily than me to the new menu. They love the treats the Airmen often pass out. I think they're much too sweet and limit them to one piece each.

A few of our men speak reasonable English, but most of the women and children speak none at all. I volunteer to teach a class on English. I must do something to alleviate the boredom of long days and longer nights. I quickly have more students than I can accommodate. The children seem to learn quickest and are soon speaking some English among themselves.

More Vietnamese people pour into Guam each day. Soon, the tents we occupy are full, and more tents are erected to accommodate them.

American civilians interview each of us, making sure we still want to go to the United States. I'm surprised when I learn quite a few elect to return to Viet Nam. Within a month we are back in a large airplane for the long flight to freedom in the United States. Mai is on the same plane, and we manage to move next to each other during the flight.

The airplane lands at another immense military base they call El Torro. I'm struck by the cold air when the big rear ramp opens. We walk out into what we would call winter in Viet Nam, but it's even colder here. The children are shivering.

"Mother, it's cold here. Is all of America this cold?" Anh asks.

"I don't know. The Americans I knew thought what we called winter was warm. Maybe it is," I answer.

"We'll just have to get used to it," Bao says.

"I wish I had my warm jacket," Anh says.

The soldiers herding us toward busses wear the same uniforms I'd seen on the aircraft carrier. This must be a Marine base. There were no Marines at Bien Hoa, but I heard stories about how cruel they were. So far, they've only been kind to us. We board the busses, and I'm happy for the warmth inside.

After only a short drive we arrive at another Marine base, Camp Pendleton. Here, we're herded into a large building where we form a line.

"What are we in line for?" Mai asks me.

"Look up there. They're giving out army coats to keep us warm," I say.

We reach the Marines handing them out.

"Sorry, we don't have any small enough for the kids," one Marine says. "This is as small as I've got."

He hands me a coat that swamps Anh. I roll up the sleeves, but the hem reaches to her ankles. She holds her arms out straight at her sides and models it to the laughter of her brother.

"It may be funny, but it's warm," Anh says.

"I think the same size might actually fit your son," the Marine says. He gives me another of the same size. It's too big for Bao, but it doesn't look so silly as the one on Anh.

"At least I can stop shivering," Bao says.

The Marine eyes me for a moment and selects a slightly larger size. "Try this on."

The coat is a bit loose, but I can't complain.

Farther down the line we're also given a book about America and how it's different from Viet Nam. It's written in English, but each line is followed by the same words in a form of Vietnamese I can barely understand. I think it must be a northern dialect.

The same bus takes us to a vast tent city. Drab green tents stretch as far as I can see to the left and right. Buildings I learn are called Quonset Huts break the tent city into several sections. We are assigned to one of the Quonset Huts along with several other families. Once more we are separated from Mai and her family.

I quickly make friends with a woman named Lien. The family name is Dahn. Her husband, Lahn, had been a minor official in the Nguyen Van Thieu regime, and he and his family were part of the helicopter lifts from the American embassy in Saigon. They have two children—a girl named Mai and a boy named Tran. Both are much younger than my children being 5 and 4 respectively, but Anh and Bao take them under their wings.

"Isn't it exciting, Tuyết? We're finally in the United States," Lien says.

"Yes, but we're not on our own yet. I'm afraid of what may happen to us once we leave this place."

"The Americans have been good to us so far. I'm sure they won't let us down. Lahn says we will soon have money just like the Americans we saw in Viet Nam. He says America is such a rich country there is plenty of money to go around."

I shake my head in disbelief. "I know the Americans very well. There is nothing free here. We must work hard for whatever we get. They will not grant us any special status."

"You're too pessimistic, Tuyết. Wait and see. Things will be much better here than back home."

*

In the morning, the first order of business is medical examinations for me and my children. Fortunately, we pass all of their tests. They tell me the next step will be interviews with immigration people and social workers, but it might take some time to get around to us.

They were not wrong. I find Mai and her family the next day, but there's not enough small talk to fill the afternoon. We vow to keep in touch. Her tent is a long walk from our hut, but walking helps fill in the empty space in my life from time to time.

I don't need to worry much about the children. Bao learns the American game of baseball being taught by some Marines. He fills his time with that sport. Anh and Mai, the Dahn's girl, spend their time playing with the other children. They've found a hill and use old boxes as sleds. They don't seem to tire of the game.

The food here is no better than on Guam. They still serve scrambled eggs for breakfast, and another meal is what they call corned beef hash. They dump it cold from a can to our trays. The vegetables are tasty, and they soon replace the potatoes with rice. Toilets are outside affairs in booths or open latrines.

To kill time, I wander the camp seeking people I might know or someone who might tell me something about my parents or Chinh. I find that many here are wealthy members of the Thieu regime or the families of prosperous business men. The military men are all senior officers, Dai Ta's or generals. None of them have any information I need. The Marines set up a bulletin board where we can post notices about people we're looking for, and I put up notes for my parents and Chinh.

The next morning, I take the children to breakfast. We get our trays and follow Lien's family in the line.

"They've got eggs again today," Lien says.

"Maybe they'll have oatmeal or that other hot cereal," I reply.

"I like the eggs," Bao says.

"I like the bacon," Anh says. "I think the oatmeal is slimy."

"The Marines at the baseball diamond say eggs are good for you. They say eggs help grow hair on your chest," Bao says.

I've heard that expression from one of my old clients, and I need to put Bao straight right away. "That's just an American way of saying they help you grow strong. It doesn't really make any hair grow on your chest."

We reach the man serving eggs, and Bao takes three scrambled. The rest of us pass the eggs and opt for the oatmeal.

At the table Lien speaks. "We'll be leaving the camp soon. They found Lahn a job as a chauffeur for a limousine service."

"Is he happy with that?" I ask.

"No, but he says he'll take anything to get us out of here. A friend of ours thinks we can find a place to live on Bolsa Avenue, wherever that is."

"You're lucky. I only know of one man who may be able to help us, and I hope he's still where he said he'd be when he left Viet Nam."

The PA system comes alive in Vietnamese. "Classes in English, American history and government will begin tomorrow. Please register at the reception center after ten o'clock today. We will try to form as many classes as needed. Once again, that's…"

I don't pay any attention to the rest. I'm glad there will be something to fill the long hours of waiting during the day.

I manage to get the children into English classes while I enroll in the history and government class. I offer to help with the English classes and become a teacher's aide in three morning sessions. The history class fills one hour in the afternoon, and I also volunteer to help with two more of those classes. I have to stay busy or I'll go crazy. Luckily, Lien can help with my children. She says it will still be a few weeks before they can leave.

Evenings after dinner are the worst. Lien and I have run out of small talk, and there's not much gossip to hash out. There is television in the mess hall, and the children enjoy it more than I do. I've seen some of it while entertaining my clients back in Viet Nam.

My first interview comes a month after our arrival. A rather stern woman with flaming red hair is very glad I speak English, but she keeps the translator around just in case.

"Mrs. Vien, I'm Shirley Vasquez." She doesn't rise or offer her hand to me. She just sits there with a bored expression, concentrating on the papers before her. "Do you have any formal education or special training?"

"No, I married my husband after I finished what you call high school." She makes a note on her paperwork.

"I see. I take it your husband is not with you. Is that correct?"

"He was killed at Nha Trang." Another note.

"I'm sorry for your loss. Do you have any special skills?"

127

"I can cook and sew that's all." I didn't think she should know about my other special skills. Again, she makes notes.

"Do you have any family members currently living in the United States?"

"No."

She sighs heavily and sits back in her chair. More notes.

"You are here under the refugee provisions of the immigration act. Normally, you would not be qualified for entry into our country, but the President has made a special exception in the case of Vietnamese refugees. You and your children will be allowed to immigrate as aliens with temporary visas for up to one year. You will have to qualify as permanent resident aliens by the end of that time in order to remain longer. Do you understand your status?"

"Yes, what do I need to do to be…what you said?"

"Permanent resident alien?"

"Yes, that."

"You will have to learn English, and I see you already speak our language well enough. Do you read and write English as well as you speak and understand it?"

"Not as well as I speak English. What else?"

"You will have to pass a test on American history and government, but I see you're already enrolled in that class."

"My children are taking English classes, and I'm already teaching them about American history and government. Will they be able to go to school once we leave this camp?"

"Your children will not be admitted to American schools until they can speak some English."

"They're learning very quickly. Is it expensive? I don't have much money."

"The public school systems are free," she replies.

"When can we leave camp?"

"That will be up to your social worker. You will have to have a sponsor willing to help you until you get your work permit. Your work opportunities will be limited until you have a green card. The only other way, since you have no relatives here, would be if you have $4,000 or more as assurance that you will not become a public liability."

This news is a complete surprise. My American lovers always stressed the fact that America was a land of opportunity, yet this woman describes so many obstacles to that dream, I'm afraid I'll never be able to achieve it.

"I don't have $4,000."

She adds, "Of course, your sponsoring family will take care of you until you can be self-sufficient. Do you have any other questions?"

I sit back stunned. What family will welcome three more mouths to feed even in a land as rich as America?

I go back to our tent and collapse on my bed. Mrs. Danh comes over and sits down next to me. "What's wrong Tuyết? You look worried."

"I just met with the immigration lady, and she was very depressing."

"I know what you mean. Lanh was just as discouraged after that interview. It seems he has no special skills that would qualify him for any meaningful work here in America. He had to take work as a chauffeur. Would you believe that's all we can get?"

"I'll just have to find some way to make a living for my family. In Viet Nam I worked two jobs to make ends meet. I can do it again."

"You're very brave." Her face brightens. "I do have some good news."

"Oh?" It's good to hear that someone has good news.

"Yes, I found my uncle and aunt this morning. They're close-by, but I never would have known it if not for the bulletin board."

"I put up one for my husband, but one of his fellow pilots told me he talked to a man who saw Chinh's helicopter crash. I don't hold out much hope of ever seeing him again. I would like to find out if my parents are alive. They had to stay behind, and I don't know if the Communists would let them live, or not. I put up one for them too."

The next day, Mai and I meet to compare notes. They are lucky. Thoung has a bank account in Europe with enough money to get them out right away after he transfers it to the

United States. She tells me he's also confident he can get a job as a pilot. They have found an apartment in the area everyone calls Bolsa, and she gives me their address and phone number. I promise to call her when I get out of the camp if I can afford a telephone and somebody shows me how to use it.

*

My next meeting is a month later. The social worker is a stocky, middle-aged, black woman named Maya. I don't quite know what to make of her at first, but she seems to be pleasant enough. She asks many questions, but the most important one was if I had anyone in the United States I could call on who might sponsor me. I immediately think of Mel, he told me he would be willing to help. I know what he will want in return for his help, but I have little choice. If I have to be his mistress again, I'll do it. I came to enjoy my time with him in Viet Nam, after he professed his love for me. That is, until it became clear that his apparent affection was only skin deep. I may have to tolerate him again, but I will also do whatever it takes to leave him as soon as I can. I don't have any idea how long that will take, but it won't be forever.

"I know an Air Force officer, a Lieutenant Colonel. His name is Melvin Jenkins. He told me he was going to March Air Force Base when he left Viet Nam three years ago," I say.

She consults a book and smiles. "I see March Air Force Base has a liaison officer assigned to the IATF (Inter-Agency Task Force, an organization set up to help settle the refugees.) March Air Force Base is nearby, in Riverside. I'll contact them to see if they can give us any information. Did I get his name right? I have Melvin Jenkins."

She spells it out, and I remember seeing Mel's name tag on his uniform.

"That's right."

"I'll talk to you again in three days." She writes a date and time on a pad, tears off the sheet and hands it to me. "Come back then."

All I can do now is hope Mel will be willing to help. I return to our hut and my children. I'd left Bao watching Anh, and I wasn't sure about doing that, but Lien said she'd also keep an eye on them.

As I walk in, I notice there are two more families sharing our already cramped living space. I find both Bao and Anh reading their English books.

"I see you two have been keeping busy."

"We want to learn our new language as fast as possible," Bao answers.

Anh puts down her book and says, "And we had hamburgers for lunch."

"They were good," Bao adds. "You have to put a lot of their ketchup and mustard sauce on them, but I like them."

I smile at the children already becoming Americans. Mel introduced me to American hamburgers back in Viet Nam, but I didn't bother to make them for the children as they required beef which was very expensive.

"As soon as you think your English is good enough, we'll begin speaking in English whenever we can. What do you know so far?"

Anh says, "Good morning Mother. How are you?"

"Very good. How about you, Bao?"

"Today is Wednesday," he says. "I can name all the days of the week."

"Show me."

"Sunday, Monday, Tuesday, Wednesday, Thursday, Friday and Saturday."

"I'm proud of you two. Keep studying."
*

That night I think of Viet Nam as I lay in bed unable to sleep. My life here in America has not yet begun, and I wonder what life is like for my parents. I'll try to send them a letter once I get settled. I can only hope the Communists won't treat them badly.

I also think of Chinh. If he's dead, I know his spirit will try to find me, and I dread that. My only consolation is that spirits cannot cross water, and a vast ocean lies between us. I still love him even though I'm sure he's lost his love for me. But, I must leave his memory behind just as I've left Viet Nam behind and my life as a whore. I can be a true mother again, but that will require a new husband to complete a real family.

There are a few single Vietnamese men in the camp. I've talked with two of them, but neither one seemed to want anything more than a sex partner. Perhaps Mel will be the one to make my dreams come true. I know he'll want me as a lover. Would I be willing to take on that role again? No, but I could tolerate it for a while if I felt he truly loved me and was willing to divorce his wife. Who am I kidding? I'll do anything to get out of this camp, even being Mel's mistress again. Once I'm on my feet in America, I can sever our relationship and hope to find a husband as an American woman and not a pitiful refugee.

Chapter 14

At my next meeting with the social worker, she smiles cheerfully as I enter the room. "Good news, Mrs. Vien. We found Colonel Jenkins at March Air Force Base. When I told him about you, he was very excited. He's waiting in the next room. He wants to speak with you privately." She points to a door on her right. "Do you want to see him now?"

Mel's my best opportunity to begin a new life. I know what he'll demand in return for his help, but what else can I do? I don't relish rotting away in this camp while the bureaucratic process grinds slowly to find us someone else. "Yes, I'll see him?"

I open the door, and Mel stands to greet me. He's the same tall, handsome officer as in Viet Nam, but he's even more impressive in his blue uniform than he ever was in the drab fatigues he wore then.

"Hello Mrs. Vien," he says as he offers his hand.

The formality of his greeting catches me off guard, but I play along.

"Hello, Trung Ta. It's good to see you looking well."

His eyes shift to the Social Worker. "Thank you, Ms. Wilson. May Mrs. Vien and I speak privately for a while?"

"Certainly, just call when you're ready." She closes the door, and Mel takes me in his arms. He stares into my eyes as a warm smile spreads across his face.

"Snow, I thought I'd never see you again, and here you are."

I let him embrace me but turn my head away to refuse his kiss. "It is good see you too, Mel, but we need to talk."

We sit down at the table, and Mel takes my hands in his. He nods toward the door. "She tells me you're here with your children. Couldn't you get your parents out?"

I tell him the story of our deception by General Quang, and my parents' willingness to stay behind.

His face takes on a look of anger and disgust. "That lousy rat, taking all your money and leaving you to the VC. He's probably basking on the Riviera now enjoying the good life with his Swiss bank account to back him up."

"I don't care about him. I'm going to start a new life here in America, and I need someone to help me. You once told me to call on you if I ever got to the States, and here I am."

His smile grows broader, and he pats my arm. "You can count on me. It'll be just like in Viet Nam."

I knew this was coming, and I need to make my position clear to him. "We need to get one thing straight, Mel. Unless you want to marry me, I'll put up with being your mistress only as long as it takes me to be on my own here in the States. Do you understand me?"

His smile melts into a grim line. "You have to understand something, too. Things have changed since I saw you last."

"What kind of change?" I can only hope it's good news.

"My wife had a stroke a year ago that left her a vegetable. She's in a nursing home in Riverside and not expected to live much longer. I'll be a free man soon. You'll only be my mistress for a little while, then we can be married. After I left Viet Nam, I discovered I really do love you. You don't know how much I've regretted what I said to you back then. It took the realization I'd never see you again to bring out my true feelings. I love you, Snow."

His words strike a chord in my soul, and his eyes convey a sincerity I've never seen in Mel before. Can I believe him? Is this just another deception? If he means it, I can be his mistress for as long as it takes, but even if he's lying, I have no other option for getting out of this camp. I'll have to play along with him until I can be sure.

Having resigned myself to a carnal relationship with Mel, the financial part of the arrangement now becomes the dominant factor. I know I'll need a lot of help for a long time, and Mel is the only source of that help. "Can you afford to help me and still take care of her?"

"That's not a problem. You and the kids can move in with me. It's a big house. There's plenty of room. I'll sign as your sponsor, and you can be out of here in a day or two. It'll be a little hard for us until she's gone, but we'll get by. I'll be able to retire from the Air Force next year, and I'll go to work for a civilian company after that. Then, we'll have a good life together because I'll make a lot more money as a civilian, and I'll have a retirement check from the Air Force on top of that."

"Mel! How can I move in with you while you're still married? Besides, I have the children to think of."

"I've never met your children, but they're certainly welcome. I'd be like a father to them."

"That's not what I meant. I know you'd like them, but what would they think of me sleeping with you?"

Mel sits back with a surprised look. "What did they think in Viet Nam?"

"They thought I only cooked for you."

"How old are they now?" His face shows a mask of disappointment.

"Bao's 14, and Anh's 11."

"Okay, I've got three bedrooms. You can sleep with your daughter if you like."

"Mel, I couldn't live in your wife's house." I shudder at the thought of her presence pervading the atmosphere. "I'd feel like an intruder. I'd never be comfortable."

Mel sags in his chair and despair clouds his face. "I'd sell it, but she owns half. With the mortgage the way it is, I wouldn't get enough to be able to buy another house. I'm stuck there until she dies, and full ownership goes to me."

"Even if I did agree, would my children go to school with other Vietnamese students? They don't speak good English yet. They need Vietnamese friends. A man in my tent says he knows someone who will give us a good deal on an apartment in the Bolsa area. We'd be better off there."

"Why pay extra money for rent? I'm sure your kids would be okay in the base school."

"Yes, it would be cheaper, but the American children might pick on them for being different. They need to have other Vietnamese kids to help out with the transition to American life. Even if I have to work two jobs, I'd rather be in Bolsa than Riverside."

He sighs and turns away. "I've heard of that area. They're already starting to call it 'Little Saigon'. That's in Westminster, 50 miles from Riverside. You can't come to see me because you won't be able to afford a car, and I can't take off from work to see you during the day when the kids are gone at school. It's impossible. Besides, if I have to help you with your rent, I won't be able to do much else as long as my wife's living."

The room is silent while we both fall into a pensive mood. I'm afraid I'll lose his support if I don't offer him some way to make our trysts possible. Fifty miles seems like a long way, and that distance will mitigate the frequency of our meetings, which is a good thing. I know it won't be like Viet Nam. I don't have my parents to care for the children, but they're both old enough to be alone for a few hours. There may be some ruse I can employ to keep them from knowing about us, but all I can think of is a two job situation. I could work during the day and claim I have to work a night job also and meet Mel on that night. But, what if I have to work nights? I'll tell them I'm working six nights when it's only five and meet Mel on my night off.

"I think I know how we can do it." Mel's face brightens at this news.

"How's that?" he aks.

"The children are used to me working two jobs. If I get a day job, I'll tell them I also have a night job once a week, and we can meet on that night. If I work nights, I'll tell them I'm working six nights instead of five. The sixth night will be you and I."

His smile returns immediately. He relaxes and sits back in his chair. "Well, it looks like our first job is to help you get settled in Westminster."

He calls the social worker back in. She congratulates me and thanks Mel. Some official paperwork follows, but in a short time we're finished. Mel speaks, "I'll be back tomorrow around noon to help you find an apartment. If we find one, I'll take leave for all next week so we can get you moved in as fast as possible."

"I'll see you tomorrow," I say and leave the room.

*

The next day Mel arrives a little before noon. The children are at lunch, but I've explained to them that I'll be house hunting this afternoon. I'm too excited to eat. Mr. Danh gives me the name and address of the apartment manager he'd spoken to me about earlier. They aren't moving in until next week because they're waiting on her mother to join them from Guam.

"You ready to go?" Mel asks.

"Yes, I'm very ready. We can go now."

"What about your kids?" he asks.

"Lien will watch them while we're gone. It's okay."

"This way to my car," he says and waves a hand toward the door.

I'm excited about leaving the camp. It's all the United States I've seen up to this point, and I'm anxious to see what the city looks like. Mel leads me to what he calls a station wagon, a car sized on the same scale as the aircraft carrier and the giant planes that brought us to the States. He opens the door for me, and I sink into soft leather seats that exude a smell unlike anything I'd ever experienced before. It's so luxurious.

He sits down behind the wheel and starts the engine. A rush of chilled air assaults me from vents in the dash. I cringe a bit in surprise.

"Oh, I'm sorry," he says as he reaches over and redirects the flow. "Riverside's out in the desert, and I like plenty of air now that it's getting to be summer." He twists a knob and the air flow slackens a bit.

"Where is this apartment you have a lead on?"

I pull a paper from my pocket and give it to him. "This is the address. I'm to see a Mr. Bui there."

"Does he know you're coming?"

"No."

"Then we'll just have to hope he's in when we get there."

He pulls away from the main building and drives out the front gate of the Camp. The Marine guard on the gate snaps a salute as we pass.

After a short drive, he accelerates up a long ramp to a very high speed. I think he's going much too fast, but as we reach the top of the ramp, I see the other cars going every bit as fast. He maneuvers into the high-speed flow of traffic very smoothly. He must have noticed me stiffening up.

"I'll bet you've never gone this fast in a car your whole life. These roads are called 'freeways', and after you learn to drive you'll get used to the speed very quickly."

"How fast are we going?" I ask when my pulse returns to normal.

"A little over 70, that's miles per hour, it equates to around 110 kilometers per hour but there's not much traffic now. The 405 slows to a crawl at rush hour."

"Are there more cars on the road then?" I can hardly believe so many cars.

"Lots more. It'll be full in all lanes and moving at 30, if you're lucky."

I finally grow used to the speed enough to carry on an intelligent conversation.

"How far is the apartment?" I ask.

"Not far."

The car falls silent for a while. I watch the brown scrub flash by. It seems like a dead land, and I think how different this is from the alive, verdant green of Viet Nam. This must be what people call desert. Why would anyone want to live here? But the number of cars around us now tells me many people do. What draws them here? Ah, maybe that's not it? Maybe there are so many people in America some of them are forced to live here? That's the only reason I can think of for people to inhabit such a barren space.

After a while we enter a more built-up area where some green trees peek above pastel colored walls surrounding housing areas. I can't tell much about the houses, but it's obvious they're huge. America is truly as wonderful as all my clients said it was.

Mel points to a sign in the middle of the freeway. "Bolsa Avenue's the next exit."

We turn off the freeway and enter normal traffic. I see a McDonald's restaurant and almost shout.

"I see a McDonald's. Can we get a hamburger?"

Mel laughs as he changes lanes and signals for a left turn into the restaurant. "Sure, whatever you like. Where did you hear about McDonald's?"

"An American Colonel I knew in Viet Nam said he wanted to own one when he retired. I remember one night when you made hamburgers for us in Viet Nam, and I was wondering if these were the same thing."

Mel laughs and pats my leg. "No, they're not the same thing as I made, but I think you'll like them. Your kids will want to try them too, I'm sure. I'll take them to one after you get settled in."

"They had hamburgers at the camp, and liked those, but I'm sure they'll want to try these too."

He parks the car and we go inside. It's not busy, and I marvel at the sights, sounds and smells of the place. A combination of hot coffee and grilled meat assails my nose while the cacophony of customer conversations and shouts from behind the counter combine in organized chaos. Behind the counter people in uniforms are busy filling orders for a window in the far wall. Others are serving people waiting at the counter. Mel points to a sign board above them.

"You can see what's available up there," he says.

I study the pictures and decide on one dish they call a "Big Mac". "I'll have a 'Big Mac'. The Colonel said that was the best thing they serve."

Mel addresses the clerk, "Make that two Big Mac meal deals."

He pays the bill, and in only a moment a clerk appears with a tray holding two boxes, French fried potatoes in cardboard sleeves and two paper cups. He fills the cups from a machine and adds lids and straws, then he finds a table. I have a lot of questions I hope he can answer and begin with the one weighing most on my mind.

"Do you think one job will be enough for us to live on?"

He takes a sip of his Coke before answering. "Well, that depends on the kind of job you get. What can you do?"

"I worked in the BX at Bien Hoa, and I tended bar sometimes in the advisor's club."

He thinks for a moment before answering. "Bar tending would be the best paying job, but the hours would be lousy. Retail, like your BX job, doesn't pay that much, and the hours are no better. That kind of job would be easier to find. Those places are always looking for people, but they only pay a little above minimum wage. I'd say you'd be looking at $100.00 a week, at most from the retail and fast food jobs. A good bartender can probably make twice that."

"I worry that one job will not be enough in America?"

"A lot of people do manage on that income, but in most low-income families both the husband and wife work. They each bring home around $150 a week for $300 total. I don't think you could find one job to pay that much considering you have no training. I can help you out some. I could manage, say, $300 a month."

Even the smallest number he's mentioned seems like a fortune to me. It's hard to believe it costs that much to live in America. I don't want to be a burden on Mel, but I'll have to work two jobs again without his help. Another alternative comes to mind.

"I could be a waitress. Would that be better?"

Mel smiles and leans back in his chair. "If you let me help you out, you'll only have to work one job, and you could train for something better in your off time. You could learn to type and take shorthand and be a secretary, or you could do data entry for computers. I do have to warn you that jobs are a bit scarce these days. It may take you a while to find a good one."

How will we live 'til then?"

"After we see about your apartment, I'll help you set up a bank account. I'll put some money in the account for you to use until you're on your feet again—say $1,000."

I catch my breath at the size of the amount. "Mel, that's a fortune. Can you afford to do that?"

"I've got three times that much in a savings account. It's not coming out of my monthly pay. Let's see what your apartment will cost first. Then you can see what jobs are within walking distance to start with. You won't be able to afford a car."

"I used to ride a moped. Maybe I could do that again."

"Yeah, you could get away with that most of the year here in Southern California. That might be an alternative. Finish your burger, and we'll see what an apartment will set you back before we go any further."

I enjoy the sandwich, and the first French fries I've eaten since Mel introduced me to American burgers and fries nearly three years back. I also enjoy watching the overweight Americans sit down with food-laden trays. No wonder they're fat.

On the way to the apartments I tell Mel to let me do the bargaining with the landlord. He laughs at my comment.

"We don't bargain here in the States like you did in Viet Nam. I don't think he'll lower his rent. There are so many refugees looking for homes, he can name his own price."

"Just the same, I want to try."

"Okay, give it a go."

We pass fields of some kind of crop. "What are they growing here?" I ask.

"Strawberries. Most of this part of the county grows strawberries. There's a few businesses here, but it's mostly farmland."

"Lien said this place is an apartment. I don't see anything but farm houses."

"We'll just have to wait and see," He says.

Mel begins to slow down and checks out an address on a mailbox.

"Your place shouldn't be too far now."

I look ahead and see a larger structure on the right. "That must be it," I say, pointing to the building.

Mel pulls into a courtyard surrounded by what appear to be rows of doors alternating with large windows. A small swimming pool occupies the middle of the courtyard, and a few children are swimming under the supervision of an older woman.

"This is an old motel," he says. He points to a sign high on a post. It reads, "Courtyard Apartments".

"What is a motel?" I ask.

"It's a place where travelers stay overnight. This can't be an apartment complex. Are you sure they gave you the right address?"

"Yes, unless there is more than one Bolsa Avenue."

"No, this is it. I guess we check in over there." He points to a red neon sign reading, "office."

He parks, and we enter a room facing a counter. The aroma of nuóc mắm sauce brings back memories. A bell rings as we open the door, and a Vietnamese man appears. He's rather tall and carries himself in a military manner. His gray hair and halting gait tell his age.

"May I help you?" he asks in English.

"Are you Mr. Bui?" I ask in Vietnamese.

"Please, speak English, if you can. I prefer to conduct all business in English unless you don't speak anything but Vietnamese."

I switch to English and notice Mel's obvious relief.

"Yes, I speak good English," I say. "My name is Vien Nouk Tuyết, and this is Trung Ta Jenkins. Mr. Danh tells me you have an apartment."

"Ah yes, that unit was rented yesterday, but you are fortunate, Ms. Vien. I have another unit that just became available this morning."

"I'd like to see it, please."

"Certainly, this way."

He leads us to a door on the other side of the pool and unlocks it. The smell of old diapers hits me immediately. I recoil a bit.

"I need to air this out," he says. "The previous tenant had two small children."

"Where did they go?" I ask.

"They went up to El Segundo when the husband found a job at Northrup."

I give him a quizzical look, and Mel says. "That's an aircraft manufacturer."

The condition of the floors and cabinet tops tell me they moved out very quickly. The place needs a thorough cleaning.

It's small even by Vietnamese standards. It reminds me of Mel's trailer.

A couch, a coffee table and two chairs face a television set. It has a refrigerator and a range with a small oven on the far wall. The window curtains are a bit shabby, but they will do. A well-worn carpet covers the floor, except for the kitchen area, which is tile. A small table and four chairs near the range serve as a dining area.

"The bedroom and bath are this way." Bui leads us down a short hallway to a large bedroom with a bathroom on one side.

"It's only one bedroom," Mel says. He turns to Bui. "Don't you have any two bedroom units?"

"I'm sorry. They're all just one bedroom," Bui responds.

"You can't stay in a place with just one bedroom," Mel says.

"We're all in one tent with three other families now. We can make do with this," I say.

"I can give you a folding bed for the living room if you like," Mr Bui adds.

"I think that would do it. How much is this one?"

"I give Vietnamese people a special price because I know you need help, at first. I ask $200 a month for the first six months and $350 a month after that. There is no lease. I rent month-to-month. Most people move on to something better as soon as they can."

I glance at Mel and see him nod slightly before he asks, "What about utilities?"

"I pay for the water, gas and electric, but the tenant pays the phone, of course," Bui answers.

I remember what Mel and I discussed about wages. At least for the first six months I could afford it, but I don't want to give in without at least making a stab at bargaining.

"It's a nice place Mr. Bui, but it needs some work. What would you say to $100 a month for the first six months?"

"Mrs. Vien, do you know how many refugees are coming into Camp Pendleton every day?"

"I don't know," I reply.

143

"There are hundreds, and they all want a place to live. You're very lucky. This apartment became available only this morning. If you don't take it, I will have a dozen other people wanting it by tomorrow. This is not Viet Nam. Americans don't usually bargain on things, but I don't demand a bribe either."

"I see it needs a good cleaning. If I clean it for you, would you give me the first month rent free?"

Bui thinks for a moment. "If you will clean it to my usual standards, I will waive your security deposit."

"How much is that?"

"$200, a month's rent."

I look at Mel, and he smiles as he nods his approval. "Okay, when can we move in?"

"As soon as the authorities will allow you to leave the camp."

"I can leave any time, now that I have a sponsor. Let's see, today's Tuesday. I'll clean tomorrow, and we'll move in Thursday."

Mel speaks, "Wait a minute, not so fast. You'll have to get some pots and pans plus some groceries. You'd better plan on moving in next week."

"You're right. I just want to get out of the camp as quickly as possible." I suddenly remember Bao's baseball game. "I almost forgot. Bao has a ball game on Saturday. It will have to be Sunday. Will that be okay, Mr. Bui?" I ask.

"Fine." He offers his hand to me to seal the bargain.

We go to Bui's office where I sign the rental agreement with Mel as a co-signer. Mel gives him a check for the first month's rent, and Mr. Bui hands me the keys to the apartment.

"I wish you every happiness in your new life here in America. You can take the keys now. If you need me to open-up for any deliveries, just call." He hands me a card with his office phone number.

In the car Mel says, "That place was a mess. I don't see why you don't stay at my house. It's much cleaner and a lot more room besides being rent free."

"We've been over this before. You know why I can't live with you."

"I know. Anyway, it was a good ploy offering to clean the place."

"It's because I'm Vietnamese. We must always bargain some."

"I guess the next order of business is finding a job you can walk to. I didn't see much on the way in except that old bar across the street."

"I used to tend bar in the advisor's club at Bien Hoa. I guess we could see if they need any help," I say.

He drives across the street to a one-story, stucco building that's seen better days. Neon signs in the windows proclaim the brands of beer on sale inside while a painted sign over the door reads, "Kozy Korner Bar & Grill". There's a hand-written sign in the window saying they want a bartender.

"Looks like you may be in luck." he says.

I walk into the bar where a young man is busy going from booth to booth checking the condiments. I approach him.

"I saw your sign wanting a bartender. Do I talk to you?"

He laughs and stops his work. He looks me over thoroughly. "No, but I sure wish it was me. You need to talk to Luigi over at the bar." He points in that direction.

I approach the bar and speak to an overweight, balding man with a stubble of beard who's busy polishing a glass.

"That man said I should talk to you about the bartender job."

Luigi continues to polish his glass, but his eyes scour me from head to foot. I get the definite impression he's more interested in my physical assets than my job knowledge.

He finally speaks. "You got any experience tendin' bar?"

"I tended bar for an American officers' club at Bien Hoa Air Base." He doesn't need to know how small that club was. Chances are he's never seen an officers' club.

"This ain't no officers' club. Most of the customers here just want beer, but some guys want a fancy drink every now and then. Tell me about the bottles behind the bar over there." He uses the glass to point to a triple row of bottles behind him.

I study the array. I've seen most of the brands at Bien Hoa. "I know *Galliano*, and all the whiskey brands. Your bar bourbon's cheap stuff and the Scotch too, but you have *Canadian Club* and good vodka in the second row. The gin's okay, and I see a bottle of *Crown Royal* on the back row, and..."

He stops me there. "Say, those GIs must have pretty good taste in whiskey." For the first time he puts down his glass and studies me carefully.

"This neighborhood is filling up with Vietnamese people. My bartender quit because there's too many fights in here these days. The gooks tangle with the biker crowd. I got a good bouncer, but I need somebody who aint gonna be a target when the beer bottles start flyin'. The gooks'd leave you alone 'cause you're one of them, and the bikers'd try to protect you 'cause you're a woman. You okay workin' nights?"

"I'll work whatever shift you need."

He reaches a hammy hand across the bar, and I take it. It's coarse and dried-out from too much time in the soap suds. "You got the job. What's your name?" he asks.

"Vien Nouk Tuyết."

He makes an attempt to pronounce my name, "Too-yet is it?"

"That's close but pronounce it more like 'Do-**yet**' and let your voice rise on the last syllable."

"Do-**YET**, is that it?"

"Don't worry about it. Most Americans have trouble saying it correctly. Just call me Snow. What do you pay?"

"Okay, Snow. I'll start you at $3.50 an hour. If you can keep the place quiet and bring in business, I'll raise it from time to time. You okay with that?"

I do some mental calculations and come up with a number that might allow me to work only one job, if Mel helps out as much as he mentioned previously. "Okay, I'll take that."

"Good. When can you start?"

"I can start next Monday night."

"Okay, weekdays it's five PM to one AM. The shift is five PM to two AM on Fridays and Saturdays. I don't open on Sunday."

I hadn't planned on six days a week, but the extra hours make the wages even more attractive. "That's fine," I say.

"You buy your own uniforms, but you can make that anything you like. The bikers who come in here like to see some skin, but that's up to you. You're easy on the eyes in that kind of thing." He points to my ao dai.

"This is an ao dai. I only have two, but maybe I can find someone who'll make me more."

"Yeah, look into it. It's kinda sexy even though you're all covered up. Come on into the office, and we'll make out the paperwork." He turns to the man who was checking the condiments on the tables and booths. "Hey, Mickey."

"What is it boss?"

"Look after the bar while I get Miss Snow signed up." He turns to me, "I'll introduce you to Rick Mullins when you start work next week."

"Sure, boss. Glad you decided to hire her. She looks like she'll bring some class to the place."

"Who is Rick Mullins?" I ask.

"He's the bouncer. A good man for you to know. He doesn't come in until we open tonight."

"What is a bouncer? What does he do?"

Luigi laughs pleasantly. "I guess you didn't need bouncers in 'Nam' 'cause you had MPs. Rick is the guy who makes sure nobody creates a problem in here, and he deals with it if things get out of hand. He'll protect you from the horny bar flies."

I smile and nod my understanding. "Thank you for telling me about him."

*

Mel is happy I got the job, but he has reservations. "This looks like a rough kind of place. You sure you want to work here?"

"The manager says they've got a good bouncer, and it's across the street from the apartment. The pay is okay, but you might have to help me out a little until I can get a raise."

"How much are they paying?" he asks.

"$3.50 an hour. I'll work 50 hours a week and that's $175 a week. I think that's okay?"

"The pay's a little low for a bartender, particularly in a place like that." He nods toward the bar.

"Should I have asked for more?"

Mel exhales loudly. "He probably wouldn't give it to you. Any hope for a raise?"

"He said there was if I could bring in more business."

"You should be able to do that with your looks, but who's going to keep the wolves at bay?"

"What do you mean?"

"Who's going to keep you from being raped?"

"I told you, they have a good bouncer, and Chinh taught me how to protect myself before he had to leave me alone at Bien Hoa."

Again, he snorts his disbelief. "You haven't seen the kind of scum that comes into a place like this. If you think you can trust that bouncer, make sure he walks you home after they close."

"I'll be fine. The only problem is it's a six night a week job."

"That blows your plan for our meetings. We could only meet during the day, and I have trouble leaving work." He snaps his fingers. "Except for Wednesday, that's my golf afternoon." He smiles. "That's it. I can meet you on Wednesday afternoons. I'll tell the guys I've got a permanent game at Mile Square with a possible employer. It'll only be once a week, but that's what we had in Viet Nam. Okay?"

"We can't do this until the children are in school."

"That's a long time to wait, but I guess it will have to be," he says.

I'm glad for the limitation of once a week. I don't know why I'm dreading our sexual encounters, but some sixth sense keeps painting horrible pictures of our time together. I push it aside again. I know all about Mel in bed, and I've made up my mind that this won't continue any longer than it has to, unless it's as man and wife. "Fine, now that that's settled, can we go back to Camp Pendleton? I can't wait to tell the children we're moving into our own place."

"We've got a lot more things to buy before you can do that, but that's another day. I'll pick you up around ten tomorrow morning, and we can clean the apartment. Bring your kids along. I'd like to meet them." Mel smiles at me, and I plant a big kiss on his cheek.

"I've got all day. Would you like to go to a motel for a while?" he asks.

Again, a small voice in the basement of my mind screams "no", so I use the first excuse that comes to mind. "I don't want to burden Lien with the children too long. I think you'd better take me back now. I'm sorry."

He sighs before answering. "Okay, maybe next time."

"Next time for sure," I say.

*

I tell Anh and Bao the good news.

"We have a sponsor now, I have a job, and we have a place to live."

"Who is our sponsor?" Anh asks.

"His name is Colonel Jenkins. I knew him back home in Viet Nam."

"Is he one of the officers you cooked for?" she asks.

"Yes, I cooked for him each Wednesday."

"It'll be fun to meet him," Anh says.

Bao is the practical one. "Where did you find a job, Mother?"

"I'll be working as a bartender at the 'Kozy Korner Bar'. It's right across the street from our apartment."

"Does our apartment have a swimming pool?" Anh asks.

I'm silent for a moment while her unexpected question registers in my mind. "Where did you hear about swimming pools?"

"Tiep said her apartment has a swimming pool. Will it be like the one you told us about?"

I'd told them about the pool at the Vung Tau hotel Mel took me to once, and they have a vague idea of such a thing. "No, this one is filled with clean water. Maybe we can all learn to swim there."

"I'd like that," Bao says.

"We have to spend tomorrow cleaning the apartment, and I'll need you children to help. Colonel Jenkins, our sponsor, will also help us out."

"You mean it's dirty?" Anh says.

"It's not bad. It won't take us long to clean it up. We can move in Sunday."

"Good, that won't interfere with my baseball game," Bao says.

I know a little about baseball from my clients, but I learn even more after the Marines here at the camp teach a bunch of the boys how to play.

"Well, it's good exercise for you. Maybe you can play again after we move."

"Where will we go to school?" Anh asks.

"I don't know, but I'll find out as soon as we move in. Colonel Jenkins will pick us up tomorrow at ten, right after your English class.

"Did you see any other children there?" Bao asks.

"There were a few around the swimming pool. They were younger, but I'm sure you'll find some friends your age there."

I pull them both into an embrace. "Are you ready for our new adventure in America?" I ask.

"Yes," they respond in unison.

*

That night I lay in bed taking stock of my life. I didn't want to be a mistress again, but here I am. Why am I always hemmed in like this? Mel says he loves me and wants to marry me, but he has to wait for his wife to die. Can I believe him? What choice do I have? If not Mel, who else could I turn to?

What do I feel for him? Is it love? No, not like the love I had with Chinh. No one will ever rise to his level in my affections, but I know it's too much to expect from any man. If it isn't love, what is it? I don't know how to classify my feelings. I've never really loved anyone but Chinh. I vowed not to fall in love with any of my clients, but Mel broke down that barrier.

How? What was it about Mel that caused me to feel a bond between us? He seemed to care about me more than the others. I was a person to him and not just a woman. I really thought he was sincere, until he shattered that bond with his denial. That night he destroyed the modicum of love I'd come to feel for him. In spite of that, the seed of love he left in my soul began to sprout again.

But, this is a new life. He says he loves me now, but I have to be sure. I have to give myself an alternative. As soon as I can stand on my own two feet, I'll say goodbye to Mel if we're not married by then. I don't know how long that will take, but I'll not be his mistress any longer than I must.

I wish Chinh were with me. I miss him so much. I've received no response to my posting on the camp bulletin board. I'll be leaving soon, but if he's alive, he may yet manage to reach America. He'd try to find me if he still loves me, and I'd welcome him here with all my heart. I can hope, but I know it's a false hope.

The children are now the only chance for someone to soften the declining years of my life. To do that, they will need the best education I can get for them, no matter how many jobs it takes.

Chapter 15

Mel picks us up promptly at ten the next day. The back of his station wagon is loaded with cleaning supplies. I introduce him to the children, and they cheer their approval when he suggests we have lunch at McDonald's later on.

As we pull on to the freeway, Bao remarks in Vietnamese, "Wow! I never knew there were so many cars, or they could go so fast." I translate for Mel.

"Get used to it, Bao," Mel says. "You'll be driving before you know it."

That statement catches me entirely by surprise. I never thought about either of the children driving a car before, and a sudden surge of fear rises in my soul at the realization we'll all have to learn to cope with this danger eventually. "You'll have to learn well before I'd let you be exposed to this traffic," I say. Mel notices my concerned expression.

"Don't worry, he'll probably have driver education in school, and I'll also help him out." Again, I translate for Bao.

"When do I do that?" Bao asks with more excitement in his voice than I've ever heard in the past. I give Mel the English version.

"How old are you now?" Mel asks.

"I'll be fifteen next spring." Bao answers.

"You have to be sixteen to get a beginner's permit, so you've got nearly two more years to wait," Mel says.

I translate this for Bao, and his response is the Vietnamese equivalent of "Shoot."

We manage to clean the apartment to Mr. Bui's satisfaction by 6:00 PM. Mel drives us back to McDonald's for dinner at the children's insistence.

*

The next morning, I leave the children in Mrs. Danh's care, and Mel takes me to a store selling used kitchen equipment; pots, pans, dishes, silverware. I can't believe that people would discard such lovely items. Each one seems fit for a king as far as I'm concerned.

We load our purchases into his station wagon. On the way to the apartment Mel says, "I've checked into a motel until we get you settled in. It saves a long drive from Riverside every day. We could go there after we get this stuff into the apartment, if you like."

I stiffen a bit. I knew it was coming, and I'm not looking forward to beginning my sexual obligation. It isn't that he's a bad lover. He's actually very good, but the pleasure derived during the experience does not compensate for the disgust I feel for falling back into the same life I endured in Viet Nam. "Not today, I'm really not in the mood."

"I guess I'll have to understand, but we won't get many chances like this until the kids are in school."

"I'm sorry but thank you for understanding."

"I guess I need to get you back for your last nights in that Quonset Hut. Sunday, we move you into your new home. I'll pick you up at nine Sunday morning, if that's okay?"

"That's fine. We'll be ready."

"Oh, by the way, I've talked to a lawyer about a divorce. You seemed to be worried about what will happen to my wife after that. You don't have to worry. He says she can qualify for California's medical welfare program. I'll have to pay some amount of support, but after I retire from the Air Force, I'll be able to afford it easily."

This is great news. For the first time the future looks bright. There's an end in sight, and a new beginning as Mrs. Mel Jenkins. I'm beginning to think he really may be sincere in his protestations of love.

"I thought you didn't want a divorce."

"I've thought a lot about us over the last few days. I want us to be man and wife as soon as we can, and Meg may go on like she is for years. I don't care what it costs. I want to marry you as soon as the divorce is final.'

"Oh Mel, how long will that take?"

"I don't know right now, but I'll let you know what the lawyer says."

*

That evening I watch Bao and the boys play baseball. I'm just beginning to appreciate the game when one of the Marines coaching the boys comes over to me.

"Is Bao your son, ma'am?" he asks.

"Yes, he is." The marine is dressed in fatigues, but I finally find a Sergeant's emblem on the uniform.

"I'm Gunnery Sergeant Barnes, Rick Barnes, I'm in charge of the youth athletic program here at Camp Pendleton." He offers his hand, and I take it.

"My name is Vien Nouk Tuyết, but Americans call me Snow."

"I know a little Vietnamese. I had two tours there, and one was as an advisor. I came over to tell you that I think your son has some talent for baseball."

"He loves the game. It's all he talks about."

"He has a good eye for the ball, and a natural swing at the plate. He should continue playing after you leave the camp. When will you be leaving?"

"We're moving into an apartment tomorrow."

"Are you living nearby?"

"Yes, in Westminster, on Bolsa Avenue."

He nods knowingly. "Ah, Little Saigon. I know the neighborhood. A lot of the Vietnamese families go there. Your son will probably go to Westminster High School when he's ready. They have a good baseball program there—keep him playing. There's a good chance he can earn a baseball scholarship to some university."

"Thank you, Sergeant."

"He's got talent." He hands me a card. "Well, if you ever need any baseball help, just call me. I've got some connections, and I may be able to open some doors for him." He salutes and walks away.

*

Sunday comes, and Mel takes us by a supermarket to pick up groceries on the way to the apartment. Like everything else in America, it's huge. The children are in awe of the vast selection of fresh and canned foods. I tend toward the fresh foods, having been used to open-air markets in Viet Nam, but

Mel points out several frozen items he thinks might interest me. The variety of frozen Chinese dishes is amazing, and I take several to try.

We enter the apartment and place the perishable items in the small refrigerator before arranging the other things on the kitchen cabinet shelves. The children explore their new home and move their meagre possessions into the Spartan furniture and small closet. I just stand in the kitchen area surveying our new home and wondering what the future holds for us. Mel interrupts my dreaming.

"A penny for your thoughts," he says as he takes me in his arms from behind.

"I'm sorry. I was thinking about the future." I turn and smile. "Thank you for all you've done for us." I kiss him, but he breaks it off too quickly.

"I don't want to get anything started. The kids are too close. I think I'll leave you alone to settle in now. If you need anything, just call me." He hands me a card from his motel which also includes his room number penciled in on the back.

"I don't know how to use a phone."

"I just assumed you knew about telephones. Come over here, and I'll show you."

He leads me to the instrument and points out the components.

"This is the handset, and this is the base. To use it, you just pick up the handset and listen for a dial tone. Go ahead and pick it up."

I do as he asks and listen to a buzzing sound. "I hear it buzzing. What's next?"

"Okay, this is an old motel, so you have to get an outside line." He consults a chart on the base. "Just hit the button marked '9'."

The dial tone changes after I push the button. "Now what?"

"You just punch in the number you want to call. Try my office number." He hands me one of his cards. "It's long distance, so you have to dial a '1' first, then the area code, then the number."

I punch in the eleven numbers and hear a set of tones like music playing. I laugh.

"What's funny?" he asks.

"These sounds, it's playing a tune."

"It's dialing the number. Wait a bit and you'll hear a new tone, the ring tone."

The sound does change to a raucous buzz in short spurts. A woman answers.

"Chief of Maintenance Office, this is Dottie."

Mel takes the phone gently. "Hit Dot, this is Colonel Jenkins. Any messages for me?"

He nods his head and mutters some answers before putting down the handset.

"That's all there is to it. I'm sure Mr. Bui charges something for each call, so only use it when you have to. Okay?"

"I don't have anyone to call but you."

"You'll have more as you get settled. Your boss at the bar will want your home number, and you may have to talk to other people in immigration. You'll get used to it."

"I start work tomorrow. I can pay for my calls, if it's not too expensive. You need the money for your wife."

"Goodbye for now, Snow. He leans closer to me and whispers, "I can't wait for school to start?"

Once Mel is gone, the children descend upon me.

"I'm hungry. Let's have lunch," Bao says.

*

I clean up after lunch and sit in the kitchen taking stock of my new life. I have a job, but I'm not sure it will be enough. I might have to find something else sooner or later, and I fear it may be sooner. I have to find out how to get Bao and Anh enrolled in school, but they'll need a lot of tutoring in English before school starts. I've also promised Luigi I'd bring in Vietnamese customers, and I haven't yet figured out how to do that. If my second job's too far to walk to, I'll have to purchase some form of transportation, and I have no idea how to go about that or how to comply with the rules and regulations I'm sure apply to such activity in America. I steel myself by realizing I'd conquered worse in Viet Nam on my own, and I have help here. A knock on the door brings me back to the present.

I open the door to an older Vietnamese woman carrying a stack of bamboo trays. She smiles warmly and speaks in Vietnamese. "Chào bạ. I'm Mrs. Nguyen from next door. May I come in? I want to welcome you to Little Saigon."

She's a most welcome sight given my current state of mind. Mai's apartment is too far away for us to meet often. If she turns out to be sincere about being a neighbor, it will be good to have someone close by to call a friend. "Chào bạ. Of course, please come in," I respond in Vietnamese, not knowing if she speaks any English.

She walks to the kitchen and sets the containers on the counter. She produces a bottle of wine from a bag she carries over her shoulder and says, "I brought you something for dinner. It doesn't need to be refrigerated. Just heat it up later." She holds up the wine bottle. "Do you have any glasses?"

"I don't have any wine glasses, but I have some small regular glasses we can use."

"They will do," she says as she produces a corkscrew from a pocket in her dress and begins to open the wine.

She pours two glasses and nods toward the small table. After we sit down she offers a toast. "Một cuộc song mói ở Mỹ."

"To a new life in America," I respond.

We each drink then she says, "You speak English?"

I laugh and respond, "Yes, I do. I was afraid you didn't."

"I no speak very well, but speak English now. You help me?"

We laugh together, and I speak in English. "Yes, I'll help you all I can. My name is Tuyết."

She smiles warmly and responds, "My name Tam. My husband name Sang. We here two month. He Dai Ta in VNAF." She blushes a bit and corrects herself. "Was Dai Ta. Now he work factory, make parts for rockets. Zoom!" She moves her free hand up toward the ceiling in a quick motion. "What your husband do?"

"My husband was killed in Viet Nam."

Her face drops. "Oh, I sorry."

"You didn't know. I'm not offended. Do you have any children?"

"What mean 'offended'?" she asks.

I translate to Vietnamese for her, "xúc phạm." She nods her understanding.

"Ah yes, mean you no mad. I have two girl, Yen and Truc. Yen 15 and Truc 12."

I understand a girl being named Yen for swallow, but Truc, a wish, surprises me. "Why Truc?"

Tam laughs. "It because Sang wish for girl when she born. He say he want both same. He no want two different kind problem."

We both laugh at the remark, and Tam speaks again. "I see your children leave. What their names?"

"My son is Bao and my daughter is Anh. Bao is 14 and Anh is 11."

"They go same school like Truc in fall. You go school soon, sign children up."

"I don't know how to go about doing that."

"I help you. I home all day. You call you need help."

"I'll be working at the Kozy Korner Bar across Bolsa during the evenings, but I'll have my days free, at least for a while. I may have to work two jobs, but I'm putting that off as long as I can."

"I hope you no have work two jobs. Children need you."

"I'm teaching them English during the day. They need a lot of help with that."

Her face brightens. "School have English class for Vietnamese children. My children there now."

"How much does it cost?"

"It free. School free in America.

"Free? That is a relief. By the way, do you know anyone who makes ao dais?"

"Shop sell them that way, but long walk." She points to the East.

"That's too bad. I don't have a car."

"We have car. Car cost much money. Sang drive. I no drive. He take car work every day."

"I had a moped in Viet Nam. Maybe I could find one here."

"I have moped in Viet Nam, too." She thinks for a moment then suddenly adds, "Must have helmet in California."

I sigh, it seems the costs kept adding up, and I haven't even received my first paycheck yet.

"Maybe Mel can take me to the ao dai shop one day."

"Who Mel? He man I see you with today?"

"Yes, he's my sponsor."

"You know him in Viet Nam?"

"Yes, he was an advisor to my husband's unit."

She cocks her head to one side. "What is 'advisor'?"

"Co van," I translate for her.

"Ah, I see. He good looking man. He marry you?"

"Someday, but not real soon. He has some things he has to do before we can marry."

She nods her understanding and smiles. "He got wife now, eh?"

I'm not sure if I should confirm her suspicions, but I hate to keep up a pretense just to save face. It's obvious she knows about some Vietnamese women and the Americans."

"Yes, but she's very ill. We may have to wait until she dies."

"Very sad thing. He help you here? Maybe buy you moped?"

"He probably would, but I hate to keep asking him for money." I decide to change the subject. "You called this 'little Saigon', I guess a lot of Viet Nam people live here."

"All people here Viet Nam. Mr. Bui very good to us."

"He seems like a good man," I say.

"He keep rent low, but I think he raise it when good times come."

"At least I didn't have to bribe him." We both laugh at the difference between America and Viet Nam.

"We be friends, please?" she asks.

"I'd like that very much."

She glances at her watch. "I go now. Girls come home soon."

She rises to leave, and I stand and embrace her. "It is so good to know I have a friend nearby."

She pats my shoulder and smiles. "All Viet Nam people help each other. You meet other people here soon."

She leaves, and our prospects in this strange land seem to take on a brighter glow.

Chapter 16

The first night at the Kozy Korner, Mickey introduces me to the bouncer.

"Snow, this is Rick Mullins. He's a guy you really need to keep close for a while."

Rick extends a meaty hand, and I take it. His grip is soft for a man who looks like he could take on a bar full of tough guys. He must be two meters tall with a build to match. His bald head sits directly on his shoulders. I can only find the hint of a neck.

"Pleased to meet ya, Miss Snow," Rick says.

"Nice to meet you too, Rick. I hope I won't need your assistance too often."

"We got two kinds that come in here, the bikers and the gooks." He catches himself immediately. "Oh, sorry, I mean Vietnamese. The bikers all think they're tough guys. You'll know who they are just by the looks of 'em. They make the most trouble. The go...er Vietnamese guys just come in to drink. They don't cause any trouble unless the bikers start something. The funny thing is the Vietnamese usually finish it. Don't take no shit from either bunch. You just call out, and I'll handle 'em."

"Rick was a Green Beret in Viet Nam," Mickey adds.

"That was a long time ago. I was down in the Delta in III Corps. Where are you from?" Rick asks.

"Bien Hoa, my husband was a helicopter pilot."

"You said 'was'. Ain't he yer husband anymore?" Rick asks.

"His helicopter was shot down in the last days of the war."

"Sorry to hear that," Rick says. "See you later." He ambles off to a corner where he can keep an eye on the whole room. It's early, and only a few people sit in the booths along the North wall.

Luigi acquaints me with the rest of the bar features, but they're almost identical to the things at the old advisor's club. There's no one at the bar yet, so I busy myself inspecting the inventory of glasses and cleaning the ones that don't meet my expectations.

Toward nine I get my first bar customers. Two biker types sit down at the far end, well away from Rick. Rick was right about me knowing them by sight. I place a coaster in front of each one.

"What will it be, gentlemen?" I ask.

The one wearing only a leather vest and black jeans turns to the one with the blond mullet. "Get that, Bull, we're 'gentlemen'."

"Well, if a good lookin' gook says so, it must be true. Bring us two **Miller** drafts," blond mullet says.

"And your phone number," leather vest adds.

I go to the taps and pull two large mugs. I take them back to the bikers and set them down on the coasters.

"Hey, our order ain't complete. We ain't got yer phone number," leather vest says.

"And you're not going to. Let's get a few things straight, gentlemen. I'm Vietnamese, not a 'gook', and I don't date the customers. If you have any questions about that, take it up with Rick."

Leather vest reaches across the bar and grabs my hand. "I think you're the one who needs to get something straight. We're **Death's Disciples**, and we don't take 'no' for an answer. People get hurt when they don't do what we want."

This is a new experience for me. In Viet Nam the officers hit on me, but it was all verbal. I decide I need to figure out how to handle this kind of situation without Rick's help, if I can. I use my free hand had to pick up a soaking wet bar rag I'd just used to clean up a mess of dubious origin only a moment ago.

"Well, in that case, lean closer and pucker up for a big kiss. Close your eyes."

He leans across the bar, closes his eyes and puckers up just before I push the filthy rag in his face. Spitting out crud and slobbering with rage, he starts to climb over, but Rick is behind him before he can accomplish the feat.

"That's enough, Milt," Rick says as he slams the biker back on his bar stool.

I find a clean bar towel and hand it to leather vest. "Sorry, Milt, but please don't try that again."

With Rick's heavy hand on his shoulder, leather vest assumes a much more subdued attitude. "What's the matter, you queer or something?" he asks.

"I've got a boyfriend who pays my rent, and I'm not interested in anyone else. Nothing personal."

"He must be one helluva guy to rate you," blond mullet says.

"He's a Lieutenant Colonel in the Air Force, and he doesn't like people flirting with me."

"Oh, a baby killer, eh?" leather vest says.

"What did you do in Viet Nam?" I ask him.

Leather vest takes on a hurt expression that is so fake a blind man could spot it from a mile away. "I was 4-F. I got hemorrhoids."

Rick breaks in. "I don't want any trouble with you guys. Miss Snow here's a nice lady, and she don't date the customers. Now that you know that, I expect you ass holes to treat her like a lady. Got that?"

Both men mumble grudging responses, but leather vest adds, "See you later, tough guy." in a low voice.

"I heard that Milt. Don't think I'm afraid of you **Death's Disciples**. I got friends too, all of them ex-green berets. Any time you wanna rumble, just say so."

Blond mullet reaches his open hand across the bar. "I ain't gonna cross Rick. They call me Bull."

"Just call me Snow." I take his hand.

"Glad to know you, Snow. We'll let the rest of the gang know you're okay. Right, Milt?"

Leather vest finishes cleaning the mess from his face and chest and nods, "Yeah, Snow, you're okay, as long as Rick says so."

Rick pats both men on the back. "Okay, guys. Your beer're on the house tonight."

Rick nods toward the other end of the bar, and I follow him. When we're away from Bull and Milt he says, "I'll walk you home for a while until I'm sure those jerks mean what they say. Don't leave without me."

I nod my understanding, and I'm grateful for his help.

*

The word must have spread to the other members of the motorcycle club. Over the next two weeks, several more come in to have a look for themselves. I get teased a lot, but I give them as good as I get. I thank whatever gods there are for my experience tending bar in Viet Nam.

Rick continues to walk me home, but I have no more trouble with **Death's Disciples**.

*

The children start school, and my first Wednesday with Mel comes too soon. I've done everything I can to prepare for this, but the physical preparations are easy. Reconciling myself to the job of mistress again is the problem. I keep telling myself that it's just like Viet Nam, but it isn't.

Mel arrives promptly at one. His face lights up as he sees me wearing only an old pajama top I picked up from the donated clothing at Camp Pendleton. It's a man's top, but it's a thin fabric with a low neckline. It's the sexiest thing I can find in my limited wardrobe.

"Wow, I wasn't quite expecting this." He closes the door behind him and takes me in his arms.

He's wearing his uniform, and the metal trim items press into my skin. The flimsy fabric of the pajama top isn't much protection. "Ow, that hurts."

I pull away, and he sees the problem when the insignia on his lapel sticks to the top.

"Sorry, I'm just so happy to be here I didn't think."

I lead him to the bedroom where he's out of his clothes in short order. He's obviously ready for sex. He embraces me again and we kiss, but not as passionately as he's expecting. He draws away a bit. "What's wrong?"

"I'm sorry. It's just been a long time. Be patient with me for a while, please," I say.

He lifts off my top and stares at me for a moment. "You're as lovely as ever." Once more we embrace, and he gently lowers me to the bed.

We make love, and I perform well. He doesn't seem to sense it's more act than passion, and I'm glad of that. Luckily, he can't stay too long as the children will be home from school by four, and I need to fix them dinner.

As he dresses he says, "That was just like old times. I'll let you know if I can't make it next week. Otherwise, I'll be here about the same time, okay?"

"Sure, Mel. I'll let you know if there's any problem on my end also."

He kisses me briefly before he leaves, and I flop down on the sofa. It's begun again, but there's some hope of a marriage now, some hope for a stable life with someone to take over the job of keeping our bellies full and providing a roof over our heads. I'm so tired of carrying the full burden of a household. I just hope that comes to pass soon.

*

One of the first things I notice about the Kozy Korner is that there are no Vietnamese ordering food. I ask one group of men at the bar why that is. I ask in Vietnamese so Luigi won't understand, if he's listening.

"It's all greasy hamburgers or deep fried whatever. I eat at home. I only come here to get out of the house for a while," one man says.

"Don't you think your wife would like to eat out every now and then?" I ask.

"Sure, but nobody's opened a Vietnamese restaurant around here yet," another remarks.

I understand the problem now. The items on the menu are strange to them, and few have had the courage to try the American selections. The bar trade is vigorous, however. It's mostly Vietnamese men, and a few Vietnamese women preying on the men, hoping to find a husband. Luigi seems to be happy with the situation, but it often generates fights between the bikers and the Vietnamese men. The result of those brawls is a lot of broken glass and shattered furniture. I'm sure he could do better without them. After all, replacing the losses has to cut into his profit margin. I approach him one day before the bar gets busy.

"Luigi, I've got a suggestion."

"What is it, Snow?"

"I think I've got an idea to end the brawls and bring in some more money."

"Who do I keep out, the gooks or the bikers? They both run up good-sized bar bills, and Rick can break up most of the set-tos before they do too much damage. I call the cops if I see he's outmatched."

"Neither one. The answer is we serve some Vietnamese meals. The Vietnamese men will bring in their families, and that will keep them calm. I'll introduce Vietnamese food to the bikers, and they'll learn to appreciate our culture more."

Luigi laughs at the idea. "How you gonna get those biker types to try gook food?"

"I know of three or four Vietnamese dishes the Americans liked in Viet Nam. We'll start with those and work into some more exotic meals later on. What do you think?"

"You could try it if you could get Johnnie to cook gook-style. Would it be expensive?"

I stare at him with a stern expression. "I've told you once before, I don't like being called a 'gook'. I won't take it from the bikers, and I'd rather not hear it from you, please."

He looks at me with a scowl, and I think I'm a few seconds from being fired, but he snorts and starts to smile.

"Okay, I'm sorry. It's a hard habit to break, but I'll do it to keep you from quitting."

"Thanks. No, it won't be expensive. I'll start out with one dish and offer free samples to the bar crowd. If they like it, we can add it to the menu, and I'll start on a new one, doing the same thing."

Luigi lapses into a pensive mode for a moment. "Okay, you got $200 to try it with. We'll see how it goes."

"Thanks, boss. I'll get with Johnnie on it."

*

Johnnie, our cook, is a slender black man with a wild hairdo he keeps tucked up inside a stocking cap while he cooks.

I've only talked to him once or twice, but I found he's a good person and serious about the quality of his food. It would be a while before the kitchen got going, so I approach him with my idea.

"Johnnie, would you help me with a cooking project?"

"Why sure, Miss Snow. What you got on your mind?"

"I've got a recipe for a Vietnamese dish I know Americans like, and I'd like to try to introduce it to our customers. The ingredients aren't expensive or exotic, and it isn't complicated to make. Luigi's given me a small budget for the trial period."

"Get me the recipe, and I'll try it."

"Thanks, I'll bring it in tomorrow."

The next day I borrow some paper from the children and write down the recipe I'd used so often for my clients. I wasn't sure about the exact amounts for the ingredients, but I know I can convey the portions to Johnnie using things like; a handful, what will fit in your palm, a pinch and other imprecise measurements. That night I give him the recipe.

"Mmmm, this sure looks good. What do you call it?"

"It's called Bò Sốt Cam, but just call it beef in orange sauce."

"I may need your help with the amounts to use. How much does this make, and how do you want to serve it?"

"You may have to double or triple the amounts to get enough to serve the bar crowd one piece of beef each. This is enough for two people for a meal. I usually serve it over steamed rice as a dinner, but I think doing it as an hors d'oeuvre would be the best way."

"Okay, I'll pick up what I ain't got here in the kitchen and make you some up for Thursday night. That's when we get the biggest biker crowd. Okay with you?"

"Sure, Thursday. I'll come in early to help you out.'

Bò Sốt Cam
(Beef with orange sauce)

1 lb beef sirloin or tenderloin

2 oranges
1 Tbsp orange juice
1 Tsp rice vinegar
1 Tbsp soy sauce
1 Tsp minced ginger
1 Tbsp sugar
2 Tbsp corn starch
2 Tsp tapioca starch
3 cloves of garlic
Salt, pepper and sugar to taste

Grate the orange peel

Mix tapioca starch with a little water and add soy sauce, minced ginger, orange juice, orange peel and sugar. Mix well.

Cut the beef into bite-sized strips and salt and pepper to taste.

Dredge beef slices through corn starch.

Heat some oil in a pan and fry the meat for 30-60 seconds.

Remove the beef and place it on a paper towel to absorb excess oil.

Peel and mince the garlic.

Slice one orange into small pieces.

Add garlic to some oil and sauté until fragrant.

Add sauce prepared above and cook until boiling.

Fry meat in the sauce for 3-4 minutes.

Serve with steamed rice.

Thursday, I help in the kitchen to make sure it all turns out the way I remember. Johnnie is my final judge. He takes a piece and chews it thoughtfully a while.

"Mmm, this is delicious. The bikers'll go wild for this stuff."

"Put it on a tray, and I'll give them a taste of Viet Nam."

I put a toothpick in each piece of meat and carry the tray out to the bar. The bikers are there in force which means there are few Vietnamese present. I approach the one I now know as Aaron, called Bull, and hold out the tray.

"I thought you guys would like to have a taste of my country's food, Bull. Try this."

"You sure it ain't roast dog?" one asks.

"Just good beef. Give it a try."

Aaron takes a piece and savors it for a moment.

"Hey, this stuff's good. Try it, Chuck.'

Two more bikers pronounce the meat edible, and the tray is soon empty.

"Got any more?" Aaron asks.

"You can get it as a dinner served with steamed rice for only $4.95. Any orders?"

*

I follow that dish up with two more suitable for American palates then introduce some of the more exotic recipes. The food is also drawing more Vietnamese customers once the word gets around. We put an ad in the local paper for a Vietnamese cook, and I interview several before finding Nhung, an older woman with a vast repertoire of genuine recipes stashed securely in her head.

Once the bikers taste Vietnamese food and find the cycle repair shop owned by some Vietnamese mechanics charges less than the Harley-Davidson dealer, the brawls end. The Kozy Korner is soon doing as much food business as bar business, and Luigi is a happy man.

*

The children are speaking reasonable English now, and Bao makes the Little League roster at second base for a team sponsored by a local farm implement dealer. Anh enjoys her classes and begins playing soccer on the school team.

Luigi raises my salary to $4.50 an hour after I get my 'green card', and part of that money, with some help from Mel, goes to purchase a used moped, a helmet, insurance and license plates. I mostly use the bike for shopping. Since I work evenings, it's all I need. Traffic on the city streets is light during the day. Mopeds aren't allowed on the freeways, but I don't need to use them.

*

Mel and I meet each Wednesday at my apartment. One week he suggests we have lunch before we have sex. We go to a Mexican restaurant, and I find I like the food. It's spicy hot like many Vietnamese dishes.

When we go back to my apartment he says, "You've got new drapes."

I almost fall over in surprise at a man noticing new drapes. "I made them. Do you like them?"

"Yeah." He moves to the window and checks them out. "Good workmanship, too. Do you need me to pay for the material? It looks expensive."

"No, Mr. Bui reimbursed me for the material, and I used Tam's sewing machine, next door."

"Very good," he muses as he leads me to the bedroom.

*

He hasn't mentioned anything about his wife in weeks. I get the distinct impression he's avoiding the subject, so I bring it up one Wednesday.

"How is the divorce going?" I ask.

"I have to wait six months to establish residence in California, so I can't start divorce proceedings until April of next year."

"You haven't mentioned that before. Why didn't you tell me we had to wait so long?"

"Hey, I didn't know myself 'til a few days ago. The damned lawyer just assumed I was a California resident, but my home of record for the Air Force is Missouri. I kept it that way to keep from having to pay California taxes, but now I'll owe the State money on top of the lawyer fees."

I lay back in bed mad at Mel and discouraged at the wait. His explanation is a bit over my head, however. "I don't understand all of this. Aren't you a resident of California. You live here."

"Military people are considered to be residents of the state they entered service from. I enlisted in Saint Louis, and that's my home of record. As far as everyone's concerned, it's just like I'm still living there."

I have no way of knowing if he's telling the truth. I make a mental note to check with some of the patrons at the Kozy Korner. He takes me in his arms.

"The time'll go by so fast you won't know it." He kisses me softly.

"I don't mind the wait, but I hate to keep asking you for money."

I'm getting by, but only that. Mel gives me what he can, but most of his money goes to the care of his wife.

"You could always move in with me," he says.

"We've been all through that a dozen times, Mel. You know I can't."

Mel kisses me again. "I know, but I have to ask in case you've changed your mind."

"I may ask for a raise soon. The children need a lot of things for school."

"Don't worry about money. I'll give you whatever you need. Besides, I'll retire in January, then I'll get a job paying more than I make in the Air Force. I'll also have a nice retirement check each month. After that we'll have plenty of money, and you won't have to work."

I smile at the thought of not worrying about money for the first time in years. "That would be very nice."

We fall into another passionate embrace.

*

The next week Mel calls on Tuesday afternoon.

"Hi beautiful, I've got some bad news."

"Oh Mel, is it serious?" I'm afraid his news is something very sinister.

"No, nothing like that. It's just I won't be able to take you to that Vietnamese opera you wanted to go to this Sunday. I have to attend a big meeting in Oklahoma City that starts on Monday morning. I'll have to fly out Sunday afternoon."

"You shouldn't scare me like that." Even though I'm relieved to hear it's something so trivial, I'm still a bit angry that he gave me a wrong impression of the problem.

"I'm sorry. It's just that I knew how much you wanted to go."

He sounds sincerely apologetic, and I forgive him immediately. "What will I do with the tickets you purchased?"

"Maybe your neighbors would like to have them. Don't worry about the price. They were only $10 each. I won't miss the money. They don't have to pay you for them if they don't want to."

"We only have two, and I was so looking forward to going myself. I'll ask around. Maybe there's someone who needs just one ticket, and I could go with them."

"That might work. You see a lot of Vietnamese at the Kozy Korner."

I switch to a more important subject. "How long will you be gone?"

"The meeting's scheduled to last for two weeks. It's all about some major modifications to our airplanes, and it may last longer. SAC Headquarters has asked me to sit in on the source selection team for the contract, and I've never done anything like that before. Usually, they just use people from Materiel Command Headquarters and the depot, but SAC insisted they have some field input, and I'm that guy."

"I'm proud of you, getting such an important assignment." I'm not sure what he's talking about, but it sounds very impressive.

"Thanks, it is somewhat of an honor. I'm just sorry I have to be away from you that long."

"I'll miss you, but you can call me after you get settled in."

"It'll be right before you go to work. There's a two-hour time difference, so five my time will only be three for you."

"Just call me whenever you can. You know my schedule."

"I'll do that. Just know I love you no matter what."

"I do, but I'll love you more if you remember to call."

I hear a voice in the background, and Mel holds his hand over the phone for a moment before speaking again.

"That was Sergeant Millhouse. I'm needed in the CO's office. Sorry I gotta go."

"I understand. "I love you, darling. Have a good trip. Goodbye."

"Goodbye, beautiful."

I hang up and linger a while to think about our situation. I'm tolerating Mel now because he's helped us so much, and I know he's serious about the divorce, but I don't really love him like I did Chinh. I can't shake the feeling that he's not really serious about us. I look at my watch and see it's time to get ready for work and stop worrying about it.

*

That night I'm very surprised to see a man in a sharp navy blazer and khaki slacks walk into the Kozy Korner. He is obviously in the wrong place. This is the night the biker crowd comes in after their club meeting at the Harley-Davidson dealer down the street, and he stands out like a cherry in a martini.

He walks to the bar and calls, "Excuse me Miss, but is there a phone in here I could use?"

I'm not usually attracted to blonds, but his eyes are a striking sky blue, and his face raises my heartbeat ever so slightly. He's clean shaven and about my height. The blazer hides his build a bit, but he appears to be on the slight side. I wouldn't guess him at any more than 80 kilograms.

"Yes, there's a pay phone on the wall over there." I point to the unit.

"Thanks," he says and walks to the phone.

I watch him go. He has a military bearing and a purposeful stride. He reaches the phone and searches his pants pockets before slumping in disgust and walking back to the bar.

"Can you give me change for a dollar?"

"Sure," I open the cash register and exchange four quarters for his dollar.

He returns to the phone and makes a short call. As he starts for the door I call to him.

"Don't go, sir. The beer's two for one tonight," I call.

I don't know why I want him to stay. Some impish impulse deep in my soul fights its way past my good sense, and I yield to it without questioning my motive. He smiles as he turns and takes a seat at the bar.

"I'll take a *Miller Lite* please."

"Bottle or a draft?" I ask.

"Draft sounds good."

"The two for one deal is only on the bottles," I say.

"That's okay. I prefer the draft," he says.

I walk to the taps and draw a large mug of the beer. He hadn't specified a size, so I make it a point to find the largest container in the house. I set the huge, frosted mug in front of him, then I notice the logo patch on the breast pocket of his sport coat.

"Are you with Mercedes?" I ask.

"Yes, I'm the new area representative for Mercedes."

"They're great cars," I say.

"Yeah, except for the one I'm driving now. I started smelling diesel on the 405 and got off at Bolsa. This is the only place open at this hour to call for help. Are you interested in cars?" He takes a big pull from his mug.

"My husband always wanted a Mercedes," I answer. "It was his one big dream."

"Does he still want a Mercedes?"

"Oh no," I smile. "He was killed when the communists took over Viet Nam." I'd grown accustomed to the indirect question attempting to reveal my marital status, and have no trouble talking about Chinh's death now.

"I'm sorry," he offers.

I change the subject, "I don't think you'll find many Mercedes customers in here tonight."

He laughs and takes another sip of beer. "You never know. I've learned never to judge a prospective buyer by his outfit or where he chooses to drink."

He points to my ao dai. "I love your outfit," he says.

"Thank you, it's a Vietnamese ao dai. A lady in Little Saigon made it for me." I turn to model it for him. "We get a lot of Vietnamese customers in here on other nights. Want anything to eat? The kitchen's pretty good."

"No, thanks, I'm okay for now." I figure he's run out of small talk and leave to serve other customers while he pretends to be interested in the *Lakers* game playing on the big TV behind the bar. Still, I manage to check him from a distance to be sure he doesn't just walk out after his first beer. As he drains the mug, I make sure to be there before he can make up his mind.

"Need another beer?" I ask.

He pushes the mug toward me. "Sure, the mechanic said it'd take him a while to get here."

I pick up the mug and dump it into a sink full of dirty companions. I look around the bar and see that most of the usual customers are on their last one. It won't hurt to spend a little time with him. I draw a fresh mug, set it in front of him and lean against the bar. "Is your car problem serious?" I ask.

"He doesn't seem to think so. He said he could get me back on the road in no time." He extends his hand across the bar. "I'm Jerry."

I wipe my hand with a clean bar towel and take his. It's warm and surprisingly soft for a man. "I'm Tuyết."

He tries to imitate my pronunciation. "Doo-yet is it?"

"Make the 'D' softer and let your voice rise as you say the last syllable. Tuyết."

"Tuyết," he finally manages, after a few tries and some coaching.

"It means 'Snow'."

He looks at me with a wry grin. "You're kidding?"

"Actually, it's Vien Nouk Tuyết, but Snow's easier for you Americans."

"Ah, Vietnamese."

"Yes, I came here in '75."

"I always wanted to meet a Vietnamese. The war has been something I wanted to get their slant on.

"That's the best pick-up line I've heard since I got to America."

He actually blushes and smiles wryly. "That wasn't my intention, but I would like to get to know you better—strictly for research purposes, of course."

"And what would Mrs. Warren have to say about that?"

"There isn't any Mrs. Warren," Jerry's answer contains no hint of surprise at the question. Men lie about such things as a matter of habit when they're looking for sex, and they often think a woman tending bar is an easy mark. Any reference to their wives usually draws some sort of reaction, but he's not at all uncomfortable. His expression does reflect disappointment, however. Evidently, he's taken my remark as a 'brush-off'.

"I'm sorry. You'll have to excuse me. I don't see many genuinely single men in here."

He changes the subject. "Your English is very good."

"Thank you. I've worked at it for a long time."

"Your English is pretty good for only getting here last year?"

"I had to get good at English a long time before I came to America."

"How's that?"

"I worked with the Americans in Viet Nam." I figure he doesn't need to know any of the details about my *work*.

"Do you have children?"

"Two, a boy and a girl. I managed to get them out with me."

"It must have been tough," is the best he can muster.

"You do what you have to do," I answer staring at a dark spot on the bar. I rub at it with my towel in a fruitless effort to remove the stain and drive away the memories of that escape.

"Hey Snow, how about another pitcher?" A bass voice rings out from the one booth still occupied.

"Sure, Rusty." I turn to Jerry. "I'll be right back."

My mind works overtime while I fill the pitcher and carry it to the table. What am I doing? I don't need another man in my life, but there's something about this guy that draws me to him. I shake him out of my mind. I'll never see him again after tonight, but he'll help me pass the time until last call. I collect the money and return to Jerry.

"Is there any man in your life now?" he asks.

"Yes, there is. We plan to be married as soon as he can divorce his wife."

He sighs. "I think I've seen that plot in an old movie."

"What do you mean?"

"Man and woman fall in love before woman knows man's married. When he finally owns up to it, she threatens to leave him, but he says he'll divorce his wife. She stays with him, but he keeps giving her excuses about the divorce. Turns out, he has no intention of divorcing his wife. She finally leaves him, but her heart's so broken-up over it she commits suicide."

"That's a very sad story. I knew Mel was married before I came to America, and I'm sure he's not stringing me along about his divorce. I'm not worried about becoming that lady."

"I hope not. I'm sure he's a nice guy."

"I am a little angry with him right now. We were planning on attending an opera this Sunday, and he called me today to say he has to leave on a business trip Sunday afternoon. I've wanted to see that opera ever since it was announced, and now I'll just have to give the tickets to a neighbor, or something."

"What opera is it? I love opera. I could buy the tickets from you."

I laugh a bit at his eagerness.

"What's funny?"

"This is a Vietnamese opera, Cái Lương."

"Oh," his face falls, but it brightens up again quickly. "Well, I go to Italian operas and don't understand a word. I don't see why this would be any different. How much are the tickets?"

"It's just an amateur production at the local high school. They're $10 each."

He reaches for his billfold and pulls out a twenty. "Here, I'll take them."

"That's very generous of you, but it's not necessary."

"Well, I have to admit the reason I want the tickets is that I'd love to have you come along and translate for me."

I give him an off-center look. "Didn't I tell you I was engaged?"

"You did, but this isn't like it's a real 'date'. I'm going to an opera and I'm hiring a translator, that's all."

I laugh at his definition of a "non-date". He seems to have a great sense of humor. I really do want to see the opera, so why not?

"Okay, I'll go with you, but strictly as a translator. Do you understand that?"

"Sure, no obligations attached, and I promise to behave like a gentleman." He raises his right hand in the air to emphasize his point. "When should I pick you up on Sunday?"

"The opera starts at seven Sunday evening. You can pick me up here at six. It'll take about 15 minutes to get to the high school, but it's open seating, so I want to be there early to get a good seat."

"Isn't this place closed on Sunday?" he says.

"Yes, but I have a key."

"How about dinner before the show?"

"No thanks. I've got to feed the kids, and I'll just eat with them."

"Okay, I'll see you at six on Sunday. How about another beer."

At that point, a man enters the bar in a mechanic's uniform. "Mr. Warren?" he calls.

"Over here," Jerry calls. He turns to me. "I guess I don't need that beer. How much do I owe you?"

We settle his tab, and he leaves with the mechanic. I watch him go and wonder if I've made a big mistake.

*

That Sunday Jerry walks into the Kozy Korner at six sharp and finds me at a table near the door. He's wearing a suit and tie, but I'm dressed in one of my every-day ao dais.

"Am I overdressed?" he asks.

"No, there'll probably be other men there in suits. I just hope I'm not underdressed, being escorted by such a sharp-looking man."

"You're gorgeous no matter what you wear. Are you ready?"

"Yes, let's go."

We get into a diesel sedan, and I give him directions to the high school.

"I've always wanted to see one of these operas," I say as we drive.

"You didn't see them in Viet Nam?"

"No, they didn't perform at Bien Hoa City, only in Saigon, and we couldn't afford to go."

"Well, then this is a first for both of us."

"Yes, I really don't know what to expect. I only know what I read about them and seeing one or two on TV back in Viet Nam."

We arrive at the high school along with many other Vietnamese families, and I lead Jerry to the school auditorium. Young girls are handing out programs. Luckily, they are in English. We find seats, and Jerry reads the story of the opera in the program.

"This is real soap opera stuff," he says.

"Most of them are, but this one looks like it will also be funny."

"How will I know when to laugh?" he asks as he winks at me.

"You won't, but I'll explain it to you as we go along so you'll know what the rest of us are laughing at. Just enjoy the music. Isn't that what you do at an Italian opera?"

"I go to a lot of operas, but I'm familiar with the story and know when to laugh even if I don't speak any Italian."

The house lights dim, and the opera begins. The costumes are very well done, and I whisper to Jerry what each character signifies. He seems to be into the music, and he catches most of the funny parts even before I translate for him. This one has a happy ending, and the crowd begins to leave after demanding three curtain calls from the cast.

"How about a drink somewhere?" he asks.

"One drink, and that's all," I demand.

"Your bar isn't open on Sundays. Where shall we go?"

"No, Luigi doesn't open on Sunday, but there's a nice place about ten blocks east of here. I'll give you directions."

We drive to the bar, and Jerry selects a booth. I order a Chevas Regal and water, and he asks for a **Miller Lite**.

"I'm surprised you drink Scotch?"

"Why?"

"I didn't expect it, that's all."

"Scotch was cheap in Viet Nam, and I just got used to it."

He leans back in his seat. "Tell me about your life in Viet Nam."

I'm a bit taken by surprise by the question. Why should he want to know about ancient history?

"What do you mean?" I ask.

"Oh, where you were born? Where did you go to school? What was life like? How did you meet your husband? That kind of thing."

"Why do you want to know?"

"I'm interested in everything about Viet Nam. The news was so biased here in the States, we never got the real story. I like to hear about it from the people who were there. I'm afraid I make myself a nuisance to any vet. Some of them don't want to talk about it, but some tell me a lot of interesting things the media filtered out of their reports."

"I had a pretty dull life." I don't think this is the time to disclose any of the more exciting aspects, particularly my life as a mistress to the Americans.

"How can any life in the middle of a war be dull?"

"Okay, you asked for it. I was born in Saigon just as the Japanese were occupying Viet Nam. I don't remember much about that war except that I was terrified of the Japanese soldiers. They were so fierce looking, and I'd heard tales of them doing horrible things to girls."

Jerry interrupts, "Did you have any brothers or sisters?"

"I was the youngest of three girls. My sisters were two and three years older than me."

"Did the Japs really rape little girls?" he asks.

"I really don't know. I was just a toddler, but I gave the soldiers a wide berth."

"Did you have a happy home life?"

"Yes, we never experienced the depravations of the war. Father had a good job with the Vichy French colonial government. I was very happy."

"After the war?"

"I never noticed much change. I was still very young when it ended. I remember my parents were very happy to see the war end, but there was still a lot of fighting against the

French and protests in Saigon. I saw one Buddhist monk burn himself to death. It was horrible. I had nightmares for weeks."

"How did you meet your husband?"

"When we were in what you call high school, my oldest sister used to sneak out of the house from time to time to meet her boyfriend. One night I insisted she take me with her or I'd tell father about it. We went to a bar where a lot of Air Force people went to meet girls. I had no idea what I was getting into. I'd barely kissed with boys, but these men had more in mind. I was so frightened, but I couldn't go home alone.

"One of the officers started pawing me, and I tried to fight him off, but he was too strong for me. Chinh saw what was happening and pulled him off me. He also grabbed my sister and forced us both into his jeep. He took us home and informed father about our escapades. As you can imagine, father was livid, but Chinh asked for permission to call on me. As you say in America, 'the rest is history'."

"So, you married Chinh?"

"Yes, we were married when I was 19 years old. He was transferred to Bien Hoa not too long after that. Bao and Anh were both born at Bien Hoa."

"Were you happy there?"

"Oh yes, life was good. Chinh flew helicopters, and I was very worried about him every time he flew. He was wounded once, but it wasn't too bad. Just a small scar on his right leg. Things were fine until he was sent to Nha Trang."

"What changed then?"

"He needed money there, and we still needed to live at Bien Hoa. Things were fine for a while, but inflation became very bad. I had to go to work for the Americans at their BX. Luckily, father had a good job working construction and mother sewed. They could care for the children while I worked. Inflation got worse, and father lost his job on top of that. At one point, we were reduced to eating rats."

"Ewww!" Jerry reacted to the idea.

"They aren't bad if you don't think about what you're eating. Then mother caught typhus and the medicine she needed wiped out our savings…" I stopped. Continuing on from there would mean telling him about my American lovers, and he didn't need to know about that phase of my life.

"And then...?" he leaned forward in his chair and looked into my eyes, begging for more.

"Well, it wasn't long after that we had a chance to get out before the Communists took over. My current fiancé serves as my sponsor, and here I am."

"How do you like life in America?"

"I think we've adapted to it pretty well. We had nothing when we arrived at Camp Pendleton. Mel was very good to my family in Viet Nam, and he's been a lot of help since I came to the States. The fact that we live in a neighborhood with a lot of other Vietnamese is also a big help. The children seem to be adapting very easily, but they also have a lot of Vietnamese children in their schools."

"Mel must be a pretty nice guy."

This remark takes me aback somewhat. It makes me think about my true feelings for Mel. Yes, he's been a big help. We couldn't have made it this far without him, but would I classify him as a "nice guy"? How would he react if I denied him sex? I often feel sex is the only thing holding him to me, yet he seems sincere in his pledge to marry me. Would he make a good husband? I think so. He likes Bao and Ahn, and he treats me with respect. That's it, he respects me. He says he loves me, but his actions aren't those of a lover. I feel he's still one of my clients. Jerry becomes impatient waiting for my response.

"Is he a nice guy? I mean, he doesn't mistreat you, does he?"

"No, it's nothing like that. I think I know what you mean by 'nice guy', but I don't think I'd put him that category."

He raises his eyebrows in surprise. "You wouldn't?"

"Well, he's more formal than "nice". I guess it's his military background. No, he's more caring than "nice"."

"But you love him anyway?"

I saw that question coming, but I'm not prepared to answer it. I give the first thing that pops into my head.

"I believe I do."

"How did you know him in Viet Nam?" he asks.

I knew this was coming, but I haven't prepared an answer. I give him the most logical one I can think of."

"He was an advisor to my husband's unit. When Chinh was reassigned, he helped my family out financially. I think he was only trying to impress me."

"I can understand that. Maybe he really will divorce his wife and marry you. She can't be as beautiful as you are."

"Thank you. I've only seen pictures of her, but she's a nice-looking lady in those pictures. She's in a nursing home now. She had a stroke which left her little more than a vegetable. Mel tries to see her every day. He says she doesn't know who he is half the time."

"I'm sorry. That's really tragic. The poor guy. He's lucky to have you. You seem like a strong enough woman to help him through all of this."

"He's a good man, and I give him all the support I can."

"You will invite me to the wedding, won't you?"

I can't help but laugh as he hands me one of his cards. "Of course."

We finish our drinks with the usual small talk, and he drops me off at my apartment. As I watch him drive off, I think some woman will be lucky to snag him, but I don't put myself in that category.

Chapter 17

The time seems to pass so slowly waiting six months for Mel to be a resident of California. Jerry doesn't call or come into the Kozy Korner, and I'm not sure if I'm happy or sad. I solve my dilemma by convincing myself Jerry cannot be interested in marriage, and Mel is.

Mel only takes me out to nice places for lunch each Wednesday, but when the children aren't in school, he takes all of us to fast food places because that's what the children want. He also comes for Sunday dinner, and I prepare Vietnamese food I know he likes. He's made a good impression on the children, and they seem to like him.

I'm so happy with my life now. That warm glow inside me is almost totally rekindled. I'll never forget Chin, but I can't deny myself a new romance. Even if I must be patient with Mel, I know the comfort of marriage will be worth the wait.

Mel also gives me information on an organization that helps me locate my parents. I've worried every moment since leaving them behind. The organization gives me an address, and I write. I can only hope they're alive. I fear the Communists killed them because of Chinh being an officer and my services to the Americans.

I send several letters but receive no replies. I wonder if they've found my parents or another family with the same names. I know many people in Viet Nam have the same names. Maybe they've made a mistake, or maybe they don't want to write to me. I know they were aware of my whoring, even though they never said so explicitly. Now that I'm gone, they don't need to hide their true feelings about me. They probably don't want to hear from me. Tears fill my eyes as I think about losing them forever. I resolve to write about the children even if they never respond. They deserve to know how wonderful they are.

I seldom see Mai any more. She calls from time to time, but she's busy with her children and English classes for all of them. Tam, along with a few other women in our apartment complex are now my main support.

December comes, and I invite Mel to celebrate Christmas with us. He agrees as long as he can get back to the nursing home in time to see his wife for dinner.

Christmas time means a break from school for the kids, and some extra time off for me. My family embraces the Christian holiday, though we continue to practice Buddhism. I put up a small tree near the household shrine and presents for each of the children sit beneath the scraggly branches.

Mel and I decide not to exchange presents. I tell him his love and support are all the presents I need, and he says the only present he wants is for his wife to pass on peacefully. He did say he'd buy something for the children, and he'll bring the gifts when he comes that morning.

The children have not yet acquired the habit of waking up at the crack of dawn on Christmas morning, but I'm awake and dressed early, preparing a quick breakfast because they wtill want to get to their presents as soon as possible.

As I expect, they wolf down breakfast and drag me to the tree.

Bao distributes the presents, and we decide Anh should go first. Her package is a rather small box, and she tears it open quickly.

"Oh, Mom, a Malibu Barbie doll. I really wanted one. Thank you." She holds it up for Bao and me to see.

"I knew you did, merry Christmas, darling." She doesn't need to know I found it at a second-hand store.

Bao tears open his small package and finds an autographed baseball. "Hey, they're all here—Ron Cey, Davy Lopes, Steve Garvey all of them. Thanks, Mom."

"You're welcome. I'm glad you like it."

"Like it? Someday this'll be worth a fortune."

He doesn't need to know one of the bikers stole it from a sporting goods store after he heard Bao loved the Dodgers. He was hoping to bribe me into his bed with it.

"Here, Mom. Open your present."

"For me? I told you kids I didn't want a present from you."

"I didn't buy it. It's something a buddy of mine made for me," Bao says as he hands me a package the size of a shoebox.

"Oh, it's very heavy," I comment as I heft the gift in both hands before opening it. I remove the ribbon carefully and undo the wrapping so the paper comes off in one piece. It is a shoebox. "It's too heavy to be shoes." I pause and shake the box a bit to heighten the suspense.

"Go ahead and open it, Mom. The suspense is killing me," Anh says.

I smile and lift the lid of the box to reveal a lot of tissue paper.

"What *is* it, Bao?" I ask as I lift the tissue paper—then I see it. "Oh, it's beautiful." I can't help but gasp as I reveal the ceramic figurine of a Vietnamese woman dressed in an ao-dai.

"It's you, Mom!" Bao says.

"A guy on my little league team made it for me. His mom does ceramics, and she made it using a picture I gave her. I remembered you telling us about the green ao dai you loved so much, but I wasn't sure of the color."

"It's perfect, Bao." Tears begin to well up in my eyes. Mel bought me that ao-dai just before he left Viet Nam. It and the jade bracelet are the only things he gave me I didn't sell on the black market to raise money. I set the figurine on the table and smile. I know Mel will love it.

"Why are you smiling, Mom?" Anh asks.

"It's just that I'm so happy today. Thank you, Bao. It's a wonderful present."

Anh hands me a box wrapped in paper she's made at school. I remember the project because she needed to cut a potato to use as a stamper. I open it carefully to preserve the paper in as good a condition as possible. I want to save it as a remembrance of her first year in an American school.

Inside the box I find clear plastic encasing what appears to be miniature flowers. "It's lovely, darling," I say, not having any idea what it was. She must have sensed my ignorance.

"It's a millefiore paper weight. I made it in my art class at school. Do you like it?"

I embrace her as my tears flow freely. "It's beautiful, and even more so since you made it yourself. Thank you."

"Don't cry, Mom," Bao says.

"I can't help it. I have such wonderful children."

*

Mel arrives shortly before noon and passes his presents out to the children. Anh receives another "Barbie" doll, some extra clothes for it and a fashion show stage that takes him and Bao almost an hour to assemble and get working properly. Bao gets a baseball glove and a pair of cleats.

After the meal, Mel excuses himself for a moment and returns carrying a small box.

"This is for you, Snow."

"Mel, we agreed not to exchange presents," I protest.

"This present doesn't require anything in return, except onea word from you," he says.

I suddenly realize what it is, but the children are stumped.

"Open it, Mom," Bao says.

I tear off the paper and ribbon to uncover a velvet covered jewelry store box. "Oh, Mel, is this what I think it is?"

"Open it up and see." He smiles broadly as I lift the lid revealing a yellow gold ring with a small diamond flanked by smaller emeralds.

The children even draw in their breath at the sight of it, and I'm without words for a moment. It's suddenly all real now. In a short time, we'll be married, and my life will be whole again.

"It's beautiful," I manage to say in spite of the flood of emotion spilling through my mind.

Mel stands, takes the ring from the box and slips it on my finger. "Will you marry me, Snow?"

I throw my arms around his neck. "Of course I will."

I'm firmly convinced now that Mel really means what he says. I don't know if what I feel for him is love, but it's close enough to commit to marriage.

He kisses me to the applause of the children and accepts their congratulations before leaving to see his wife.

That night, the three of us dine on a special Vietnamese meal where I substitute turkey for the usual chicken ingredient. The children call it Vietnamese Christmas dinner. That night I'm happier than I've been since before Chinh left me alone so long ago. My life is back on track.

*

In January Mel invites all of us to his retirement ceremony, and I make arrangements with the school for the children's absence. He picks us up early that morning and drives us to March AFB. Bao is quite impressed by the size of the place and Mel's office near the flight line.

"Wow, did Dad have an office like this?" he asks.

"I was never in your father's office, but I doubt it was like this. He was only a helicopter pilot. Mel is a senior officer with an important position," I say.

Mel corrects me. "Don't say he was 'only a helicopter pilot'. Those guys were the real heroes of the war. They got shot at as much as the infantry guys."

"My father got a medal for bravery," Bao says.

Mel reacts with surprise. "Oh?"

I relate the story and Mel is impressed. "That's pretty brave."

"I wish I knew more about my father," Bao says.

"I was too young to know what was going on," Anh says.

"Just know your father was very brave and very good man," I say.

"Time to head off for the ceremony," Mel says.

*

The ceremony takes place in the office of the Wing Commander. Mel is presented with a medal of some kind, and another officer reads a synopsis of his career. There's much congratulating from the people he works with, including several senior NCOs.

He takes us to the officer's club after the ceremony where a luncheon is set up in his honor. Many officers give funny speeches about him, and the meal ends with a series of toasts to his success in civilian life.

I excuse myself to use the ladies' room and enter a stall close to the sinks. I can't help but overhear two women talking as they refresh their make-up and adjust their hairdos.

"Nice party the guys threw for Mel Jenkins' retirement," a woman says.

"Yeah, really nice," another woman answers.

"Did you get to meet his fiancee?" the first one says.

"Yes, she's certainly beautiful for a Vietnamese and seems to be very nice," the second answers.

"I'm glad he found someone nice one after that bitch of a wife divorced him," the first says.

"She's also a lot better looking than that redhead he was dating," the second answers.

"I thought I saw him with the redhead at a restaurant Roger and I were at the other night," the first says.

They begin to talk on another subject. I can't believe what I'm hearing. Mel divorced? Another woman? I look at the ring on my left hand. Is it all a sham? Is this just some way for Mel to string me along for his sexual satisfaction while he pursues a more suitable wife? I must talk to him, but now is not the time or place. I feel their words burning deep inside me, and I fear they will consume me before he can quench the fire.

*

It's late afternoon before we start back to Westminster. Mel says he's okay to drive in spite of all the alcohol he's consumed. I make another mental note to have him teach me to drive.

"That was an impressive ceremony," I say as we enter the Riverside freeway. The need to confront him about the gossip burns in my chest, but I feel I must keep things cordial until we're alone.

"I guess I should feel sad about leaving the Air Force, but I don't. It was a good life, even though I never made a lot of money, but I'm ready for something else now. I start work at Orange County Airport in three weeks. It'll be good to have more than enough money for a change. My Air Force retirement check on top of a nice salary from the airport means I can help you more now, and we'll be doing alright when we're married. We can also move you and the kids to a nicer apartment."

We reach the apartment, and the children change clothes and fly out to their own obligations. Mel starts to leave, but I ask him to stay.

"Mel, I need to talk to you about something. Can you stay for a while?"

"Sure, what's on your mind?"

I point him to the sofa, but instead of sitting down beside him, I pull a chair up to face him.

"I've heard some gossip today that really upset me." It's hard for me to say this, and his reaction is a flash of anger that subsides quickly.

"What's that?"

"It's about your wife. Are you already divorced?"

"Where'd you hear that?" His voice again betrays his anger. His face sets in a grim expression, and his eyes take on a cold look.

"I overheard some women talking in the ladies' room at the officer's club."

"Don't believe everything you hear."

"They also said you have another woman besides me."

He relaxes a bit, but the fire still burns behind his eyes.

"When Meg went into the nursing home, I told everyone we'd been divorced. I didn't want a lot of sympathy and tears over it."

His explanation seems plausible. It fits his stoic personality.

"I can understand that, but what about the other woman?"

"I did date other women until you came back to me. I broke it off with her as soon I got the news you were here. Believe me, you're the only woman in my life now."

I take a moment to think about his explanation. I have no reason to believe idle gossip over his statements. I want to believe him, and I must believe in him since I plan to marry him.

"I guess it was just gossip. I'm sorry I brought it up."

We kiss, and none of that seems to matter. I know he wants to go further, but I stop him.

"We can't, Mel. The children might come home any time."

He lets me go and smiles. "I understand. Just be patient with me on this, please."

"I know you love me, and I will be patient for as long as it takes."

"I think I need to go now before my lust overcomes my good sense," he says as he rises from the sofa.

I give him one more kiss before he goes. I gain confidence in his integrity now that I know the complete story from his lips.

That night, I tell the children about my conversation with Mel and my feelings about the situation.

"I'm glad Mel's not lying to you, Mom," Bao says.

"Yes, I was afraid you might not see him anymore," Ahn says. "We'd like to have a father again."

Chapter 18

In February, Mel's busy with his new job and only has time off on weekends. It's almost impossible for us to get together given my work schedule. I can hear the exasperation growing in his voice with each call. One morning he seems particularly irritated.

"Isn't there some way we can work this out?" he says.

"I don't know how. You can't get off during the day, and I work at night. The only time we're both free is the wee hours of the morning or Sunday, and that's the only day I have with my children." I'm secretly hoping this will give me a respite from Mel's attentions. Lately, he has been acting more like a client than a fiancée.

"Early mornings won't work. You'd be worn out from working all night, and I'd lose sleep and be yawning my head off at work all the next day."

"You see me on Sunday almost all day."

"Yeah, but the kids are around, and you won't make love when they're out because you're afraid they'll come back and find us in bed."

"I wouldn't mind if we were husband and wife."

"Did you forget that I have to wait until April before I can file for divorce?"

"I know, I'm just anxious for it to be over so we can be married." I decide to change the subject. "Do you still want to come for dinner on Sunday?"

"Sure, the usual time?"

"Yes, be here around one and we'll eat at one-thirty."

"Can you make something besides Vietnamese food? I think I need some good home-fried chicken."

"I'm planning on roast beef. Is that all right?"

"Sure, anything but that stir-fried mess and rice. See you Sunday. By the way, I've got a special present for you I'll bring along. See you then."

"See you then." I hang up and glare at the phone. Mel has become a different man since we can't get together regularly. I'm beginning to wonder if I really want to be his wife.

*

Mel devours the roast beef on Sunday, and after dinner he excuses himself to go to his car. He returns with a large box and sets it on the dinner table.

"Bao asked about his father at my retirement ceremony, and a guy at the airport made this for me. I thought you and the kids might like to have it."

He opens the box and lifts out a large model of a Huey helicopter.

"See, it's painted in VNAF markings, and look at this." He points to some printing near the right side of the nose. "This is why I asked you about your husband's name and rank, Snow."

I read the small print with some difficulty, but it's something I've seen hundreds of times, Thieu Ta Vien Van Chinh. I fall back into my chair and burry my face in my hands. I can't hold back the tears. I thought I'd reconciled myself to his death. All my attempts to find out about him have failed. This only serves to remind me of the man I loved and how poorly I treated him.

Bao tugs at my sleeve. I lift my head and see him pointing to Anh. She's sitting there staring at the model with a look of sheer horror on her face. I run to her side and wrap her in my arms.

"It's all right, baby. It's only a model. Don't be afraid."

I rock her back and forth for a few moments. Bao and Mel both just look on with helpless expressions.

"What's the matter with her?" Mel asks.

"She's remembering how we escaped from Viet Nam. You can't believe how frightening it was."

Anh suddenly comes to life. She grasps my arm.

"I'm all right, Mother. It just brought back so many bad memories," she says.

"For me too, darling, for me too," I say as I hug her and kiss her on the cheek."

"I'm sorry, Snow. I thought it would make you happy."

I can't let the children know the real reason for my tears. They had no knowledge of my life as a whore. Mel might understand. He has to know I loved Chinh, and how hard it was for me to do what I did. I compose myself and put on a stoic face.

"I'm sorry. It just triggered the emotions I suffered when they told me he was dead. It is a lovely thing, Mel. Thank you."

Bao inspects the model now that the room is back to normal.

"Did my father's helicopter have all of these guns?"

"I don't know if he ever flew a gun-ship, but most pilots did at one time or another," Mel says. He begins to point out the armaments. "These are rocket pods. They hold 19 rockets each. The guns are called mini-guns and fire over 3,000 rounds a minute."

"Wow, they were really cool," Bao breathes as he stares at the model with large eyes.

"Yes, they were, but they were also very fragile things. An old helicopter pilot once described a Huey to me as, 'a collection of constantly moving fragile parts with each part bent on the destruction of the parts adjacent to it'. A single bullet in the right place could bring one down, but I was always surprised by how durable they were. I've seen them come home riddled with bullet holes and still land safely."

"Except if they were hit by an RPG," I insert.

"Yeah, that was usually fatal," Mel adds before he realizes the significance of my remark. He turns to see me crying again.

"I'm sorry, Snow. I know this is painful for you. I'll take the model back to him."

I rise and dry my tears. "No, I want it. I want the children to remember their father and what a brave a man he was." The children run to my side, and we embrace as the tears roll down our cheeks.

*

April finally arrives, and I question Mel about the divorce again. "Now that you're a resident of California, how long will the divorce take?"

"I don't know. I talked with the lawyer last week, and he said he needed to do more research before he could give me an answer on that. He did talk about what it was going to cost, though."

"Will it be expensive?"

"I'll say. It'll take most of what I've got saved to get a final decree. There'll be alimony, but I'm already paying her expenses at the nursing home. I don't think the court'll require any more than that, but that'll be plenty. She'll also get half the proceeds from the sale of the house."

*

Jerry calls again in May. "Hi, Tuyết. I haven't received a wedding invitation yet, and I was wondering how the engagement's coming?"

I'm surprised he's using the Vietnamese version of my name, but I love it.

"Mel and I are still engaged, and I think the divorce is just around the corner. We're getting married as soon as his divorce is final."

"The real reason I called is, I can get some good tickets to a Dodgers game a week from Sunday. I thought you and the kids would like to see a game."

"I couldn't do that. I felt so guilty about the Vietnamese opera. I told Mel about that, and he understood, but I don't know if he'd be so forgiving this time. Besides, he usually has dinner here every Sunday, but Bao would love that. He eats and sleeps baseball. You could take him if he doesn't have a school game."

"Okay, I'll get two tickets, but if you change your mind, call me. That is, call me before next Thursday. I can't get any more extra tickets after that."

"Thank you, if anything changes, I'll call you."

I hang up almost wishing I could go with Jerry. I don't know what draws me to him, but his invitation is very tempting.

*

Sunday, Mel comes to dinner, as usual, but the children surprise us both after dinner.

"I got a game this afternoon, Mom," Bao says. "Sorry to skip out on you guys so soon, but Mr. Quan's picking me up in a few minutes."

"You didn't tell me about this. Maybe Mel and I would like to go," I say.

"Sorry, it must have slipped my mind. It's just a pick-up game. Nothing you and Mel'd be interested in. I'll be back around five." He goes to his room to get his gear.

"Can I go too, Mother? Shirley Quan's brother is playing, and she asked me to come with Bao so we could talk about the school play we're both in."

"What school play? You children have to let me know about your activities. Of course, you can go with Bao, but give me some advance notice next time."

"Sorry, Mother, I won't forget next time." Anh goes out the door with Bao.

I look after them, shaking my head. "I wonder what that was all about."

"I think it's a conspiracy," Mel says.

"A conspiracy?"

"To give us some time to ourselves," Mel says. "How shall we take advantage of it?" His eyes twinkle with a lust built up over several weeks of forced abstinence, and his mouth curves into a lecherous smile.

"Maybe we could watch some TV," I say as I lead him to the bedroom.

*

The sex is better than ever, but Mel doesn't doze afterward.

"I have to spend next Sunday with Meg. It's some kind of special day for families, or something, and the staff thinks I should be there. I won't be able to have dinner with you and the kids. I'm sorry."

"It's alright. I understand." I really don't. He hasn't cared that much about being with his wife on Sunday since we became engaged.

"Thanks, I'll be really pissed if the kids have decided to leave us alone again," he says.

"I'll let them know about this right away. Do you think they really wanted to leave us alone so we could have sex?"

"Hey, kids these days are a lot more aware of those things than we ever were. I wouldn't doubt it."

"Do you remember the man who took me to the Vietnamese opera?" I ask.

"Sure."

"He wants to take Bao to a Dodgers game on Sunday. Since you're not going to be here, would you mind if Anh and I went along?"

He gives me a wary look. "Is this guy hitting on you?"

"No, it's nothing like that. He said he can get four tickets if I decide to go. I've made it very clear to him that I'm committed to you. I just thought it might be fun."

He stares at me as he ponders my request. I feel his eyes probing me to pry out my true motive. I have no trouble projecting my real feelings about Jerry. I'm not in love with him.

His hesitation in answering tells me he's suspicious, and I rush to reassure him.

"I won't go if you don't feel comfortable with it," I say.

He seems to relax a bit. "No, I trust you completely. Go ahead and go. You'll enjoy seeing how the pros do it. It'll give you some idea of how good your son is."

"Thank you, darling." I kiss him, but he draws away.

"We'd better get dressed before the kids get back," he says.

We dress quickly, and I make the bed as smoothly as it was when they left.

*

When the children come home, I ask them about Sunday.

"Do either of you have anything important next Sunday?"

"Nothing I couldn't cancel," Anh says.

"I've got a pick-up game with some guys, but I don't have to be there," Bao says.

"Good, how would you both like to go see a Dodgers game?"

Ahn shrugs her shoulders and sighs. "If the whole family's going, I'll go along."

Bao's eyes light up, and a broad smile appears. "You bet! How did you manage that, Mom?"

"Do you remember me telling you about the man who took me to the opera?"

"You mean he's the one who got the tickets?"

"Yes, him. His name is Mr. Warren, and he wants to take us to the game on Sunday. He says they're great seats."

"Is Mel going?" Ahn asks.

"No, he has to spend Sunday with his wife."

"Mel's not too keen on baseball anyway," Bao says. "He asks me about it and he's bought me some nice stuff, but I think he only does that to make a good impression on you, Mom."

"Why do you say that, Bao?" I ask.

"I don't know. I just get the feeling he's not being entirely honest sometimes, that's all. You know, not about important things, but other things."

"He's a busy man with a lot on his mind. I think you have to make some allowances for that. Do you want to go to the ball game with Mr. Warren?"

"You know I want to go," Bao answers.

"I really don't want to go to a 'ball game'. Can't I stay home?" Ahn replies.

I know she'd be bored stiff, and I feel Mel isn't too keen on me seeing Jerry again. "Okay, you can stay home, and I'll stay with you. Bao, do you feel comfortable going with Mr. Warren to see the game?"

"I think so, and I really want to see a Dodgers game."

"Then it's all set. I'll call Mr. Warren tomorrow and say he only needs a ticket for Bao."

*

Monday evening I'm surprised to see Jerry walk into the Kozy Korner. He's dressed more appropriately this time, in a white golf shirt with an embroidered Mercedes logo and khakis.

"Jerry, what a surprise."

"I hoped you were working tonight. What made you change your mind about the ball game? I thought you were going too."

"Mel doesn't seem to feel comfortable with it, but I know Bao will be in 7th heaven at a Dodgers game. What'll you have?"

"I'll take a ***Miller Lite***."

"I remember he likes draft and draw a frosty mug full of the golden liquid. As I set it in front of him, I say, "You could have just returned my call."

"I had to visit the dealer in San Diego today, so I decided to stop in here before I went home. I checked with my secretary after lunch, and she told me you'd called. I'm sorry you decided not to go to the game with me."

"Please understand that I'd feel like I was cheating on Mel. I told Mel about the opera, and he was okay with that. When I told him about this, and he was so hesitant about saying 'yes' I don't feel like I can go.

"Well, I wouldn't want him to think I was pushing in on his woman."

"He's really not the jealous type. It'll be okay."

At that moment, a customer at the other end of the bar calls for service, and I leave Jerry for a moment while I take care of his order. When I return, Jerry seems a bit on edge. "Is there some way we can talk privately for a few minutes?" he asks.

"Dick's here tonight. I could ask him to spell me for a while. What do you want to talk about?"

"It's something you need to know." He pushes his mug back and forth nervously, and his face has a pained expression.

"Just a minute. I'll get Dick to take over." As I go to get Dick from the back office, I wonder what Jerry could have to say. I know Mel as thoroughly as a woman can know any man. There can't be any flaw in his personality I haven't seen. The only thing I can think of would be something to do with his wife, but that's a pretty straightforward situation.

Dick agrees to take over the bar for 15 minutes, and I lead Jerry to a booth.

"Okay, what do you want to tell me?" I ask.

"As I said, I was at the San Diego dealership today, and one of the customers I was serving is a big divorce lawyer. He was talking to the Service Manager while I was inspecting a flaw in his paint, and I overheard them talking about divorces. I caught him later and asked him how long they take. He told me a simple divorce was a two-week process and the worst he'd handled only took six weeks. I thought you might like to have this information."

I sit back in the booth absorbing his story. It's only been a month since Mel became a resident of California, but he's been a bit dodgy about the progress of the divorce. If it's as simple as Jerry says, he shouldn't feel that way at all.

"It's only been a month since he could file as a California resident. Your wedding invitation should be arriving very shortly," I say.

He laughs and finishes his beer. "Just thought you'd like to know. I gotta be going." He rises to leave, and I go back to the bar.

*

On Sunday, Jerry arrives right on time, and I introduce him to the children.

"Children, this is Mr. Jerry Warren."

Bao offers his hand. "Pleased to meet you, Mr. Warren."

Jerry takes his hand. "Please, just call me Jerry."

"Sure, Jerry," Bao replies.

I interrupt. "That's Mr. Warren to you, son."

"Okay, Mom." Bao gives a good imitation of being scolded.

Anh offers her hand too, and Jerry takes it gently in both of his. "I'd have known you were your mother's daughter without an introduction. You have all of her beauty."

"It's a pleasure to meet you, Mr. Warren."

"Well, now that introductions are out of the way, let's go see a ball game," Jerry says.

*

The ball game is a big success with Bao. When they get home, Bao and Jerry feel the need to give Ahn and I a play-by-play of the game, but the conversation is meaningless to us. I watch Jerry as Bao tells all about the game. His smile tells me he's as proud of Bao as Chinh would have been. Bao finally winds down, and Jerry rises to leave. I let him say goodbye to the children and lead him outside to the courtyard surrounding the pool. I sit him down in a chair and take one next to him.

"Jerry, it was very generous of you to take Bao to a ball game, but please don't ask to see me or the children again. I'm engaged to be married."

He exhales sharply, and his body slumps as if he was a tire losing air.

"I admit it was an excuse to see you again, but you saw the look on Bao's face and heard how he talked about it. Customers give me tickets from time-to-time, and I'd like to take him to another game sometime."

"He loves baseball, and you can take him to a game any time you want to, but I won't ever be going along, and I won't spend any time with you before or after the game."

"I understand."

He deflates even more than I thought possible. I have to look away from him to hide the feeling of disloyalty to Mel darkening my face.

"Thank you for understanding. Mel and I are going to be married, so please don't ask me to damage that relationship."

He looks at me with resigned eyes. "I guess this is goodbye, then."

"You're a nice guy, but it has to be."

"Let's just make it goodbye until the wedding, okay?"

"Okay."

We shake hands before he leaves. I watch as he walks to his car, trying to quell the feeling he's created in my heart. Deep inside me a voice urges me to call him back, but the practical part of my brain takes over. I don't know Jerry that well, and I do know Mel. I may have some doubts concerning the story about his wife, but I really don't doubt his love for me.

Jerry waves to me as he gets in the car, and I wave back. I know I've made the right decision, but I need to get the truth from Mel. As he drives away, a small voice reminds me to keep Jerry's number.

Chapter 19

In June, the children are out of school and in and out of the apartment sporadically—Bao with his baseball, and Anh with swimming lessons at our apartment pool. One of the other Vietnamese wives is a lifeguard at a country club and gives lessons on her days off. Bao thinks he's too old to take lessons with the "little kids". He and another boy sign up for lessons at the YMCA because the other boy's father will take them and pick them up.

One Sunday, the children both have activities that will tie them up all afternoon. Mel has dinner with us, as usual, and is overjoyed to see them leave us alone for several hours.

"Okay, baby, now's our time to shine," he says as he almost pulls me into my bedroom.

"Easy, Mel. Bao won't be back until six, and Anh'll be later than that. We've got plenty of time."

He relaxes his grip on my arm and draws me into an embrace.

"Oh God. I'm treating you like a whore instead of my fiancée. I'm sorry."

He leads me to the bedroom more gently this time, but the reappearance of his Viet Nam attitude troubles me. Maybe it was just because we've been apart longer than he expected, but maybe it's his true feelings showing from under the cloak of romance?

*

Afterwards, we dress and make the bed in anticipation of the children returning. We move to the living room and enjoy a glass of wine from the bottle Mel brought to go with dinner. I decide a blunt question is the only way to open the most critical subject on my mind.

"How's the divorce coming along?" I ask.

Mel grunts in disgust and takes a sip of wine. "Not very well. The damned lawyer the court appointed for Meg keeps coming up with new demands, and that costs me more money in fees for my lawyer. I'm beginning to think all of those guys are in cahoots to line each other's pockets."

"It's been going on so long now. Your six-month wait was up in April, and it's now June. I didn't think getting a divorce could be such a lengthy process."

"I didn't either, but it's turning out to be a nightmare."

I decide any further discussion of the divorce is fruitless and change the subject. "Have you thought any more about moving closer to your work? You know that would also make you closer to me."

"Yes, but it won't work. I'd have to sell the house to get the cash to buy another one, and my hands are tied until after the divorce is final. Let's talk about something else pleasant."

"Okay, how about house hunting some Sunday?"

This subject draws almost the same bitter response as my query about the divorce.

"Why look if we can't buy? I can't do a thing until this divorce is settled."

He turns on the television and pretends to be engrossed in an old movie.

"Want another glass of wine?" I ask, but he only stares at the set. Further discussion of the divorce is useless now and getting angry won't improve the situation. I decide to leave the subject to another day, but I sense I've struck a nerve here, and I do not intend to leave it alone.

*

Monday night at the Kozy Korner one of the regulars sits down at the bar.

"The usual, Josh?" I asked.

"No, I think I'd like some champagne tonight, Snow."

"What's the occasion?" I ask as I take a bottle of the cheap stuff I know he has in mind from the wine cooler and find a suitable glass.

"Get a glass for yourself, too." He turns to the sparse crowd at the booths. "Hey, anybody else want to help me celebrate? My divorce is final today. Whooo Hooo." He grabs the bottle and waves it over his head.

"Easy, don't shake it up too much," I warn as two men join him at the bar. I place glasses in front of each new drinker and pop the cork on the champagne. Luckily, it doesn't fizz too much.

After all the glasses are full Josh says, "Here's to being rid of the bitch." He raises the glass in the air before putting it to his lips. We all join him.

"Just curious, but how long did it take from start to finish?" I ask.

"It was hell. The witch fought me all the way for custody of our son. We were at it for a solid three months," Josh says.

"Wow," one of the other men says. "Mine only took six weeks." Another said, "My ex and I didn't dispute anything. There weren't any kids, and no house to argue over. We got our decree in a month."

"You guys have a good time. One glass is all I'm allowed." I empty my glass and move to help the waitress waiting at the bar station reserved for her.

So, a tough divorce only takes three months. Maybe Mel *is* stringing me along. The fact that his wife is incapacitated may stretch things out a bit, but there are no children, and Mel said he'd take care of his share of the nursing home costs anyway.

I can't believe he'd deceive me about this. He's spent a lot of money on our transition to life in America, and I don't doubt he loves me. He's given me an engagement ring, hasn't he? I try to suppress it, but a black specter of doubt rises in the back of my mind.

*

I go about my usual chores the next morning, but Mel is constantly on my mind. The only conclusion I can come to is that he's lying to me about the divorce, but why? He must have some reason for it, but why isn't he telling me? The only reason I can think of is that if he revealed his secret, I'd leave him.

That's it. It has to be so bad that I'd give up his financial support. He knows I rely on that money. If I didn't have it, I'd have to take on a second job. Can the truth be so terrible? The realization casts a black fog over me.

The children sense my attitude. Bao corners me in the kitchen as I'm cleaning up after breakfast. He's dressed in his baseball uniform and carrying the duffel bag containing his gear. He drops the bag on the kitchen floor.

"What's wrong, mom?" Bao asks.

"What do you mean? Nothing's wrong."

"You haven't been your usual happy self this morning. Something bothering you?"

"It's nothing. I'll be all right."

"Is it something I've done?" he asks.

I take him in my arms and hold him close, but he's obviously uncomfortable. Since he turned fifteen, he's not much on hugs these days. I release him quickly.

"Heavens no. You children are my anchors in this strange sea of America. No, it has to do with Mel and me."

"I hope it's nothing serious. I'd hate to see you two break up."

"It's okay, don't worry about it."

"Okay, I gotta go to my practice game now. I'll be back in time for dinner." He turns to pick up his duffel bag.

"What will you do for lunch?" I ask.

"Don't worry. The coach always buys hot dogs for us. See you later."

He's out the door before I can quiz him further.

Anh has been listening in the bedroom, and she comes into the kitchen.

"Don't be mad at Mel, Mother." I see tears starting to form in her eyes, and take her in my arms.

"I'm not mad at him, darling. This is just a small bump in the road for us. Don't worry."

This seems to calm her a bit. "I think Mel would make a good father," she says.

"Yes, he would. Now go back to what you were doing. Everything's okay."

*

Mel calls on Wednesday.

"Hello, beautiful, is there any possibility of us getting together this week?"

"I don't see how, but I really do need to talk to you in person."

205

He, obviously, senses a hint of anger in my voice.
"What's the matter?"
"It's about the divorce."
"What about the divorce?"
His voice betrays his sense of guilt.
"I'd rather talk to you face-to-face about this."
"I'll come to the bar tonight. We can talk about it then."

He hangs up abruptly. This is so unlike him. I know I've hit a nerve.

*

Mel walks in around nine. He sits at the far end of the bar, and I walk the few steps past the remaining bar patrons to him.

"Hi Mel, what will you have?"
"A Scotch and water, and use the good Scotch, please."

I mix his drink and place it before him.

"You wanted to talk?" he asks.

I look around the room. There are only two other people at the bar, and they have a lot left on their draft beers. Two booths are occupied, and the waitress is lounging at her bar station watching them finish their meals.

"Yes, it's about your divorce. I've talked with a few people, and they all say no divorce takes this long. What's happening, Mel?"

He avoids my gaze and looks at the TV behind the bar. "You've got to be patient with me, Snow."

This reply exhausts my patience. He's lying about something, and I have to find out what it is. I throw my bar rag on the floor and glare at him.

"Patient? I've been patient for nearly a year now. There's some reason you're not pressing this divorce. What is it?"

He licks his lips and takes a sip of his drink before he answers.

"I haven't told you about the money. She's sitting on half a million in a trust fund from her parents. I'll get it when she dies, if I'm still married to her. If she knew about you, she'd change her will so I couldn't get it. Thankfully, she's incapable of doing that now, but I can't divorce her. The money goes to her sister if I divorce her. That money means a secure future for you and me. Can you understand that?" His face is a mask of contrition. If he were a puppy, I'd pick him up and hold him, but I've seen this act before. He's still lying.

"Yes, I can, but why did you tell me you were getting a divorce? Why didn't you just tell me the truth?" I pick up the bar rag and throw it into the sink so hard the suds splash on my apron.

He hangs his head and takes a deep breath before answering. "I was afraid you wouldn't stay with me if I told you the truth, so I lied about the divorce."

"What about the engagement ring? Is that real?" I hold my hand out in front of him.

"Yes, that's real. I really do want to marry you."

"But, not until she's dead. Is that it?"

"The medics say she could go any time. She keeps having what they call mini-strokes, and they say one of them will eventually kill her, but like I told you, she could go on like this for another two years."

"You expect me to wait two more years so you can get your hands on half a million dollars?" I resist the urge to retrieve the bar rag and throw it in his face.

"It'll be our money, darling. We'll have a half million to let us do all the good things. We can take cruises, see the world. Live the good life."

I close my eyes and shake my head. All men ever think of are money and sex. Why can't they have some sense of what a woman wants? Suddenly, a hot flash of anger runs up my spine.

"What's more important to you, our love or the good life? You once told me all you wanted was to marry me. You told me you were pursuing a divorce, but you aren't. What am I supposed to believe, Mel?" I'm so angry foam from my mouth splatters on the bar in front of him. Now I must retrieve the bar rag.

"Believe that I love you, and I want to marry you as soon as possible. I figured if I waited until she died, I'd get her money, there'd be no nursing home cost and she wouldn't get half the house. I thought she'd die before you got suspicious about the fake divorce."

I fight back the urge to slap his face. Getting physical won't solve anything. I'd feel better for an instant, but I'd regret it forever. Every good opinion of him begins to melt away in the face of his lies, leaving only the skeleton of my gratitude for his help. I concentrate on cleaning the bar in front of him.

"I didn't think you'd care as long as we were together," he said.

"How many times have I told you? I didn't come to America to be your mistress again. When I found you, and you agreed to be our sponsor, I thought you understood that. Then you asked me to marry you, and said you'd divorce your wife. Now I find it's all built on a foundation of lies." I begin to cry in spite of my determination not to. Mel reaches across the bar to touch my arm, but I draw away.

"You must know I love you. I never lied about that," he says.

"Do you? Love should mean more than Sunday dinner together and sex every now and then. Money shouldn't matter if you love me. You say you're making good money now. That and your Air Force retirement money should be enough for a good life without her money."

"What do you want me to do, Snow?"

I take a deep breath to calm myself before I answer. "I want a husband who loves me more than money. Someone to take care of me and the children. A house in a nice area, and not having to work day and night just to have enough to eat. I thought when you asked me to marry you I'd get all that, but now you ask me to *be patient* and wait for your wife to die so you can have a little more money."

"Half a million is a lot of money, Snow."

"I don't care, Mel. To Hell with the money. Divorce her now and marry me, damnit." In spite of my better judgement, I let my voice rise a bit.

I glare at him in a white-hot rage. If looks could kill, Mel would be a dead man. We must have been talking too loudly because we attract the attention of the bouncer. He comes up next to Mel.

"Hey Snow, is this guy bothering you?" he asks.

"No, it's all right, Rick. This is my fiancée, Mel Jenkins. Just a lover's quarrel."

"Oh, sorry." He extends a hand to Mel. "I'm Rick Mullins."

Mel takes his hand. "Mel Jenkins, nice to know someone's looking out for Snow."

"Yeah, I make sure nobody messes with her. The biker crowd's pretty well behaved now, but sometimes the Vietnamese guys have to be cooled down. Know what I mean?"

"I can imagine. Nice to meet you, Rick.'

Rick leaves and Mel continues in a more subtle tone. "Don't you want a chance for the good life? Yes, I could give you what you want now, but it could be so much better if you can be patient just a while longer."

"I'm sick of waiting, Mel. I waited for Chinh to come home, and now you're asking me to wait again. I don't want to wait any more."

"I can afford to give you more money now. You can move into a nicer apartment, but I won't divorce Meg."

"This is about more than money, Mel. I want a full-time husband. Bao needs a man's hand on his shoulder now. I want a solid, permanent relationship. All of this is more important than money as far as I'm concerned."

Once more his face becomes a slack mask of despair. "It's not more important for me. I struggled with money all those years in the Air Force. Now that I can see a future free of money worries, I don't want to give it up. Now that I've found you again, I don't want to give you up either. Can't you understand that?"

I look at him and see he's determined to have that money. Is security enough reason for me to continue my relationship with Mel? If he's lied to me about the divorce, what else would he lie about? Yes, I still feel some degree of love for him, but is it enough to overcome the breach of trust his lies have generated.

If I left him, what would I do? Jerry is a possibility, but I need more time to be sure he's not just another Mel.

"I can't give you an answer now. Give me a few days to think. Good night, Mel."

"I need to pay you for my drink."

"It's on the house."

He takes the hint. "Can I still come over for Sunday dinner?"

"No, just leave me alone for a while. I'll call you next week."

He leaves the bar, and I find it hard to be civil with my co-workers the rest of the evening because of the rage boiling inside me.

That evening in bed I think over my situation. How can I believe anything Mel says now? I can't break off our engagement because I still need his financial help, and I really don't want to break it off. I still believe he loves me in his own way, and I feel something more that gratitude for his help. He's still my best hope for a good life here in America.

A good life—in Viet Nam that was a home, family and enough to eat. Over the past year I've learned what *the good life* is here in America. The images I see on TV are still a fantasy world to me, but that's obviously what Mel wants. Why don't I want it too?

Yes, I would like to have it all, but my bed has been empty too long. Too long I've been without someone to share the details of my day. Too long without the touch of a hand on my shoulder, a random kiss, a smile to brighten a cloudy day, an unchanging rock of love to lean upon when life seems hopeless. These things must come first. What good is money without them?

Would Mel give me that kind of love after our marriage? Maybe American men are different. My only experience is as their whore. No, I don't believe they are different, and I won't settle for less than what I had with Chinh. I fall asleep thinking of our wonderful life together so long ago.

Chapter 20

The next morning, I get the children off to school and clean up breakfast before I sit down to think about Mel. Yes, he's a gentle lover, but he's not at all what I would call romantic. He's been very good to me and the children, but he doesn't touch me just because he's nearby. He doesn't kiss me for no reason at all. I remember Chinh, and how he used to stroke my hair and tell me it was like fine silk.

Surely, there can't be that much difference between American men and Vietnamese men. There must be American men like Chinh. Why should I settle for Mel? I still have my looks, and I'm not that old. I slump into the sofa. How would I find such a man? The kind I want doesn't come into the Kozy Korner, or did he?

I go to the bedroom and dig through my top dresser drawer to find Jerry's card. I call his office.

"Good morning, Mercedes North America, this is Jerry Warren. How may I serve you?"

"Jerry, this is Tuyét."

"What a surprise. Is this an invitation to the wedding?"

"That's the problem, and I need to talk to someone about it. Can we get together for coffee, or something?"

"That would be nice, but I'd rather talk about it over dinner sometime? What would be a good day for you?"

"Jerry, I don't want you to spend a lot of money on this. Can't we just do lunch somewhere?"

"Look, from your tone of voice it sounds serious, and that calls for a serious atmosphere. It has to be dinner, I insist. What night?"

"I can manage to get off this Saturday night, if that suits your schedule."

"It certainly does. I'll see what time I can get reservations at Chez Jacque and call you back."

"Jerry! That's a very expensive place. I won't let you spend that much money for this meeting. I won't go if it's Chez Jacques."

There's a pause on the other end of the line. "Okay, do you like Mexican food?"

"Yes, that would be fine."

"How about the Red Onion? It's a family restaurant. You could bring the kids."

"Thank you, but I don't want them to hear this. It'll be just you and me."

"Fine, I'll make a reservation there for 7:00 PM. The restaurant's in Torrance, so I'll pick you up at six. Is that alright?"

"I'll be ready by six."

We both say goodbye and hang up. I can't help feeling a little guilty about this, but I need to talk to someone in a neutral corner. I know Jerry's interested in me, but I think he can put his feelings aside to help with my problem.

*

Saturday evening, I stand in front of the mirror checking out the dress I found at the second-hand shop. I don't think an ao dai would be appropriate for a Mexican restaurant, even though Jerry said it was a family place.

"God Mom, you look gorgeous. This is the first time I've really seen you in an American dress." Anh steps up behind me and stands on tiptoe to adjust a bit of hair, more out of habit than necessity. "You look like the dangerous women in the movies I watch on Saturday afternoon."

"I hope I didn't overdo it, but this is the only thing I could find I thought appropriate"

"If the food's good, be sure to bring back a doggie bag for Bao and me."

We laugh at the joke just as the doorbell rings

I answer it and find Jerry standing there with a bouquet of roses. He wears a dark blue suit accenting his blonde hair and sky-blue eyes.

"Hey, you look great!" He seems to be stunned by my appearance. He's never seen me dressed more than casually.

I reach for the flowers. "How sweet of you, Jerry. Come on in." I call to Anh, "Anh, come say hello to Mr. Warren."

"Hi Mr. Warren," Anh says.

I hand her the flowers. "Here, Anh. Please put these in some water for me, will you?"

"Sure, Mom." She leaves us alone.

"Where's your son?" he asks.

"Bao has a baseball practice game. I'm ready to go, Jerry."

I shout at Anh, "I won't be late, honey. Take care of yourself."

"I'll be okay, Mom. Bao will be home from baseball practice in a little while. Have fun."

We walk out to Jerry's car, a medium sized Mercedes sedan. He holds the car door open for me and closes it when I'm inside.

As we pull away, he says, "Why don't you tell me about your problem as we go, that way we can concentrate on enjoying dinner?"

I stare out the window at the setting sun painting the San Gabriel Mountains pink and think about it. Do I really want him to know all the gory details? I kick myself, mentally. Why did I get him to ask me out if I didn't?

"It's about Mel and me."

"That's what I imagined. What's the problem?"

"I don't know if he's the man I really want to marry."

"Isn't it a little late to have any doubts about that?"

"I know, but I don't want to marry a man who only thinks about money."

"You have to admit that money is important in a marriage."

"It is, but love is just as important to me."

"Doesn't Mel love you?"

"He says he does, but saying it isn't enough. Besides, he's been lying to me."

"Hmmm," is his only reply.

I interpret his response as pensive and not mocking. I wait for more from him.

"What kind of lies are we talking about?"

"Mainly, his divorce. He's already admitted he lied about that. He's not getting a divorce. Now he says he's due to inherit some big money if he doesn't divorce her."

"And, he expects you to wait for her to die, is that it?"

"Yes."

"Do you love him?"

This question is the one I was dreading. Did I ever really love Mel? "You have to understand about Mel and me."

"What is there to understand? You either love him or you don't."

"It's not that simple."

"Then, explain it to me."

He's being very patient about this, and I'm searching my soul for some way to tell him about my days as…as a whore. No matter how I try to phrase it, that's what I was. Maybe he'll understand.

"I was Mel's mistress in Viet Nam." I look at Jerry for a reaction, but he's concentrating on the road ahead. I feel the need to add more. "I had a job, but the pay couldn't keep up with inflation. I couldn't find a second job without paying a large bribe, and I didn't have the money for that. My family was slowly starving. I had to do something."

"Go on. I can understand that."

"I made my living by sleeping with the Americans. Basically, I was a whore, and Mel was only one of my clients. Does that shock you?"

"Tuyết, I was never in Viet Nam, but I can imagine how hard it was to live during the war. I won't judge you for that. Please go on."

"I vowed not to have feelings for any of my clients, but Mel somehow broke through that barrier. He said he loved me and offered to help me if I ever made it to America. Naturally, I asked the people at Camp Pendleton to find him when I got here. He was at March Air Force Base near Riverside, and he came immediately. I was glad to see him, and he said he was hoping I'd find my way back to him someday. He's been so good to us. He paid for all of the things I needed to get my start here."

"So, you feel obligated to him. Is that it?"

"Yes, but it's more than that. He said he loves me and wants to marry me, and I do feel something toward him, but…"

"But you're not sure it's love?"

"It's not the same feeling I had for Chinh, but I thought I might come to love him the same way once we were married."

"You were his mistress in Viet Nam, are you sexually involved with him now?"

"Yes, but I only agreed to it after he said he'd divorce his wife and marry me. I thought it would only be a short wait, but he kept stretching it out and giving me excuses. Now I know he lied about it. He never filed for divorce."

"You still haven't answered my question. Do you love him?"

The car falls silent for a long time as we speed down the 405 toward LA. Jerry doesn't press me, but I feel the crush of the silence demanding an answer.

"I'm not sure. I don't know if I'm expecting too much from American men. Maybe they're all like Mel?"

He seems to stifle a laugh before he speaks again.

"I can assure you we're not all like Mel. I know I'm not like that. If you were my fiancée, you wouldn't have any doubt about my love. I'd show you I love you in every way possible. Now tell me if you love him."

"No. I don't think I do. I'll always be grateful for his help. We could never have made it without him, but I don't love him. Am I being ungrateful if I leave him now?"

"You can always be grateful to him even if you don't love him. What happens to you and your children if you don't have his support?"

"My job at the Kozy Korner isn't quite enough yet. I'd have to find a second job doing something."

"Would you let me help you?"

It's a very tempting offer, but it would be just another "Mel" situation. "No, Jerry. I don't want to jump from one obligational relationship to another one just like it."

"I don't mean with money. I mean by helping you find a better paying job, like as a cashier or a clerk in one of my dealerships."

"Those would all be day jobs, and I'd probably need a car. They'd have to pay a lot more than the Kozy Korner if I'd have to have a car."

"If something comes up I'll let you know. As for a car, I can help with that too, but my advice to you right now would be to dump Mel as soon as possible. He sounds like a real jerk."

I saw this coming, but it still hits me hard. I know that's what I need to do, but I dread doing it. Changing the subject is the only strategy open to me now.

"Thanks, Jerry. Let's talk about something else."

He exhales audibly. "I was hoping we could lighten things up a bit. What else would you like to talk about?"

"Do you have a woman in your life now?"

He snorts in response to the query. "I did, but she was expecting me to stay with my father's firm. She dumped me when I quit."

"What does your father do?"

"He's Walter H. Warren of Walter H. Warren and Associates, one of the largest investment firms in Los Angeles. His company handles a lot of big movie mogul accounts. He's filthy rich."

"Oh, I see. Daddy would make you a vice president, or something equally rewarding, is that it?"

"Yeah, I went to work for him right out of UCLA."

"Sounds like it would have been perfect for you."

"Perfect, except I was working for my father. I want to make it on my own."

"Is this job 'making it'?"

"Not quite. I stood it with his outfit for five years then took a job just like this one with Ford. The Ford position was a dead end, but it landed me this job with Mercedes. I've been at it for about a year in this area. Before that I was in the San Francisco office. The big boys assure me I can get a job at North American headquarters after this. From there I can work my way up to some really big money."

"Hmm, ambitious, eh?"

"What are your ambitions?"

"To find a husband who loves me and provides for me so I don't have to work anymore."

"And, you thought you had that with Mel."

"I did once, but not now."

"Well, here I am, a free and single guy whose only intention is to buy you a great meal. Speaking of which, we're here."

He turns off the freeway and up to a modestly-sized restaurant with parking in the rear. It's a little up-scale from the Mexican places Mel took me to in Westminster, but I don't think I'm overdressed.

An Hispanic lady leads us to a table. After we're seated and provided with water and menus, Jerry begins, "Tell me about Viet Nam."

Before I can answer the waiter arrives asking for drinks.

"Would you like your usual Chivas and water?" Jerry asks.

"Why don't you order whatever goes with a Mexican dinner," I reply

"Bring us two Dos Equis, please," Jerry says.

"What's 'Dos Equis'?" I ask

"It's a Mexican beer. You'll like it. Tell me more about Viet Nam," Jerry says.

"Viet Nam is such a beautiful country, too beautiful to be torn apart by war. I imagine it's starting to get beautiful again by now. Nature has a way of hiding its scars quickly. It was so green. I've never seen anything that green here in the States. Sometimes I miss it very much and want to go back, but I couldn't live under the communists."

"What about the people? How did they feel about the war?"

"Most of them didn't want the war, but they didn't want the communists either. We had a good life even though we didn't have much money. You never got the true story here in America. Your press was so biased against the war they painted a very ugly picture of us. What they called graft and corruption was our way of life. Your government here is just as 'corrupt' as ours was. The only difference is your graft is well hidden while ours was out in the open."

"How did you get out of the country?" he asks.

I shudder, recalling that horrible day, and he notices.

"You don't have to talk about it if you don't want to."

"No, it's alright. One my neighbors, really my best friend, helped. She talked her husband into taking us along in his helicopter. We drove to the helicopter in a truck with armed men in the back. They had to kill people to keep them from jumping on, but that was only the start. The gunners in the helicopter had to kill many more to keep the mob away. Even after we were aboard and lifting off, people grabbed the skids, hoping to escape. The gunners crushed their fingers with rifle butts and let them fall to their deaths. I was terribly frightened, and the children were crying so hard I couldn't console them, but we made it to an American aircraft carrier at sea."

Jerry's face is frozen in amazement. He doesn't speak for several seconds.

"Oh my God," was all he could manage for a moment. He finally recovers.

"I saw some of that on television, but they only showed the choppers landing on the carriers and being pushed over the side. I never realized it was that bad. You're a very brave woman."

The beer arrives, and we pause to order dinner, after Jerry gives me some help understanding some of the Mexican dishes on the menu. I know about tacos and enchiladas, but this menu is more extensive. The waiter suggests carne asada, and we both agree to that.

"What about you, Jerry? Tell me something about yourself."

"I grew up in Bel Air. As I told you, my father owns a big financial firm in Santa Monica, so I went to the best schools then to UCLA. I got a BA in accounting. Walter wanted me to go to Stanford for an MBA, but I thought it was a waste of time when I could just work for him right away and make good money. I told you the rest of the story."

"I guess you travel a lot in your job."

"I'm gone about three fourths of the time, but not often overnight. Most of the time back at the office is spent with paperwork."

The arrival of tortilla chips and alsa stops conversation for a while as we dig into the spicy sauce with our corn chips.

The waiter brings more chips, and Jerry speaks, "Tell me more about your Vietnamese husband, Tuyét."

"He was a helicopter pilot, and I was always afraid for him. They lost a lot of helicopters during the war, but he was only wounded once, and that wasn't serious. He said he had a charmed life because of me. I loved him very much, but he's dead now. I miss him, but I have to go on with my life."

"And, you thought Mel was the way to do that?"

"I was sure of that until I found out he was lying about the divorce."

The entrees arrive and stop conversation for the moment as the waiter asks if the food's to our liking.

During dinner Jerry changes the subject. "Was Southern California much of a change from Viet Nam? I mean, as far as climate's concerned."

"Not that much. It's cooler here in the summer and about the same in the winter. Maybe a little cooler. I think that's why our people settle here. In Viet Nam, I used to think sixty degrees was cold. When the smog lifts, and you can see the mountains, I love to look at the snow on the mountain tops. It's my name, after all, and I'd never seen it before moving here."

"It can be very beautiful, like you. Here's to a beautiful lady." Jerry raises his glass in a toast, and I respond in kind.

We both take a sip and resume the meal.

After the waiter clears away the plates and we refuse dessert, Jerry orders an after-dinner drink, and we continue the conversation.

"The food was excellent, Jerry."

"It's better at Chez Jacques, and a woman as beautiful as you should eat someplace like that every night."

I laugh. "You are so romantic, giving such charming compliments. I can't believe some woman hasn't snapped you up by now."

"I know a woman who could snap me up in a heartbeat." He looks directly into my eyes, and I see a sincerity in his gaze I haven't experienced since Chinh. He means what he says, and I'm sad to turn him down.

"Jerry, you're a good man, and I might come to love you, but I'm too old for you." This seems to revive him a bit.

"You are not. I'm 36, and I know you're younger than that."

"I guess I shouldn't tell you, but that's my age too."

"I don't believe it."

"You've seen Bao. He's 15. I was not a child bride, Jerry."

"I don't care how old you are. I still think you're the most beautiful woman I've ever seen, and not just on the outside."

"Thank you." He takes my hand in his and smiles so warmly I almost want to let him love me forever. "I think you need to take me home now, please.

He pays the check, and we leave. The drive to my apartment is consumed with funny stories about Jerry's Mercedes customers. He walks me to my door.

"Goodnight, Tuyết. I want you to know that you can rely on me for anything that may come up in the future. All you have to do is call."

"Thank you, Jerry. I'm grateful for that."

"Is a goodnight kiss too much to ask?" he says.

His eyes seem to sparkle in the dim light of the entryway, and his lips seem so inviting, but I turn away. "Yes, I'm still engaged to Mel, you know."

"I know. Goodnight, Tuyết, but please keep my phone number."

"Goodnight, Jerry. I will."

Chapter 21

The next morning I'm surprised to hear the doorbell just after the children leave for school. I open it to find a statuesque redhead dressed in a very fashionable business outfit and wearing expensive jewelry. The professional aura is only spoiled by a shoddy job on her makeup and the motion of her jaw as it works on some chewing gum.

"You Snow?" she asks.

"Yes, may I help you with something?" I answer automatically just as I would at the Kozy Korner, though I have no idea who this woman is.

"I'm Veronica Howell. We have something in common, honey, and we need to talk."

"I don't know you. What could we possibly have in common?"

"How about Mel Jenkins, honey," she says.

"Mel? Are you related to him?" I instantly know it's a foolish question. This is not about a family matter, I'm sure.

She throws back her head and laughs. "That's a good one. I wish I was." She regains her composure before continuing. "No, we ain't related." She looks past me and says, "I don't think you want me to explain this standing here in the doorway. Can I come in?"

I'm beginning to have an idea what this is all about. She seems to have some knowledge of Mel, but how she knows is a mystery. My brain spins trying to make sense of this, but I know the only way to do that is to let her say her piece.

"Yes, please come in." I lead her into the living room, and she takes a seat on the sofa. I sit in a chair across from her. I decide to be civil, but also decide to keep up my guard.

"This won't take long," she says. "It wasn't hard to find you. Mel didn't do a very good job of covering his tracks. I know he's a womanizer, but he said he'd given all that up since he met me. Lately, I figured he was at it again, and tracked him down to you."

Now I know beyond all doubt she's about to convince me to dump Mel. "You mean...?"

Before I can finish she answers, "Jeez, do I have to spell it out? Honey, we're both screwing the same man. He has a Harley-Davidson tattoo on the left cheek of his ass, hasn't he?"

I sit back in my chair smiling. It's not hard to believe he's having sex with other women after lying about the divorce.

"You're taking this pretty calmly," she says.

"Miss Howell, I know Mel's a liar, and it doesn't surprise me that he's having affairs with other women. The only thing I'm curious about is how did you find out about me?"

"Mel quit coming to see me on Sundays and gave some lame excuse about having to see his wife each time. I staked out his house one Sunday and followed him here. I saw him go into this apartment, and someone who lived here told me it was Miss Snow's place. I've been trying to find the nerve to knock on your door ever since."

"How long have you and Mel...?"

"Been screwing?" she interrupts. "About four years now. I met him at a party just after he got back from Nam. It wasn't hard to get in bed with him, as you probably know. We hit it off right away. He told me he loved me and would marry me as soon as his wife died. He even gave me this engagement ring." She flashes a diamond at me.

I interrupt. "He's told me the same story and made me the same promise." I extend my left hand to show her my ring. The two are identical.

"I figured as much. Was he screwing you in Viet Nam?"

"Yes, we were together for almost his whole tour."

"I thought so. He never admitted to having a mistress in Viet Nam, but I couldn't see a horny bastard like him toughing it out for a whole year over there."

"He's been very good to me. We'd never have made it in America without him."

"Hey, he's got his good parts as well as the bad."

"I think I only saw the good side of him in Viet Nam. He didn't have to lie to me there."

She licks her lips and clears her throat. "Say, you got anything to drink?"

"Certainly. Would you like iced tea or something a bit stronger?"

"You got any bourbon in the place?"

"No, just Scotch. Is that all right?"

"Okay, I'll take some Scotch and Coke."

She doesn't move to help me, but I didn't expect her to. I mix her drink and carry it to the coffee table. She takes a tentative sip.

"Good, you didn't make it too strong. Mind if I smoke?"

"No, go ahead." I move to find something to use for an ash tray as she retrieves a pack of cigarettes and a lighter from her purse.

"Now that I have your news, I'll give him back his ring the next time I see him," I say as I put down a saucer for her ashes.

She laughs. "I came here to ask you to do just that, but I guess I didn't have to."

"I'm not willing to wait on his wife to die, and I told him so. He said he'd divorce her, but he lied about that. I'm through with him."

"He's only strung you along for a little while. I've been waitin' on the bitch to die for four years, but I found out he's lying about that too."

"What do you mean?"

"She's not in any nursing home suffering from ministrokes. She's in Las Vegas living the good life off the money she inherited from her parents. She divorced him in '74."

"How did you find out?"

"I had a private detective check out the story. Cost me $800, but it was worth it."

"Why didn't you leave him then?"

"I love him in spite of all his lies. I don't need the fictitious money he says he's going to get when she dies. I'm a widow, and my first husband left me pretty well off. I never told Mel about my money. I wanted to be sure he wasn't after me for it. Besides, I love the big dumb bastard."

It's hard for me to imagine a woman knowing about the lies and loving him anyway. Is she really that desperate to have a man in her life that she'll accept him on those terms? It's beyond my comprehension.

"And, you never confronted him with this?"

"I was going to do that and tell him we could have the good life on my money if he'd marry me, but then you came along. I needed to know what kind of problem I had, so I looked you up." She snuffs out the cigarette and immediately lights another.

"You don't need to worry about me. I'm dumping him as soon as I can. Are you sure I'm the only competition?"

"It wouldn't surprise me if he has more women besides us, but I don't think so. Not even a professional liar like him could keep that many balls in the air at one time."

We've exhausted the subject of Mel and me, but she doesn't seem ready to leave. We sit in silence for a moment as the room begins to fill with a blue smog of cigarette smoke. The odor has a familiar tang. I've smelled it on Mel's clothes from time to time, but I always assumed it was from his work. I shake my head in wonderment at Mel's audacity. "What made him think he could get away with this?"

She laughs and takes a sip of her drink. "Mel likes to watch old movies too much. I think that's where he got the idea about the wife in the nursing home."

"That's what one of my customers at the bar said."

She laughs again as she stubs out her second cigarette and lights a third. "You got any kids?"

"Two, a boy 15 and a girl 12."

She sets her drink on the coffee table and stares at the wall behind me.

"I envy you that. My first husband couldn't get me pregnant, and I'm too old for kids now."

I see the pain in her expression, and I can understand how she feels. What would I do without Bao and Anh?

"And, you still want Mel in spite of his lies?"

"Want him? Honey, I want him so bad my hair hurts. I do love him, and I'm glad you're dumping him." She looks at her watch and stubs out her cigarette. "Sorry, I gotta go. I'm meeting Mel for lunch today, but I won't tell him about our little conversation."

I stand, and she downs the remains of her drink in one gulp. "Thank you for coming by," I say.

"My pleasure, honey. I'm just glad to know you're out of the picture now."

We embrace briefly before she goes. I open every window in the place and leave the door wide open to clear out the smoke stench.

*

Mel calls me on Thursday.

"Hey, I can take the afternoon off today. Can I come over?"

"Yes, we need to finish the conversation we started in the bar."

"Oh, sounds serious."

"I'll tell you when you get here. We can't do this over the phone."

"All right, I'll be there around one."

The rest of the morning I rehearse my speech a dozen times, each time imagining a different reaction from Mel. I'm ready when he comes in the door.

"Where's the fancy negligee?" he asks, trying to lighten up the cold atmosphere.

"Sit down, Mel. We have to talk."

"I know, but what's so serious?"

"It's about Veronica Howell."

You'd think I hit him with a baseball bat. His eyes pop wide open and his jaw drops an inch.

"Who's she?" he asks.

I could almost believe him.

"Don't try to con me, Mel. She was here Monday, and she knows about your tattoo."

"Oh, now I remember. It was a long time ago, before you came here. I had an affair with her for a few months, but I broke it off in '73. I haven't seen her since, honest."

"Just like you were pursuing a divorce, is that it?"

"Hey, I'm telling you the truth now. I haven't screwed her in three years."

"Why would she come see me now if you left her three years ago?"

"She's crazy. She just wants me back as a meal ticket."

"She says she doesn't care about money just wants to marry you."

His face falls into a grim expression. "She's a hooker. I found out about her being a call girl, and that's why I left her."

"I don't believe you, Mel."

"Why would I lie to you?"

"Why did you lie about the divorce?"

"I mean about this."

I see the pleading expression on his face, and I'm almost ready to forgive him, but my good sense takes hold. "Veronica also told me your wife isn't in a nursing home."

His expression hardens, and his mouth takes on a grim set. I don't know if it's an act or real.

"That lying bitch."

"Then take me to see your wife, Mel."

He suddenly becomes placid. "I can't do that. She's not allowed to have visitors except for family."

"How convenient. You could at least let me talk to the administrator of the home to verify she's there."

"He wouldn't do that. California law says he can't divulge any information on his patients."

"Again, how convenient." I'm seething inside, but I use all my self-control to stay calm.

A period of silence follows. Mel is obviously going to stick to his story. He's admitted to one lie but only after I confronted him with evidence from sources he couldn't refute. I have to balance my gratitude against a mountain of lies. The scales fall heavily against gratitude.

"I'm sorry, Mel. It's over. I don't want to see you again." The words come hard, but they seem to hit him even harder.

"Oh my God, Snow. You can't be serious. After all I've done for you."

I have to look away. I can't face him. I pull his ring from my finger and hand it back to him. "Here, I mean it."

He doesn't take the ring, and I place it on the coffee table before him. He looks down at it and begins to cry.

"Turn off the crocodile tears, Mel. Just tell me why you dragged Veronica along with the same story you gave me."

He pulls out a handkerchief and wipes his eyes. "I love Veronica, but when you came back into my life, you rekindled my love for you. I didn't know what to do. I'd been holding off Veronica with the nursing home story, so it came in handy again for you. I guess I always knew I'd have to decide between you, but I couldn't. Now I guess you've decided for me."

I look at the man who once stood proudly in a blue uniform. I had such hopes for Mel and me.

"I think you'd better leave now, Mel."

He rises, holds his arms out to me, and puts on his best lost puppy expression. "One last kiss…please."

The nerve of this guy. He knows exactly what he's done, but he still wants me to think he's worth my time.

"No, Mel. We're finished. Just leave."

He drops his arms and goes out the door, slamming it closed behind him. I can hear his voice even through the closed door.

"Starve, bitch!"

I expected anger, but this reaction is disappointing even for Mel. I plop on the sofa.

"Damn all American men. Is sex all you want…all you ever think about?" I know he either can't hear me or doesn't want to hear me, but it feels good to shout it out.

I must be foolish to think I can find a husband like Chinh here? I decide that pursuing this route to happiness is a dead end. I'll just have to make a good life here on my own.

I look around at our shabby excuse for an apartment and decide a better place is the first step toward a new beginning. I'll ask Luigi for a raise and find a second job then look for a new apartment. Leaving this behind will sever all ties with a bleak past.

A knock on the door interrupts my thoughts. I look through the peep hole to make sure it's not Mel and see a very nervous Tam from next door. I open for her, and she rushes in to embrace me.

"I hear much loud talk and slammed door. You okay?" she says.

"It's alright. I just broke up with my fiancé."

Her expression turns from concern to consolation. "I so sorry. He look like good man."

"He wasn't. He lied to me about everything, and he was seeing another woman while he was engaged to me."

"Oh, he very bad man. Good thing you send him away."

I close the door and she takes a seat on the sofa. She's all ears and eager to hear the gory details. I mentally shrug off my inhibitions. Why not let her hear it all?

"Can I make you some tea?" I ask.

"Tea be very good."

I put on the kettle and return to the living area. "Mel and I were together in Viet Nam."

Tam interrupts, "I know. He co van for husband."

I smile, and she seems to understand. "Ahh, he more than that, eh?"

"Yes, after Chinh was killed, I thought he might be my next husband. He said he loved me while we were together in Viet Nam, and I assumed he'd still feel the same way about me now. I naturally turned to him for help here, and he became our sponsor in return for resuming our relationship."

"Why he not marry you now?"

"He said his wife was in a nursing home, and he couldn't divorce her because she controlled a large sum of money. If she died as his wife, he'd get the money. If he divorced her, the money would go to her sister. At least, that was the story he fed me. It was all a lie."

"How you know he lie?"

"A few days ago, a woman visited me. She's also been in a relationship with Mel. She told me the truth about his wife. She's not in a nursing home. She divorced him years ago. I confronted Mel with this, and he tried lying again. This time I knew he was lying and broke it off. That's what you heard us arguing about."

The kettle whistles, and I make tea.

*

The children come in just as Tam is leaving. She greets them in Vietnamese, but quickly switches to English before vanishing into her apartment.

I embrace them as they dump their things on the coffee table.

"We're hungry," Bao says.

"I know. Come into the kitchen, and I'll fix you something. We need to talk about something while you eat."

When they're seated and digging into their food, I begin, "You know I was going to marry Mel, don't you?"

Bao replies with a mouth full of sandwich, "Yes, Mother."

"Well, we're not going to be married now."

Both react with quizzical expressions, and Anh speaks first, "Why not?"

"He's been lying to me for a long time on things that are very important to me. I asked him about them today, and he admitted he's been lying. I can't marry him now, and I told him so."

"Gee, Mother, I thought you two were really in love," Bao says.

"I did love him until I found out about his lying. Now, he's destroyed that love."

"I'm going to miss him," Anh says. "He seemed like a nice man." Tears begin to form in her eyes, and I move to embrace her.

"It's alright, darling. I thought he was going to be nice too. Sometimes people are not what they seem to be. I'm sorry you had to learn this lesson so early in life, but it's a good thing to know. Many people will try to deceive you as you grow up. You must be very careful about who you trust with your love."

"I'll miss our trips to McDonalds," Bao adds.

"Yes, we will have to be very careful with our money. Mel was helping out, but that's gone now. Maybe we can do McDonalds once in a while, but not as often as with Mel."

I dry Anh's tears with her napkin, and she seems to recover.

"It's okay, Mother, I just thought we might have a father again," Anh says.

"We will, someday, I promise, but for now, we'll have to go on as best we can. We must learn to rely on each other."

Chapter 22

It takes some cajoling topped with a hollow threat to quit, but Luigi finally gives in and makes me an assistant manager. It's enough of a raise to almost replace what Mel was giving me. The next task is to find a second job I can fit into my Kozy Korner schedule, one that pays enough for us to upgrade our standard of living.

None of the local shops seem to be hiring at the moment, and the jobs advertised in the paper either require experience I don't have, or they're too far away to commute on a moped. Each day I pass the Bàn Tay Đẹp nail salon, but they never post any notice of needing extra help. Nails are something I think I do very well, so I stop in one day, hoping I can talk them into hiring another manicurist. The shop has four work stations, but only two are functioning, and two women are waiting to be served.

I approach one of the workers and ask for the manager in English. The manicurist shakes her head and ask if I still understand Vietnamese. I answer in Vietnamese, and she calls out to the back room of the shop, "Miss Hoa, someone to see you."

A woman in her 40s appears, wearing a lovely blue ao dai.

Judging by the manicurist's lack of English and the frustrated expressions of the waiting American customers, I assume they need a translator badly.

"Do you need anyone to work here during the daytime? I speak excellent English." I ask in Vietnamese.

Her face brightens at the question. She waves a hand at the waiting women, both of whom are Americans. "As you see, I am beginning to gain a lot of American customers. They like the way we do nails, but they have trouble communicating with my Vietnamese women. I could use someone who speaks English well. Have you done nails before?"

"Not professionally, but I do my own, and I've helped other women with theirs." I hold out my hands for inspection.

Hoa looks them over carefully. "You do a good job. I'll give you a trial period of one month. If you're reliable, and the customers like you, I'll make it permanent."

"You don't have to worry about me being reliable. I'll be here every day."

She motions for me to join her in the back room. Once we're away from the front area of the shop, she switches to English. "I have trouble with these women. They don't show up for work and call in saying they have a sick child. I'm often down to one girl, and I have to do nails myself to keep the customers happy. You'd pick up for one of them when they aren't here and take on any new customers for yourself. When could you work?"

"I work at the Kozy Korner in the evenings, but I'm free most of the day. I just need to be home to prepare dinner for my children before I go to work at five o'clock."

"Perfect. I could use you from ten to three every day if you could do that."

That's five hours. If I'm going to give up that much more of my day, I need to know it will be worth my time. "How much does it pay?" I ask.

"You get paid for each job by the customer. We charge $8.00 for a manicure or a pedicure. I take half because I furnish the shop space and the supplies. You get to keep any tips."

I figure an hour a customer, and at least three each day. That's $12.00 a day before taxes, maybe $60 a week? It isn't that much, but anything will help. "That sounds good. Can I start tomorrow?"

"Yes, come back to my office, and we'll fill out your paperwork."

*

The nail work is brisk after the customers find I speak English fluently. The other two women resent me, at first. I'm constantly given to understand what customer belongs to which manicurist. Most of those women are glad to wait for their usual manicurist even though I'm sitting idle. I also take over for the missing women on the days they don't show up. The other girls soften a bit after I help them with translating the customer's

English. One wants me to give her English lessons, but I refuse citing two kids and two jobs.

*

With my raise at the Kozy Korner and the new money from the nail shop, I've replaced what Mel was giving me with enough additional that I begin to look for a new apartment. Bui's place still has a lingering aura of Mel about it, and we're all beginning to feel claustrophobic with the miniscule closet space and phone-booth-sized bathroom.

A brief ride West on Bolsa leads me to a new apartment building under construction and nearly finished. I find the rental office and park outside.

An older Vietnamese woman greets me in Vietnamese after I enter.

"Please, do you speak English?" I ask in Vietnamese.

"Not good. We speak Vietnamese, please?" she asks.

I continue in Vietnamese. "I saw you're building new apartments. When will they be open?"

"We think in three or four weeks. Are you interested in renting?"

"Yes, if I can afford it. How much for two bedrooms?" Bao needs a real bed instead of that sofa-bed. Anh can continue to share a room with me. I know three bedrooms will be out of my price range.

"Let me show you the floor plans."

She opens a binder to a diagram showing a two-story layout. The ground floor is all one room divided into a living room and kitchen by a long breakfast bar. There's a laundry room and half bath off the kitchen, and a small patio outside the sliding doors forming one wall of a small dinette area. Stairs lead up to a hallway with a bedroom at each end. One of the bedrooms is large enough for Anh and me to share. It has a full bath and ample closet space. There's another closet in the hallway and one for the water heater and the heater/air conditioner combination. A full bath next to the second bedroom completes the upper floor. A plan of the entire complex shows a large swimming pool surrounded by a concrete deck.

"This unit will rent for $400 a month, and we have two left."

It's $100 a month more than I'm paying now, but I'll have money left over to cover the monthly payments for the furniture we'll need. I hate going into debt, but the chance for a better apartment is too good to pass up. We've been stuffed into that converted motel too long.

"What about utilities?" I ask.

"We pay for the gas and water, but you pay for electricity and phone."

The extra costs involved will be a strain on my budget, but Bao can take a summer job to help out. I still have some money left from what Mel gave me back when we started out, and I really want to move into a nicer place.

"I'll take it."

"We require a small deposit of $100 that is refundable if you change your mind. The lease is for one year, and you sign that when you move in. A security deposit of one month's rent is also due at that time, but your $100 is applied to that."

I write her a check and ride back to our apartment wondering all the way if I've taken on too much.

*

The next morning, Jerry calls.

"How are you doing?" he asks.

"I'm fine, but I can't talk long. I'm due at my nail salon job in two hours, and I need to finish getting ready."

"Nail salon? Did you take on a second job? I thought Mel was supporting you so you didn't need a second job."

"That's all over now. I'm not engaged to Mel anymore."

"Whoo hooo!" He holds the phone away from his mouth, but I'm sure they could hear his celebration in San Diego. "That's the best news I've heard since the draft ended, but I hate to see you having to work two jobs."

"I pass the nail salon every day on my way to the Kozy Korner. It's only part time, and it meshes well with my main job. Besides, Luigi made me an assistant manager, and gave me a nice raise."

"If you got a raise, why do you need a second job?"

"I need the second job so we can afford to move into a better apartment. This place reminds me too much of Mel." I'm sure he hears the disgust in my voice, though I'm trying to stay civil.

"I know what you mean. Have you found anyplace yet?"

"There's a new bunch of apartments opening up in a few weeks, and I put a deposit on a two-bedroom unit."

"Let me know when you're ready to move. I'll take some time off and help you. You'll need a truck of some kind, and I can talk one of my dealers into loaning me one. Just give me a few days' notice."

"Thanks, I'll keep you posted, but I really have to go now."

"Is it all right if I call you again for a date?"

The excitement in his voice causes me to smile. I know he wants to bed me, but it's more like a schoolboy lusting after his teacher. Mel's approach was pure business compared to Jerry.

"Yes, but please give me some time to settle into our new place before you do."

"I'll do that. Would you mind if our date included the kids?"

"No, why do you ask?"

"There's a special day coming up next month, and I think the kids would like it a lot. You may have to take off one evening to do it. Could you manage that?"

"If I have enough notice. What kind of date are we talking about?"

"I want it to be a surprise, if that's okay."

"I guess so, just give us plenty of warning. The children have their own schedules too."

"I'll give you plenty of notice when I know the exact date. I'll call you then."

We say goodbye, and I wonder what the date could be.

*

I tell Tam, our neighbor, about the new apartments, but she has some news for me.

"My husband say we move soon too. He want place closer to work. We go look for new place this weekend."

This eases my mind a lot. I wasn't looking forward to leaving her alone here.

"I'm glad. Please let me know if you do find something. I'll let you know our new address as soon I have it. I also plan to have a phone put in so we can stay in touch."

"I like that very much. We still be good friends."

She makes some tea, and we spend an hour talking about our days back in Viet Nam.

Chapter 23

Jerry walks into the Kozy Korner Wednesday night. I place a mug of **Miller Lite** in front of him and start the conversation before he has a chance to say "hello".

"I have some good news. The lady at the apartment called and said we could move in early. The section our new apartment is in just finished construction. I was just going to call you about that truck you mentioned. Could you possibly make it Monday? I've got Monday off at both the nail salon and the Kozy Korner."

He smiles, takes a sip of beer and thinks for a moment before pulling out a pocket calendar.

"I'll have to re-arrange some appointments, but that shouldn't be a problem. I've got some time off coming, so that's not a problem either. Sure, what time?"

"Is 9:00 AM too early?"

"Not for helping you out. How big a truck will you need?"

"We don't have that much in the apartment. The furniture belongs to Bui, except for the sofa bed."

"I think I can get a small van. If none of my dealers has one, I'll rent one."

"That's a lot of expense--"

Another customer calls for service before I can protest further. He wants a drink that requires considerable time to mix, and when I turn back, Jerry's gone.

A half-finished glass of beer sits on top of a five-dollar bill and a note that reads, "See you Monday, Jerry."

*

All week I plan the move. Knowing I have to buy some furniture, I dig out Mel's ring and take it to a pawn shop on Bolsa Avenue.

The pawnbroker looks it over carefully using a jeweler's loupe and tests the metal on a touchstone. "I can give you $100.00 for it," he says.

"Is that all?"

"Hey, it's only gold plated, and the stone has a lot of flaws and poor color. That's all it's worth to me. I have to have some room for profit on my end," he says.

Knowing what I now know about Mel, it's no surprise. I think about Veronica but decide she doesn't care about the ring's value and doesn't need to know any different.

"I'll have to take it, I guess."

He counts out the money, and I go on my way.

*

Jerry calls on Friday to confirm his availability, and Monday morning he arrives with a medium-sized van. He and Bao load up what few possessions we have and the four of us drive to the new apartment.

I open the door to the fresh construction smell which is such a contrast to the old taxi cab aroma of Mr. Bui's places. Jerry and I, along with the children, inspect the place before unloading.

"Nice place," Jerry says. "But, you're going to need a lot of furniture."

"I know. I found a furniture store that'll give me a year to pay for the furniture, and the interest rate isn't too bad. They're going to deliver everything this afternoon."

Jerry looks at me for a moment before he speaks. "Look, I know you don't want another 'Mel' relationship, but I'd like to help you with this?"

"No, Jerry. Thank you for offering, but I want to do this on my own."

The children notice the tension. Bao says, "Hey Ahn, why don't you and I go check out the pool?"

Ahn gives him a quizzical look. "We haven't unpacked our swim suits yet."

Bao nods toward the door. "I don't mean to swim. We just need to see what kind of pool it is."

Ahn gets the message. "Oh, yeah, we do need to look it over. Do you mind, Mother?"

"No, you children go ahead."

They leave us alone to argue.

Jerry starts the discussion. "I respect you for wanting to be independent, but you're working at two jobs now to afford this place. How are you going to make payments on furniture on top of that?"

"It's only for a year. We'll have to do without some things for a while, and Bao will have to take a summer job, but we'll manage."

"After you told me about your escape from Viet Nam, I knew you were a very brave woman. Now I know you're also a very stubborn woman. Haven't you known me long enough to realize I'm not Mel?"

His voice rises a bit on the last statement, and I sense his frustration. "I think I know that, but I don't want to become indebted to you. How do I know you won't demand repayment in the same currency as Mel?"

He sighs heavily and plops down on the old sofa-bed. "I guess you don't, and nothing I say will convince you otherwise. I guess we just need to spend more time together."

I sit down next to him, and he starts to put his arm around me but thinks twice about that and pulls back. He continues, "Well, maybe we could get better acquainted two weeks from Tuesday. That's the date I was telling you about. You and the kids and me on an adventure."

I turn and look at him. "What kind of adventure?"

"Don't worry. It's not dangerous, and the kids will get a big kick out of it. Just see if you can get off that night."

"This sounds very mysterious."

"I want it to be a surprise, that's all."

"Okay, I'll see if I can get off. By the way, how should we dress for this adventure?"

"Just casual. It's nothing formal."

I stand up. "We need to get the food into the refrigerator before it spoils."

Jerry stays until the new furniture is arranged to my satisfaction then says goodbye.

"Don't forget, two weeks from next Tuesday," he shouts as the van pulls away.

*

The big day finally arrives, and we're eager to find out the nature of Jerry's surprise. The children assail him as he comes through the door.

"Where are we going, Mr. Warren?" Anh asks.

"Yeah, what's the big surprise?" Bao echoes.

Jerry's face takes on a proud expression, and a broad smile shows his white teeth. "That's a secret, you'll know when we get there. Come on, we don't want to be late."

He herds us into his car and turns East on Bolsa. He threads his way through the city streets to a huge parking lot.

Bao knows where we are at once. "Wow, this is Disneyland."

"Disneyland?" Ahn echoes.

"Yes, its Mercedes Benz night," Jerry shouts. "We get free admission and we can ride all of the rides free. Come on, let's get started."

We pass into the park where we all stand, mouths agape. It is a wonderland.

All evening we intersperse exciting rides with marvelous food and snacks. Jerry often has to explain the significance of the ride themes, but they would have been very impressive even without his synopses of the movies they are based upon.

I was not so much concentrating on the rides as observing Jerry with the children. He treats Bao like an adult and yet acts like a protective father with Anh. He high fives' Bao and embraces Anh. The only frightening ride is the Matterhorn, and he prepares Anh for it so the impact is more excitement than terror. He almost ignores me, but I understand. This outing is for the children.

As we walk to the car when it's all over, the children re-live every adventure only asking for our concurrence in the wonder of each one. We reach our new apartment, and the children rush upstairs to give Jerry and me some time together. He leads me out by the pool.

The full moon shines through the row of trees at one end of the pool, casting lacy black shadows on the pool deck. We sit down there.

"You were wonderful with the children today," I say.

"They're good kids."

"It surprises me that a man of your age would be comfortable with children."

"They come with you, don't they?"

"Yes, but..."

"No buts. Even if they were spoiled brats, and I had to discipline them until they were human, I'd take on that task to have you."

"You're talking like you want to marry me."

The statement seems to surprise him, but his shocked expression melts into a broad smile.

"That first night I saw you at the bar, a door opened in my heart I never knew was there. Everything in my being screamed at me to go through that door. I knew that if I walked away without getting to know you, I'd miss my best chance for happiness. I'm so glad I didn't walk away."

"So, it was only because you thought I was beautiful that you stayed around?" Here it was again. In Viet Nam I was glad of my beauty because it made finding clients easy, but at the end I began to think of my beauty as a curse. Mel's actions here in American only reinforced that feeling. Now, when I thought Jerry was different, he proves to have the same motives, but he continues.

"Any man would want you for your beauty, but since I've come to know you, I've found your beauty goes far beyond good looks. I love you for the proud, independent woman you are. I love you for the way you've raised wonderful children. You've survived a war and adapted to a new country. I've known a lot of women, in college and later, but none of them can compare to you. They wanted me to set them up in life with all the good things just because they consented to marry me. You're not that kind. You've never asked how much money I make, or how much I have in the bank. I know you want security, but I also think you'd be happy no matter how much money we had as long as we were together. I know you haven't known me long enough, but I'd marry you tomorrow if you'd say 'yes'."

A warm, sweet wave of relief washes over me. Dare I begin to think of Jerry as a possible husband? The demon of caution inside my brain forces my response.

"Don't press me on this, Jerry. I do like you, and your actions with the children today only make that feeling stronger, but something inside me says to wait."

"What more can I do to convince you?"

"I don't know. I just feel it's too soon. I haven't even met your parents yet."

"My parents, hmph. I don't think you'd want to meet my parents." He looks away and hangs his head.

"Why not? I'm sure they're nice people." He turns back to me, and his sharp expression startles me a bit.

"Nice, eh? They wouldn't think the same about you."

"Why not?" I think I know the answer to my question, but I hope to be surprised.

"They won't think much of me marrying an Asian woman."

I'm right, but if he truly loves me, he needs to know how I feel about family. "Family is very important to we Vietnamese. I need to meet them if you're going to talk about marriage."

He sits back and sighs. "I understand, but I'd better try the idea out on them first. I know what they're going to say, but I really don't care what they think. I haven't been there in six months. Not since Jacquie's birthday."

"Who's Jacquie, your sister?"

"No, my Mother."

"And you call her by her first name?"

"That's what she wants. I've called her Jacquie ever since I could talk."

I sit back in silence for a moment. It takes me a while to absorb the idea of a child calling its mother by her first name. I realize it's a moot point now and chalk it up to American culture. I'm still appalled by the idea of it being six months since he last saw his parents.

"Okay, I can accept that, but you say you haven't seen your parents in six months? Where do they live?" I expect an answer justifying such a long absence, but Jerry surprises me.

"In Bel Air."

"Bel Air? You can't live more than an hour's drive from Bel Air. This is LA, we've got the freeways, you know. Where do you live?"

My question seems to shock him. His face takes on a sheepish grin as he responds. "Torrance."

"That's terrible. You should honor your parents. They deserve your respect."

"You sound like I should erect a temple, or something. Some parents may deserve that kind of respect, but mine don't."

"Don't be silly. If you don't give them the respect they deserve in life, their spirits will come back to punish you after they die."

He stifles a laugh. "Sorry, did I just hear you say you believe in ghosts?"

"You call them ghosts, but to us they're real. Even Christian Vietnamese honor the spirits of their ancestors. They'll say they don't believe, but they do. They make the sacrifices at Tết Trung Nguyên just like the Buddhists."

"What is that, that tet trung nwen?"

"It's a day when you feed and clothe the spirits of your ancestors who still roam the Earth."

"Wait a minute. How can you feed and clothe a ghost?"

I know he thinks it's silly, but I've learned to let the American attitude roll off my back.

"You set out the food and you burn paper effigies of the things the spirits need, like clothes, money, cars, that kind of thing."

His smothered laughs have turned into a broad smile, and though he still thinks I'm foolish, he's learned that I take the subject seriously.

"Well, I respect your beliefs, even though I don't believe the same way."

"I think we'd better leave it at that." I know he will never see these things the way I do.

He settles back in the couch and brushes back his hair. "Okay, I believe you, but you really don't want to meet my parents."

"Yes, I do. Do they even know about me and you?"

"No, I haven't told them about you." He turns away and exhales sharply.

"Why not?"

"It's none of their business who I want to marry." His response holds a tinge of anger I want to de-fuse as quickly as possible.

"Don't get angry. We haven't discussed marriage seriously yet, but if you do want to marry me, I will need your parents' blessing. At least feel them out about us. I need to know what I'm up against."

He turns back to me and smiles. "I'll go see them this weekend, but don't expect much."

"Please understand. You only have to let me know how high a mountain I would have to climb if I did decide to marry you."

"You'd better buy some good climbing equipment is all I've got to say." He smiles at me with love in his eyes. He's so different from any other man I've met here or in Viet Nam.

He leans his face close to mine. My mind says no, but my heart says it's time to let him kiss me. I surrender to his lips. It's a brief thing. He pulls away quickly.

"I need to get going. I'll have to buy a case or two of **Miller Lite** to steel my nerves before I see Jacquie and Walt."

We both laugh at the joke. We say goodbye, and I watch as he drives away.

Can I feel love for Jerry? I certainly feel more for him than I did for Mel. Marrying Mel was more of an obligation and, I thought, my only chance for happiness. Jerry is different. I almost have the same stirring in my soul for him I had for Chinh. The children like him, and that's very important. I've seen two kinds of American men before Jerry. Mel is one, and the crowd at the Kozy Korner is another. I know I don't want either of those choices. Is Jerry different? Do I love him? I think the answer is yes on both counts.

Chapter 24

I think of Jerry often over the weekend. I'm glad he's seeing his parents, but somewhere inside me a voice keeps reminding me they will probably talk him out of a relationship with a 'foreigner'. I wonder if I'll ever see him again.

He doesn't call on Monday, and I hear a nagging voice deep in my brain shouting, *I told you so.* I go to work ready to blot Jerry out of my memory and consign him to the same Hell as Mel. When he walks into the Kozy Korner that night, I'm certain this is his goodbye speech. I fill a mug with his favorite beer and place it in front of him.

"How did it go?" I've rehearsed several first phrases for this meeting, but none want to come out of the hiding places they've retreated to. He takes a drink of beer before replying, and I feel sure he's just putting off the inevitable.

"Boring. I'd rather have been with you."

Hope raises its head above the dark clouds, but it quickly sinks down again. I don't speak for a moment. From the tone of his voice I know his parents are not receptive to their son loving an Asian woman. I decide to get right to the heart of the matter. "What did they have to say about me?"

"Well, they weren't too happy, but I told you they wouldn't be. They don't like the idea at all, but they've agreed to meet you."

"So, I'm on probation. Is that it?" I can't help my outrage over being considered some kind of lower-class human.

"I understand how you must feel, but it was your idea for me to tell them. I told you, I don't give a damn what they think. I want to marry you, if you'll have me."

"That's a pretty indirect proposal. Even if I wanted to say 'yes', I can't marry you while your parents are opposed to it. I can't explain it. You'll just have to accept it as part of my upbringing."

"Right now, all they're seeing are the stereotypes of Asians. They think you wear a conical straw hat and wade through rice paddies. I hope they'll change their minds once they see what a beautiful, articulate and resourceful woman you are."

"Okay, what else do I need to know?'

"There's not that much you have to know. My father is a demanding bully who's used to getting his way, and I'm his black sheep. Jacquie's just as big a snob as he is. She's an Alabama society girl who married right and never looked back. There's not much else to know about them. They don't like you because you're Vietnamese, and the fact that you tend bar only makes things worse."

"Tending bar is honest work." I feel as if he could see smoke rising from my head. I've worked hard to make a new life here, and his parents attitude rankles.

"Look, Tuyết. I love you, and that's all that matters to me. To Hell with them."

"Don't say such an ugly thing, Jerry. If I agree to marry you, I want to like your parents, and I want them to like me. We Vietnamese value our families. I couldn't live with you, knowing your parents hate me. Maybe you're right. Once they see me in person and get to know me they may change their minds. When can we do this?"

"How about two weeks from this Saturday? Jacquie says that will work for her, and Dad doesn't care. We can have dinner with them at Dan Tana's. That's fashionable enough for Dad and still neutral ground."

"I think I can re-arrange my work schedule. If I can't, I'll let you know. Do you think it would help things if I brought Bao and Anh along?"

"I don't think anything will help, but it might be best if you left them home. My parents can be cruel, and I wouldn't want your kids exposed to that."

"Will it be that bad?"

"You won't believe it until you experience it for yourself. They're snobs of the first order, and they think I'm wasting my life as it is. To them, you're just another one of my big mistakes, but you're the first woman I've ever felt this way about. I love you, and nothing will stand in the way of our happiness, not even my parents."

"Call me next week to set the time."

"I will, but the other reason for my call is I'd like to have a real Vietnamese dinner with you and the kids. What would be a good day for that?"

"Sunday's the only day we could be together as a family."

"Let's make it this Sunday, then. Okay?"

"How authentic do you want this meal to be?"

"No cats or dogs, okay?"

"Don't be such an ass. You know we never use those ingredients, but I'll be sure to fix something I know you'll like." My experience with Americans in Viet Nam and at the Kozy Korner gives me confidence in preparing something to please his pallet.

"I'm just kidding. See you Sunday."

He finishes his beer, and we say goodnight.

I watch him leave. Would I really turn him down if I can't bring his parents around? I don't know. Do I love him? I don't know. Do I want the chance to love him? Definitely. That being the case, the only thing that can keep the relationship meaningful is to impress his parents. I vow to do everything in my power to accomplish that end.

*

Jerry rings the doorbell at noon Sunday, as we'd arranged, and Bao lets him in.

"Come on in, Mr. Warren. Mom's working on dinner." He calls toward the kitchen. "Mom, Mr. Warren's here."

As I walk out of the kitchen area to greet him, he sniffs the air and smiles.

"What's that smell?"

"It's a surprise. Can I fix you a drink?"

"Have you got any **Miller Lite** in the house?"

"In the refrigerator. Sit down, and I'll bring you one."

I deliver a beer and a glass to Jerry and return to the kitchen as Anh comes down the stairs.

"Hi, Mr. Warren. Mom's got a real treat in store for you today."

"I'm looking forward to the meal. Any hints about it? Your mother wouldn't tell me anything."

"Let's just say you'll like everything in it," Anh says.

"Yeah, no dogs or cats," Bao adds.

Jerry laughs at the comment. It's an old supposition where oriental food is concerned.

"One of the guys in the office told me that some Vietnamese eat dogs."

"Not Vietnamese," Anh corrects him. "Those people are 'Montagnards'. They're a different race. They live up in the mountains and don't associate much with the true Vietnamese," Anh explains.

"I've got a lot to learn about your country."

"You already know about my country," Bao says. "We're all going to be Americans pretty soon."

"Of course, I meant your native country. Aren't you proud of your heritage?"

"Yes, we are," Anh says, glaring at her brother. "Bao wants to forget he was ever Vietnamese, but Mom won't let him."

"Good for her!" Jerry says.

Coconut Lemon Grass Chicken

Ingredients:

    2 tablespoons butter
    1 large onion, halved and sliced
    3 cloves garlic, chopped
    1 tablespoon kosher salt, optional
    2 teaspoons freshly ground black pepper
    1 tablespoon sugar
    1 1/2 tablespoons minced fresh ginger
    3 pounds boneless chicken (thighs or breasts), diced
    1 tablespoon minced fresh hot red chili peppers
    4 stalks lemongrass, green tops removed then pale ends finely chopped*

2 tablespoons curry powder
3 tablespoons soy sauce

4 tablespoons fish sauce (nuóc mắm sauce)
4 ounces unsweetened coconut milk

Shaved fresh coconut, for garnish, optional

Directions

Melt the butter in a medium skillet over medium heat. Add the half the onion and all the garlic and cook, stirring frequently, until both begin to soften, about 7 minutes. Add the salt (if using), black pepper, sugar, chopped ginger and chicken. Cook over medium-high heat until the sugar melts and the onion mixture and chicken begin to brown, about 15 minutes.
Add the remaining onion, the chili peppers, lemon grass, curry powder, soy sauce, fish sauce and coconut milk. Stir, reduce the heat to medium-low, cover, and cook until the chicken is no longer pink at the center, about 10 minutes. Remove the lid and simmer (adjusting the heat if necessary) until the sauce thickens and the chicken is tender, about 10 minutes more.
Serve warm garnished with coconut shavings if desired. This dish tastes even better the next day!

"Dinner's ready," I call from the kitchen.
I set the table Vietnamese style with bowls and chopsticks. Jerry views the scene with some apprehension. He told me a date once forced him to use chopsticks in a Chinese restaurant, and he wasn't very good with them. I think we can probably help him achieve some degree of proficiency. We sit down around the table, and Bao begins to pass the bowls of food.
Jerry is at a loss as to how to proceed, but I come to his rescue.

"Put the rice in first, Jerry, then put the food in on top of that. Like Bao's doing." I point to his bowl.

"I see, but will someone show me how to hold these things?" Jerry asks as he picks up the bamboo chopsticks.

Anh obliges him. "Put one like this," she positions one of the sticks in his hand. "Hold it like a pencil. Then put the other one here. Now just move them together like this." Anh squeezes his hand so the chopsticks come together.

"I think I've got it."

All eyes are on him as he attempts to lift a piece of chicken from the serving bowl into his own. A sigh escapes each throat as the chicken drops back into the broth.

"Keep trying, you'll get it," I encourage him.

"Couldn't I just have a fork?" Jerry pleads.

"You wanted a Vietnamese meal, and you have to eat it Vietnamese style. Get busy!" I command.

On the third try, Jerry manages to get the bit of chicken into his rice bowl. His achievement elicits applause from the rest of the table. The move from the rice bowl to his mouth is done much more proficiently.

"This is delicious!" Jerry exclaims. "It's kind of spicy, though."

"That's the nuóc mắm sauce," Bao explains.

"I've heard of that stuff, but everyone says it smells so terrible," Jerry says.

"Only the cheap stuff smells bad," Anh says. "The good stuff doesn't stink."

During the meal, Jerry quizzes the children on their lives and their likes and dislikes. He even seems to be able to identify with their taste in music, which always escapes me. They laugh and joke about his proficiency with chopsticks and he seems to bond with them easily.

After the second piece of chicken falls in his lap, I offer him a fork.

"No thanks, I think I'm getting the knack of these things now." He clicks his chopsticks together to emphasize the point.

Desert is crème brulée, and he's relieved to see he can use a spoon.

After dessert, Jerry sits back in his chair. "That's one of the best meals I've ever had. The crème brulée was as good as any I could get in Paris, but is that Vietnamese?"

"I'm glad you liked it. No, it's French, but you have to remember the French ruled our country for a long time. Some of the good parts rubbed off on us." I say.

"If you'll excuse me, Mr. Warren, I promised some guys I'd shoot hoops with them after dinner," Bao rises to leave.

"I have to leave too, Mom," Anh says and rises to follow her brother.

"You kids have fun," Jerry says. "And, thanks for giving us some time alone."

"No problem. See you later, Mom," Bao says.

They leave the apartment, and I lead Jerry to the living room sofa.

"I like your kids. They're well-mannered and self-confident, just like their mother. You should be very proud of them," he says.

"I am. They've adapted to their new life easier than I thought they would."

"I'm sure their mother had something to do with that."

"I helped them with their English a little, but they've surpassed me in that area now. We don't speak Vietnamese in the house any more. They only use it with their Vietnamese friends on rare occasions. Most of them want to just speak English too."

"So, you're now American in every respect except citizenship."

"And, except for wanting your parents to like me."

"We'll work on that next weekend."

He moves to kiss me, and I cooperate, but when he wants to go farther, I push him back.

"What's the matter?" he asks.

"Please understand, Jerry. If I let you make love to me now, it'll be confirmation that I'm just a whore, at least in my mind. You may not think of it that way, and I'm not accusing you. It's just me. I'd feel like it was Mel all over again."

He leans back on the sofa and sighs heavily.

"I have to respect your wishes if I call myself a gentleman, but you know I'd marry you in an instant, don't you?"

"I know, but you know the barriers to my agreement."

"Are there more than my parents?"

"Only the ones in my mind you haven't broken down yet."

"And those are?"

"I can't put them into words. All I can tell you is it will take some time for me to get used to a man who wants me for myself and not just my looks or my skill in the bedroom."

"That good, eh?" He smiles.

I put on my best coquettish expression. "You'll just have to wait and see."

He sighs and seems to slump a bit. "Touché. I just didn't think you'd have a problem with sex before marriage."

I stiffen a bit. "Did you think I'd be an easy mark after I told you about my life in Viet Nam?"

He lowers his head and almost whispers, "You know I don't think of you that way."

I place my hand on his arm. "Jerry, please understand. I have to be sure about you, and that will take time. Ever since Mel, it's like I've built a thick wall around my soul, and you have to break through it a brick at a time."

He takes me in his arms and turns my face to his. "I hope I've made some progress."

I smile. "You're more than half way through."

We kiss, and a wave of sweet warmth washes over us. His soul seems to reveal itself to me in that kiss. Now I'm sure this is not Mel all over again. We break the kiss.

I sit back and exhale sharply. "There goes another brick"

Chapter 25

All week I agonize over what to wear to meet Jerry's parents. I know we're going to a fine restaurant, and there's nothing in my closet that will do. I ask the women in the Bàn Tay Đẹp nail salon about places to buy decent clothes at a reasonable price, and they give me several shops to check out. One is a consignment shop, and I check it out first.

The clerk sees me pull up on my moped and assumes a condescending attitude. "Good morning, ma'am. What are you interested in today?"

"I'm having dinner with my prospective fiancée and his parents on Saturday, and I need a dress appropriate for that occasion."

"Are you dining at their home or at a restaurant?" she asks.

"It's at Dan Tana's, and I need something a little nicer than usual."

Her face takes on an incredulous expression. Evidently, she can't make the connection between a moped, a consignment shop and a fine restaurant.

"That's where all the stars go. Is he in the movies?"

I laugh. "Heavens no, he works for Mercedes."

The mention of the high-priced car brand seems to help her fit the pieces together.

"I have some nice things over here, but I'm afraid it will be difficult to fit your figure. You're so slender."

She leads me to a rack of cocktail dresses, and I begin to check them out. I don't want to show too much skin or a deep décolletage, and long hemlines won't be appropriate. I finally find a green sheath with some embroidery on the top in gold. It looks large, and when I try it on, I confirm my original assessment.

The clerk pulls at a few places to tighten the fit, and I'm pleased with the result.

"There's an alteration place next door that can make this fit you nicely, and they're not expensive," she says.

"I can do the alterations myself. How much is it?"

She consults the tag. "Thirty dollars. That's a very good price for this quality."

It's a fortune to me, but I like the look.

"Is it really good quality?" I ask.

"Oh, it's a Bullock's dress, and they only sell the best."

I have to take her word for that. I have no way to shop the LA stores.

"You'll need some shoes to go with that, and the lady who brought in this dress also dropped off her shoes. I doubt they're your size, but you can try them on."

I change back into my own clothes, and she produces the shoes. Considering the size of the dress, the shoes are not that large. Chinh always said I had feet like a duck, long and wide. By far, my feet are my worst feature. I slip on the right shoe, and it fits like it was made for me. The other one is just as comfortable.

"How much are the shoes?" I ask.

"The lady wants $30 for the dress and $30 for the shoes."

Being Vietnamese, I always have to bargain. By now, I know many Americans won't come down on their prices, but this shop seems different to me. I make an offer.

"I'll give you forty dollars for the dress and the shoes."

She thinks a moment. "Well, they've been here for a while. I'll call and ask her."

She enters an office area at the rear of the store and makes a phone call. Without putting the phone down, she turns to me with her hand over the mouthpiece.

"She says $45 is her minimum price."

It'll mean a week of economizing, but I can do it. "I'll take them."

She ends the call and wraps up the things so they'll fit in the saddlebags of my moped, and I'm off to the nail shop. One of the women there works in a hair salon as her second job, and she's offered to do my hair for the big event. Her name is Ngon, and we agree she'll come to my apartment Friday morning to do the job before we report to the nail salon. I can hardly wait to see what magic she'll do.

*

Before Friday I give myself a good manicure and do my nails in a color to compliment the dress. Anh helps me tailor the dress, and I stretch my budget even farther for some sheer pantyhose in the right shade.

On Friday Ngon comes equipped with all her tools. I sit on a dining room chair, and she drapes a sheet around me and places another one on the floor. She lifts my long hair and tucks it under to show me the length she proposes. I look into my hand mirror and gasp.

"Do you really think it should be that short?" I ask."

"Do you want to look like you just came off the boat, or like a sophisticated American lady?" she says.

"The sophisticated lady, of course."

"Well this is the current style. I'll cut it short and curl it a bit at the end so it clings to your neck but still gives you a soft look. You're lucky, you don't have a wide face. This is the style a lot of American women want these days."

I agonize over the loss of my beautiful long hair, but I've seen the fashion magazines in the nail spa, and I know she's right. "Okay, go ahead."

I put down my mirror. I'm afraid to look until the job is finished.

Ngon works for a half hour cutting and shaping, then uses a large curing iron to complete the work.

"There, you look beautiful," she says.

I hold up the mirror and see a new woman. I doubted I could be beautiful without long hair, but the face in the mirror is even lovelier than I could have imagined.

"You've done a wonderful job Ngon. How can I ever thank you?"

"Someday I may need your help to land a man. You can pay me back then."

We embrace before cleaning up the mess of long, black hair.

*

Jerry calls promptly at six on Saturday. When I open the door, he's frozen for a moment.

"Wow! You look like you just stepped out of a movie screen. I never thought you could be any more beautiful than you are, but you did it. I love your hair."

"Thank you, Jerry. I'm ready to go now. I just need to get my purse." Fortunately, I had a small purse one of the nail spa customers gave me as a tip. it matches my outfit well enough, even if the color isn't quite right. I call to Anh. "I'm going now, honey."

She calls back from our room. "Okay, Mom. Have a good time."

I only hope I will.

We arrive at the restaurant, and a valet takes the car. The place doesn't look fancy on the outside, but Jerry assures me a lot of movie stars eat here.

The maître d' hotel leads us toward the back of the restaurant. As we pass by the tables, I feel eyes on me and hear muffled conversations. Jerry whispers, "You're drawing a lot of attention. These people probably think you're some kind of movie star."

"I'm sorry to disappoint them," I say. My insides are shaking from the fear of Jerry's parents, and this added attention isn't helping a bit.

"Don't be. Maybe one of them's a producer or director looking for new talent."

We stop at a table where a distinguished-looking, older man in an expensive suit and a lady of comparable age with impeccably coiffed white hair and designer gown sit sipping cocktails. She's wearing enough diamonds to finance a revolution, and her make-up is expertly applied. The man rises as we approach.

"Tuyết, this is my father, Walter Warren."

He extends his hand, and I take it in a firm grip.

"It's a pleasure to meet you, **Too**-yet," he says as he grips my hand again before releasing it. He murders my name, but I don't think correcting him would be appropriate at this time.

"And, this is my mother Jacqueline, we all call her Jacquie."

"A pleasure to meet you, Mrs. Warren," I say. I don't think calling her Jacquie at this stage of the game is appropriate. She doesn't offer her hand and only nods her acknowledgement before speaking with a faint southern accent.

"What a lovely dress. Where did you find it, deyah?"

Her accent reminds me of an old client in Viet Nam. He was from Alabama, and it took me a while to understand him, but after I got used to it, I thought it was charming. At least he spoke slowly enough for me to understand him easily. Her tone of voice, however, tells me the compliment is only half sincere. I don't want to start out with a lie, so I tell the truth. "It's from Bullock's, but by way of Nancy's Consignment Shop. I bought it there and altered it myself." She cocks her head to one side as she scans me.

"You did an excellent job."

"Thank you," I say.

"Let's all sit down. Tuyết, why don't you sit next to Mom, and I'll sit next to Dad," Jerry says.

"Oh no, Gerald. It's man, woman, man, woman. Sit next to Waltah, **Too**-yet," Jacquie says. Again, I ignore the terrible pronunciation.

I take the seat Jacquie indicates, and Walter pushes my chair up to the table. A waiter arrives and asks for my drink order.

"I'll have a Scotch and Water, please," I say.

"What brand of Scotch, Madam?" he asks.

"Chivas Regal, please," I respond.

Walter reacts with surprise. "I didn't think a delicate lady like you would drink Scotch."

"I learned to like it in Viet Nam. It was readily available and inexpensive."

"It's still pretty good Scotch." He turns to the waiter. "I'll have the same thing."

Jacquie orders another Mai Tai, and Jerry calls for *Miller Lite*.

"Gerald, why don't you ordah a decent beer? They have some good German brands here," Jacquie says.

"It's good beer, Jacquie. You should try it sometime."

"I nevah drink beer," she says with a slight shiver.

After the waiter leaves, Jacquie speaks to me. "Tell us about yourself, **Too**-yet."

It's a pretty open-ended question, but I feel I should start at the beginning.

"I come from a loving family who provided for my every need. I attended school through what you call high school here in America. I was 19 when I married my husband. He was a helicopter pilot in the Vietnamese Air Force. We had two children, Bao, a boy and Anh, a girl. He was decorated for bravery by Nguyen Cao Ky himself, but he was killed in action in 1975.

"My neighbor's husband flew my children and me out of the country along with his family, and we made our way to the United States and Camp Pendleton. An American officer I knew in Viet Nam was stationed at March Air Force Base in Riverside, and he agreed to be our sponsor.

"I met your son last year. You've raised a fine man, and you should be proud of him. I'm sure your parenting had a lot to do with that. He gets along well with my children, and they seem to like him."

Jacquie sits silent for a moment. She takes a sip of her Mai Tai then speaks, "I'm sorry for the loss of your husband."

"Thank you."

Walter Warren interrupts the conversation. "We'd better figure out what we want to order before the waiter has us thrown out." He's joking, of course, but I'm not sure about what might happen in a restaurant this fancy.

We study our menus, and I notice mine has no prices.

I whisper to Jerry, "My menu has no prices. How do I know what to order?"

He whispers back, "Order anything you like. I can afford it, besides Walter will insist on paying the bill anyway."

The waiter takes our orders and brings another round of drinks, then Jacquie continues her inquisition.

"And what do you do now?" she asks.

"I tend bar at a local pub in Westminster and do nails at the Bàn Tay Đẹp nail salon. It means 'beautiful hands' in Vietnamese."

"Who takes care of your children while you work?" Jacquie asks.

"They're in school during the day, but I'm there when they come home. Bao, my son, is almost 16, and Anh, my daughter, is 12. I'm there to give them a good breakfast and see them off to school in the morning, and I fix dinner for them after my work at the nail salon and before I have to go to my job at the pub.

"Anh is a good student and spends most of her evenings studying. Bao plays baseball for his high school team and spends a lot of time at practice or in the school's weight room. He thinks he'll be offered a scholarship to UCLA for baseball. I'm very proud of my children. They speak excellent English now, and both are B+ students."

"Yes, and what would you do if you didn't have to work?" she asks.

"I don't know. I've worked two jobs for a long time. I'm used to it now. I'd have to do something. I think I'd go crazy just sitting at home."

Walter breaks in. "I know how you feel. Jacquie's been after me to retire and turn the business over to my oldest son, but a man can only play so much golf."

"You once told me the business was interfering with your golf game," Jerry says.

Walter laughs at the obvious joke. "I know, but I was younger then, and I could play 36 holes every day. I'm lucky to manage 18 in a golf cart now."

Jacquie brings the conversation back on focus. "I don't suppose you have time for any hobbies, do you?"

"I'm afraid not. I love to sew, and I used to make some of my children's clothes, but besides not having time for it these days, what they want in clothes now is beyond my skill level."

"Don't do well with leather and rags, eh?" Walter says.

We all laugh at that remark.

The waiter brings the salads, and conversation ends for a moment as he grinds fresh pepper for each of us.

Between bites Jacquie continues. "Our other two sons married very well. Their wives are both professional women. One is a doctor, and the other is an accountant. She does the books for her husband's business. He has a construction company that builds houses. Did you ever think about pursuing higher education?"

"No, it was impossible in Viet Nam. My family could not afford university, and I'm too old for that now."

"Without a college degree, what could you possibly do?" Jacquie asks.

Jerry breaks in. His posture stiffens, and a red glow begins creeping up the back of his neck. "She could do anything she put her mind to. She's a very resourceful lady."

I step in. "Thank you, Jerry, but I'd probably start my own nail spa or alteration shop, something like that. I wouldn't need higher education for that, and with a good staff, I wouldn't have to spend that much time away from the children."

"I like your entrepreneurial spirit," Walter says. "You'll need capital for that, but I know just where you can get it."

"Waltah, don't be so crass. We're not talking business here," Jacquie reminds him, using the Southern pronunciation of his name.

He goes back to his salad but slips me a sly wink. I think I now have an ally in Jerry's father.

The entrees come, and once more the conversation shifts to other topics. As the bus boys clear away our plates, I decide to add another piece of sincere flattery. "You two are such wonderful parents. It's no wonder your children turned out so well. A father who grew a very successful business and a charming lady for a mother."

"Thank you, deah," Jacquie says. "We tried our best with Gerald, but he's had a stubborn streak ever since he was born. I don't know wheah that came from."

Walter gives her a sideways glance. "I can take a wild guess as to where he got it." He points surreptitiously to Jacquie.

260

"Are you suggesting he got it from **my** side of the family?" Jacquie says.

"Well, who was it that drove the club manager crazy insisting on floral wallpaper for the ladies' lounge at the country club? And, I remember who wouldn't vote to approve Father Reilly's plan for a soup kitchen in our church," Walter said.

"Those were different matters and totally unrelated to this discussion."

We finish the dinner wine in awkward silence, and I make one more try.

"Jacquie, I know you don't approve of me as a prospective daughter-in-law, but should I decide to marry Jerry, I'd want you and Mr. Warren to like me. Even if you didn't, I'd still respect you as Jerry's parents and give you all the love I can, even if it's not returned. I'd see that my children were just as respectful toward you."

"Thank you. If Gerald asks you to marry him, there's not much we can do to change his mind. I've learned that much over the last thirty years. You seem like a very resourceful lady, and we should spend more time together. Perhaps, we can come to share his feelings about you."

She turns to Walter, "I think it's time to go, Waltah."

She takes my hand and smiles at me. "You must have Gerald bring you to see us soon."

A pat on my hand, and she rises. The men rise with her.

"Goodnight, **Too**-yet, goodnight, Gerald."

Jerry rises and helps me with my chair then reaches into his billfold.

"Don't worry about that, son. I've taken care of the bill," Walter says.

Jerry puts his billfold back in his pocket. "I'll see you both tomorrow," he says.

We leave the restaurant, and on the way back to Westminster Jerry and I discuss the dinner conversation.

"Do you see how bigoted my mother is now?" Jerry says.

"I do, but I'll try to change her mind about me." I wonder if that's even possible. I have to say it, but I'm not confident I can do it. What could I do to penetrate her wall of prejudice?

"Don't worry about her. I want to marry you no matter what Jacquie says, if you'll have me."

"You haven't even proposed, but don't take the ring back to the jewelry store just yet," I chide.

Jerry reacts with honest surprise.

"How did you know I have one?"

This statement and his serious expression take me aback. I know he wants to marry me, but a ring? I'm at a loss for words and answer with the first thing that pops into my mind.

"I didn't, it was just an expression."

His face melts into a smile, and he laughs to lighten the mood.

"At least I can get a full refund if you say no."

I fall into his arms, and we kiss.

Chapter 27

Sunday morning the children assault me asking about the dinner with Jerry's parents last night. I fill them in on the meeting, and they react as I expect.

"If they don't like you, that's their problem," Bao says.

"How could they not like you after seeing you in that outfit with your new hairdo?" Anh says.

"I think his father likes me, but I'm sure his mother doesn't."

"Why not?" Bao asks.

"She was expecting her son to marry someone more professional, more sophisticated, I guess."

"Has he asked you to marry him?" Anh asks.

"Only indirectly, but he will if I give him any encouragement at all."

"I think his mother's a jerk," Bao says.

I have to agree, but I can't let that comment go uncorrected.

"Don't talk that way, Bao. She may not think much of me, but she's Jerry's mother and deserves respect."

He hangs his head for a moment and says, "I'm sorry, but if she doesn't like you, she's not very smart."

I think this is a good place to end the conversation. "We'd better clear the table and get the dishes done before Jerry gets here," I say.

We get busy restoring the apartment to its normally neat condition and finish just as Jerry rings the doorbell.

He greets the children and we all find places in the living room. Jerry begins.

"I think you wowed Dad even if Jacquie's still a bit cool toward you. They want to meet all of you. Could you come to their house next weekend?" Jerry asks.

"For the whole weekend?" I ask.

"Yes, we could go up on Friday and come back on Sunday, if you can arrange your work schedule," Jerry says.

I can imagine Jacquie's reasons for inviting us. They must have an impressive house, and she expects that to help "put me in my place." On top of that, I'm sure she has planned several more opportunities for me to understand how far below her social strata I rank. I will be running a gauntlet of challenges to my fitness as a daughter-in-law to the wealthy and sophisticated Warren family. In spite of my misgivings, there's only one answer I can give Jerry.

"It's short notice, but I think I can. I'll let you know if I can't do it."

"Do they have a pool?" Anh asks.

"Yes, they do, a heated one," Jerry says.

"That's great, I'll bring my swim suit," Anh says.

With that news, the children excuse themselves to go off to their own Sunday functions, Bao to a pick-up baseball game and Anh to a homework session with some friends. When they're gone, Jerry and I sit on the sofa together. He produces the box holding the engagement ring.

"I didn't take it back to the jewelry store. I'm still hoping you'll decide to say 'yes'."

"Not yet. I want your parents to accept me, even if they don't like me."

"I think all Jacquie needs is a bit more time with you to win her over. This visit with your kids along should do it. She loves her grandchildren, and this gives her a chance to spoil two more without having to wait for them to get out of diapers."

"I think you're very optimistic about this. Even if I do manage to win her over', I don't want to marry until after I'm an American citizen."

Jerry reacts as I expected he would. "What? Can't we get married first and work that out afterwards? It might make your path to citizenship easier."

"No, I want to be American first. I don't want people to think I only married you to get American citizenship the easy way."

"I can respect that even if it does mean waiting longer to use this ring"

"We mustn't get ahead of ourselves. I have to get through this weekend first."

*

Jerry picks us up Friday morning, and drives to one of the richest neighborhoods I've ever seen. The streets are lined with Royal Palms, and the lawns are professionally landscaped and impeccably groomed. He turns into a driveway and stops near the front door of a two-story Spanish colonial style mansion.

I knew such wealth existed but seeing it up close makes my stomach churn uneasily. Facing them at a restaurant was on neutral ground. Now I must face them on their home turf. I know Jacquie expects me to be overwhelmed by the opulence of her home, but I make up my mind to take it in stride no matter how impressive it is. I take a deep breath to buck up my courage.

"Welcome to my family home," Jerry says.

"Wow, it's a mansion!" Bao says.

"Your parents must have a ton of money," Anh adds.

"Yes, they do have a lot of money, and yes, it is a big house, but don't let it get to you," Jerry says. "Act like it's no big deal. It's only a place to live, just like your apartment. It's just bigger and fancier, that's all."

"How long has your family lived here?" I ask as Jerry removes our luggage from the trunk.

"Since 1947 when my father moved his firm here to handle a movie mogul's account. It was his first big break, and he made the most of it. Well, are you ready to enter the lion's den?"

Jerry leads us to the front door where an attractive, older black woman is waiting for us.

"Tuyết, this is Lydia, one of the best cooks in Southern California. Lydia, this is Tuyết and her children, Bao and Ahn," Jerry says.

She smiles broadly at the sight of me and my family. "Welcome, Miss **Too**-yet. It's good to see y'all."

She has a hard time coping with my name, so I give her a break.

"Thank you, Lydia, but please call me Snow. It's easier for Americans."

The children greet Lydia who comments, "What lovely children you have, Miss Snow."

"Thank you, Lydia," I reply.

Lydia points the way down the hall. "Come on in! They's waiting for ya in the living room. I'll take care o' your bags."

We step through the door into a large entryway, and I'm immediately captivated by the large sculpture standing in the middle of the hardwood floor.

"That's gorgeous, Jerry."

"It's not the real thing. It's a replica of some famous artist's Lida and the Swan. Jacquie bought it on her last trip to Europe. She refers to it as, 'A little souvenir I came across in Florence'."

"It must have cost a fortune." I pick up on the sarcasm in his voice, but I'm still awed by the presence of something so obviously expensive as the first thing one sees upon entering her home. Once more, I have to calm my inner turmoil.

"The livin' room's this way," Lydia says.

She leads us through a long hallway with an impressive runner spanning the entire length. Oil and watercolor paintings cover the walls. I don't know anything about art, but I'm sure all of them are valuable.

About half way down, Walter steps out of the living room. Lydia continues up the stairway with our bags.

"I figured that was you," he says as he folds me in his arms and gives me a hug before welcoming Bao and Anh.

"Welcome to our home," he says as he shakes Bao's hand and kisses Anh on the cheek.

"Oh Mr. Warren, I'm so nervous. I've never met any rich people before," Anh says.

Walter laughs. "We're just people, like everyone else," he says.

"The only difference is you have more money," Bao inserts.

Walter laughs and turns to me. "Come on in. My wife really wants to meet your kids."

I'm sure she does. I only hope she'll be thwarted in her purposes by their excellent English and courteous behavior.

He leads us through double sliding doors into the spacious living room. The furniture is contemporary design with textured rose upholstery, and the end and coffee tables are a rich walnut. Plush white carpet covers the floor. A full bar stands in one corner of the room just inside the doors, and a baby grand piano poses regally before a wall of sliding glass doors. Transparent drapes shield the room from direct sunlight, and darker versions wait in reserve on each side. The wall on my right is half floor to ceiling book shelves and half a gallery of oil paintings divided by a closed door.

"Jacquie, they're here," he announces.

Jacquie looks up from her book and rises to greet us. "Well, it's good to see y'all again, Tuyết." She embraces me warmly. Jerry has, obviously, coached them both on the correct pronunciation of my name.

"You too, Jacquie."

"And these are your children?" Jacquie turns to them with a softer but still very intimidating expression. I begin to wonder if Jerry was right about her attitude toward prospective grandchildren. She extends her hand to Bao who shakes it carefully.

"I'm Bao, Mrs. Warren, and this is my sister Anh."

"Don't be so formal, dear. Both of you, please call me Jacquie. All of my grandchildren do."

"They have been raised to respect their elders," I insert. "I don't want them to be informal with adults."

"A very admirable quality," Walter says. "Quite a difference from today's American youth."

"Oh, Waltah. You know how I hate people treating me like I'm an old woman." She turns to me. "Please don't be concerned about your children using my first name. All of my children and grandchildren call me Jacquie. You've heard Gerald doing it, I know.'"

I don't want to add another barrier to our relationship, but I need to make it clear to Bao and Anh that this is an exception to my rules.

267

"You children may call her Jacquie because she's given you permission to do so. This exception does not apply to any other adult."

"Yes, Ma'am," they both reply.

Jacquie embraces Anh. "You're as lovely as your mother."

"Thank you, Jacquie, and you're every bit as lovely as mother said you were," Anh replies.

I'm very proud of her because it is an entirely un-rehearsed comment, even though it doesn't do anything to help the hurricane in my stomach. I'm sure she spends a lot of money on her appearance and expects people to notice but hearing such a compliment from a child seems to surprise her.

"Thank you dear," is Jacquie's response to the compliment as a genuine smile briefly softens her usually stern expression.

"I understand you're a baseball player, Bao" Walt says.

"Yes, I'm on my high school team, sir."

"What position?" Walt asks.

"Anything in the infield, but second base is my favorite."

"Maybe you can come help the Dodgers after college," Walt jokes.

"That would be great," Bao says.

"Would anyone like something to drink?" Walter asks. "Let's see, it's Scotch and water for Tuyết, a martini for Jacquie and a **Miller Lite** for Jerry. How about a **Miller Lite** for you, Bao?"

Bao looks to me for approval.

"I don't think he's old enough to have beer," I say.

Bao's face shows his disappointment.

"Maybe not as far as the law's concerned, but one beer in the safety of my home won't hurt him. He should know what it tastes like and how it affects him while he's among adults who won't let him get into trouble, but I'll respect your wishes."

The question is clearly addressed to me. Will it offend Walter if I say "no"? There is a certain logic in what he says. I relent. "Okay, but only one beer. It's cola or something else non-alcoholic after that."

"Thanks, Mom," Bao sighs. "I will have a ***Miller Lite***, too, Mr. Warren."

"I'll just have a ***Coke***," Anh says.

"Coming right up. Everybody find a seat. It'll be a while until lunch."

"You children come sit next to me," Jacquie says as she pats the sofa cushions on either side of her. Bao takes the seat on her left, and Anh sits on her right.

"And what is your favorite subject in school?" she asks Bao.

"I like math. I want to be an engineer, ma'am."

"As I told you, please call me Jacquie."

"Yes, uh, Jacquie," he stumbles to say.

"How are your grades?" Walter asks Bao. "You'll need a good GPA to get into a first-class engineering school."

"I have a B+ average. If it wasn't for baseball, I'd have straight As."

"I understand," Walter says. "If you're a player the major universities want, you may get a scholarship."

"I hope so. I won't have to work too hard over the summer if I do."

"My goodness," Jacquie picks up on this opening quickly. "You shouldn't have to work while you're in school."

I can see where she's taking this. I don't mind her making me feel small, but I draw the line when it comes to my children.

"It won't hurt him to help with his college expenses," I speak up. "He needs to know what work is and how to get along with people outside of school and his family."

I'm surprised when Bao echoes my thoughts.

"It's alright, Mrs. – I mean, Jacquie. Mom's an inspiration for Anh and me. She's worked hard to make a good life for us here in America."

Jacquie looks at Bao for a moment before turning her attention to Anh.

"And, what grade are you in now?" she asks.

"I just finished sixth grade. I'll be in seventh in September."

"Do you like school?"

"Oh yes, now that my English is better. It was hard, at first, but there were a lot of Vietnamese kids in my class, and we helped each other a lot."

Again, I feel the need to add my two-cent's worth.

"Anh is a straight A student. Her teachers are very proud of the way she's mastered English."

"Yes, they both speak excellent English," Jacquie seems to choke on the compliment.

Lydia interrupts announcing lunch.

We move into the dining room. Lydia comes in from the kitchen carrying a large tray.

"A terrine!" I express my delight. "I haven't had a good terrine since Viet Nam."

"You've eaten terrine before?" Jacquie asks with a note of amazement in her voice. The dish was, undoubtedly, designed to make me ask what it was.

"Oh yes. I used to make terrines for my husband, especially during Tet. His favorite was ham. What's in this one?"

"Taste it and tell me," Jacquie says as she holds a hand up to silence Lydia.

I take a dainty bite of the jelled loaf and savor the morsel for a moment. "It's rabbit, and very good rabbit too."

"That's right, ma'am," Lydia beams.

"Wow, that's one of my favorites," Bao says. "Why don't you fix these any more, Mom?"

"I don't have time these days, Honey. My jobs keep me hopping just to have a warm meal for you kids every day."

"What kind of meal do you fix for them?" Jacquie asks.

I sense the motive for this question is developing a criticism of my children's diet, but I know she can't win on that score.

"Many Vietnamese meals are very nourishing yet simple to prepare. During the week, they often get a stir-fry with rice. Sometimes we do hamburgers or hot dogs, if they ask for that kind of meal. On Sundays, I have time to fix more elaborate dishes." I turn and smile at Jerry. "Jerry's had one or two of my big meals. He's even learned to eat with chopsticks."

"That took a while," Jerry comments. "You'll have to give Lydia some of your recipes. I'm sure Walter would enjoy them. He likes Chinese food."

"What about you, Jacquie?" I ask.

"I'm really not a fan of oriental food," Jacquie says.

"Maybe Lydia would let me work with her this afternoon, and I could make you a dish the Americans loved when I used to cook for them back in Viet Nam?"

I've thrown down the gauntlet. Jacquie gives me a suspicious look but calls for Lydia. The combination cook, maid and butler responds quickly. "Yes, Mrs. Warren?"

"I want you to work with Tuyết on this evening's dinner. Did you have anything planned?"

"Yes, Ma'am. I was goin' t' have that pot roast y'all like so well."

A smile widens across Jacquie's face. She thinks she has me buffaloed, but she's dead wrong.

"Perfect. Would you mind if I worked with you to make Vietnamese style beef?" I ask Lydia.

Jacquie nods toward Lydia, indicating her approval.

"Why sure Miss Snow. I'd be glad to work with y'all on dinner."

"Good, I'll get with you after lunch to see if you have everything we'll need."

The rest of lunch proceeds without incident. The children want to test the pool, but I force them to wait until their lunch digests a bit. I join Lydia in the spacious kitchen and check for the ingredients I need.

"What we gonna cook, Miss Snow?"

"It's a dish called Bo Luc Lac, but in English we just call it Shaking Beef. I know you have sugar and garlic, but how about soy sauce?"

"We got that."

"Okay, we'll also need sesame oil?"

"That too."

"Oyster sauce?"

"Yup."

"I know you don't have nouc man, but do you have any kind of fish sauce?"

"Mmmm? I think I got somethin' that'll work."

Lydia opens a cavernous refrigerator and produces a bottle of Thai fish sauce.

"I used this one time about two months back when Mistah Warren wanted some kind of Chinese meal. Had to look up the recipe in one of Wanda's cook books. She's the cook for the Bighams next door."

"That'll work. Let's get busy. The beef needs to marinate for two hours."

We cut the beef into cubes and prepare the marinade then set the beef to marinate while I brief Lydia on the preparation. The Warren's kitchen does not possess a wok, but Lydia finds a large skillet that works just as well.

Bo Luc Lac
(Vietnamese Shaking Beef)

Ingredients:

Beef Marinade:

1½ lbs beef cut into 1" cubes
2 Tbs minced garlic
1½ Tbs sugar
2 Tbs oyster sauce
1 Tbs fish sauce
1 Tbs sesame oil
1 Ts thick soy sauce

Vinaigrette:

½ cup rice vinegar
1½ Tbs sugar
½ Tbs salt

Dipping Sauce:

Juice of 1 lime
½ tsp Kosher salt
½ tsp fresh cracked pepper

Preparation:

Combine marinade ingredients and set aside for two hours
Mix vinaigrette ingredients.
Thinly slice red onions and use 3-4 tbs of the vinaigrette to pickle the onions. Set aside for 10 minutes.
Prepare a bed of watercress and thinly sliced tomatoes on a serving platter.
Heat 2 Tbs of cooking oil in a wok or large skillet until it begins to smoke. Add a layer of the beef and sear for about 2 minutes. Shake pan to sear other sides of the beef and cook until brown on all sides and bouncy to a spatula. (You may have to do this in batches.)
Transfer beef to serving dish and drizzle 3-4 Tbs of the vinaigrette over the beef and greens. Top with the pickled onions. Serve dipping sauce in a small ramekin.
While the beef marinates, I wander out to the pool. The children are having a wonderful time with all the pool toys. Bao appears to be particularly enjoying the diving board.
Walter and Jacquie recline on chaise lounges in their bathing suits. Walter sports a golf tan featuring reddish arms, head and neck with a barely tanned torso. His legs show a pattern consistent with wearing shorts from time to time.
Jacquie has obviously paid more attention to achieving a perfect tan. Her white one-piece suit fits perfectly over a figure too slim for her age. She lays back in the chaise lounge wearing dark sun glasses. She doesn't acknowledge my arrival, but she may be asleep. Walter speaks first.
"Aren't you going to enjoy the pool?" he asks.
"I don't swim, Walter. I never learned."
"Your kids seem to be doing pretty well," he says.

"They learned at our first apartment. A lady there was giving lessons. She didn't charge too much, so I let Anh learn there. Bao learned at the local YMCA."

I take a chaise lounge next to Walter. Bao notices me first.

"Hey, Mom! Watch this." He bounces on the diving board and curls up into a somersault before extending to hit the water feet first. I applaud as his head surfaces.

"Mr. Warren taught me how to do that. Isn't it great?"

"You looked good," I say, though I really wasn't sure what I was saying.

"He's a quick learner," Walter says. "And, a real athlete. I can see why he likes baseball."

I smile at his compliment. I watched him play soccer in Viet Nam, but never thought of him as athletic then. As he climbs out of the pool to dive again, I notice how his body has developed in the last year. He's lost his gawkiness and is beginning to look like his father. Tears well up in my eyes as I remember Chinh. I'm glad my son will never have to go to war.

"If you didn't have to work two jobs, what would you *really* like to do Tuyết?" Walter asks.

"I don't know. Doing nails doesn't pay that much unless you own the shop, and I don't have enough money for that. I could also do alterations, but that would also take money for a shop. I know Jerry would help me if we were married."

Walter sits up in his chair and turns to me. He speaks in a low voice. "I know Jerry will marry you, if you'll have him, and I also know someone who would be willing to finance whatever kind of shop you wanted." He points to his own chest for emphasis. "I've always been a good judge of character, and I see in you the kind of person I can invest in with confidence."

The remark surprises me. Just when I've managed to calm the hurricane in my stomach to a tropical storm, Walter hits me with a typhoon. I know this is a serious compliment. I'm obligated to respond, but I can't find the words right away. He notices my consternation.

"Don't bother to say anything just now. We can talk about this later but keep my offer in mind. Your children will soon be to a place where they won't need their mother full time. When you get to that point, we'll talk again. Want something to drink? Lydia's made some great iced tea."

"Yyyyes, I'll have a glass of tea." Maybe some tea will help cushion the impact of Walter's offer on top of all the other mix-masters churning up my insides.

He calls for Lydia and orders our tea.

Jacquie finally stirs.

"Oh, hi, Tuyết. I was having a nap. Did you and Lydia work out ouah dinnah?"

"Yes, we did. I think you'll really enjoy the meal."

"Will I have to use those horrible stick things to eat it?" she says.

"Oh no. A knife and fork will do very nicely."

*

I guide Lydia through the preparation of dinner before changing and inspecting the children's' outfits. We all sit down together, and Walter says grace before Lydia arrives with a platter of meat. She places it in front of Walter who sniffs if noisily.

"That smells great," he says as he lifts four pieces of beef to his plate and passes the platter to me. Lydia returns with a bowl of rice and another bowl of steamed broccoli.

I watch as Jacquie places one cube of the beef on her plate along with some tomatoes and watercress from the platter. She places a small serving of broccoli beside the beef but passes on the rice. She daintily cuts a small bite from the beef cube and chews slowly, savoring the spicy and piquant flavor. The room is silent except for the click of Walter's silverware as he attacks his plate. Jacquie finally swallows, mops at her lips with her napkin and speaks.

"Congratulations, Lydia. You did an excellent job with Tuyết's recipe."

Lydia was quick to correct her mistress. "Oh no, ma'am. Miss Snow did most of it. I only followed her orders when she let me do anything. She gets all the credit, if you like it."

Jacquie turns to me with thinly disguised frustration. "Then it's congratulations to you, Tuyết. I didn't think I'd like anything from Viet Nam, but after this, I'm willing to try almost anything in that style."

"I thought you might like it." A voice deep in my consciousness laughs in triumph, but I quell it rapidly. This was a minor victory, and I should not start celebrating yet.

"Like it? This is great. Pass me that plate again." Walter reaches out toward the half empty platter, and Bao passes it to him. "Anybody want more besides me?" he asks.

"I'll take some more," Jerry says.

Walter indicates that Bao should pass the entrée the other way. Even Jacquie takes another piece on the way by. Walter consumes what remains.

After dinner, the children sit down in front of the TV while the adults gather in the card room.

"Do you play Bridge?" Jacquie asks me.

I should have known this was coming. How could she pass up another chance to prove how un-refined I am.

"No, the only card game I know is Gin Rummy. One of the American advisors taught me." They don't need to know that he used it to kill time between sex sessions.

"Gin Rummy?" Walter comes alive. "You and I will play Gin. Thanks for saving me from an evening of Bridge." He moves to an octagonal table set up for poker and pulls a deck of cards and a score pad from a drawer on his side.

"What can Gerald and I do?" Jacquie says.

"He loves Backgammon. Why not challenge him to a friendly game, say for a half cent a point?" Walter says.

"Sounds good to me," Jerry says.

Jacquie huffs to the other side of the room and produces an elaborate game board and a box of tokens and dice. "I don't like to play for money, Gerald, if that's alright with you?"

"Fine with me," he replies.

"Are we going to play Hollywood?" I ask.

Walter quits shuffling and looks at me with a surprised expression.

"Whoever taught you to play must have been used to men's grill Gin."

"I don't know that, but he was a very good player. I seldom beat him."

Again, he doesn't need to know that I let him win about half the time.

"Okay, here we go. Cut for deal."

He deals first, and after three hands, I can tell he's every bit as good as the American Colonel who taught me. I soon learn his style of play and decide to accept the challenge of defeating him. The first game ends with me in the lead by 600 points. Walter tears off the score sheet and hands it to me.

"At Bel Air Country Club that would be worth $6.00 in our usual penny a point game. Your teacher was very good."

"Yes, he was, in every way," I smile at Walter who doesn't need to know what other ways were involved, "but it still took all of my skill to defeat you. You aren't so bad yourself."

"Thanks. Tell you what. I'm used to having some skin in the game. We'll play for a penny a point. If you win, I pay off, if you lose, you pay nothing."

I should feel demeaned, but I don't feel badly about taking his money after seeing how he lives. I need to make at least an attempt at being noble.

"I don't want to take unfair advantage of you, Walter."

There, I've satisfied my conscience.

"How much can I lose? I've dropped $500 in the men's grill at a nickel a point. Believe me, I can afford it."

At this point, my mouth betrays my brain.

"I still don't feel right. If I lose I'll pay off at .1¢ a point."

"As long as you think you can afford it?"

I really don't want to risk even that amount, but I've made the offer.

"It's your deal," I say.

At the end of the evening, Walter owes me $50.00.

*

When the games are over, I see the children off to bed and bid goodnight to Jacquie and Walter. Jacquie placed Jerry and I in separate bedrooms, as I expected she would. Jerry walks me upstairs to my door.

"How did you manage to take Walter for that much money?"

I wasn't going to tell him, but Walter announced his payoff to all as the games were breaking up.

"He's a good player. I was just having a run of good luck."

We stop at my door, and I feel the heat of passion radiating from his touch. He'd love to be sharing a bed with me, but I just don't feel comfortable about sex with him at this point. Maybe it's a hangover from Mel? Whatever it is, I'm not inviting him in.

"Goodnight, Jerry,"

He takes me in his arms, and we kiss. An old familiar urge rises from my stomach, but I quickly suppress it. He breaks off the kiss when I don't return his passion.

"Goodnight, Tuyết. By the way, Jacquie's planned a dinner at Bel Air Country Club tomorrow night. Do I need to take you shopping in the morning?"

Here's another chance for Jacquie to humiliate me. I should have anticipated this, but it would have made no difference. I doubt another trip to the consignment shop would produce anything suitable.

"Yes, I didn't bring anything but the dress I wore to Dan Tana's. I don't think it's fancy enough for this occasion."

"Okay, we'll go out right after the shops open at ten. See you in the morning."

We kiss again, and I enter my bedroom quickly. If I hesitate, I might give in.

*

The next morning after breakfast, Jerry takes me out to shop. My first worry is about how to behave at the country club.

"I'm really worried about tonight, not so much as what to wear as how do I behave?"

"I guess I should give you some pointers about those things since Jacquie will certainly be introducing you to some of her friends. You're very poised and mature, so I'm confident you can take in stride anything they throw at you. We'll have a coffee and discuss it, after we find you a suitable outfit."

Jerry pulls up in front of a shop featuring elegantly dressed mannequins in both windows. This is a first for me and the thought of spending the kind of money these things surely cost is almost making me sick. I follow him into the shop where the clerks greet us with the deference due a couple stepping out of a Mercedes.

"Good morning, I'm Madeline, how may I help you?"

A woman who could have just come off a fashion show runway flashes a smile that's only half genuine.

"Hello, Madeline. I'm Jerry Warren, and this is Tuyết."

I offer my hand to Madeline who takes it in a warm but gentle grip.

"It's a pleasure, Miss Tuyết. What can we do for you?"

Jerry speaks up. "She needs an outfit for dinner at Bel Air Country Club tonight. Do you have something that might fit her without alterations?"

"Oh, yes. A figure like hers is easy to fit. Come right over here, please."

Madeline shows us several outfits, and I try on three. With each new ensemble, Jerry offers his opinion as Madeline stands behind him nodding yes or no. They narrow the field down to one navy blue dress and one slacks and jacket set in white.

"I think I like the slacks and jacket," I say. "What do you think, Jerry?"

"Looks great to me. What about you, Madeline?"

"We'll need to find the right thing to wear under the jacket. I think something in a red or fuchsia." Madeline thinks a moment then disappears from the dressing room and returns with several blouses. I try on three before she declares a winner.

Jerry pays with a credit card, and Madeline recommends another shop for shoes to go with the outfit.

He takes me to another shop where we select a pair of dress sandals.

On the way to the coffee shop, I express my concern about him buying my outfit.

"I really feel like a charity case with you buying these things. They cost so much."

"Don't feel badly. It's worth every penny to keep Jacquie from embarrassing you tonight. Besides, Walter will probably insist on reimbursing me. I think he's taken a liking to you."

Jerry drives to a small coffee shop nearby. He orders black coffee while I ask for hot chocolate. We manage to find a booth that offers some privacy, and he begins.

"The club is composed of a lot of very rich people who don't act like they have any money at all, most of the time. Because you're there, they'll think you have money too, but you're so attractive, they won't dig too deeply beyond your looks. You're Walter Warren's guest. That will be enough to put them on their guard. All you have to do is be your charming self."

"I'm afraid someone will ask what I do or where I went to college."

"Your bar serves food, doesn't it?" he asks.

"Yes, we have a very good menu for a small tavern," I say.

"Then just tell them you're in the restaurant business. It's true as far as it goes, and they probably won't pursue it beyond that. As far as school is concerned, just say that you never finished college. Tell them you got married before you were able to get your degree."

"But isn't that lying?"

"You married your first husband before you went to college, didn't you?"

"Yes, but..."

"No buts! You'll probably never see any of these people again, and they don't know anything about you. I'm sure none of them have ever been to your bar, so you don't have to worry about anyone blowing your cover. Just think of the people you meet as being customers."

But, I am worried about seeing them again. If I decide to marry him, we'll be visiting his parents more often than he has in the past, and they'll probably invite us to their club again. The lies are something I can live with for the present, but there could be complications later. I don't think this is the time to bring that up, though.

"Okay, but I won't be comfortable with it tonight."

Chapter 28

That evening I come downstairs in my new outfit to find the Warrens, Jerry and my children waiting in the living room. The children are wearing the best clothes I could find in the second-hand store, but they look very nice. Walter and Jerry rise as I walk in.

"How do you like it?" I turn around to show the whole outfit.

"Tuyết, you outdid yourself," Walter says.

"Wow, Mom!" was all Bao could manage.

Anh fingers the material. "This is beautiful, Mother."

Jacquie sits in her chair with a look of borderline approval on her face.

"When you start with someone as lovely as Tuyết, it's easy to be successful. You're going to wow everybody at the club," Jerry says as he kisses me gently on the cheek.

"I'm so nervous about this evening," I whisper to him.

"You'll be fine, Darling. Just be yourself and remember that you're with Walter Warren. Nobody's going to risk getting on the wrong side of my father," he whispers back.

*

We take two cars to the club. The Warrens ride in the Cadillac while Jerry drives me and the children over in his Mercedes.

The club is even more intimidating than I imagined. The parking lot is full of Cadillacs, Lincolns, Mercedes and Jaguars with a few Rolls Royce thrown in, and the people I see going in the door exude wealth.

"Wow, what a great place," Bao says.

"It's been around a long time, and it's very expensive, but they're only people just like you and me. You couldn't tell most of them have any money at all, but there are a few who like to flaunt their wealth. Just don't let any of this get to you. It's just a big, pricey Kozy Korner," Jerry advises him.

We meet Walt and Jacquie in the entry to the dining room, and the headwaiter leads us to a round table in one corner of the large dining area. I sit between Jerry and Walter while

Jacquie is on Walter's left with Bao next to her. Anh is between her brother and Jerry.

I open the menu and almost faint at the prices. I turn to Jerry and whisper, "Jerry, these prices are outrageous."

"It's nothing Dad can't afford," Jerry whispers back. "Order whatever looks good to you."

I can't believe anyone can afford the prices, but the dining room is nearly full. I suddenly feel very poor. Jerry grew up with this lifestyle, but it's a far cry from even the best in Viet Nam. I have to shake off this feeling of super-inferiority. I know Jacquie will find some way to reinforce it. That method becomes obvious very soon.

The waitress takes drink orders and Jacquie says to me, "Come along, Tuyết. I want to introduce you to some of our friends."

"I think I'd like Jerry to come along," I say.

"I'll go too," Walter says.

Walter's expression and tone of voice tell me he's fearful of what Jacquie might do and wants to be there to help defend me.

"Oh yes, Gerald, of course, but we don't need you along, Waltah. Stay here with the children and get to know them better."

Jacquie leads us to a table of six where a bald-headed man rises to greet her.

"Jacquie! How have you been? Haven't seen you for a while."

"Roger, you remember my son, Jerry?"

"Sure, how are you doing, Jerry." Roger shakes Jerry's hand heartily.

"I'm fine, Mr. Simpson. I'd like you to meet my friend. This is Miss Vien."

Roger turns to face me with a broad smile on his face. "It's certainly a pleasure, Miss Vien."

I offer my hand to Simpson who takes it eagerly.

"This is my wife, Fran," Simpson says.

A plump lady with ample bosoms and red hair smiles in my direction.

"And this is Joe and Carol Higgins." Joe rises to acknowledge me while his wife asks, "Are you Vietnamese, Miss Vien?"

His wife is half his age and has an aura about her reminding me of the women who frequent the Kozy Korner.

"Yes, I am," I reply. "I was able to make it here in '75, and I'm working on my US citizenship now."

"Welcome to our country," she says.

"I see Jerry has his father's good taste in women," Joe says as he scans me with the eye of a practiced lecher.

"Roger's a big Cadillac dealer here in Los Angeles. Waltah buys all of our cars from him," Jacquie explains.

"I'm always afraid he's going to switch to Mercedes someday to tip some business his son's way," Roger responds.

"Not much hope of that," Jerry chimes in. "He still remembers World War II."

The joke brings polite laughter from the group.

"Mr. Higgins owns a construction company, and Mr. Sanders, there, deals in the commodity market." Jacquie describes the other two men in the way most important to her—money and position.

"Mrs. Higgins does a lot of work with the homeless in Los Angeles through a mission downtown," Jerry adds.

"That's very good of you," I say with genuine admiration in my voice.

"It's not much, but the mission does some wonderful work. We have several of your people on the mission staff," Carol says.

"Yes, I know there's a large Vietnamese community in Los Angeles." I say.

"I have to give the Vietnamese credit," Joe adds. "They'll do any kind of work, and they stay off the welfare rolls."

I feel a stinging sensation in my chest at his words. I almost say something in response but keep silent out of respect for Jerry.

"What do you do, dear?" Fran Simpson asks.

I remember Jerry's advice and say, "I'm in the restaurant business in Westminster."

I can feel Jacquie's reaction even though I can't turn to view it. I expect her to chime in with more detail about my work, but she stays silent.

"Is it a Vietnamese restaurant?" Simpson asks.

"Well, it's kind of half and half," I answer.

"Isn't that unusual. I'd have never guessed a Vietnamese woman would own a restaurant," Fran says.

"I don't own the restaurant," I say. My conscience demands I set the record straight.

Jerry steps in. "Not yet. She's in the process of buying it. Tuyết always says the bank owns the place until she pays it off."

The table relaxes, and I know I shouldn't say anything more. Jacquie brings a close to the interview. I can tell by her stoic expression the encounter did not turn out the way she intended. Jerry's advice made all the difference, and I feel even more love for him now.

"We'd better get back to our table. I see Kathy's brought our salads, and Waltah will want to start eating," Jacquie says."

"A pleasure meeting all of you," I say.

As we walk back to our table, Jerry whispers, "See, I told you they were just people like everybody else. I know Jacquie wanted you to feel inferior, but I think it backfired on her."

"Thanks to your advice and help," I whisper back.

We return to our table, and Walter asks, "Did she introduce you to Congressman Clawson?"

"No, she didn't."

Walter leans closer and whispers, "I manage his money. He may be a man you'll need on your side someday. Just let me know if you ever need some political clout."

Jacquie interrupts, "What are you two whispering about?"

Walter winks at me and turns to her, "Only giving her a little advice, that's all."

The arrival of dinner halts conversation.

After dinner, we spend more time in the bar with Walt introducing me to more of his friends.

On the way home, I can't hold back my reaction.

"I was so nervous, Jerry. I really didn't like pretending to be somebody I'm not."

"It's okay, Mom," Bao breaks in. "You'll never see any of those people again, anyway."

"If you do, it will be as my wife," Jerry says. "That will be enough explanation for those people, but I don't plan to see them that often."

"If I consent to be your wife, we'll see your parents frequently, and they'll probably invite us to their club again," I protest.

"I don't visit them more than a couple of times a year," Jerry says.

"That's something we've already talked about, remember?"

My tone of voice tells Jerry that if we marry he will be seeing much more of his parents in the future.

Chapter 29

Sunday, we sleep in. Bao and Anh are up before Jerry and me, and they race to the pool again. They've lost their aversion to suntans, and I don't discourage them. Back in Viet Nam people avoided getting too much sun because they didn't want the dark skin that came with the exposure.

Walter goes to the golf course for his usual Sunday game. Jerry decides to join the children in the pool. Jacquie suggests she and I have brunch at her favorite café, and I agree.

I climb into the passenger seat of the Cadillac Eldorado as Jacquie starts the engine. She doesn't say a word as we pull out of the drive and turn down the residential street toward a posh shopping area I'd noticed on the way in.

I decide to break the silence. "Your home is lovely, Jacquie."

"I did most of the decorating myself, but I did have some professional help."

"I'm sure you have excellent taste in everything. Would you be willing to help me learn how to be a good wife to Jerry?"

Jacquie starts a bit at my request. "What do you mean?"

"I mean teach me how to be an elegant lady like yourself."

Jacquie relaxes visibly. I think she's afraid I was asking about the intimate part of my life with Jerry, and she obviously has no intention of discussing that. Besides being too delicate for her tastes, I know she has absolutely nothing to offer me in that area.

"You are already an elegant lady, Tuyết."

The compliment takes me by surprise. It's the first time she's said anything like that to me.

"Thank you. I try to be a lady all the time."

We arrive at a small restaurant where Jacquie is greeted with the deference due her checkbook. The place is crowded, but the head waiter finds us a table along one wall. We order breakfast and she opens conversation.

"Gerald told us how to say your name, but I don't know if it's your first name or your last name. Which is it?"

287

"My full name is Vien Nouk Tuyết. We say our names backwards from the way Americans do. Tuyết is my first name."

"Vien Nouk Tuyết," she says my name several times as she commits it to memory. "I think I have it now. Tell me, did you ever try to find out about your husband?" Jacquie says then takes a sip of her coffee.

"I tried to find him at Camp Pendleton and through a refugee organization after I left there, but I never had any success. I finally had to accept the fact of his death when those tries failed. When your son came along, I knew I'd found someone who could make my life a joy again."

Jacquie stares at me for a moment before speaking.

"I don't know what I'd do if I lost Waltah. At my age, I'd probably not marry again, but I don't know if I could stand the loneliness. My children are all living their own lives now, particularly Gerald. I doubt they'd spend any more time with me than they do now. I think it would be a very hard time for me."

I smile a bit as I think of my past hardships. "It seems like there've been nothing but hard times for me over the last few years. The fall of my country and escaping the Communists. I thought things would be better in America, but Camp Pendleton was bleak until an American Officer I knew in Viet Nam agreed to be our sponsor. He helped us get situated in our new life. I thought I loved him, but he turned out to be a fraud. I broke up with him when I discovered he'd been lying to me from the beginning."

Jacquie shakes her head. "You make me ashamed to admit I'm an American, Tuyết. I never had to sacrifice for anything. My life's been handed to me on one silver platter after another. First, my family was well off, and I lived a life of luxury until I married Waltah. His father owned the firm, and he was already a partner by the time I graduated from college. I had servants to wait on me and take care of the boys. The only time I ever got my hands dirty was when I gardened."

I reach across the table and take her hand. "I know you were a good wife because I see the love Walter has for you. I know you were a good mother because I can see it in Jerry. I haven't met your other sons, but Jerry tells me they're both successful men. We just had different sets of challenges in our lives. Yours were all about raising boys in an atmosphere of abundance so they became good human beings and not spoiled brats while I had to struggle just to put food on the table. I really think you had the harder task." For the first time since I've known her I see her blush a bit.

"It's very sweet of you to say that, but I never had to flee my own country just ahead of a vicious enemy. I never had to learn a new language or a whole new life-style. You are truly a remarkable lady."

By the time we finish brunch and return to the Warrens' home, Jerry and the children are finished in the pool and come into the living room from the kitchen where they've finished lunch. At my insistence, he and I go through old photo albums of Jerry's youth. Jacquie sits nearby reading. One picture shows Jerry and his brothers as late teens. They're all handsome, but Jerry is the only blonde.

"Isn't that strange?" I direct the question to Jacquie. "Jerry's the only blonde. Walter has dark hair, were you a blonde?"

She joins us on the couch and takes command of the album.

"I'm surprised you wanted to see these old albums, Gerald," she says.

"It wasn't my idea it was Tuyết's," he replies.

"Well, you'd better get a look at all of them now," Jacquie says. "God knows, Gerald only gets here once a year."

"I'll remedy that, Jacquie," I say. "We Vietnamese value family. You would be highly respected as the matriarch of the family back there. I guarantee you'll see Jerry and me much more often if I ever agree to marry him."

"You are truly a formidable lady if you can manage that," she says.

She turns to another section showing her and Walter much younger.

"To answer your question, I was a platinum blonde as a younger woman. I think that's what attracted Waltah to me. He was crazy about Jean Harlow. I always thought she was cheap and **vulgah**."

"Your boys are all very handsome," I say.

"Yes, they all have the best of both Waltah and me."

I turn to another section and find pictures of a family gathering.

"What was the occasion for these pictures?" I ask.

"It was our 25th wedding anniversary party. We had the whole family here." She points to a woman in one photo. "That's my sister Judith. She's two years younger than me."

"She's very lovely," I say.

"She lives in Palo Alto, but we don't get to see her and her husband very much. It has to be a special occasion for them to make the trip."

"Aunt Judy always had the best Easter baskets for us boys. They used to live in Malibu, but Uncle Harry was transferred to Palo Alto when he made vice president."

"Who is the man in the wheelchair?" I ask.

"That's Waltah's Uncle Thomas. He lost his legs to a land mine on Iwo Jima during World War II," Jacquie says.

"I lost a friend to a mine at Bien Hoa. It was one the French left behind."

Jacquie turns solemn. "I'm sorry. I didn't mean to bring back sad memories."

"It's alright. I'm just happy to be where I don't have to worry about those things," I say.

We finish with the photo albums, and Jacquie goes back to her book. Walter comes in from the golf course and heads for the bar.

"Anybody ready for a drink?" he asks.

"Waltah, have you had any lunch? I don't want you drinking on an empty stomach."

Walter embraces his wife and plants a wet kiss on her cheek. Jacquie grimaces and pushes him away.

"You smell of perspiration, go take a showah," she says.

Water laughs. "I'll shower later, and I had a burger at the club. What I need now is a double Scotch. Who wants what?"

Jacquie declines, Jerry orders a ***Miller Lite***, and before Bao can answer I step in.

"Nothing but soft drinks for the children, please. I'll have a Scotch and water."

Bao makes a face and Anh smiles at him. Evidently, Bao and his sister discussed the drink situation beforehand. I think Bao was sure of another beer, and Anh knew I would veto his request. They order ***Coca-Cola***.

While Walter fixes the drinks, I notice the book Jacquie was reading. I don't have time to read anymore, but I recognize the poet's name.

"Do you like Byron?" I ask.

"Why yes, do you know Byron?" Jacquie asks.

I look out the large glass doors at nothing in particular. Sad memories flood my brain. Memories of Chinh and the sad faces at Camp Pendleton. I begin to recite the only part of any Byron poem I ever memorized:

> Yet did I love thee to the last
>   As fervently as thou.
> Who didst not change through all the past
>   And canst not alter now.
> The love where Death has set his seal,
> Nor age can chill nor rival steal,
>   Nor falsehood disavow:
> And, what were worse, thou canst not see
> Or wrong, or change, or fault in me.
> The better days of life were ours;
>   The worst can be but mine:

Jerry and Walt stand in stunned silence. This is a side of me Jerry has not seen up to now, and Walt's amazed that anyone bothered to memorize such mushy poetry.

"Is that Byron?" Jacquie asks.

"Yes, it's from a poem he wrote when he was convinced he was dying, the title is 'And Thou Art Dead, as Young and Fair'."

Jacquie thumbs through the index until she finds the title, then turns to the poem. She reads for what seems to be a long time before closing the book and staring at me.

"How did you know that poem?"

I smile at her. It helps my nervousness that she's surprised at my knowledge.

"When we were at Camp Pendleton a woman came around with a box of old books people donated. No one read much English, and the books were all very old. I selected Byron not really knowing what it was. I just liked the sound of the name.

"I had a lot of trouble with the old-style words, but one of the social workers helped me understand it. Once I knew what he was saying, I fell in love with his work. He seemed to capture all the emotions I was feeling at the time. I was worried about my husband, but everyone kept telling me that, if he were alive, the communists wouldn't let him live long. You see, he was an officer, and we were told the officers were singled out for special tortures. I resigned myself to his death while I was in that camp, and Byron helped me. This poem seemed to sum up my feelings."

Jacquie stares at me for a moment. The room is eerily silent as everyone watches us, not knowing quite what to expect.

"How did you ever overcome such sadness?" Jacquie asks.

The question makes me think. I can't recall worrying about "how". I only knew I had to go on for the children's sake.

"I concentrated on my children and their welfare. I still think of Chinh from time to time, but Jerry's taken his place in my life, though he can never take his place in my heart." I turn to Jerry. "I hope you understand. I can never forget the father of my children."

Jerry moves to my side and kisses me gently. "I do understand. Don't worry about it. I love you with all of my heart," he says.

Walter is obviously uncomfortable with the conversation and changes the subject. "This sounds pretty serious. You two should get engaged?"

Jerry answers, "I've offered her a ring, but she hasn't said 'yes' yet."

I break in, "It's hard for me after the failure of my first relationship here in the States. I guess I'm afraid of having my heart broken again. I do love you, Jerry, but I just need more time to get over my own misgivings." I turn to Walter, "Your objection to our marriage only adds to those misgivings. We Vietnamese value family, and I wouldn't feel right marrying Jerry while you two were opposed to it."

"Don't count me as one of those opposed to you and Jerry," Walter says.

His comment is no surprise to Jerry and me, but Jacquie stiffens a bit on hearing it.

Walter turns to Jacquie, "I know you wanted to wait until after this visit to make up your mind, but Tuyết is a courageous woman who's overcome more hardship in her life than any woman should have to bear. She's adapted to a strange country and learned a new language. She's not afraid of hard work, and I think that, with a little help, she could be a very good business woman. Besides, she's one of the most beautiful women I've ever seen. I would be proud to have her as a daughter-in-law, and I can't understand your objection to her, especially when she can quote Byron."

All eyes in the room turn to Jacquie. She seems to sag a bit under the weight of the stares but recovers quickly.

"Well, I never said I was permanently opposed to Tuyết and Jerry. I, I, I…"

Jerry cuts off the conversation by kneeling in front of me. He produces the jewelry box. I look into those sky-blue eyes, shining with nothing but sincere love for me, and all my apprehensions melt away. Even the lump in my stomach vanishes under the spell of our love. I can't restrain the tears any more.

"Tuyết, I've been seeking a dream all my life, never thinking it would ever come true, and here you are. You're everything I ever wanted in a wife and a whole lot more. I can't believe how blessed I am to have found you. Now that I have, I can't imagine life without you. I love you with all my heart, and I want you to be my wife. Will you marry me?"

I glance at the children for their approval. Anh smiles and nods firmly.

"Good grief, Mom, say yes," Bao almost shouts.

I look at Jacquie, but her face is still stern. She takes a deep breath and exhales sharply.

"I guess I'm outvoted. All I ask is, please try to find a job other than *bartending*?"

The room is quiet for a moment until a broad smile appears on Jacquie's face. She stands and puts an arm around me, and the room breaks into applause.

I pull Jerry to his feet. "Yes, I'll marry you."

My tears flow freely as I embrace the man I now admit to loving. He holds me for a long time then offers his handkerchief, and I dry my eyes. He slips the ring on my finger to more applause. I pull him to me, and we kiss again.

We break off the kiss, but Jerry keeps his arm around my waist.

"Looks like Jacquie gets to plan another big wedding," Walter says.

"I don't know what Tuyết wants, but I was thinking more of a civil ceremony and a small reception for close friends," Jerry answers.

"Oh Gerald, you wouldn't deprive me of the chance to do a big church wedding, would you?" Jacquie gives the impression of disappointment.

"Jerry and I can't afford a big wedding, Jacquie," I offer.

"Nonsense! Waltah and I intend to pay for everything, don't we Waltah?"

The older man looks at his son with the resignation of one who has given his wife her way for nearly fifty years. He shrugs his shoulders. "I don't see why not. We paid for your brothers' weddings."

"And they were extravaganzas worthy of Hollywood," Jerry says. "We don't want that, Dad."

"Well, you're our last child to marry, and your mother won't get another chance to show off like this. Humor her, Son, for my sake."

I'm sure Jacquie will make Walter's life miserable if she doesn't get what she wants. Jerry looks at me for support, but I only shrug in response.

"It's settled, then," Jacquie says. "You set the date, and I'll start making the arrangements."

"It won't be for a while. I want to be an American before we get married," I say.

Jacquie frowns and asks, "How long will that take?"

I hate disappointing her now that I finally have some indication of her agreement, but I've made up my mind on this.

"The children and I have a few more classes before we'll be able to pass the tests. We can get that out of the way by the first of the year. The main problem is the fees. I've got a long way to go to save that kind of money."

Walter jumps in. "Don't worry about the money. I'll take care of that."

"I wanted to do this on my own," I say.

"Well, let me, at least, make up the difference between what you have now and what you need," Walter says.

I don't answer him for a moment. Jerry sees my frown. He knows I don't want charity.

"I can do that, too, if you'd feel better about it. After all, you'll be my wife." Jerry says to me.

I don't know what to say. Help with the money would be nice, and Jerry's offer fits best with my personal preference, but letting Walter help would go a long way to helping seal the bond between Jerry's family and me. Jacquie steps in.

"Gerald, we don't have to rush into this. There are many things we have to resolve before you can be married." She turns to me. "Are you of the Catholic faith, Tuyết?"

"No, I'm Buddhist, why?"

"To be married in the Catholic church you would have to convert. Are you opposed to that?" she says.

Here's her final obstacle to our marriage. Is my love for Jerry strong enough to overcome my revulsion toward the Catholic church? Jerry solves that problem for me.

"Jacquie, you know I haven't been to Mass since I was eighteen. I don't consider myself a Catholic any more. This is another reason for a civil ceremony. Tuyết wouldn't need to change her life for that."

"You haven't answered my question, Tuyết," Jacquie says.

Now I must choose. I know Jacquie's heart is set on a big church wedding. Denying her that might drive a permanent wedge between us. On the other hand, I know Jerry wants to marry as soon as possible. I finally hit on a possible solution to my dilemma.

"I'm sorry, Jerry, but I want to be an American before we marry. Jacquie wants a big church wedding, and I can't deny her that. Catechism will take a while, and citizenship will also take some time. I can do them together and satisfy both Jacquie and my own conscience. You can help with the money when that time comes, and I won't feel obligated to anyone but my husband. I think that's fair to everyone."

Walter applauds my decision. "Good girl. That's a deal worthy of Wall Street. How can anyone refuse it?"

"It makes perfect sense," Jacquie says.

Jerry has a sour expression, but it soon melts into a smile. "Okay, I can go along with that."

I embrace him and feel the warmth of his love in his kiss. I'm not looking forward to converting, but I'll do it gladly to mollify Jacquie. I know Jerry won't insist on regular church attendance once we're married. I don't intend to force Bao or Anh into converting, but Jacquie hasn't mentioned the children. It looks like I finally have a solid path to happiness in America.

Chapter 30

The drive back to our appartment is festive. We even stop at an ice cream parlor for treats.

Anh and Bao are both excited about the marriage. They like Jerry, and they feel I will, at last, be able to live without working.

"Will you work after you and Mr. Warren are married?" Bao asks me.

Jerry breaks in. "Your mother won't have to work after we're married unless she wants to," Jerry says.

"I don't know what I'll do," I say.

"What do you mean, Mother?" Bao says.

"I don't know what I'd do with myself if I didn't work. You children are older now, and you don't need as much help as you used to. Yes, I'd probably do a better job of cooking for you, and I'd certainly be a better housekeeper, but I can't see myself sitting in front of the television or gossiping with the neighbors when I wasn't busy. I think I'd go crazy with too much time on my hands."

"Maybe you can find something better than bartending or doing nails?" Anh says.

"And what's wrong with bartending and doing nails? They've kept a roof over our heads for a long time now."

"Nothing, Mom, but I think Jacquie would have a cow if you kept on tending bar after the wedding," Bao says.

"What else would I do? I don't have the education for anything else."

The children sit in a pensive mood for a moment before Bao asks Jerry, "She could get a job in a Mercedes dealership, couldn't she? That should be respectable enough for your Mother."

"I think I could at least get her an interview at one or two of the dealerships I work with," he answers.

"No, no, it has to be something more high class," Anh protests. "Something like concierge at a fancy hotel."

I know she doesn't have any more idea of what a concierge is than I do. She must have heard the term somewhere or seen something on television.

"I couldn't do that. I don't even know what a concierge is."

"You just take care of the hotel guest's special needs, like show tickets and airport transportation and things like that. You could learn it all in no time. You're an intelligent woman, and you're good at working with people," Jerry says.

"I've thought about having a shop of some kind. I think I'd like to sell women's hats. I could even make some myself."

"You'd need money for that, and I think Walter would advance you as much as you like," Jerry says.

"Whatever you decide to do, you'll do it well," Bao says.

"I agree," Anh adds.

We arrive at the apartment, and Jerry drops us off.

*

Monday morning, the ladies at the nail salon are thrilled about my wedding. They want to help in some way, and I promise they will all have some part in the ceremony. It seems so far away, yet I know the time will pass quickly.

That evening I break the news to Luigi, and he is not thrilled.

"I hate to lose you, Tuyết. You bring a lot of business in here."

"I'm afraid they don't get much encouragement to hang around from me."

"Don't kid yourself. Those bozos aren't going to give up until one of them has you in bed. I'm just glad none of them succeeded."

"You're sweet. By the way, the whole gang here is invited to the wedding in Bel Air."

"I'll see if the wife and I can make it, but Bel Air? I don't think anybody else'll go. I'll put the word out, though."

*

The next morning, after my work at the nail salon, I visit the local Catholic church and make arrangements for my conversion. This will be a conversion in name only. I still remember the tyranny of the Catholic politicians in Viet Nam. Besides that, I know something about the Catholic faith, and I cannot take it seriously. I do this only for Jacquie's sake, knowing Jerry and I will never be true adherents to those beliefs.

Tuesday, Jerry calls with an invitation to a very posh event.

"The LA opera company is putting on **Carmen** and I got two great tickets for this Saturday's performance. If you can get off, would you like to go?"

"I can probably get off, but I don't know anything about American opera."

"Well, then this is payback for you taking me to that Vietnamese opera. This one's French, but it's one of the most popular operas in America. It has great music and a good story."

"I'll let you know if I can get off. I'll talk to my boss tonight."

"Good. I'll be out of the office, but I check in regularly. I'll call so often I'll probably drive my secretary crazy."

"You drive carefully, and I'll call you tomorrow."

I blow him a kiss into the receiver before I hang up. He won't know it, but I feel better for doing it.

*

The next morning, I tell the children.

"I've got a date with Jerry this Saturday. He's taking me to the opera. It may be a late night. Will you kids be okay?"

"Yeah, Mom. I'll take good care of Anh," Bao offers.

"I'm old enough to take care of myself, thank you," Anh responds.

"If you need anything, Mrs. Perkins, next door, said she'd be home."

They leave for school, and I leave a message for Jerry.

*

Saturday afternoon I'm ready by one. I have a two hour wait until he's scheduled to pick me up, but I don't want to have him waiting on me. I turn on our small TV, but nothing seems to cut the boredom. It seems an eternity before the doorbell rings. I open to see Jerry in a very nice suit.

"You look very handsome," I say.

"And you look very sophisticated yourself. Turn around."

I model the dress for him. It's a second-hand store special that I modified myself.

"Yes, sophisticated and stunning. Just the right combination of cleavage and modesty for the opera. Let's go."

This time he has a large sedan. It seems very elegant, but it smells of diesel fuel.

"It stinks a bit," I say.

"It had a small leak, but I fixed it. I didn't have a chance to wash the engine down, but the smell will go away in a while."

We drive to a restaurant in LA for dinner then to the opera house. I can't believe the elegance of the place. The fountains outside play a concert of sound and color in the twilight. We walk past tables where people are lounging and sipping drinks, then into a huge reception area. The ceilings are at least 20 meters high, and the chandeliers are huge arrays of crystal.

"This is the Dorothy Chandler Pavilion," Jerry says. "It's named after a woman who was instrumental in building a home suitable for the opera company."

"I think I've seen this on television."

"You have. This is where they hold the Academy Awards each year."

"I can't believe I'm standing in the same place where movie stars have been."

"Have you noticed how many people think you're a movie star?"

"So, that's why my cheeks have been burning."

He laughs at my comment. "I'm the luckiest man in the world tonight. I'm escorting a beautiful woman to a grand opera. Shall we take our seats?"

An usher leads us to seats on the main floor. Jerry says this is the orchestra. I look up at several balconies and wonder what the people can see from way up there. We sit down just as the lights dim for a moment.

"This is the overture," he says in a whisper. "It's a combination of the music in the opera."

The music begins, and I'm touched by the emotion it conveys. It's so grand it overwhelms my senses. I've never experienced anything like it. The curtains part, and the immense stage is covered with people who begin to sing as soldiers march across the stage. I can't understand a word, but the feelings come through so passionately I don't need them. Jerry whispers the plot to me just the same.

Act two involves some intrigue Jerry has to explain, but the Toreador song is stirring.

The rest of the opera seems to follow a familiar pattern of love found and lost and bitter revenge for unrequited love. I almost cry when Jose stabs Carmen, his song is so sad. The audience applauds wildly as it ends

We walk out of the opera house and Jerry asks, "Would you like a drink?"

"What time is it?" I didn't wear my usual watch as the ***Timex*** didn't quite go with the outfit.

"Just after midnight, but I know a place not too far from here where we can get a drink. Shall we?"

"Okay, but only one drink. I have to get home to the children."

We drive to a hotel a few blocks from the opera house. A valet opens my door and another one takes the car keys from Jerry. He leads me to a booth in the cocktail lounge.

"How did you like the opera?" he asks.

"It was very tragic, but the music was wonderful. Jose was very much in love, and Carmen was so cruel to him. He gave up everything for her, but she didn't appreciate his sacrifice."

A waitress interrupts our conversation, and we order drinks. Jerry reaches across the table and takes my hand. "I was hoping it would put you in the mood for romance."

The drinks arrive, and Jerry raises his glass. "A toast to true love."

I respond, "True love." We touch glasses and take a sip of our drinks.

"It was very romantic in spots, but the ending dampened that feeling quite a bit."

"I was hoping you might agree to my getting us a room here."

Here it is. All this time he's been a gentleman, but now he feels like he has the right to ask about sex.

"Oh, so now that we're engaged, you think we can jump in bed together whenever you like. After I sleep with you, what's going to be **your** reason for putting off our wedding?"

For the first time, I see Jerry angry. His face becomes red and his jaw sets in a grim line. He speaks haltingly through clenched teeth.

"I don't plan to put off the wedding. I thought I'd planned a very romantic evening I hoped would end with you and I making love for the first time. I'm sorry, I thought you wouldn't have any objection to it now that we're engaged. I'll take you home."

He rises to leave and offers a hand to me.

I can't move for a moment. I'm too busy thinking. The voice in my head screams at me, *What are you doing?*

Why should I deny him? I know he's sincere about our wedding. I don't have the lingering doubts I had with Mel. He's been so patient with me and hasn't pressed any advantage until now. I don't feel obligated to him for anything, and I do love him.

Yes, I have to admit what my heart has been telling me for a long time, but my brain was unwilling to go along with the idea. I love this man almost as much as I loved Chinh. He will never replace the father of my children, but I can have a good life with Jerry. For the first time in years I can go to bed with a man purely for love's sake. Why not?

"Sit down Jerry. Let's talk about this a minute."

He resumes his seat and says nothing but looks away with a disappointed stare.

"You have to understand how I feel. I was a whore in Viet Nam. It disgusted me, but it was the only way to feed my family. When I left Viet Nam, I thought I'd left all that behind me. I vowed I'd never do that again. When Mel came to our rescue, I succumbed to his wants in the hope he would marry me. When he proved to be a liar, I cursed all men. I vowed I'd never lie with a man again until after we were married. Breaking that vow is hard for me to do. Do you understand that?"

His face softens a bit, but it's still stern.

"Yes, I can understand how you feel, but I thought I'd broken down those barriers. I hope you've seen I truly love you with all my heart. I hope you understand this night was not motivated by lust, but only love for you. I'm sorry. I assumed too much."

I fear I've hurt him terribly, and I probe for some confirmation his love is as strong as ever.

"Jerry, please know I love you. I don't refuse you because I don't love you. I don't want to hurt you either. This night has been very romantic, and I don't see how any other woman could refuse you after such a wonderful evening. You just have to know that it isn't you, it's me. I promise you the most wonderful wedding night you could imagine, but please tell me you still love me."

His lips form a crooked smile as his eyes brighten. He reaches across the table and takes my hands in his.

"Yes, I love you with all of my heart."

We finish our drinks, and he pays the bill before we retrieve the car. The drive back to Westminster is quiet, but at my apartment door he pulls me to him and kisses me gently.

"Goodnight Tuyết. Please know I love you forever."

"Goodnight Jerry. I don't doubt your love for a moment."

He starts to walk back to his car but half way there he turns, smiles and blows a kiss my way. I'm sure he understood my feelings, or, at least, I hope he did.

Chapter 31

Jerry calls the next day, his usual cheerful self.

"Good morning, beautiful. How do you feel this morning?"

I know what he's driving at.

"Guilty," I say.

He laughs a bit then says, "I just polled the jury, and they were 8 to 4 'not guilty'."

I relax and fall into the mood of the joke.

"Only 8 to 4? Who were the four?"

"Easy, the jury was eight women and four men."

It's my turn to laugh.

"That's not why I called you so early."

"Oh, what's up?"

"One of Dad's lawyers checked into the citizenship process, and since you've come this far already, it's easier if you proceed under the normal circumstances. I never realized, the fees associated with applying for citizenship are so high."

"I know, I've been trying to save as much as I can, but it won't be enough any time soon. Thank you for offering to make up the difference."

"My pleasure. It only means I'll have to put a little more back each month, but I'm happy to do it. I also wanted to let you know I'd be gone on a business trip for a few days and won't be able to have Sunday dinner with you and the kids. I'll call you as soon as I get back."

*

All through the summer, Jerry arranges one adventure after another for the children. We have occasional dates, just the two of us, but he doesn't mention sex again. Every time we're alone, I feel a sense of guilt about denying him my body. He's gone above and beyond in proving his love and has never mentioned one word about delaying our wedding. In fact, he always asks me to marry sooner. I often wonder if it isn't me making up excuses just like Mel.

The citizenship process grinds on with training for all of us, consuming all of our free time. Bao and Anh are ready for the tests long before I am. They have more time to study. By November all we lack are the funds to pay the fees.

I wade through my catechism training. I can't begin to accept the church doctrine, but it's something I must go through to keep Jacquie happy. I know Jerry and I will not see the inside of a Catholic church after we're married.

We've talked about religion, of course. He's told me he isn't a practicing Catholic, and I shouldn't worry too much about that aspect of our marriage. He's seen our family shrine in the apartment, and he has no problem with that carrying over into our home. So far, we haven't found any wedge issues that might imperil our marriage, but I always worry that something will come up to spoil our happiness. I constantly urge Jerry to drive carefully. He reminds me that he drives a Mercedes, and they are the safest cars in the world. That information does little to assuage my fears about him being on the road a good percentage of the time. The blow to my expectations comes from another direction.

Chapter 32

One weekend in November we're at Jerry's parents' house when Lydia informs Jerry his mother is in an agitated state about the plans for the wedding. We find Jacquie on the telephone in her combination office and art studio.

"Father Collins, it's impossible for her to obtain any kind of death certificate for her Vietnamese husband. Besides he hasn't contacted her in nearly two years. If he were still alive, he'd surely have tried to get in touch with her."

She waves a perfunctory greeting to us, and Jerry signals for us to leave her alone. We walk to the kitchen where Jerry secures a **Miller Lite** from the big refrigerator.

"I learned long ago not to bother Jacquie in the middle of an argument. It only results in her being mad at me as well," he says.

Lydia is cleaning up after lunch but greets Jerry warmly.

"Mr. Jerry, you're sure spendin' a lot more time round heah since you and Ms. Snow got together. Good to have you. You two want some lunch?"

"I'm not hungry," I say.

"No thanks, Lydia. As soon as Jacquie's off the phone, we have to talk about wedding plans."

"Mrs. Warren sure is workin' that weddin' awful hard. She been on that phone all day non-stop."

"She's in her element, Lydia. Any time she can order people around, she's happy," Jerry says.

At that moment Jacquie appears in the kitchen, and I think I see smoke coming from the top of her head.

"Honestly, that man would drive a saint crazy! What did you two want?"

"I was just interested in how our wedding was coming along. Tuyêt would like to know some details, if it's not too much trouble."

Jacquie senses the sarcasm in her son's voice and sits down across the table from us.

"Can I get you anything, Mrs. Warren?" Lydia asks.

"I'd like some iced tea, Lydia, please."

Lydia prepares Jacquie's tea and sets it before her on the table.

"Thank you, Lydia." Jacquie turns to her son. "Well, Dr. Collins is giving me a hard time about a church wedding since Tuyết can't produce a death certificate for her Vietnamese husband."

"There's no way he's still alive. All the news channels say the Communists are either killing officers or sending them to 're-education' camps, and that probably amounts to the same thing. If he got out of the country, he'd have found me by now. Besides, two people in his unit said they saw his helicopter shot out of the sky," I say.

"I told him all of that, but he's adamant about it. Your father makes a very generous contribution to that church every year, and you'd think he'd be able to bend a little in our case. I hate it that he's cheating me out of a big church wedding." She takes a long drink of iced tea to cool down.

I decide I'd better let Jerry handle this, since he knows his mother better than I do.

"You know we only want a simple civil ceremony. Judge Wilkinson can do it, and we don't have to tell him about Tuyết's husband. You can plan a gigantic reception at the country club with all the bells and whistles. That's what all the guests are looking forward to, anyway," Jerry says.

Jacquie's sets down her tea and stares out the window for a moment. "I suppose that's what we'll have to do since that damned clergyman won't give in."

"Easy, Jacquie. I wouldn't want lightning to strike the house," Jerry says.

"Well, he's maddening to deal with, and completely unreasonable."

"Meaning he won't cave in to your demands?"

"Meaning he's not willing to budge an inch on anything!"

"A civil ceremony would save us a lot of money for a wedding dress. I could just wear something nice I could also use for special occasions after we're married," I say, trying to help mollify the situation.

"Don't you two want to be married in the church? What would God think?"

"Jacquie, the next time you care what God thinks will be the first time, and you know it. God will bless Tuyết and me no matter how we're married, or where. I'm sure Dad will thank you for saving him the money, since he's paying for the whole thing anyway," Jerry says.

"You have a point about the dress. My wedding dress is only a reminder of the figure I lost after having three children."

Jacquie's purses her lips together in a thoughtful expression. "It would have been nice to have another good dress instead of a white elephant taking up half a closet. With Tuyết's figure, it should be easy to find something attractive. You may have a point there."

"Have you pinned down a date with the club yet?"

"I was waiting on the church, but I don't think that will be a problem now." Jacquie rises and kisses Jerry on the forehead. "Excuse me, I have to tell a minister to go to hell."

Jacquie breezes out of the kitchen just as Lydia places another **Miller Lite** in front of Jerry.

"I thought y'all might need this. That woman sure do change her mind fast," Lydia whispers to Jerry. "This mornin' she was dead set on a church weddin' for you and Miss Snow."

"She'd rather tell Father Collins where to get off. It's much more satisfying to her."

"I guess I've been going through catechism for nothing?" I say.

It's more the time I've spent doing it than the actual process itself. I could have used those hours more productively, not to mention that they cost me several day's pay at the nail salon.

"Looks that way. At least we've talked her into a civil ceremony at the club, though."

"I should be grateful. I can drop catechism classes, and we avoid a big church wedding."

At that point, Jacquie bustles into the kitchen carrying a note pad and pen.

"Malcom has the 22nd of January available at the club and Judge Wilkinson is okay for that day also. You wanted the 15th, Tuyết. Are you okay with the 22nd?"

"That date will be fine, Jacquie, and a civil ceremony will save you and Walter some money. I assume that's fine with you, Jerry."

"You know it is! I really don't want a church wedding."

"Then Saturday, January 22nd it is. Any preferences on the menu?"

"Whatever you decide on will be fine with me, Jacquie. You have such good taste in that kind of thing," I say. "By the way, later on I'd like you to help me pick out a wedding dress too."

Jacquie's face lights up with joy at my acknowledgement of her good taste and the invitation to help find a suitable dress.

"Thank you, Tuyết. We should start looking sometime before Christmas. It takes a while to get the dress you want if it isn't sitting in the shop," Jacquie says.

"Now that we have a wedding date, Jerry and I can start house hunting. It will be good to have a family again. I've missed my parents so much, and I don't think I'll ever see them again. You and Walter will be my family from now on," I say.

"We're looking forward to it, Deah. We can't wait to have you and your children close to us. It will be so nice to be around young people again," Jacquie says.

*

Jacquie takes me wedding dress shopping over the Thanksgiving holiday.

I try on dress after dress and find it hard to make a selection. Some are complete rejects, but none of them fit into Jacquie's acceptable category. I'm afraid we'll never find anything until we walk into "Marsha's Bridal Gowns".

The shop exudes expensive from every rack. The décor is expensive tasteful. The mannequins are expensive chic. The carpet is expensive Persian. The air is scented with expensive perfume. Even the sales clerks look expensive.

A lovely, slim blonde in a tight-fitting blue dress welcomes us.

"Good morning, I'm Marsha. How may I help you this morning?"

"I'm Mrs. Waltah Warren, and this is my son's fiancée, Miss Vien. We're looking for a wedding dress. Nothing in the traditional line, it's only going to be a small wedding at our country club with a reception to follow immediately. Expense is no object."

"I think we have some things you'll like. I didn't catch your name." Marsha addresses me.

"It's Tuyết" I say as I accept Marsha's extended hand.

"You must be Vietnamese?"

"Yes, how did you know?"

"From the name. The Vietnamese have such a lovely way of naming their daughters." Marsha studies me for a moment then motions for me to follow. "I think we have something you might like. Let's go back to the dressing room and try a few things on."

I'm curious as to how she knows my Vietnamese name, but I decide to leave delving into that question until after we select a wedding dress. She leads me into a room with a low pedestal surrounded by mirrors and vanishes behind one of them. She emerges carrying several dresses in plastic bags. Jacquie inspects her selections.

"Won't these be a bit on the loud side?" Jacquie asks.

Marsha laughs. "Heavens no, these colors are perfectly acceptable for someone with Tuyết's dark hair and skin tone. She'll look stunning in them. I think this one."

Marsha pulls a dress from its bag and holds it up in front of me.

"Yes, I think this should do nicely, and I'm sure it's your size. What do you think?"

I feel the fabric and study the lines of the gown. "I'll try it on."

In a few minutes, I stand in front of the array of mirrors and inspect the result. Jacquie is awed.

"You look absolutely gorgeous! I didn't believe you'd look so good in that color."

"It won't take much in the way of alterations, either," Marsha says as she pulls at a seam here and there. "You have such a wonderful figure. Anyone might think the dress was made for you, and it's a bargain at only $1,500.00."

"Jacquie, that's a lot of money for a dress. I wouldn't feel comfortable in something this expensive."

"No, Darling. This one suits you fine. Remember, Waltah's paying for it, and I have to like it. In the first case, money is not a problem, and in the second, it's a good thing it isn't."

"What would you think if I told you I was really thinking about an ao dai for the wedding? I could buy a fabulous ao dai for a third of that price."

"What does an ao dai look like?" Jacquie asked.

"It's the traditional dress of Vietnamese women," Marsha says. "I know a woman who makes beautiful ao dais. I'll give you the address of her shop if you'd like."

I react to Marsha's suggestion. "How do you know about Vietnamese names and clothes?"

Marsha blushes a bit. "My husband is Vietnamese, that's how I know. I think you'd be stunning in an ao dai, Tuyết."

I look at Jacquie. "Are you game?"

"Why not? We can always come back here and buy this one. Will you save it for us, Marsha?"

"Certainly, just give me a call when you've made up your mind." She hands Jacquie a card after writing the ao dai shop's address on the back.

We drive to a less fashionable part of Los Angeles but find the shop with no trouble. Once inside, I take over. I speak Vietnamese to the older woman in charge who vanishes for a moment before returning with cloth samples for inspection.

"What wonderful silks," Jacquie says as she marvels at the selection.

"I show you pictures," the Vietnamese proprietress says. She hustles to the back of the store returning with a photo album. Jacquie flips through the pages and stops at a page showing a beautiful Vietnamese woman in a light blush version of the traditional garb trimmed in darker rose-pink embroidery.

"I think this one, Tuyết. What do you think?"

I peruse the photo substituting myself for the model. "I love it."

I speak to the woman in Vietnamese before turning back to Jacquie. "She says the price is only $450.00."

"Well, if that's what you really want. I can't wait to see Gerald's face when you come down the aisle."

Chapter 33

In early December, the day finally comes for the children and I to take our oaths as citizens. Jerry and his parents are there to congratulate us afterward, and a reporter for the **Los Angeles Times** is there to do a story on the new Americans. I worry that my name appearing in a big paper might be the trigger for some new disaster.

The oath ceremony begins as the judge asks the group to rise and raise their right hands. Then it begins.

I hereby declare, on oath, that I absolutely and entirely renounce and abjure all allegiance and fidelity to any foreign prince, potentate, state or sovereignty of whom or which I have heretofore been a subject or citizen...

I think about this part for an instant. What does it matter? There is no more South Vietnam.

...that I will support and defend the Constitution and laws of the United States of America against all enemies foreign and domestic; that I will bear true faith and allegiance to the same; that I will bear arms on behalf of the United States when required by the law...

I hope Bao never has to see war again.

...that I will perform non-combatant service in the armed forces of the United States when required by law...

I wonder how many people here know the true horror of war when they take this oath.

...and that I take this obligation freely without any mental reservation or purpose of evasion, so help me God.

I say the words, and I can embrace nearly all of them, but deep in my heart I will always be Vietnamese. America has been quite a shock to me, and I had some preparation for it through my American clients. I can't imagine what it must be like for someone who had to take it all in without that advantage. I am an American now, and I must change my self-perception from that of visitor to one of native.

I embrace my children. "Well, you're Americans now. How does it feel?"

"I don't feel any different," Anh says.

"Learning English was hard, but it was well worth it," Bao says. "I feel great."

Jerry and his parents find their way to us through the crowd.

"Congratulations citizen Tuyết," Jerry says as he embraces me and plants a long kiss square on my mouth. He hugs Anh and shakes hands with Bao.

Walter follows Jerry with a fatherly kiss on my cheek and an equally fatherly embrace.

"Good to have you as one of us," Walter says. "You've already made America a more beautiful place to live."

Walter moves on to the children as Jacquie embraces me, being careful not to crush her hairdo or wrinkle her blouse. "Welcome to America, officially," she says. "Now your journey is complete."

Walter announces that the next stop is lunch at Bel Air Country Club.

*

The next evening Jerry and I are alone in my apartment. Bao is spending the night at UCLA. They're interested in him for their baseball team. Anh is at a sleepover with some girlfriends.

"Well, I don't see anything in the way of our marriage now. You're an American, and you don't have to convert to Catholicism. Let's just cross over into Nevada and get married. We can honeymoon in Las Vegas."

It sounds lovely, but it would upset his parents as well as all the people I've told about our wedding.

"We can't do that. Your mother's made elaborate plans for January. Besides, who'd watch the children while we were gone?"

"I guess I didn't make myself clear. I mean we could get married secretly in Nevada and still have her big wedding in January."

I see his plan. We get married secretly so I'll have sex with him before the formal wedding.

"Very clever, you Americans." I use a phony accent to emphasize the sarcasm. "Marry innocent foreign woman and have your way with her, then say marriage no good and go 'way."

He laughs at my humor and holds me closer.

"That might be the way Mel would do it, but I only propose Nevada because there's no waiting period there. I must confess, though, the motive was purely sexual."

"I know you're not Mel, and I admire you for respecting my wishes. Don't you think I want to make love to you as much as you want to make love to me?"

"Then let's go upstairs right now."

I haven't had any misgivings about having sex with a man since after my first client in Viet Nam. Why should I feel this way about Jerry? I think I'm sure of him. It's not like Mel. To have sex now seems cheap in some way. Anh and I share a bedroom. How would I feel with her sleeping in the same room we used for sex?

"Not here, Jerry. I can't do it here if we're not married."

He thinks for a moment before saying more. "Okay, Bao's gone until tomorrow afternoon, and Anh won't be back until after breakfast tomorrow. I know of a very nice motel

"That's even worse. I'd really feel like a whore with you and I checking in for a few hours."

Jerry goes pensive then snaps his fingers. "I know, can I use your phone?"

"Of course, but what are you going to do?"

"If it works out, I think you'll like this option."

"What is it?"

"It'll be a surprise, just trust me."

What more can I say? "Okay.'

Jerry goes to the phone and speaks very softly with one hand covering his mouth and the phone. I see a broad smile as he moves his hand away.

"Thanks, Mike. I owe you one." he says then hangs up. "it's all set. Come on."

He takes my arm and leads me out the door to his car.

"Where are we going?" I plead.

"It's a surprise, but if you don't like it, we'll turn around and come back here. Okay?"

"I guess so." I do trust Jerry. He's shown me he respects my wishes many times.

We drive for what seems forever on the San Diego Freeway. Then he crosses to the Santa Monica. We pick up Highway 1 at the coast and wind up at Malibu. Jerry pulls off at a very luxurious beach house and parks under a pergola.

"Here we are," he says.

"Whose place is this?" I ask.

"One of my movie star Mercedes customers. He said I could use it any time he wasn't. Come on inside."

He leads me to a door and punches in some numbers on a keypad. "He doesn't use a key here, but you have to know the code out here and another on the inside or the police will be here before you know it."

The door opens onto a beautifully designed room. Jerry moves to a panel on the left-hand wall where a red light is blinking. He punches in more numbers and the light changes to green.

"Now we're okay. I don't know where anything else is in here. We'll just have to explore."

"I feel like a burglar, Jerry."

"It's okay, don't worry about it. Just enjoy. I think there's a bar over there."

I stand fixed to the spot feeling like a home invader. Past the entry is a large room with modern furniture. To my right is a glass wall of sliding doors facing the ocean and opening onto a large deck furnished with umbrella tables and chairs. Lounge chairs line one side of the deck. The sky is darkening, and the sun hangs just above the ocean like a huge orange balloon. Ropes of purple clouds try to keep it from falling into the water. I hear the tinkle of glassware and ice. Then Jerry puts a drink in my hand.

"Let's go out and watch the sunset."

He opens one of the doors, and we step out onto the deck. He takes one of the lounge chairs and sets his drink on a small table. December in LA is hardly warm at this time of night. I'm wearing a light sweater, but it isn't enough.

"It's cold out here, Jerry." I wrap my arms around myself for emphasis.

He spreads his legs and says, "Come sit with me. I'll keep you warm."

I take him up on the offer and nestle into the warmth of his arms. My drink is unexpectedly mild, and the Scotch warms me from the inside. The sun grows larger as it sinks into the horizon. There's only a slight breeze and the sound of the surf is soothing. The salty, fish smell of the ocean is like a perfume to me. I'm almost asleep when he nuzzles his face into my hair.

"You smell so wonderful, like sweet incense burning in an Asian temple. I love everything about you, Snow"

It's the first time he's used the translation of my name in a long time. Somehow it seems to emphasize his need. The warmth of his body, the Scotch and now his words arouse a need burning deep in my soul. I turn my face to his, and we kiss passionately. I feel my breathing quicken as his arousal makes itself plain.

"Let's go inside," he says.

I rise from the chair and he follows, leading me to a plush bedroom. He dims the lights and punches some buttons on a panel in one wall. The room is flooded with soft music, and he embraces me again. For the first time since coming to America, the sky rockets explode inside my head. I don't resist as he pulls off my sweater. He sheds his jacket and we kiss again as he unbuttons my blouse.

I know what I told him before, and a voice deep in my consciousness scolds me, but I quickly silence it. This is the man I'll love for the rest of my life. He deserves to have his way. My bra follows the blouse, and he lays me on the incredibly soft bed.

He kneels beside me and kisses each breast.

"God! How wonderful you are," he gasps as he lays his head on my chest. I rub my hand through his hair.

"It's alright," I assure him.

He kisses me again then removes my shoes and jeans. He removes the rest of his clothes, and I smile at the sight of his naked body. How many men have I seen this way? He's not the most beautiful, but he has a pleasant body almost devoid of hair.

Only a blonde wisp surrounds his private parts. He removes my panties slowly and hesitates a moment as he discovers that I still shave there.

"Oh, my God. How wonderful," he says then buries his face in me.

A wave of passion washes over me, but I resist enough to pull his head toward me. He understands and embraces me as we fall into a blue abyss, losing all reason and logic to the spell of the moment.

*

I awaken under the softest blanket I've ever felt. Jerry rests on one elbow watching me.

"Hello," is all he says.

"Hello to you. I really enjoyed that."

"I've had sex with five women in my life, but you're the most wonderful woman I've ever known. I'm a very lucky guy because you agreed to marry me."

I love him, but I hope I haven't made a big mistake. Now that we've experienced sex together, will he expect it every time we get the opportunity? Our wedding day is still a month away. Will he be content to wait?

"You're a good lover, too."

"I take that as a real compliment, coming from you,' he says.

I'm not quite sure how to take that remark. I know he means it sincerely and not sarcastically, but it still stings a bit. He notices my slight flinch.

"I'm sorry. I meant that in the best way."

I pull him to me, and we kiss.

"Don't worry. I'm not offended."

He rises and begins to dress. "Want a drink?"

"No, thanks, but I'd love some tea if there's any available."

"I'll see what I can do." He leaves the room, and I head for the bathroom.

The bath is even more luxurious than the bedroom. I notice it's fully equipped to take care of a woman's needs. After I use the toilet, I take advantage of that equipment to make myself presentable. I dress and walk to the main room where Jerry's brewing tea.

The moon is just now appearing in the windows. It casts a dim silvery light on the beach and makes the surf glow white. A million stars are visible now that we're away from the smog and city lights of LA. I take a seat on a leather sofa to take in all the beauty. Jerry soon arrives with two cups and sits beside me.

"Isn't it beautiful?" I say then take a tentative sip of the tea.

"I love the seaside. I wish I could afford a place like this. I'd never leave it."

"Where do you want to live after we're married?"

"I don't know. Would you like a house or an apartment?"

"Could we afford a house?"

I know houses in LA are expensive, but apartment rent is just money down the drain. Yet, I would love a freer lifestyle which lawn care and house payments would surely restrict.

"If you wouldn't mind continuing to work, we could easily afford a house. I could help you find work more suitable to Jacquie, but we'd probably also have to have two cars. You can't take your moped on the freeways."

"I think I'd like to continue working. The children are used to it, and they're old enough to be latch key kids without that causing problems for them."

He hasn't brought up the subject of continuing our sexual encounters, and I don't want to seem callous and broach that subject now. I decide to handle any future situations as they arise.

"Your kids are great. I'll adopt them after we're married."

"I don't know why I'm talking about moving. Bao needs to finish high school before I move, and Anh probably won't want to move after she starts high school. They've both made a lot of friends at school. Maybe we should find a bigger apartment in Westminster?"

"That's fine with me. I don't care where we are as long as we're together."

"We'll have a good life, won't we?"

"It may not be this good," he waves a hand at the luxury around us, "but, I'll make it as good as I possibly can. You deserve the best of everything."

Chapter 34

The holidays don't make much difference in my schedule. The nail salon shuts down on both eves, but the Kozy Korner only closes on the actual holidays. Since Christmas and New Year are both on Saturday, it does give me a real weekend on each one. Randy and I have few opportunities to meet until Christmas day. He brings the children his gifts, but we agree not to exchange presents and save our money for the honeymoon. We plan a week in Hawaii at a resort on Maui. I'm looking forward to some warm weather after the chill of December and January in LA.

Of course, Walter and Jacquie ask us over on the Sunday after Christmas. They have a huge tree that I discover is not real, but it's beautiful just the same. As expected, the gifts are expensive for the children, while Jerry and I open red envelopes to reveal large checks.

"They're for your honeymoon expenses," Jacquie assures us.

Jerry's brothers and their families are also there giving us a chance to meet the rest of his family. Everyone is very welcoming to me and the children. Their kids are older than Bao and Anh, but they accept them readily.

January is consumed with final preparations for the wedding and honeymoon. He seems to be spending a lot of time away from his office, and the secretary won't tell me where he is. I find this unusual since she can always tell me which dealership he's visiting or what training he's attending. I write it off to honeymoon planning.

*

The wedding day dawns warmer, and Jacquie says God must truly be blessing this union to perform such a miracle.

There are over two hundred people in one half of the country club's large ballroom. Jerry's relatives and the Warren's friends are there in force.

Mai and Thoung are there, of course, as are the Nguyens and a few other people from the apartment complex. Luigi and Rick from the Kozy Korner are there with their wives. Anh is my maid of honor and two of the nail salon girl are bride's maids. One of Jerry's older brother serves as best man, and his younger brother and Bao are groomsmen.

Walter Warren stands in the hallway waiting for me to emerge from the dressing room. He's agreed to stand in for my father. When I appear he almost whistles with admiration but holds back just in time.

"You look wonderful. I didn't think you could ever be more beautiful than the first time I saw you, but you've done it."

"Thank you. Do you really like the ao-dai?"

He studies me for a moment. My top features a close-fitting bodice with a high collar and long bell sleeves all in a soft pink. Darker rose-pink embroidery circles the bodice from the waist to just above the bust line with the same design half way up the sleeves. The front and back panels end in the same embroidery as the bodice, running from the hem to just below the knee. Slits down both sides show loose-fitting white silk pants. White low-heeled shoes complete the outfit. I carry a bouquet of pink roses.

"You couldn't have made a better choice. Are you ready?"

I nod, and we walk slowly into the ballroom.

*

Of course, I invited both Mel and Veronica to the wedding. They come through the reception line together, much to my surprise.

"Veronica, I'm glad you came, but I'm surprised you're with Mel."

"We're back together. He's promised his womanizing days are over, and we plan to be married next month. You and your husband are invited, of course."

"We'll be back from our honeymoon by the tenth. Just make it after that."

"No problem, we're planning a date toward the end of the month."

She kisses me on the cheek. "I wish you all the happiness in the world."

"Thank you." She passes me off to Mel.

"Am I allowed to kiss the bride?" he asks.

"Of course. It's the custom here in America, isn't it?"

We embrace, and he gives me a kiss that attracts Jerry's and Veronica's attention.

"Whoa, that's my job," Jerry says.

Mel pushes me away and shakes Jerry's hand. "You're a very lucky man, Mr. Warren. You have a 'pearl of great price' here."

The line moves on, ending what could have been an awkward moment.

Mai and Thoung are next. Thoung is handsome in a dark blue suit and paisley tie, and I've never seen Mai looking prettier. She's learned to do make-up, and her hair is expertly done. Her English is also greatly improved. We embrace for a long time.

"I'm so happy for you, Tuyết," she whispers in Vietnamese.

"I think I've found a wonderful man, but I want to stay in touch with you. Will you and Thoung and the children come to see us after we get back from the honeymoon?"

"Oh yes, it will be just like back in Viet Nam again."

She releases me, and I introduce her to Jerry.

"Tuyết's told me so much about you," he says.

"We very good friends in Viet Nam. We be very good friends again here, if you agree."

"Of course. You will be welcome in our home any time."

The rest of the line mostly consists of people Jerry had to introduce me to. They're his family's friends and some people he works with.

It seems to take forever before we get to our table for dinner. I'm grateful to see a full glass of water sitting before me, and I drink half of it before the first in an endless line of toasts.

Dinner is a steak of medium quality, but the wine is great and there's plenty of Champagne after dinner. The party goes on well into the night. The disk jockey plays a lot of older tunes in keeping with the age of the principles. Jerry and I dance together after the obligatory dances with relatives. My dance with Walter

Warren confirms his special fondness for me, as he holds me a bit too closely. I notice Jacquie scolding him afterward.

Appropriately, Anh catches the bridal bouquet while one of Jerry's relatives snatches the garter. Since ao-dai's don't really lend themselves to garters, I had to pin one to a leg of my slacks. Jerry takes the microphone to say goodbye.

"Tuyết and I want to thank all of you for sharing this happy occasion with us. You've made it so special. Tomorrow we'll be leaving for a long honeymoon in the Pacific. We're going to start in Hawaii and, this is a surprise for my new wife; she doesn't know anything about this; end up in Viet Nam."

The room breaks out in applause with the exception of Mel, myself and the few Vietnamese who stayed for the reception. I know Jerry means well, but I also know Jerry's naive about the communists. Taking me back at this time could be a fatal mistake. Even if I am an American citizen, that would make little difference to those vermin. As far as they're concerned I was born Vietnamese and will always be subject to their control.

I'm in shock. I know the ruthlessness of the Viet Cong and their communist friends from Hanoi, and I'm not confident my American citizenship will afford any protection from them. In spite of that fear, I'm more worried about finding Chinh alive. What if he is? What if I happen to run into him? I put those thoughts from my mind. Chinh's dead, and that's that, but I pull Jerry close to me and whisper, "Why did you do this? Are you insane?"

"We'll talk about it later, but don't worry. I've checked this out very thoroughly. I'll explain it all later."

I put on a forced smile and act like I'm pleased, but I know this discussion is going to cloud our wedding night.

*

Jerry and I leave the party around eleven o'clock. The drive to the Bel Air Hotel is short, and I decide to wait until we get to our room to discuss the Viet Nam portion of our honeymoon. I can't believe he thinks I would be safe there. Once the bellhop leaves I start.

"Jerry, I don't want to go to Viet Nam."

"I thought you'd want to find out about your parents."

"I don't think it's safe."

"Walter worked pretty hard with Congressman Clawson on that part of our trip. Clawson assured him you'd be safe."

"Does Clawson know what I did in Viet Nam?"

"No, Walter doesn't know. I never told him."

"The Communists may think I'm some kind of war criminal. You have no idea how cruel they are. They could be waiting to arrest me the moment we land."

I sit down on the bed and begin to cry. Jerry sits down and puts an arm around me.

"Clawson says the new President wants to normalize relations with Viet Nam. He's planning on relaxing all travel restrictions as soon as he's inaugurated. Clawson says the Vietnamese government's indicated they're willing to talk about it. The State Department people have assured him you'd be safe. They've told him the Communists have no charges against you."

"Just the same, I don't feel good about it. Please, can't we just cancel that part of the trip?"

Jerry looks at me. I can read the disappointment in his eyes.

"Walter went to a lot of trouble to arrange for that part of our honeymoon. He called in a lot of IOUs so you could find your parents. I think it would really hurt him if we cancelled."

"Would it hurt you if your new wife was locked up in a filthy Vietnamese prison?"

He takes hold of my shoulders and turns me toward him.

"Look, if I thought there was even a chance of that, no matter how small, I wouldn't have agreed to it. Have some faith in your government. Don't you want to see your parents?"

"Of course, I do. I want to know why they haven't answered my letters, but I don't trust the Communists."

He releases his grip and pulls me close to him.

"I'm going to take a shower. Do you want to take one?"

"No, I need to think about this some more. You go ahead."

"Should I plan on going to sleep right away after I shower?"

He looks at me with a lecherous grin that melts my heart. I kiss him passionately.

"I promised you a wonderful wedding night, didn't I? That's exactly what I have in mind after your shower. I won't let this Viet Nam thing spoil our happiness tonight."

I use his absence to put on the special Fredericks of Hollywood things I'd purchased for the wedding night. As I admire myself in the full-length mirror I think of my wedding night with Chinh. It was far different from this one.

Chinh wanted a traditional wedding in traditional dress. The ceremony seemed to last forever. I didn't mind that. I was dreading the thought of the marriage bed. No one gave me any formal training on sex. All I had were the giggly tales of my unmarried friends and the steamy novels I hid from my parents.

I remembered how frightened I was. Sex was a mystery to me, and I hadn't allowed Chinh to even touch my private parts before the wedding. Other boys tried to seduce me before Chinh, but I'd resisted them on stern warnings from my mother that such conduct was more than wrong and would only result in shame for the entire family. I was a good daughter, but now I must be a good wife. Chinh was so gentle with me. He made it wonderful in every way. I was glad I chose him as my husband.

Jerry's lustful rendering of a popular song from inside the shower brings me back to the present. I'm glad I'm an experienced and skillful lover now. This wedding night will be one of pure erotic enjoyment. I smooth out the bed sheets and strike a provocative pose near the headboard. Jerry emerges from the bathroom glistening with lust. We make love several times, and each one is lovelier than the last. As we lay side-by-side, weary to the bone, I think how wonderful it is to have a man next to me again. Of all things about being married, I missed that the most. I roll over and kiss his forehead. He doesn't stir; he's sound asleep.

Chapter 33

The flight to Hawaii is routine, but long. I hadn't been on an airplane that long since I came to the States with the children. Jerry books first class tickets, making the journey much more tolerable than being packed like sardines into troop seats on a military airplane. I enjoy the free wine and the meals that, even at first class prices, are little more than glorified TV dinners. I do manage to sleep a little on the flight in spite of the feeling of elation sending bolts of anticipation through my body. They contrast with stern misgivings about spending so much money. Jerry doesn't seem to care about the money, but my inner soul rebels at the thought of how much food a first-class ticket would buy. The complete mental make-over of my life is quite a challenge.

*

Hawaii is more beautiful than I imagined. We only had a short layover on my trip from Guam, and it was at night, so I never got a chance to view the scenery. I'd heard there were parts of Viet Nam that look like this, but I never saw more of my country than the flat fields around Saigon and Bien Hoa. The salt smell on the air is invigorating and I'm eager to get to our hotel room.

The hotel is wonderful. Right on the beach and close to some lovely shops. The bellboy puts down our luggage and shows us the various features of the large third floor suite before leaving with a more generous tip than I thought his services merited. I'll have to teach Jerry frugality, but our honeymoon isn't the time for that. But, why should I worry about that and spoil my illusion? I'm a queen for the few days of our honeymoon. I can return to the old Tuyết when we get back home.

I throw my arms around my new husband and kiss him passionately. "Do you know how happy I am to be Mrs. Jerry Warren?"

"I'm glad. I want to make you the happiest woman in the world."

"Then make love to me right now. Here, with the doors open and the sea pounding in our ears and everything." I kiss him again as he carries me to the bed.

*

Hawaii is like home to me. The people here are all some admixture of oriental genes, and I fit in like a native. People are friendly and can't believe I'm a tourist. The floorshows in the evenings, the little trips during the day, all of these are great, but I enjoy just lying on the beach with Jerry as much as anything.

We hadn't spent any long periods of time together before the wedding. I find he has several annoying quirks, but I'll only have to adjust a little to live with them. He's finding it hard to wait for me to get ready to go somewhere, but he will have to learn a woman needs time to be beautiful.

Sometimes we talk money. I have none, but Jerry has managed to save some and invest a bit. A good chunk of his savings will be eaten up by the honeymoon, but he says he's happy to do it for me. His salary is more than I thought anybody made except the President of IBM. I won't have to work for the first time in years. I offer to continue working, but Jerry thinks his father has something in mind for me when we get back to the States.

Thankfully, Jerry doesn't want any children. He tells me he plans to adopt both Bao and Anh, and they will be his children. He admits that changing diapers and preparing formula are not his idea of fun. I know I'm too old for children, but I would've tried, had it been important to him.

Too soon the time comes to leave for Viet Nam. I dread this part of the trip because a vision of disaster keeps haunting my thoughts. I've coped so far by trying to think only of the present here in Hawaii, but now I have no choice but to face reality.

*

There is no direct flight from Hawaii to Saigon. We must go to Manilla and switch to a Chinese flight.

Jerry can't wait for the plane to land at what once was Tan Son Nuht air base. He can barely contain his enthusiasm as he tells me, "I'm really excited about this. I've heard and read so much about your country. I can hardly wait to see it."

"I doubt they'll give us a tour of the country," I say.

"I can't imagine a war going on here," Jerry says as he scans the verdant countryside slipping by under the plane. I insisted he take the window seat so he could take in the view.

"It was a horrible time," I stare past Jerry and through the window. "The VC hit Bien Hoa Air Base with rockets every morning just to remind us they were out there. They never hit much, but it made you think. You couldn't be sure the next one wouldn't be the one to kill you and your children. I worried about Chinh so much, particularly after he was wounded."

Jerry tries to change the subject. "At least, you'll get to see your parents."

"Yes, that will be good." I wonder if they'll be glad to see me. I'm sure they know what I did to feed them, they may want no part of me now. Maybe that's why they haven't answered my letters. Jerry assures me the Communists know where my parents are and will take us to them. I can only hope they're telling the truth.'

The plane lands and we make our way to the immigration and customs area. I notice people looking at me and hear their conversations. They obviously think I can't understand Vietnamese because they don't bother to lower their voices.

The immigration official is a thin, austere-looking man with a wispy mustache. He wears gold-rimmed glasses perched just above the tip of his nose.

When it's my turn he speaks to me in Vietnamese, "Ba Warren, I think you may be Vietnamese."

I answer in Vietnamese, "Yes, I was born here; but I am a U. S. citizen now and married to a U. S. citizen."

"I see," he continues, "Was your husband in the American military here?"

"No, he never served in the war."

Jerry is beginning to get a bit nervous since he doesn't understand what we're saying. He breaks in, "What is he talking to you about?"

The little man turns to Jerry. "I apologize, Mr. Warren. I was only asking your wife if she were Vietnamese and if you served in the war. Just curiosity, that's all. Your papers are in order." He stamps the passports and gives us an oily smile as he waves us on.

Customs is perfunctory, but they do open my cosmetic case and inspect it thoroughly. The female customs officer doing the search confiscates several items of my cosmetics, explaining that they contain ingredients not allowed in the country. I know that's a lie and that she will take those things home with her tonight. In the lobby, a Communist official in a uniform greets us. He speaks fairly good English.

"Good afternoon, Mr. and Mrs. Warren. I Colonel Pham Duong Lanh. Please follow me."

He directs a porter to carry our bags and leads us to a sedan waiting outside the terminal. The streets are abuzz with the sound of mopeds and motorcycles, but this is the only car I see. We get into the back seat while Colonel Lanh takes the front seat next to a surly-looking driver. He turns to us and continues to speak in English.

"I take you to Mekong Hotel, as arranged for you by Swiss embassy. Please no leave hotel. I not sure Americans safe on streets of Ho Chi Minh City. You have guards outside door all time. They for your security only. You may use hotel dining room any time. You understand?"

"Yes, but would it be possible to arrange for a tour of the city?" Jerry asks.

"No, sorry. You only here so Mrs. Warren see parents."

"You know where my parents are?" I ask in Vietnamese.

Lanh smiles at me and answers in Vietnamese, "Yes, but you know too. You've write to them many times."

"They never answered my letters."

"Your letters were delivered. If they don't answer, that their concern. Many Vietnamese-Americans correspond with relatives through American organizations. Many send money." A greasy smile spreads across his face at this statement.

"Since they haven't answered my letters, I wonder if they will see me."

"We've spoken to them, and they've agreed to meet you. We also spoke with your ex-husband, but he doesn't want see you."

"Did you say 'ex-husband'?" I say.

"Yes, Colonel Chinh divorced you last year. He give no reason, but we know why."

The greasy smile grows even larger.

"I thought he was killed in the war."

"He was badly burned, but he recovered under the excellent care he received in our Peoples' Re-education Camp. He re-educated successfully and flies helicopter for the Peoples' Army. He was very brave in the War of Liberation in Laos. He's been promoted many times and now commands a helicopter wing."

I'm stunned. He never tried to reach me. I can understand while he was in their filthy camps, but he could have written me later. He could have, but he didn't. Now I'm sure he knows what I was in those last years of our country. At least knowing about the divorce eases my mind about marrying Jerry. I translate the conversation for Jerry.

"I'm glad to hear that," Jerry says. "It wouldn't have made any difference to me if he didn't divorce you. You assumed he was dead, and that was good enough for me."

"It probably would have made a difference to your mother," I say.

"Look, if we came here and found him alive and not divorced, Mother never need know about it."

"I'd be living a lie again, but I guess it would have been a lie I could live with. In a way I was hoping he was alive until I met you. We're married now, and I wouldn't change that, but Chinh still has a place in my heart no other man can fill. I hope you understand."

Jerry takes me in his arms. "I know I can never take his place completely, but I'll do my best to make you glad you married me."

Lahn continues in English, "I take you to your parents tomorrow. Be ready ten o'clock in morning. This car pick you up at hotel and take you to them."

*

The next morning. I awaken Jerry, "Now you've done everything any of my other lovers have done. You've made love to me in Viet Nam."

"And it was great," Jerry mumbles. "After a night like that I understand why Mel wanted to take you home with him."

We laugh as we dress for the day, but my stomach is churning. I'm anxious about how my parents will react to me since they never bothered to answer my letters, and I dread the possibility of encountering Chinh.

Breakfast in the hotel is Vietnamese style. I order for Jerry so he will not be faced with food he would find distasteful. Over breakfast, I brief Jerry on how to behave in a Vietnamese home. There are several things he should astutely avoid, such as crossing his legs or exposing the sole of his shoe. I coach him on how to treat my father and mother and on things he should say and not say.

There is no check. The waiter explains that all meals are added to our hotel bill.

The car is out front promptly at ten. Colonel Lahn greets us in English.

"Good morning, Mr. and Mrs. Warren. You sleep well?"

"Yes, very well," Jerry answers.

The hotel is anything but first class by American standards, but it is clean, and the air conditioning worked well enough. Vietnam is not boiling hot in February. We could just as easily open the window to be cool enough.

"Good, we go parent's house now."

Chapter 34

We drive through the streets of what was once Saigon to an area near the old American base of Tan Son Nuht. I was only a child when we lived in Saigon, but I remember much more traffic that we encounter today. I remember the slums writhing in squalor, but we pass none of that. Even the people on the street seem less cheerful than I remember. The Communists have made some drastic changes in the city.

We turn a corner into a street showing a bit more prosperity. Pastel colored cinder block buildings with stout wooden doors line the street. There are no windows. Some of the doors are padlocked at two places with formidable looking pieces of hardware. Each one has a small window that only opens from the inside.

We stop at a house with a large, red door, and Lahn indicates this is my parents' house.

"Your parents live here. You knock. You may have one hour."

I knock. A voice from inside calls in Vietnamese, and I answer. The little window opens, and my Mother's face appears. She immediately breaks into a broad smile, and I hear the rattle of locks opening. The door swings open, and my mother rushes to embrace me.

"Tuyết, Tuyết it's so good to see you," she almost takes my breath away with her bear hug. She finally lets me go and steps back to look me over.

I do the same with her. I expected she would have gained some weight, but she's as thin as when we parted two years ago. Life under the Communists appears to be no different with the war over.

"You look so beautiful," she says. Then, she finally notices Jerry. "Who is this?"

"This is my new American husband, Jerry Warren. I'm now Mrs. Jerry Warren."

Jerry breaks in now because all of the conversation so far has been in Vietnamese. "She seems to be glad to see you."

"I'm sorry, Jerry. She is happy. I'll introduce you." I switch back to Vietnamese and make the introduction to Mother before turning back to Jerry. "Your turn," I say.

"Chao Ba Vien. Rất vui được gặp bạn mẹ," he says while he bows to her.

He butchers it a bit, but Mother smiles and embraces him uttering a sting of Vietnamese so rapidly that I'm hard-pressed to pick it all up.

"What did she say?" he asks.

"She said she's glad I've found such a handsome man, but don't get a big head over it."

At that point, Father comes from the house. I rush to embrace him, but he seems cool. We go through the introductions again.

Lahn speaks, "I wait in car. Remember, one hour." He gets back into the sedan.

Father ushers us into the house where we all take seats.

"We never thought we'd ever see you again, and here you are," Mother says.

"How are our grandchildren?" father asks.

I reply in Vietnamese. My parents speak very little English. "They are well, and you'd be very proud of them. They do well in the American schools. I've brought you a lot of pictures." I produce an envelope full of pictures, and they comment on each one as it's passed between them.

Father finally asks the question I've been dreading, "Did you know Chinh was alive when you married this man?"

"No, not until Lahn told us yesterday. I was sure Chinh was dead. Thoung and another pilot from Nha Trang told me Chinh's helicopter was shot down. I tried to reach him from America, but never heard a word. I was sure the communists killed him. Father, I married this American believing Chinh was dead. If you would have answered my letters, I would have known he was alive, and I would not have married him."

Father speaks, "My daughter, I could live with your prostitution. I understood why you had to do it, but when you show up here with another husband you married not knowing if Chinh was alive or dead, I can't overlook that. You are fortunate

334

Chinh divorced you after he was released from the re-education camp."

Father looks at me with an expression of disgust. Mother breaks into a sobbing fit.

"Do not be cruel to our daughter. She is here for a short time only," Mother manages through her tears.

Jerry taps me on the shoulder for an explanation, but I brush him aside. "Not now, this is crucial. Give us a moment."

I begin to cry but compose myself for Jerry's sake. "Is Chinh here, Father?"

"No, he will be at the base all day. He knows you are coming, but he doesn't want to see you."

Jerry whispers in my ear, "Tell me what's happening. Your Father doesn't look very glad to see you."

"It's okay, Jerry. He just needs some time to adjust to our marriage. Let me handle it for a little longer. Be patient."

I continue in Vietnamese. "Father, you know I didn't want to leave Chinh behind, but Thoung told me he did not return from his mission with the other helicopters. Besides, we heard the VC were killing every officer they captured. On the big ship Thoung found a man who saw Chinh's helicopter hit by an RPG. He said he doubted Chinh was alive. You encouraged me to leave and take the children with me. I tried to contact you and Chinh, but none of my letters were answered."

"Chinh burned your letters without reading them. We wanted to write to you, but he forbade it. We were glad to see you safe in America, and we were sad when you stopped writing. We knew we would never see you again even though our hearts longed for the sight of you. Now here you are with an American husband."

To my surprise, Mother steps in. "Don't be old-fashioned, husband. We cannot change the past. What's done is done. Our daughter is here with us—happy at last. We need to put the past behind us and enjoy our daughter again."

"I am still your daughter," I sob.

"Yes, I can't deny that. We can forget the past, but Chinh will not. He wants nothing to do with you. He's glad you're thousands of miles away in America. He does not want to see you, Tuyết. He has put you out of his mind. His only regret is that he will not see his children grow up."

Mother speaks. "Tuyết, my little girl. You look so beautiful. I thought my daughter was gone forever, and now she's here by my side. No matter what you have done, I love you still."

Jerry is sure the conversation's not going well. He doesn't understand a word, but the tone is unmistakable. He breaks in, "Tuyết, tell me what they're saying. I don't like the sound of it."

"It's okay, Jerry. Like I told you, they're just shocked at seeing me here with an American husband. They're also ashamed of what I was during the war. It's very hard on all of us; just give me a little more time. I'm sorry I have to do this in Vietnamese, but they speak very little English."

He sits back in his chair; being careful not to cross his legs.

Father starts to hand back the photos, but I tell him to keep them. "I'll send you more pictures if Chinh will let you have them."

"I will speak with him," Father says. "Perhaps he will change his mind when he sees these?"

I'm busy talking with my parents when a younger woman comes in and rushes to greet me.

"This is my cousin, Linh," I tell Jerry. I speak to her in Vietnamese.

"Co Linh, this is my American husband. My father will tell you all about it later."

She nods at Jerry.

"Chou Co," Jerry says. Linh smiles and nods again.

"I speak some English," she says haltingly. "Good morning, sir. How are you?"

"I am fine," Jerry remembers to speak slowly and distinctly without raising his voice. I'd told him about my experiences with Americans who think that anyone will understand English if it's spoken loudly enough.

Linh excuses herself and comes back with a tray of fruit punch in tall glasses. I tell Jerry it's okay to drink it. It turns out to be quite tasty.

The conversation in Vietnamese goes on for what seems to be an eternity before I stop to translate for Jerry.

"They've been telling me about all my relatives. Most of them are fine. One of my uncles is still in prison. He was a major in the ARVN, and they don't think he will ever get out alive, but he's the only one. Thank you for making this possible, Jerry."

"It's mostly Walter's doing, but I'll take some credit also."

Colonel Lanh walks in and greets everyone in Vietnamese before turning to me. "Hour up. We must go back to hotel. You ready?"

"I think so. We can go any time now," I say.

Jerry interrupts, "I do have to do one thing before we go. Where is the bathroom? I'm about to bust after all that orange stuff."

Lahn nods his approval, and I laugh and lead Jerry to a small, closet-like enclosure with a hole in the floor. "Here it is," I laugh. "The Americans used to call this 'Twelve O'clock High'. Think you can hit it?"

"Not with you looking at me. Go away."

"No, I want to watch. Go ahead. I've seen it before, you know."

I giggle as Jerry plays his stream around the hole only managing to hit it about half the time.

I'm surprised to find another person in the living area when we return. It's Chinh in the tan uniform of the North Vietnamese military. He's as distinguished looking as ever even though his face bears hideous scars. I fell in love with him in his VNAF uniform, and even though this is the uniform of the old enemy and his face has changed from the scaring, he still makes my heart race. His expression is stern yet can't entirely cover a hint of pain. I gasp for breath, and he speaks to me in Vietnamese.

"Hello, Tuyết. Are you surprised to see me?"

"Chinh, Father said you didn't want to see me, but I'm glad you came."

I want to run to his arms, but his face tells me I'm not welcome.

"Your father has been filling me in," Chinh says. "I was sitting in my office, knowing you were here, and I finally changed my mind about seeing you. Even if I didn't want to see you, I wanted to find out about our children. There is much for us to talk about, Tuyết. Can we be alone for a while?"

"Yes, I certainly owe you that," I stammer. I switch to English and turn to Jerry, "This is Chinh, but I'll introduce you later. Would you mind if we talked in private for a while?"

"No, Darling. Take all the time you need." He can't take his eyes off Chinh. His expression is more one of curiosity than resentment or jealousy.

I turn to Linh and ask her to translate for Jerry while I'm gone. I follow Chinh across the atrium to one of the sleeping rooms.

"Sit down, Tuyết. We need to get a few things straight before we go back to your husband." We sit on the ledge that serves as a bed.

"Oh, Chinh. I was sure you were dead, and I never heard from you. What else could I do?"

"It's all right; I decided a long time ago you were lost to me. I divorced you last year. I thought about marrying again, but no one could ever take your place in my heart.

"I learned of your infidelity while I was at Nha Trang, and I felt it was more than I could ever forgive. Then I learned you'd gone to America, and I swore I would never take you back even if you returned to Viet Nam. Now, here you are, and the sight of you makes me wish I'd never gone through with that divorce. My heart still tells me I love you as much as ever. I decided I don't care about the past. I had to see you one last time."

I burst into tears and throw my arms around the husband lost to me forever. "I dreamed of you so often. It was hard raising the children without a father, but they're good children. You'd be proud of them."

"I'm sure I would. I miss them very much. Bao must be a big boy now."

"He is. He plays baseball for his high school, and I think he will get a scholarship to a large American university because of baseball."

"And, Anh must be blossoming."

"She's prettier every day, and an honor student." I show him the pictures in my wallet. "Father has better pictures."

He smiles as he holds the pictures for a long time. "They are lovely," he says as he hands back my billfold.

"Will you let me write to you and my parents?" I'm hoping his change in attitude will extend to allowing correspondence.

"Yes, I've decided to forget the past. While I was in the filthy cells of the re-education camp, the thought of you kept me going. When they offered me a chance to get out I jumped at it even though it meant joining the Communists. After a while I ran into a man from my old outfit at Bien Hoa. He told me you'd escaped with Thoung. I threw myself into my work to forget, but I never did. Does your American husband know about your life here?"

"Yes, he does; and he loves me anyway. America is different from here. They are much more tolerant of these things, but the children never knew about any of it."

"Then I'm happy for them, Tuyết."

"I'm glad my parents are with you."

"I searched for them once I'd established myself in their Air Force. I found them at Bien Hoa, living hand to mouth. They also thought I was dead but were happy to live with me again."

"They look so thin. Is there enough food now?"

"Life under the Communists is not much better than it was during the war. Food is just as scarce, and only shoddy Communist goods are available in the markets." He smiles broadly. "I miss the Americans, but I dare not say so."

"I'm glad they're with you. I could send you some money, if that would help?"

"It would never get to me. The Communists open all mail from America and take what they want. Is there anything else I can tell you?"

"Father and Linh have told me all about my sisters and the rest of the family. Now that I know you're safe, I'm satisfied."

He rises and holds out his arms, "Then, our business is finished, but may I hold you one last time?"

I rise and extend my arms. He folds me into an embrace I remember so well. I feel secure, but I know I cannot have this feeling again, ever. I can't help the tears. I wish things had been different, but I know I cannot change the past. We each did what we had to do to survive, and we must accept the consequences. Jerry is my future now, and his embrace is every bit as warm as Chinh's. He pushes me away.

"Shall we go back now?" he says.

"Yes, we must both return to the present, no matter how the past calls to us. We cannot go back in time."

I rise and walk back to the living room. Jerry stands as I enter.

Chinh offers his hand to Jerry, who takes it hesitantly. "I am Colonel Chinh," he says in English.

"Tuyết's told me so much about you. Your children are also very proud of you."

"I'm glad to see her happily married in her new life. I must be honest and say that I would forget the divorce and marry her again if I thought that was possible."

"I can't blame you. I know how I'd feel in your place."

They drop the handshake, and Chinh pats Jerry on the back.

"I warn you. If you ever mistreat her, I'll hear about it and come bomb your house."

Jerry looks at him with surprise until Chinh breaks into laughter.

"I see your escort is Colonel Lanh," Chinh says. "You are in good hands."

I say a tearful goodbye to my parents and Linh, then Chinh and Lahn escort us to the waiting government car.

Chinh exchanges some words with Lahn, then turns to us and speaks in English.

"I told him you are important people to me. If you have any trouble, let me know." He hands me a business card and switches to Vietnamese. "Good bye, Tuyết. We will never meet again." He kisses me lightly, then turns and strides purposefully back into the house.

Back at the hotel I fill Jerry in on the information I'd garnered from my parents and Linh. He's amazed I can wind my way through the maze of uncles, aunts and cousins without skipping a beat. He asks me about Chinh.

"It's funny he's now flying for the communists. What saved his bacon?"

"He was in a re-education camp, but they needed helicopter pilots for the war in Laos. He said he would do anything to get out, even fly for the Communists."

"I'm a lucky man to have you after seeing him with all of those medals. He's quite a hero."

I smile softly as I reply, "Yes, he is."

*

The next morning Lahn is there with the car to take us to the airport.

"I hope you enjoy your stay," he says.

"Yes, thank you," I say. "We had a good visit with my parents and Colonel Chinh."

At the airport, there are few formalities to go through. The security check is perfunctory by American standards, but the same ominous official who questioned me when we arrived is waiting at the passport table.

"Well, Mrs. Warren, did you enjoy your visit?" he asks in English.

"Yes, we did; thank you," I reply nervously. The little man seems to be holding my passport a bit too long to suit me.

He finally hands it to me. "Come back to Viet Nam again soon, Mr. and Mrs. Warren."

Chapter 35

Once we're airborne, Jerry says, "I think I'll take a nap."

"Sweet dreams, darling." I'm glad he won't see the tears trailing down my cheeks as I watch the muddy rice paddies of my former homeland grow smaller below us. I can't help but weep for the life I once had there. A life I leave behind forever. A wonderful husband and happy memories in spite of the war. More tears flow as I recall the way I betrayed that gentle man.

A soft snore reminds me of my new husband and a new life in a new country. The boundless hope for a better life than I have ever known dries my tears. I look about me and smile. What a contrast to my first departure from Viet Nam—a plush first-class seat versus the hard floor of a helicopter, stark terror replaced by quiet serenity.

The war restricted hope to a narrow tunnel I trod with tentative steps. I dared hope for no more than tomorrow, but now I go to a life of tomorrows filled with hope.

The End

Made in the USA
Columbia, SC
23 January 2019